Perfect PROPOSALS

JUST SAY YES

D1513568

Perfect
PROPOSALS
COLLECTION

March 2016

April 2016

May 2016

June 2016

Perfect
PROPOSALS
JUST SAY YES

Mira Lyn
KELLY

Marion
LENNOX

Ann
MAJOR

First Published in Great Britain 2016
By Mills & Boon, an imprint of HarperCollins*Publishers*
1 London Bridge Street, London, SE1 9GF

JUST SAY YES © 2016 Harlequin Books S.A.

Waking Up Married © 2012 Mira Lyn Sperl
The Heir's Chosen Bride © 2006 Marion Lennox
The Throw-Away Bride © 2008 Ann Major

ISBN: 978-0-263-92155-7

09-0616

WAKING UP MARRIED

MIRA LYN KELLY

Mira Lyn Kelly lives with her husband in rural Minnesota, where their four beautiful children provide an excess of action, adventure and entertainment. With writing as her passion and inspiration striking at the most unpredictable times, Mira can always be found with a notebook at the ready. (More than once the neighbors have caught her, covered in grass clippings, scribbling away atop the compost container!) Check out her website www.miralynkelly.com

This book is dedicated with love to my dad, for always supporting my dreams—no matter where they took me! (Okay, that's far enough, Dad. No reading past here!)

CHAPTER ONE

FORCED TO LISTEN to one heaving revolt after another reverberate off the polished marble, Connor Reed cursed his conscience.

Talk about an inconvenient burden. No matter how his stomach rocked and his head slammed, there was no way he could make a bolt for the beckoning doorway to freedom at the far wall.

Wrenching his gaze back to his own slightly green reflection, he turned off the tap and wrung out a towel. Pushed some empathy into his expression and prepared to face the music.

"Hey, gorgeous," he called, crossing over to the pitiful creature half leaning into, half clutching the toilet in front of her. "Feeling any better?"

Raccoon eyes peered out from beneath a blond rat's nest as she reached for the damp cloth he held in offering. "Carter—"

"Connor," he corrected drily, torn between amusement and what, by all rights, ought to be the very antithesis of it.

"We need a lawyer," she gasped, barely finding the time to look chagrined before the next wave of revolt took her.

A lawyer. Not exactly a stellar kickoff to their honeymoon. But then, this wasn't exactly a stellar situation to begin with. Of course, in the less than fifteen minutes since the warm body sprawled beside him had moaned—once, and not in a good way—then lurched from the bed to the bathroom, he hadn't quite put all the soggy pieces of the night before into place. But based on the shocking evidence at hand—or more specifically, finger…and the band of glinting diamonds encircling hers—this was the worst-case scenario come to life. Cutting loose gone bad. Consequences in action. Yeah, in all likelihood, this was going to be a major hassle to clean up.

So a lawyer sounded like an ideal place to start. Once the upchuck portion of the morning concluded, at any rate.

"One thing at a time, babe. Let's get through this, and we'll worry about the rest later."

Whatever her choked response was, he got the gist it was an agreement of sorts.

Damn, what a disaster.

Rubbing a hand over the back of his neck, Connor gave his blanching bride a not-so-subtle once-over.

Twelve hours ago she'd been "authentic" with her sharp wit and gently rough edges. Her too-wide smile, assortment of freckles and sexy laugh. Now, with her hair threatening to dip into God only knew, she just looked…rough. No gentle about it.

Still, even as he stared at the hot mess she was before him, fragmented images bombarded his mind with hints of who she'd been the night before. The girl-next-door giving in to a bit of wild. The perfect fit for his bad-boy mood. He'd thought she looked like a few hours of fun.

So how the hell had she ended up flipped over his shoulder, giggling about how crazy he was, as he toted her into one of those all-night chapels Las Vegas was famous for?

Megan turned, giving him a full-on frontal view of the too-tight, hot-pink T-shirt she'd been wearing when he'd stumbled into the bathroom after her.

Stamped across her bust in black block letters were two words: *GOT SPERM?*

Oh, right. That was how.

Hell.

What had she been thinking!

Megan peered up at the darkening scowl across Carter's—no—*Connor's* face and then down at what was probably a combined ten carats of diamonds adorning the fourth finger of her left hand…and heaved into the bowl again.

She'd had sex. With a stranger. Someone she maintained only the foggiest recollection of meeting. And then…she'd gone and *married* him.

Or maybe they'd waited…going the more traditional route and saving themselves for after the wedding. So it would be special.

Ugh!

So *incredibly special* the only detail of the entire consummation she remembered was the soft rub of fabric between her thighs, the heady weight of him above her and her intense frustration in getting her toe caught in his belt loop while trying to wrestle his tie loose.

And now, here she was on her knees, hurling her lungs out while this man, essentially a stranger, bore witness to one of the most intimate unpleasantnesses a person could endure. She wished he'd left when she'd told him to. But he'd stayed to make sure she was okay…like the good husband he was.

It was almost enough to make her laugh, only it really wasn't funny and her body was otherwise engaged.

"There can't be much left" came the gruff voice from behind her.

As the spasms subsided, she hazarded a glance at the man she'd married. Beyond the contemplative expression, those dark eyes didn't offer up much to read.

"There isn't…" she groaned. "I've been on empty for a few rounds already. This…is just my stomach making a point…I think."

"Hmm. Really driving it home, I see." The touch of dry humor pulled her focus back to him again. To the details she'd missed in the first pass. He was tall. And not because of her near-floor-level perspective. Tall enough so as he leaned against the open doorway, his free hand hung in a loose grip from the top of the frame mere inches from his head. And he was built in a powerful, lean-strength kind of way where the muscles across his chest, abdomen, shoulders and arms were well-defined but without the extreme bulk of serious bodybuilders. This guy just looked really fit. And as if that weren't bad enough, he was classically handsome too, with a blade-straight nose, high cheekbones and an assortment of even features so appealing she suddenly wondered how long she'd been staring.

From her little hangout on the floor…by the toilet…where she'd been throwing up.

Ugh!

Really, the humiliation couldn't get much worse. But it didn't matter. This guy and all his good looks weren't a part of her plan. So what if he was handsome, or that she'd seen hints of the kind of humor she typically appreciated, or that she was, in fact, married to him? She'd had enough close calls in her life with men she'd actually *known*, and she was through with the whole business.

Still, pride had her stumbling to her feet on limbs that were clumsy and tight from the combination of dehydration and kneeling too long. Limbs that weren't quite working. Suddenly she was going right back down until two strong hands gripped her beneath her arms, holding her steady as she regained her footing.

The contact was awkward. Her, trying to hold herself apart; him, trying to support her without getting too close. "Thank you."

"Not a problem." And then after a pause, "Just one of the benefits of having a husband around, I guess."

She nodded, exhausted, overwhelmed, but somehow more grateful than words could convey for that bit of superficial exchange. As much as they needed to, she wasn't ready to talk about what happened last night. About how they were going to sort it out this morning and over the next however long it took to get an annulment processed.

Not until she'd at the very least had a shower, tooth-brushing, floss and several intensive minutes with the most mediciney mouthwash she could get her hands on. Glancing down, she added a change of clothes to her list. And then, committed to doing her part, she replied in kind, "Knew there was a reason I'd picked one up."

The low answering chuckle had her daring another look over her shoulder.

It was the smile that did it. That brought the melee of vodka-soaked images into order enough for her to see at least a glimpse of the man from the night before rather than the near stranger she'd woken beside this morning.

Oh, God. What had she gotten herself into—and how fast could she get herself out of it?

CHAPTER TWO

Twelve hours earlier...

"OH, COME ON, screw the sperm bank." Tina sighed with a dismissive flutter of her candy-apple acrylics. "Where's the fun in that?"

Megan Scott tipped her glass, swallowing the last decadent drops of white-chocolate martini, then slumped deeper into the plush cushions of the lounge chair she'd taken up residence in some forty minutes before. Contemplating another drink, she did her best to ignore the incessant bickering her fellow bridesmaids had perfected through a lifetime of practice.

That it was her womb they were battling over was of as little consequence as the fact that Megan already had a plan and she was sticking to it.

"Um...the fun comes nine months later," Jodie snipped back. "All tiny and new, wearing one of those little nursery beanies... and without any of the communicable side effects on offer with *your* plan..."

Tina's plan, as Megan understood it, revolved around the T-shirt—hot off the silk screen and sporting the slogan GOT SPERM?—folded neatly on the cocktail table between them.

"I mean, seriously, who's to say this total, random stranger enticed by your thirteen-dollar custom call for baby batter isn't attempting to walk off the early stages of Ebola or worse? Casual, unprotected sex is stupid. And you're trying to talk Megan into it. For God sake, why don't you pick up a knife and stab her."

Turning the glass upside down, Megan watched as a single last drop of martini goodness slid to the rim. Catching it with her tongue, she hoped the cocktail waitress would take her action as the plea for help it was and bring a refill. Fast.

"You're such a prude. It's pathetic."

Eesh.

"*What I am* is too much of a lady to say *what you are.*"

"Girls, please," Megan interjected before the volley of barbs got any more intense. "I totally appreciate you two looking out for me this way." Okay, she was stretching the truth, but somehow her tongue let her get away with it. Honestly, she'd have rather been of such little interest they both got her name wrong all weekend and ignored her through dinner. But courtesy of her mother's propensity to spill secrets, the family grapevine had guaranteed her Vegas arrival for cousin Gail's wedding was met with a tempest of polarizing opinion regarding her decision to undergo artificial insemination in two months' time. "Tina, I love—really love—this T-shirt, but the only place it's going is into my scrapbook. And, Jodie, thank you for the support but—"

Jodie's hand came up, cutting her off. "I don't, really. Support what you've decided to do. You ought to wait to find a husband like the rest of us."

Images of Barry and the two years they'd dated flashed through her mind, threatening to suck her into a vortex of churning emotions she wouldn't allow herself to surrender to. Shame, embarrassment, anger and helpless frustration.

"Megan, I swear I didn't even realize it myself. Not until right that minute...and suddenly I knew. I'd never stopped loving her."

She wasn't going there again, wasn't wasting another precious second on the man who'd left for a conference talking about starting a family with her and then come home married to someone else.

Spine stiffening, she reined herself in.

She didn't need Barry.

She didn't need any man to have the child she'd always wanted—well, at least not for more than five minutes of quality time with a plastic cup.

Jodie sighed, a faraway look settling over her features. "Wait for your Prince Charming and you'll have someone to share your special moment in the nursery, making it all the sweeter."

"Well, actually," Megan started, but Jodie wasn't finished.

"You're what's wrong with our society. I mean, life isn't about getting everything you want the instant you want it. Some things are worth waiting for. That said, in a toss-up between bedding down with the next patient zero or hitting the drive-thru for prescreened sperm...I'll back the bank."

Megan felt the telling wash of heat rush through her cheeks, but thinking about Gail and what kind of wedding she'd have if all three of her bridesmaids were at each other's throats, she tamped it down. "Okay. Well, thank you...for your thoughts on the issue."

Tina's less-than-delicate snort sounded from beside her, and Megan craned her neck in search of their waitress. Only, rather than the leggy server with the no-nonsense attitude, she found her attention snared by the man walking past their table. Hand raised in casual greeting, mahogany eyes fixed on someone across the room, he was tall, dark and handsome in the most traditional sense. Broad and tapered, chiseled and cut. All clean lines and classic good looks. The balanced symmetry of him so flawless, it might have made him bland.

If not for his mouth.

This guy had one of those slanted smiles going on. The kind so lazy only half of it bothered to go to work. And yet, something about the ease of it suggested a near permanence on his face, while its stunted progress implied—well, she supposed that was part of the lure. It could really imply anything.

That smile was the kind women got lost in while trying to unravel its mystery.

Only, Megan was through trying to read signs and figure guys out. Which was why she pried her eyes loose from the table where this one had settled in with a friend or associate or whomever, and forced herself to refocus on Tina and Jodie… who were totally focused on her.

In tandem they leaned forward, resting on their elbows.

"Window-shopping the gene pool, Megan?" Tina asked with a knowing smirk as one pencil-thin brow pushed high. "See something you like?"

Jodie's eyes narrowed. "His suit is too perfectly cut to be anything but made-to-measure. The suit, the watch, the links. This guy has *quality catch* written all over him. Megan, quick, cross your legs higher and give up some thigh. Tina, get his attention."

Megan's lips parted to protest, but Tina was a woman of action. "Wow, Megan, I knew you were a gymnast, but I didn't think anyone's legs could do that!"

Tina's face took on an expression of benevolence and she crossed her arms, leaning back in her seat. "You're welcome."

Needles of tension prickled up and down her back as she struggled for her next breath. Eyes fixed on the tabletop in front of her, Megan held up her empty martini glass and prayed to the cocktail gods for a refill. When she thought she could manage more than a squeak, she cleared her throat and replied to anyone within listening distance, "I'm not a gymnast."

At which point Tina and Jodie burst out laughing.

"It may not seem like it now, but you're better off without her…"

Connor Reed shifted irritably in his chair, swirling the amber and ice of his scotch as he listened to Jeff Norton forfeit his status as one of the guys. "Noted."

And not exactly a news flash.

"…You and Caro were together for almost a year… It's okay to be hurt…"

Hurt? Connor's eye started to twitch.

This wasn't guy talk. It wasn't the promised blowing off of steam with which he'd been lured to Sin City.

It *wasn't* cool.

"…a blow to the ego, and for someone with an ego like yours…"

Growling into his glass, he muttered, "We need to get your testosterone levels checked."

"Whatever," Jeff answered, unfazed. He was as secure with his emotional "awareness" as he was with his position as Connor's oldest and best friend. "All I'm saying is you were ready to marry Caro two weeks ago. I don't believe you're as indifferent as you make out to be."

"Yeah, but you never want to believe the truth about me," Connor replied with an unrepentant grin. "Seriously, though, Jeff, like I told you before, I'm fine. Caro was a great girl, but hearing what she had to say…I'm more relieved than anything else."

The following grunt suggested Jeff wasn't buying it.

And to an extent, the guy might be right. Just not the way he figured.

Connor wasn't heartbroken over the end of the relationship because his heart had never played into the equation. Callous but true. And something Caro had understood from the first.

Connor didn't do love. All too well he understood the potential of its destructive power. He knew the distance of its reach, had experienced the devastation of its ripple effect. No thank you. He hadn't been signing on for more.

What he'd been after was a family. The kind he'd only ever seen from the outside looking in, but coveted just the same. The kind his father hadn't wanted some bastard son to contaminate, and his mother had been too deep in her own grief to sustain. So he'd been determined to build his own.

There were a lot of things he'd done without as a kid. Things he'd made it his purpose to secure as an adult. Money, respect, his own home…and the thriving business he ran with an iron fist that garnered them all. But a family…? For that, he needed a partner. One he'd thought he found in Caro. She fit the bill, fundraiser ready with the right name, education and background. Coolly composed and devoid of the emotional neediness he'd spent his adult life actively avoiding. Or so he'd thought, right up to that last day when she'd folded her napkin at the side of her plate and evenly explained she wanted a marriage based on more than what they had. She hadn't expected to, but there it was.

Fair enough. He gave her credit for having the good sense to recognize she wanted something she wouldn't find with him. And most important, *before* the vows were exchanged.

So, heartbroken? No.

Disappointed? Sure.

Relieved? Hell, yes.

"…I think you're lonely. Sad…"

Throwing back the rest of his single malt, Connor relished the burn down his throat and spread of heat through his belly. If he weighed in fifty pounds lighter, it might have been enough to fuzz out the discomfort of this conversation.

But there was always the next one.

"…remember, there are other fish in the sea—"

"*Come on*, what's next—hot flashes?" Holding up the empty, he scanned the crowd for the cocktail server.

"—hell, apparently the one over there is a gymnast."

Connor quirked a brow, angling his head for a better look. "Which one?"

Jeff winked. "Just making sure you were listening. Care about you, man."

Though he'd never figured out why, Connor knew.

That caring had been the single constant in his life from the time he'd been ripped out of poverty and drop-kicked into the East Coast's most exclusive boarding school at thirteen. He'd been the illegitimate kid with a chip on his shoulder, a jagged crack through the center of his soul and a grudge against the name he couldn't escape—and Jeff had been the unlucky SOB saddled with him as a roommate. Connor hadn't given him any reason to cut him a break, but for some reason, Jeff had anyway.

Which was why, for as much as he gave his friend a hard time about being an "in touch" guy…he also gave him the truth. "Yeah, you too… Now, where's the gymnast?"

Another two rounds and some forty minutes later, Connor leaned back in his chair watching as Jeff reasserted his status

as a testosterone-driven male by smoothly intercepting the cocktail girl he'd been eyeing for the better part of an hour. Connor
didn't even want to think about the rap this guy had laid on her
to get those lashes batting and her tray cast aside so fast, but
whatever it was, it must have been phenomenal.

Jeff shot him a salute, and the deal was done.

Reaching into this breast pocket, Connor pulled out his wallet, tossed a few bills onto the table and then set his empty glass
atop the stack.

The night stretched out before him with all its endless...
exhausting possibilities.

He could hit the blackjack tables.

Grab a bite.

Pick up some company. Or not. With this apathetic indifference he was rocking—

"Excuse me."

Glancing up, he'd expected another waitress ready to clear,
but instead it was the blonde in the midnight dress from the
other table. The *gymnast*, who most definitely wasn't a gymnast if her height and the soft S-like lines of a figure draped
in one of those clingy wrap numbers were anything to go on.

Very nice. "Hi. What can I do for you?"

Her smile spread wide as her big blue eyes held his. "This is
going to sound like a line. A really, really bad one. But you've
got to believe me when I say it's not."

The corner of his mouth twitched as he readied for what inevitably was *the rest of the line*. Playing in, he gave her a nod.
"Okay, you've got the disclaimer out of the way. Go for it."

She nodded, releasing a deep breath. "I noticed you were
about to leave. And I'd be more grateful than you could imagine if you wouldn't mind walking out with me. So it looks like
we're leaving *together*."

Right. "Just *looks* like we're leaving together?"

Again her wide smile flashed, and Connor saw shades of
girl-next-door. Not usually his type, but for whatever reason,
there was something about the look of this one...

"Yes. My...friends saw me notice you earlier and...well...

and you don't even want to know what it's been like since. I told them I'd come over and see if you were interested because I want them off my back. But I can tell from looking at you, that I'm not the kind of woman you'd be interested in…which is, actually, the only reason I decided to come over. I'd love to get out of here without them following me for the rest of the night."

She'd been checking him out, eh?

Well, fair being fair, he gave his eyes the go-ahead to run the length of her and back, spending more time along the way than he'd done in his first casual glance. Very, very nice. Even with her scolding finger wagging at him on the return trip.

"None of that. You're handsome, but I'm honestly working an escape strategy here."

He shifted, the smile he hadn't quite let loose earlier breaking free with the realization she was serious. Glancing past her, he noted her friends blatantly staring back.

"Subtle."

She shrugged delicately. "So far as I can tell, subtle isn't really their thing."

He raised a brow. "*So far as you can tell?* What kind of friends are they?"

"The kind on loan until our bridesmaids' obligations have been fulfilled, sometime before dawn on Sunday. I hope. They're my cousin's best friends from kindergarten."

Ah. "And they've taken an interest in your love life because….?"

Her nose wrinkled up as she scanned the ceiling. "Any chance you might just walk me out of here?"

Connor eased back into his chair, pulling out the seat Jeff had vacated with his foot. "Not if you want it to look convincing. I'll walk you out of here…in ten minutes."

The skeptical look said she'd figured out he was thinking about more than the next ten minutes.

As different as she was from the women he usually pursued, she looked as if she really might be exactly the kind of fun this night called for.

The kind who didn't generally hook up with strangers.

The corruptible kind, he thought, feeling less apathetic by the second.

"Ten minutes. We'll talk. Flirt. You can touch my arm once or twice to really sell it. Maybe I'll tuck some wayward strand of hair behind your ear. Your voyeuristic friends will gobble it up. Then I'll lean in close to your ear and suggest we get out of here. Maybe do it in a way that has you blushing all the way to your roots. You'll get flustered and shy, but let me take your hand anyway. And we'll go."

The look on her face was priceless. As though he'd gotten to her with this bit of scripted tripe.

"That's…um…" She swallowed, her gaze darting around, landing on his mouth and lingering briefly before snapping back to his eyes. "More of an investment than I was really asking for."

"The better for you."

"Yeah, but what's in it for you?"

Connor flashed a wolfish smile. "Ten minutes to convince you to give me twenty. We'll see where it goes from there."

The slight shake of her head had his focus honing and his critical skills tuning up. Man, he'd been thinking how much he might like to see her girl-next-door smile turn sultry, but now here she was making him work for her too? It didn't get better.

"I should probably go. I'm not a casual-encounter kind of girl. And even if you were looking for something more than casual, I still wouldn't be interested."

Something about the way she said it had his curiosity standing up for a stretch. "Oh, yeah—how come?"

Her hand lifted in a sort of dismissive flutter, which stopped almost before it began. Then meeting his eyes, she said, "Sorry, it's a little too personal for a *fake first nondate*."

Connor grinned, shrugging one shoulder. "So why not make it a *not-quite-so-fake first nondate*. Or maybe a *fake first date*, though if we're already faking it, we ought to go for a second or third date…when all the good stuff starts."

Her smile went wide before giving way to a laugh out of line with the girl-next-door everything else about her. The laugh had his head cranking around for a second take. And sure enough, when her eyes were half closed, her lips parted for that low rolling sound of seductive abandon, he was the one left staring.

For a second.

Before he shifted back into gear. "Seriously, I'd like to know."

He could see it in her eyes, in the tilt of her head and the way her body had already started to turn away. In her mind, the decision was made, and mentally, she was halfway to the door. Too bad.

But regardless, he didn't want to leave her hanging after she'd mustered the nerve to come over.

"I'll walk you out," he said, but she shook her head and smiled.

"Thanks, I'll be fine, though."

"Fair enough. I'm Connor, by the way." He extended his hand, feeling like an ass offering to shake goodbye after the exchange they'd shared, but for some reason wanting to test the contact anyway.

"Megan." She reached across the table and met his hand with her smaller one—and a flash of neon pink arced through the air, coming to land in his lap.

The hand in his clenched as he looked down and read the block lettering.

"What the—?"

Peals of laughter rang from the table where Megan had been sitting. The bridesmaids she'd been trying to escape. Or so she'd said.

His hand tightened around hers as, leveling her with a stare, he pulled her forward and then down into the open chair. "Sit. Now I *need* to know."

Megan looked into his eyes, a thousand thoughts running through hers before she slumped back in the chair and said, "Okay, Carter—"

"Connor."

She swallowed. "Connor. Right. Sorry. So here it is…"

CHAPTER THREE

Nine hours earlier...

"I THINK YOUR SUBCONSCIOUS is trying to tell you something."

Megan grinned into her glass, trying not to laugh as she took the next sip. Sweet martini goodness coated her tongue, making her wonder how she'd gone through so much of her life without having tried one of these white-chocolate concoctions. They were delicious.

Oh, wait...the subconscious...

"Okay, what?"

"This trip to Vegas. It's your subconscious screaming some deeply repressed need to take a chance. Do something crazy."

They were back to this again. Megan shot him a knowing look, only to find his unrepentant one on the other end. "*Or*, this trip is about my cousin getting married."

"Denial is a powerful thing."

"Forget it. I told you already. I'm not running off and marrying you, so please stop begging."

Carter—shoot, *Connor*, why couldn't she remember!—let out a bark of laughter. They both knew marriage wasn't what he'd been getting at. Just as they both knew he wasn't actually serious.

He knew what her plans were. Had been truly interested when she'd laid them out, explaining her choice to pursue artificial insemination via sperm donor. And rather than back away slowly, he'd decided they both needed a night to cut loose and have some fun. The kind without consequences. The kind that revolved around easy conversation, harmless flirting and more drinks than were a good idea.

Knowing it would be the last, and finding a certain comfort in the utter lack of expectation from the man she was with, Megan agreed.

And she'd been near breathless with laughter ever since—milling through the grand casino, stopping at one attraction and then another, caught up in the sort of fun in which she never indulged.

Connor had been right. This was what she'd needed.

The palm of his hand settled lightly at the small of her back as he guided her toward an outcropping of slots. "I don't know, Megan. Seems for a decision this big, you want to consider every option before dismissing it out of hand."

"Maybe you're right." Then giving in to the impish grin tugging at her lips, she waved vaguely at the men around her. "And there are plenty of *options* to consider."

Connor shook his head. "If you're looking for a guy to close the deal, I'd steer clear of the slots," he offered, totally deadpan. "Nothing says *compensation issues* like a man clinging too closely to a twelve-inch rod of metal."

It took more than she'd thought she had to do it, but once Megan reined in her laughter, she pulled a mock scowl. "Seriously, how long have we known each other—and you think I'd hit the slots?"

This time it was Connor cracking the half smile that seemed his equivalent to a full-on belly laugh. "Right, I should have had more faith."

She nodded, scanning the casino floor. "Roulette tables are where all the quality swimmers hang out."

Another wry twist of lips. "I'm forced to disagree with you. Any guy lingering around a game based solely on luck is delusional. Probably believes in Santa and fairies. Doesn't bode well for mental stability. You want the probability of psychosis spiraling through Junioretta's double helix?"

Another stifled giggle. "No, definitely not. How could I have been so off base?"

"Sometimes I wonder about you."

She couldn't remember the last time she'd had so much fun. Couldn't remember a guy she'd been so instantly at ease with. Of course, that last bit probably had more to do with knowing this wasn't leading anywhere. Which took the pressure off tremendously. She could simply enjoy the attention of this incredibly attractive, charming man without worrying about... anything.

"Blackjack, then?"

They'd made it halfway across the floor when Connor caught a passing waitress, giving her their order before returning his attention to Megan. "Also delusional. He thinks he's in control when it's a game of chance. Unless he's counting...and then you have a criminal element to consider."

Playing devil's advocate, she asked, "But wouldn't counting suggest a higher level of intelligence?"

"So you're a single mom, strapped from the cost of the private academy his 'genius' demands. How much time are you going to have for all those trips to visit little Buster in juvie?"

Megan let out her best indignant cough. "You're implying my baby is going to be some kind of delinquent?"

One oh-so-arrogant brow shot high. Sexy and confident. "Not if you play your cards right."

"Fine, fine." She laughed, wiping the tears at the corners of her eyes with the backs of her thumbs. "So we've been through the slots, roulette and blackjack. If none of those are right, then what—offtrack betting?"

Connor drew to a stop, turning to consider her more closely than the question called for. Closely enough she could feel her body respond to the touch of his eyes at every point of contact. His smile was pure arrogance as he answered, "You want to win the genetic jackpot, then skip the pit stop at Gamblers Anonymous altogether. Obviously your best bet is me."

* * *

Megan laughed, head thrown back, eyes closed, and the sound of it hit him right in the center of the chest. And when those big blue eyes blinked back at him, her cheeks a rosy red, the hot rush and warm pull of attraction firing through his body nearly knocked the reason right out of him.

Fortunately, she didn't seem to notice as she turned to accept her cocktail from the approaching waitress. "In the nick of time. I'll definitely need another drink before I buy into that one."

With a jut of his chin, he urged, "By all means, then, bottoms up." Tossing back a swallow of his own, he grinned. "I've got all night."

Damn, she had a gorgeous laugh. Even after it left her lips… echoes of it lit her eyes. Those sparkling eyes that were staring up at him like maybe he had the solution for anything. And suddenly, the idea of this strong, fiercely independent woman *needing* something *from him* appealed on an almost primal level.

"What?" he asked, chalking up the low timbre of his voice to a dry throat and remedying the obvious problem with a gulp of scotch.

Megan reached for the lapel of his jacket, her slender fingers curving around the fabric in a move both needy and intimate—a move that did something to him he wasn't quite sure he should like *quite* so much.

Pearly-white teeth sank into the soft swell of her bottom lip before pulling free and he stopped breathing altogether.

"Megan."

She sighed. "I'm starving."

For a beat he stared down at her. And then those fingers tightened and she gave his lapel a little shake. *"Star-ving."*

A single nod.

Food.

Yeah, he was pretty hungry too. For something, anyway. So it was time to stop staring down into her pretty, freckle-kissed face.

"Right." Downing the rest of his glass in one swallow, he handed off the empty to a passing server. "Then I'm your man."

Seven hours earlier...

He'd thought it couldn't get any better than the laugh. But then he'd heard the laugh coupled with the squeals of delight and gotten an eyeful of Megan's sensational and perfectly displayed backside. Shimmying in some victory dance as her winning machine counted up at the far end of the waffle buffet their surprisingly reliable cabbie had recommended.

Damn.

She'd caught him by surprise. Again. Lulling him into too easy a conversation and then giving up the details of her life as easily as this machine had given up her winnings. All it had taken was the right question at the right time, and she'd opened up, revealing new insight into the engaging creature he'd managed to capture for the night.

She was a self-proclaimed recovering romantic. A woman who believed in love but had discovered through a lifetime of experience the heights of that particular romantic elevation to be beyond her reach. And she'd accepted it, wasn't interested in the futility of an unattainable pursuit. She was a brainiac beauty. A freelance software engineer, successful in her own right. Confident where it counted and modest in the most appealing ways. Independent to an extreme and unafraid to buck convention when it came to the achievement of her goals. Kind, funny and sexy.

Now he stood behind her, their latest round of cocktails set aside—which maybe wasn't such a bad thing considering the kind of detours his head had been taking—as he shrugged out of his suit jacket, giving in to the absurdly out-of-place bit of possessive insanity going nuts thinking about anyone else seeing this heart-shaped perfection.

"Here, put this on," he said, slipping it over her shoulders.

"I can't believe it!" she gasped. "I never win. I never, ever, *ever* get lucky like this."

Connor grinned, watching as the bare length of her arms disappeared within the sea of his coat. Reaching over, he adjusted the lapels, telling himself she'd looked cold. Then before he gave in to the temptation to linger near that tantalizing V of feminine flesh, or God forbid let his knuckles skim the softness there, he moved on to cuff her sleeves. Rolling up the arms until the slim band of her wristwatch shone beneath the flashing lights of her winning machine. It was a delicate band, but a little plain. The way he'd mistakenly thought about her, when really this girl glittered like a diamond.

"Carter," she said breathlessly, those blue eyes watching where his thumb stroked across the sensitive pale skin of her inner wrist.

"Connor." What the hell was he doing?

Her eyes lifted slowly, following the line of his arm, across his shoulder, to the top of his tie and then his mouth.

Did she have any idea how seductive those few beats of time were when he could all but see her mind working through the possibilities of where her gaze lingered.

This woman was hot. And sweet. And smart. And funny.

And she was staring at his mouth like it looked better than vanilla vodka and white-chocolate liqueur.

Like maybe, after all, she might want a taste.

Or even more.

Another beat and her eyes met his.

"Connor," she corrected, the good judgment wrestling in those blue pools, barely holding out against temptation.

Damn, he liked the way she said his name. Especially when she got it right.

He had an excellent idea for helping her remember too.

Repetition. And positive reinforcement—the breathless, moaning, pleading kind.

Hours of it.

He could push—turn on the seduction and he'd have her.

This flirtation he'd been playing at was nothing. For every

easy compliment, he'd kept a physical space between them. For every suggestive line, he'd avoided eye contact. Because he'd known—had a sense about what could be between them, and he'd steered clear of it. Only, now…he wanted more.

Shaking his head, he glared at the half-empty glass on the counter beside them. *Your fault.*

Pushing those thoughts aside, he put the arm's length back between them, the easy smile. The just-for-fun.

Moments later they were outside in the night air, surrounded by the bright lights, the drifting foot traffic and steady stream of cars. "You just cracked two machines in a row. We ought to head back to the casino and find you a real jackpot. Or would you like to try something different, like roulette?"

A deep sigh left her pretty mouth. "I don't think so. For someone who doesn't win very often, I'm happy to be coming out ahead the way I am. I don't want to push my luck."

"Something else in mind?" he asked. But he already knew, having seen the flash of resignation in her eyes.

Goodbye.

He didn't want the night to end, but she had a plan, after all. He respected her for it. Admired the sense of priority, forethought and commitment she'd put into it. Hell, that plan was probably half her appeal.

"I've had a really good time tonight." Megan shifted in front of him, her gaze skating away as her fingers slid down the lapels of his suit jacket, to where they idly played with the top button.

"Me too. Of course, this is Vegas. It's still early."

Her eyes pulled back to his, flickering only once to his mouth. "Early morning."

And then her shoulders were straightening, her features falling into an altogether too-polite expression. "And I've got a big day ahead of me."

"Big day of attending."

"Yes. And making up elaborate lies about our night together." This time her grin was pure imp. "Give Jodie and Tina something juicier to chew on than each other."

"Wow, you're going to lie about me?" he asked, settling his

hand at the small of her back as they approached the curb in search of a cab. "I'm flattered."

Nothing available, but one would come along any minute.

Megan shot him a wry smile. "Actually, probably not. I want to. It would be so great. But lying gives me hives. Even for a good cause like keeping the peace at my cousin's wedding, I'm not sure I'd be able to do it."

"So you're one of those perpetually honest types?" he asked as they walked in the direction of the casino where they were staying.

"Pretty much. Not always convenient. But I guess it keeps me out of trouble most times."

Uh-huh, but if she didn't stop worrying that sexy bottom lip between her teeth—nothing would keep her out of the trouble he had in mind.

Only, then she noticed the way he was watching her, and looked away.

He didn't want to lose her attention. Not yet. "With women like Tina and Jodie, I'm thinking not saying anything at all would be as effective as telling them what a stallion I am—which, incidentally, is one hundred percent accurate. Leave them to stew in their curiosity. Speculate to their hearts' content. And give them nothing."

"Oooh, it'll drive them *insane*," she gasped, nearly bouncing beside him and making him wonder how deep her wicked streak went. And if it ever blurred the line into naughty. "God knows their imaginations are more colorful than mine."

Giving in to another smirk, he offered, "I could help with that."

He was joking. Mostly.

Megan stopped and shook her head, the straight ends of her hair brushing softly across her shoulders. "I'm sure you could."

Even beneath the lights and glitz of the Strip, he could see the rise of a deep blush in her cheeks, read all the subtle signs of hesitation as they came. He could see her talking herself out of every maybe, what-if, just-a-few-more and only-this-once idea popping into her pretty head. He could feel the tension as she wrestled with her conscience about extending a night they'd both enjoyed.

He knew she wanted to… "But you have a plan."

Honest. Intelligent. Funny. Independent. Megan was all that and more, with the kind of practical approach to love he couldn't get out of his head. Eyes to the sky, he pushed out a long breath—that stopped abruptly when his focus caught on the neon sign flashing over her right shoulder.

She had a plan…but maybe it wasn't the only one.

God, she didn't want the night to end. But there was only one place it could go. And as much as the idea of falling into this man's bed appealed to her, it wasn't how she lived her life.

It didn't matter that he seemed more soul mate than stranger. Or that she'd never be in a position to let go like this again. If she gave in, she'd regret it tomorrow.

And when she thought about this night, she didn't want there to be any regrets.

So she swallowed and did what she had to do. "I have a plan."

The words opened an emptiness inside her, different from the one that had been so much a part of her every day.

"Thank you for a wonderful evening, Carter."

His mouth tilted in another one of those unreadable half smiles.

Tempting. So tempting.

"Megan, about your plan." He caught her elbow in a loose hold. "There's one thing I'm curious about."

Facing him, she asked, "What's that?"

His fingers slipped from her elbow down her arm in a soft caress and, catching her hand in his, he tucked it low against her back. Stepped in and, dropping his stare to her mouth, murmured, "Just this."

And he kissed her.

At first, the shock of contact was all she could register. And then the slow, back-and-forth rub of his mouth against hers. The firm pressure. The gentle pull. The low-level current riding all the places they touched.

Yes.

Just this.

The perfect end to a night she wished didn't have to.

Seconds later there was a breath between them—passing back and forth in a soft wash of warm and wet.

"Connor," he murmured, close enough she could almost feel the vibration on her lips.

Megan blinked, but didn't step back as she peered up into his eyes. "What?"

The corner of his mouth tipped. "Wanted to make sure you remembered my name."

"Connor." She sighed, closing her eyes to savor the moment just a little longer before she left. "That was very nice."

Catching her with a crooked finger beneath her chin, Connor brought her gaze back to his. When their eyes met, she had to blink. It wasn't the bittersweet sort of resigned longing *she felt* that was shining in his eyes. Not by a long shot. It was cocky arrogance and a sharply focused anticipation.

"Not really," he said, curving his hand so it cupped her jaw. "*That* was getting you used to the idea."

Her lips parted to protest, but before she had the chance to backtrack or reword her response, he'd swooped in again. Closing the bit of distance between them without hesitation. Taking her mouth as if it was his to do with as he pleased, making it his own in a way that had Megan's hands rising of their own volition, her fingers curling into his tailored shirt, her moan sliding free of her mouth and into his. There wasn't anything even remotely *nice* about this kiss. It was hot. Explosive. Consuming and intense.

It was the kind of kiss for behind closed doors. The kind she'd never in her life believed she would have allowed to take place in the middle of a crowded sidewalk. But then, she'd never been faced with the need to break away from something so damn good.

And then she wasn't thinking about what she should be doing at all. Where she was. Or where she was going. There was only the hot press of Connor's body as he pulled her closer. The skillful exploration of a part of her that suddenly felt like undiscovered country. The slow lick of his tongue against hers.

Delicious.

So good.

Another wicked lick was followed by a slow, steady thrust, and she was lost to it. Her hands moved against the hard planes of his torso in restless anticipation of what more he could give her.

She might regret this tomorrow…but not nearly as much as she would regret walking away tonight.

When Connor pulled back, she was breathless. Hungry. Desperate.

This time, the elusive tilt to Connor's lips was gone. He drew a slow breath, his brows seeming to draw lower through every passing second until his eyes had become fathomless depths, so dark she wondered if, once she fell in, she'd ever make it back out again.

"Okay, yeah," he murmured, as though having reached some internal understanding with himself.

"Yeah, okay," she whispered, nodding. "But we have to go back to your room. I'm sharing a suite with Tina and Jodie."

Only, then his head lowered to hers, and he pressed a single slow kiss against her lips before moving close to her ear. "I've got an even better idea."

A second later his hands had clamped around her hips and she'd been hoisted over his shoulder, where she bounced with his long strides. Delighted by this show of caveman antics, she breathlessly laughed out a demand for an explanation.

"I've got a plan…" he answered, confident and excited. "I'll tell you about it on the way. It's up here on the right."

CHAPTER FOUR

THE QUIET HUM OF THE SHOWER came to a stop, leaving only the silence of the villa roaring around him. Connor stared out over the bedroom terrace and private Caribbean blue pool below, trying to anticipate what he would face when his wife emerged from her steamy refuge.

Megan had held it together through those first minutes of realization, even managing a few joking remarks between bouts of nausea—but as soon as she'd been strong enough to stand on her own, she'd asked for some privacy to clean up.

And he'd been waiting since. Listening to the lock snap on the bathroom door as it closed behind him. Contemplating the single muted sob he'd heard before the echoing spray of the shower drowned all other sound. Piecing together the events, revelations and resolutions of the night before. Trying to reconcile them with the here and now of the morning.

Megan wanted a lawyer.

It had been the only definitive statement she'd made regarding their marriage in those few chaotic moments they'd spent ensconced in their marble-and-brass hideaway. Granted, she was probably as hazy on the finer points of the night as he was, but something possessive inside him was growling in outrage at the thought.

She was his wife.

She'd married him. And not on some lark either, but because she'd recognized the potential between them, same as him.

So yeah, the alcohol may have played into the immediacy of

his actions. But with every passing minute, the details of those critical hours they'd spent together and the woman he'd married sharpened in his mind, reaffirming his confidence in the decision to strike while the iron was hot.

And no, the irony wasn't lost on him that after his patient, methodical approach to finding a wife had failed with Caro— Megan had just dropped into his lap. Sure, sure, he'd had to sell her on the idea once he'd seen the sense in it. But he was a man with a knack for identifying opportunity and the skills to convey the benefits of said opportunity to others. He could size up a situation and break down the key factors, without waiting for the proverbial knock at his door or encyclopedic pitch most people required prior to taking action. And what he'd seen in Megan told him she was the kind of opportunity he shouldn't kick out of his bed for eating crackers— or, more specifically, downing half Nevada's monthly import of vanilla vodka in one night.

Their agendas were simply too well aligned to ignore. The timing too right. The practical approach too perfect. And she'd been like-minded enough to see it and agree.

Megan fit him to a T, so he wasn't prepared to admit he'd made a mistake. Not yet anyway. Though he supposed the next few minutes would be fairly telling on that count. A bout of hysterics, for instance, would most definitely have him reconsidering his stance.

The lock released with a loud click and Connor steeled his gut for what came next. Only, somehow the sight of Megan, towel dried, freshly scrubbed and swimming in a thick, oatmeal robe as she tentatively pushed a damp tendril from her brow, was something he had no defense against.

She was beautiful.

And the steady way she met his eyes proved she wasn't a meltdown in progress. Though taking the rest of her body language into account—the crossed arms, one hand securing the overlap of panels high at her neck and the other wrapped tight around her waist—suggested she wasn't quite ready to pick up where they'd left off the night before. She looked cautious. Alert. And cool.

She looked strong, and it had his pulse jacking as much as the sight of those sexy little pink toenails peeking out from beneath the hem of her oversize robe.

"Feeling better?" he asked, planting a shoulder against the sliding door rather than giving in to the urge to get closer. He wanted her comfortable. As quickly as he could make it happen.

"Yes, thank you." Clearing her throat quietly, she glanced briefly around before returning her attention to him. "I needed that. Needed a few minutes to get my thoughts together. I'm sorry to have kept you waiting out here, though."

Conscientious. Nice. "Not a problem. It's been an interesting morning, and it started off a little faster than I think either one of us expected."

Her brows lifted as she drew a long breath. "It did, but considering our situation, that's probably for the best. We've got a lot to cover in a short time."

And then before he had a chance to ask, that steady gaze filled with purpose and her thumb popped up like a bullet point as she began.

"So, we'll both need a lawyer to navigate the legalities involved in granting an annulment. But I'd be willing to bet the front desk has at least some cursory information available about the process, this being Vegas and all. I'll ask when I run down to make copies of whatever documentation we got from the… chapel?"

Connor offered a short nod, his frown deepening as she ticked off to-dos with her fingers.

Independent. He admired it…but she was working in the wrong direction. Megan had made it to four before he'd pushed off the wall and caught her slender hand in his own. "Hey, slow down a second."

Her breath caught and her eyes went wide. "The fourth was this," she said, her voice coming quieter as she wiggled the offending digit in his grasp. "Your ring. I was afraid to take it off until I could give it back to you."

Connor's brow furrowed as she began to slide the platinum-and-diamond-set band free.

"Wait. Let me look at it on your hand."

Her gaze lifted to his, questioning and wary.

"It looks good on you." Worth every considerable grand he'd sunk into it the night before.

Megan nodded, the corner of her mouth curving in quiet appreciation. "The most stunning ring I've ever seen. I wish I could remember more than how incredibly it sparkled beneath the fluorescent lights in the wedding-chapel bathroom."

Connor let out a low chuckle, playing with the band where it sat on her finger. And then stopped, suddenly not finding her words funny at all.

Staring down at the little crease working its way between her brows, he asked, "Megan, you don't remember me buying you this ring?"

She swallowed, and the crease deepened. "You can't even imagine how much I wish I did. But no. I don't actually—" Seeming to think better of it, she cut off her words with a shake of her head. "It doesn't matter."

Like hell. "Megan, it matters to me. Do you remember when I asked you?"

"No." Not a blink, not a waver.

"The wedding?"

"I'm sorry. No."

Connor stared at her, his mind stalled on the seeming impossibility of what he was hearing. Yeah, she'd obviously had a few too many—they both had. Hell, he'd been hit hard enough where more than a few minutes had been required for the details to shuffle into place, and he probably had at least seventy-five pounds on her...but blacking out?

"Megan," he started, working to keep the urgency out of his voice. "Exactly how much of last night *do* you remember?"

"A few minutes here and there."

Alarm spreading through him like wildfire, he waited for her to say something more. Waited for her to finish her sentence with "seem to be missing." Only, then the ring was free, being pressed into his palm, wrapped tight beneath fingers

Megan had dutifully closed for him. And she was peering up at him, those blue pools searching his eyes for something... anything maybe.

"I remember seeing you at a bar and thinking how handsome you were. I remember laughing...a lot, and at another point, talking over waffles, though about what I couldn't say except you looked serious then. I remember you joking about us picking out china patterns. And I remember knowing with all certainty you weren't serious. There weren't any maybes between us. It simply wasn't like that." Her cheeks turned a delicate shade of pink as she looked away. "I remember knowing I should slow down because I don't really drink much, but ordering another round because I didn't want the fun to end. And I remember signing my name in the chapel, thinking—God, I don't even know what. So, I guess, not really thinking at all."

Connor stared, stunned as she turned away, a flush still blazing in her cheeks even as her shoulders remained straight. The air left his lungs on a hot expletive as he watched her nudge at the decorative pillows and shams littering the floor around the bed with her foot.

No wonder she was treating their marriage like some throwaway Vegas souvenir. This woman had a plan, and she didn't remember a single one of the reasons Connor had given her for changing it. Hell, she barely remembered him. And yet, she'd somehow managed to hold it together, remaining calm and focused throughout.

She was strong. Tough.

Everything he wanted.

Her mouth pulled to the side. "I don't suppose you happen to know where I might find my dress?"

Images of that superfine, silky bit of blue hitting him in the face flashed through his mind; only, where the dress went after had been as low a priority then as it was now.

"Megan. I'm sorry. If I'd realized, I would have been telling you everything, trying to fill in the night, explaining what happened. Why didn't you ask?"

* * *

Closing her eyes, Megan drew a steadying breath.

Why? Because the details weren't important and she could decipher the broad strokes on her own. This gorgeous, carefree guy had tempted her with all the things she'd sworn she could live without…the attention of a charming, desirable man, the chance to be utterly spontaneous, the indulgence in a night of reckless excess she wouldn't even consider once she had another person dependent on her. And so her pickled mind had rationalized this one last adventure. Vegas-style.

Maybe her blocking out their time together was some sort of defense mechanism.

Looking at this man alone made her believe whatever happened between them could very well have been the kind of phenomenal a grown woman didn't recover from, and her inner psyche was simply trying to protect her.

"Megan?" The deep, rich baritone cut into her thoughts an instant before the heat of his hands settled over her shoulders, jolting her back to the now. "Why?"

"It doesn't matter."

And then those strong hands were turning her around, gripping her tight. "You're wrong. I don't think you understand. Last night wasn't just some goof to be rectified this morning."

She blinked, trying to look away even as she felt herself stumbling further into the intensity of Connor's dark eyes. He thought there was something meaningful between them? Some potential?

This wasn't what she needed to hear.

"It has to be." She couldn't invest in potential again. She didn't have the time and she didn't have the will. "I have a plan."

She'd expected him to back off a step, ask what she was talking about, but instead that single corner of his mouth turned up to the slightest degree. As if suddenly he found himself on better footing than he'd expected. "Yeah, but my plan's better. Even you think so."

She'd told him?

Her chin pulled back as she felt the sting of self-betrayal and cursed her inner psyche.

Was nothing sacred?

Images of the laughter came back to her in a sickening rush, and she couldn't help but wonder if all her goals and intentions had been a part of the joke. Only, as she looked into Connor's eyes, some instinctive part of her knew it wasn't the case.

So what, then…

"Oh, my God." Her throat closed tight, trying to strangle the words she didn't want to say. "Did you volunteer to be my sperm donor?"

He was tall and handsome, without any obvious festering infections—

"No." His brows, already drawn low over his eyes, went even lower, obscuring what little chance she'd had to try to read a man who wasn't exactly an open book to begin with. "Not really. Not like you're thinking."

Not like she was thinking? Like what, then? she thought with a fresh wave of panic.

Her eyes fell to the empty spot on her ring finger. He'd married her. So maybe it wasn't so much a donation at all. Donations were free and clear…and this guy had already tied her down with a fairly significant string.

He wanted dibs on her baby.

He wanted a claim.

Suddenly, her breath was coming faster than it should, and the air working its way in and out of her lungs felt thin and useless.

"Wait, Megan. I don't know what you're thinking, but I can tell from your face it's wrong. Let me explain."

"You're gay." What else would a guy who looked like this be doing with her?

"Uh…" That tilted smile was back and she knew she was right.

"Okay, so you don't want your parents to know? You need an heir or something to keep your trust fund?"

"No—uh—I—uh—"

Shaking her head, she closed her eyes. "Look, Carter, either way, it doesn't matter. Whatever deal we might have worked out last night is off."

She'd been heavily intoxicated. Even if she'd signed a dozen documents, they would never stand up. She could walk away, unless—

Her eyes shot wide as she stared up at him in horror. "Did you...try...to get me pregnant last night?"

Connor coughed, his amused expression morphing into shock, confusion and something she really, really didn't want to believe was guilt no matter how much it looked like it.

His hand came up between them, but she didn't care if he needed a minute to sort out his story or work through his defense. Spinning away, she banded her arms across her abdomen, sick with the knowledge of what she'd done. "Of all the stupid, self-sabotaging, dangerous—"

"Megan." The way he said her name made it half plea, half laugh.

What had she done? Even if she wasn't pregnant, she'd had unprotected sex with a man she didn't know.

...patient zero...

Her stomach pitched hard. "He could have an STD," she gasped, her own anxiety pushing the words past her lips before she'd thought to stifle them.

"Megan." This time her name sounded strained coming through his lips. As though this guy was losing his patience.

Tough. Whatever he was thinking, he'd have to put a pin in it. She had bigger fish to fry than worrying about his patience when her best-case scenario was not pregnant, not infected, but still having to push back her plan by six months to ensure enough time for any STDs to show up in the screen.

"Damn it, Megan, look at me." Those hands were on her again, spinning her around and holding her still as Connor got in her face.

"One." He let go of her to bring his thumb up. "I do not have any sexually transmitted diseases. I always use a condom and following the breakup of my yearlong committed relationship had myself tested, as a precaution, regardless. Two." His index finger was next. "Neither is there a trust fund nor some executor to appease regarding it. Every cent I have, I earned on my own. Three, where the hell do you get this stuff?" Another finger. "Four, I didn't marry you to get my hands on a baby. I married you because we had similar goals and priorities and expectations…and damn it, I married you because I liked you a hell of a lot too."

She shook her head, searching those impossible eyes. "But it doesn't make sense—"

He waved her off. "And five, I absolutely did not try to get you pregnant last night. We didn't have sex."

Her jaw dropped.

So he was gay.

And why the revelation hit her like disappointment when she ought to be turning cartwheels, she couldn't say. But she'd deal with it later.

Only. then that mishmash of backward thinking was in play again, rising up with a victorious laugh at a thought that should have spurred outrage. "But I was *naked*," she challenged, recalling she'd literally stumbled over her panties and hideous T-shirt sprinting to the bathroom. A lucky break considering how fast on her heels Connor had been.

Naked *and* puking would have been a low she didn't care to contemplate.

"Yeah, and I didn't say *nothing* happened." With that concession, his gaze burned a slow path down her body, leaving her with the sense the bulk of her robe was all but invisible. He'd seen her before. And right then, he was seeing her again.

"Connor!"

His eyes met hers, completely unrepentant. "Man, I love it when you get my name right."

"Wait…what?"

"Say it again for me."

"Okay," she swallowed. "I believe you. You're probably not gay."

"Mmm. So sure?" he needled.

Make that *definitely* not. Like they *definitely* should have steered clear of the topic of sex altogether. Because having touched on it, now those hard-to-read eyes of his weren't so hard to read at all. They were filled with a possessive sort of predatory heat…directed at her.

"I could convince you. Spend the next hour or two making my argument." Leaning into her space, he added, "I'm a pretty compelling guy when I set my mind to it."

"Connor," she warned, trying not to give in to the laugh threatening to escape. She should be horrified. Traumatized. So why was it, in the aftermath of the worst decision of her life, this man's totally inappropriate taunts and teasing were somehow making her feel safe.

As if he'd sensed the ease in her tension, something changed in the man before her. The joking and pretense were set aside. Connor was completely serious, and her soul-deep awareness of his shift in mood was more disconcerting than waking up next to a stranger had been.

"Megan, the reason we didn't have sex last night was because you went from laughing and sexy and totally in the moment to not feeling so great. So instead of taking you to bed, I put you there. Simple."

Simple. Somehow it didn't feel that way.

He took her hand. "I should have realized how much you'd had to drink. I should have stopped us earlier."

"I'm a big girl with better sense than this. I should have stopped myself. Obviously." She drew a slow breath and pressed the heels of her hands against the dull throb at her temples. "Look at where it got me."

"Married." Connor's warm palm cupped her cheek as he searched her eyes, his elusive smile nowhere to be found. "To a man who's about as perfect an alternative to your plan as you can get. And you don't even remember why."

"But you do?" she asked, the quiet words sounding too sincere for the sarcastic tone she'd intended.

Suddenly she wanted that only-half-the-story smirk back, because this straightforward intensity she could actually *feel* thrumming through the air between them, pulsing against her skin as if it was trying to get inside, was too much to bear.

He was a stranger. Only, this stranger was looking into her eyes as if he knew exactly who she was.

"More every minute."

CHAPTER FIVE

MEGAN'S LIPS WERE PARTED, revealing that bit of wet just beyond the pale swell he wanted to run his thumb across. But Megan didn't remember him. Which meant, though she'd taken vows, signed her name, worn his ring and climbed all over him the night before…this morning, she didn't belong to him.

He understood it.

Accepted it.

Only, when she looked into his eyes the way she was now. When her breathing changed the smallest degree, and the color morning had leached from her skin pushed back into her cheeks, it felt an awful lot like she was.

Like on some level she knew what they'd had between them. And wanted it again.

He could show her how it had been. Kiss her until they were both senseless and she was begging him like she had—

Her breath caught. "I should find my dress."

Or he could wait. Damn it.

Moving back, Connor shoved his hands into his pockets.

Those big blue eyes were crawling away again, scanning the space around them as though salvation could be found in some dark corner of the room. Only, then they brightened as a small squeak escaped her, and Connor realized she'd found her dress.

"Thank God. I figure I pretty well earned this walk of shame, but seriously, I didn't want to have to do it in a robe."

Again Connor felt a smile pushing at his lips. She had a sense of humor. One he appreciated.

"Walk of shame, eh. I don't know if married women qualify."

Megan cringed at the words he'd been trying out on his tongue. Testing the feel of in his mouth.

They hadn't been bad or bitter or totally out of place, and he wondered if they might be an acquired taste he was warming up to. Something to encourage his wife to try.

Megan worried her bottom lip. "Looking at this dress, I definitely qualify."

As sexy and smooth as it had been draped over her curves the night before, the wrinkled garment barely ranked above a rag this morning.

"I can call down to the concierge and get you one sent up—"

Megan choked, "Wait, don't—I'll wear one of your shirts or something"

"I like the idea of you wrapped up in one of my shirts…quite a lot. But first let's have breakfast."

This time it was Megan at a loss for words, and he savored it for the full second and a half he had before she'd found her new tack. "I can't stay for breakfast. I've got a wedding today. A real wedding."

Connor stiffened. "As opposed to the fake—and yet legally binding—variety from last night."

Apologetic eyes drifted back to him. "I only meant—"

He put up a hand, waving off her apology. "I know what you meant. One they'd planned. And I know you're freaked out and more than a little desperate to get out of here and collect your thoughts, but, Megan, we're married. We need to discuss this. You've got hours before Gail's expecting you. We'll have some food to settle your stomach. Talk. Call it a—getting-to-know-your-husband date?" At her hesitation, he asked, "Come on, you're too much of a control freak not to have questions."

The look in her eyes said it all. She had a million of them. But there was more than curiosity in those crystal depths. There was fear, as well. As if somehow, she was afraid of what she might learn.

"Megan, come on. I can't be *that* bad."

"I don't think you're bad. I'm just confused and overwhelmed and…" She squared her shoulders. "I'm not entirely sure a getting-to-know-you anything makes much sense, all things considered."

All things considered.

Code for the lawyers again. Divorce.

Connor cocked his jaw to the left and crossed his arms, looking hard at the woman he'd married the night before.

No doubt a divorce would be the simplest solution.

He could let her go. Put a couple of his lawyers on it, have the whole situation resolved quietly and quickly.

She didn't remember him. Them.

So really it would almost be as if the whole thing never happened.

Except he'd remember. He'd know.

Putting up a shrug, Connor made a decent show of nonchalance as he pulled the ace from his sleeve. "Yeah, you're probably right. Besides, if you need to talk, I'm sure Jodie and Tina would be happy to lend an ear. You've got, what, four hours to kill before they get their hands on another distraction?"

Megan's startled gaze snapped to his. "Do they know?"

Oh, yeah, wifey wasn't going anywhere. Not for a while, anyway.

"They know you and I left the bar together. And you didn't come back to the suite you were sharing last night. So I'd say they know enough to make me the lesser evil on option this morning."

"The lesser evil?" Her brow quirked, leaving her mouth to hint at the smile and laughter that had gotten them into this mess. "Wow, you sure know how to sell yourself."

Making him want more.

"Don't have to," he said, crossing the bedroom. "Not when I'm up against those two."

Her stare narrowed on him as she followed. "Fine. You win. Let's play getting-to-know-you."

Connor did his best to rein in the victorious grin working over his mouth, and swung open the bedroom door.

The master suite was situated at the end of the second-level hall, overlooking the main living space where marble and glass gleamed in contrast to rich jewel-toned fabrics, heavily carved wood and silk-covered walls.

Megan's steps faltered, the shock on her face this morning even better than it had been the night before.

"So, Megan. The first thing you should know about me…"

"Uh-huh, yes?"

"I don't want a divorce."

"Just give it a try?" Megan asked, sputtering at the insanity of Connor's suggestion, casually tossed out as he'd perused an elaborate breakfast spread in the dining room. "You're crazy."

Glancing up from the coffee he'd stirred a generous portion of cream into, he grinned. "Exactly what you said last night. Of course, there'd been a whole lot of breathless 'yes, please' tied up in 'you're crazy' then."

Her eyes rolled skyward. She could only imagine the circumstances. Didn't want to imagine them. But couldn't seem to help it. In fact, every time her gaze touched on those criminally captivating lips…she started imagining all over again. Imagining, but not remembering.

"Last night I was forty percent alcohol by volume. Last night doesn't count."

Another shrug. "It counts to me. And if you'll sit down and have something to eat, I'll tell you why it counts to you too."

Handing her the coffee, he nodded at the tray of pastries, fresh fruit, cheeses and breads he'd brought to the table. "Trust me on this, you want the food in your stomach first."

Connor selected a croissant, set it, a tiny ceramic crock of butter and another of jam on a china plate with a silver knife, and pushed it in front of her. "Eat."

She looked at it warily, not really wanting to eat anything at all after the way her morning had begun.

She was nervous. Frustrated. And more than a smidgen concerned about Connor's apparent commitment to this monumental mistake.

He didn't want a divorce. She didn't get it. It didn't make sense.

"You don't know me," she began with a slow shake of her head. "Even if I'd talked your ear off from the minute we met until my little pilgrimage to the porcelain god...you couldn't really know me. My beliefs, my hang-ups, my shortcomings."

Connor heaved a sigh and met her eyes. "I know you wanted a conventional family, and I know, while you're friends with the men you date, you've never actually fallen in love. Same as me, that fairy-tale connection people go after like junkies looking for their next fix isn't a part of your makeup. I know you're tired of making yourself vulnerable again and again, hoping each time things will end differently. And I know you've figured out what you really want is a child, and you don't need a husband to get one."

Okay, so maybe he knew her a little.

Megan sat back in her chair, watching this virtual stranger reach for her plate, rip a corner off her croissant, butter it and, as though he hadn't just relayed her deepest secret and greatest failures, hold it out in offering.

"Eat, while I clear a few things up between us."

Tentatively she took the bite, letting the flakes of rich, buttery pastry dissolve on her tongue.

"For the record, I've been interested in settling down for some time. But contrary to what the evidence might suggest, marriage isn't something I take lightly or would jump into without serious consideration."

When she opened her mouth to call him on that last bit, he lifted a staying hand and went on.

"Marriage is the foundation of a family, and I want mine to be rock solid. I want the security—for my children, and really us both as well—of knowing it won't crumble under some needy, emotional pique or the whims of a fickle heart. So I've been waiting for a woman with a specific sense of priority."

His brow pulled down as he stared at the table and then looked back to her with a knowing expression. "And before you start thinking I was just some man on the make last night, out trawling for a wife, I wasn't. I wasn't looking for anything but the good time we were having. And then, it just hit me. You were the one."

"The one." There was a whole lot of weight in that statement. More than she'd expected to be shouldering through this weekend trip to Vegas.

"Yes. Now, let me tell you how much I respect your plan to prioritize your child over the instinct to find a mate."

She gulped.

Wow, if she'd told him that, she'd really told him everything.

"It takes time to build a relationship. If you have a child, it's time you'll be taking away from him or her. And what if it gets serious?" he asked, buttering another small piece of croissant. "You introduce little Megan to this guy, but then it doesn't work out. Now you aren't the only one who's let down. It's your daughter or son, as well. Plus, there's the whole post-breakup emotional slump to contend with. No picnic for a single mom, or the little person more in tune with her feelings than anyone else on the planet. That this isn't the kind of emotional cycling you want your child to go through says a tremendous amount about you. And, like I said, I respect it."

He'd spoken casually, seemingly at ease, and yet there was an intensity about him as he relayed this bit of perspective on her plan that implied a level of empathy beyond what she'd expect.

A part of her wanted to ask him about his past. About his parents. Things she wondered if they'd discussed the night before. Only, to do so would open more doors, and she was already confused enough without adding images of this powerful man as a vulnerable child to the mix.

Connor reached out to offer her the next bite and she caught his wrist in her hand. "I don't understand. If you respect my plan so much, how did we end up married?"

Those dark eyes held with hers. "Because what I offered you was the best of both worlds without the risk of the worst."

"How?"

"Simple. This thing between us, Megan. It's not about love."

Her chin pulled back as she absorbed the words. Felt them

wash through her with the same kind of phantom familiarity she'd been experiencing on and off with Connor since she'd woken in his bed. Only, this time, something about it wasn't entirely comforting. Almost like a piece of the puzzle that was her missing experience had been put into place sideways and didn't quite fit.

Maybe it simply wasn't what she'd expected him to say, though why not, she didn't know. Surely she hadn't believed this man who married her within hours of their meeting had *fallen in love* with her. Talk about crazy. Still, somehow hearing him say it left her feeling...confused.

So she asked, "If it's not about love, then what?"

Connor gave her a satisfied grin. "All the vital components that make a relationship successful, without any of the emotional messiness to drag it down. It's about respect, caring and commitment. Shared goals and compatible priorities. It's about treating a marriage like a partnership instead of some romantic fantasy. It's about two people *liking* each other."

Liking each other. What this man was suggesting was what she'd had in most every relationship she'd attempted. With one major difference. In those relationships, neither she nor the man she'd been dating believed it was enough. Whereas with Connor... "So, you're saying it's about expectations. If we limit them, no one's disappointed."

"Embrace them," he corrected, "because they work for us."

She nodded, saying the words slowly. "A partnership."

Of course, this man wouldn't want anything more from her.

He frowned as he met her eyes. "I'm not talking about some relationship without any caring. I'm talking about improving on friendship. Without turning it into something neither of us is capable of delivering on."

"If what you're looking for is a friend, surely, Connor, you must have hundreds to choose from. Women you know better. Trust more. Women who want this."

Connor stared at her a moment, considering his words before he spoke them. "But I want you. The truth is, there isn't another woman I know better. At least not as it applies to core beliefs and priorities. You didn't have some ulterior motive when we met. You didn't know who I was or what I had or what you thought I wanted. In fact, from the start, the most consistent thing about you has been your unwavering honesty, even when it didn't suit your needs. I got to know the you who *didn't* want a relationship. I like what I've learned about you, Megan. The independence. The sharp wit. The easy laugh and intelligent conversation. The authenticity.

"Sure, the historical events that made you the woman you are today are still a mystery, but what you want and who you are and how we get along… Those things I know. I like."

She swallowed. "Because of last night."

It didn't seem enough.

"Last night. This morning. Right this minute. I like what I see."

"So even if I am the kind of woman you're looking for…"

"*The* woman."

She nodded, feeling more uncertain than she had since waking with no memory. "What makes you the man for me?"

"I can take care of you."

"I can take care of myself."

"I know," he said, that wry twist in motion again. "It's one of the many, many things I appreciate about you. You're independent and self-sufficient. Your happiness won't be contingent on the amount of attention I can give you any given week. But as fully capable as you are, my support would allow you to be more than a single parent, with a single income. Married to me, you can be a full-time mother instead of a slave to the workforce. You can work or not work, whatever you choose. I have housekeepers, so any time you want to yourself won't be spent scrubbing grout. My work requires travel. You and our children would be encouraged to accompany me. You could see the world. Meet new people. There would be little, if anything, tying you down beyond the few expectations I have for my wife."

The muscles along her shoulders pulled tight. "What expectations?"

"There's a significant social element in my business, and I want a wife who can help balance the conversation. Playing hostess and accompanying me as needed for whatever comes up. Dinners, parties, charitable events. No more than a couple times a week. Also, our children—as many as you'd like—come first. They need to be your number-one priority. And lastly it means respecting both me and our marriage vows."

She understood. "Fidelity."

"Fidelity."

No surprise Connor wasn't the kind of man to sit idly while his wife entertained herself with the golf pro from the club, but within the marriage...

Her eyes drifted to where her hand was wrapped halfway around his wrist. She'd been touching him all this time, and yet this was the first moment she'd been aware of the low charge running between them. Meeting his gaze, she could see in those dark pools an answering awareness of that connection.

Her breath caught.

"You won't be lonely with me, Megan. I know what I'm suggesting doesn't follow the norm. It's not the traditional court-ship and promise of love. But we aren't the most traditional people." Reversing her hold, he took her hand in his. "We have something good. All I'm asking is for you to give it a chance."

A chance.

She believed it could be good. Which was part of the problem. Because something good would be hard to lose.

And she'd lost so many times already. It was why she'd come up with the plan. No more waiting for the other shoe to drop. Hoping for something that would never come.

Except with Connor, love wasn't part of the equation. He simply wanted a partner. Someone who understood his priorities the way he understood hers.

He wanted to be another parent for their *children*.

As many as she wanted.

She'd always dreamed of a houseful of kids. But when she'd decided on the plan, she accepted in all likelihood there would be only the one. And one had been enough.

But what Connor was offering wasn't about *just enough*. He was offering her more than she'd believed she could wish for.

Still, the risk remained, reduced as it may be.

What if she got attached—let herself believe in a family—and he changed his mind? Left.

She couldn't go through it again.

"I need to think," she said, pushing back from the table and walking to the glass doors where the Vegas sun beat down, brutal and beautiful all at once, over their private oasis.

Moving in behind her, Connor rested his hands over her shoulders, pressing his thumbs into the tender muscles at either side of her spine. A part of her wanted to shrug him off, tell him to give her the space she asked for. But a bigger part recognized the act as an example of the kind of support he was offering. A subtle reminder she would not be alone. There would be someone behind her.

"I get it, Megan. I do. You don't remember and it's scary to take my word on something so huge." Then it wasn't merely the touch of his hands she was experiencing, but the press of his body along hers. His chin rested atop her head, his chest at her back as he continued rubbing the tension from her neck…and all she could think was how right it felt. "So I'm not asking you to believe in me right now. I'm asking you to believe in yourself."

She turned in his arms, her hands coming to rest on the planes of his chest as if it were the most natural thing in the word. "Believe in myself?"

Connor brushed his knuckles against her temple, soft and light.

"You married me. Don't you want to find out why?"

CHAPTER SIX

SHE'D AGREED.

Connor couldn't quite believe it himself—and yeah, yeah, it wasn't exactly the whole nine yards…more like a conservative six and half by his estimate—but Megan was spending the day with him. Giving him a chance to convince her of what kind of sense they made.

Which meant he was going to Gail's wedding. Fortunately, a Vegas-style seating chart had more to do with who got to the bar first than which great-aunt was too blind to figure out she'd scored a table by the kitchen.

Pouring another coffee for himself and a glass of juice for Megan, he listened with half an ear as she checked in with Gail. She'd barely gotten past hello before a suspicious silence, followed by some stuttering and then more silence, confirmed what he'd known from the start. Jodie and Tina had been running at the mouth, probably since Megan and he took off the night before.

"I did stay with him… Of course I'm fine, but that's not— Gail, you're getting married today— Yes, he is very handsome…"

This was the difference between men and women. When Connor texted Jeff to let him know something had come up and he'd get in touch next week, the guy had texted back a single word. Later. End of discussion. Granted, it might have gone longer if he'd mentioned the *something* in question was an exchange of vows, followed by a case of acute amnesia…but whatever.

"I know it's not like me... No, there weren't drugs involved—Stop! Gail, today is about you. When should I come by to help?"

Walking the juice over to the table, he set it down by her hand, running a thumb over her shoulder to make sure she saw it.

Then, covering the small of her back with his palm, he leaned close to her free ear. "Let me know if you need anything else."

Her eyes were wide when she turned slowly to look at him, and pure masculine satisfaction surged through him at the obvious impact his actions had spurred.

She *wanted* to be convinced.

"Wait, what?" she asked, her attention firmly back on the call at hand. "You don't want me—?"

Connor looked up, curious.

"Because of Jodie and Tina. Right... No, no, anything to make this day perfect for you."

She sounded uncertain but resigned. "Well, I'll see you down at the limo, then. And, Gail—could you get my bridesmaid dress sent over here?"

After a few more details were exchanged, Megan hung up and turned a hesitant smile his way. "Good news. We've got a few more hours to get to know each other."

"Oh, yeah?"

"Gail doesn't want to deal with Jodie and Tina while she's getting ready, and she can't have me if they aren't there, so we'll all meet at the limo when it's time to go."

"Come on over here," he said, patting the cushion beside him.

Megan crossed to him, a strained smile stiff on her lips, apprehension lurking in her eyes.

Good news his foot. She'd been banking on the break.

Taking her hand, he pulled her down beside him, leaving space between the crook of his knee and her hip, but keeping a light hold on her fingers. "Look, let's forget about all the reasons I'm such a stellar choice for a husband right now and relax. Talk."

Her eyes narrowed on his mouth and she pulled back the

slightest degree. "Why do I feel like you're about to sell me some snake oil?"

Connor didn't release her fingers, but tightened his hold, reeling her back in. "Because you're mildly pessimistic. Now, knock it off. You don't remember, but if there's one thing we do well...it's talk. About anything."

To prove his point, he picked up one of the papers delivered with breakfast and tossed it into Megan's lap. "So let's get this ball rolling. Check the headlines and then give me the first thing that comes to mind."

"You are so cheating!" Megan accused, her laughter doing little to back up the finger she jabbed at Connor's chest.

The finger he then grabbed and used to tow her off the knees she been perched on. And suddenly she was tucked in the small crease between Connor's half-sprawled form and the back of the couch. Again.

And again, she planted her palm on the center of his chest, refusing to admit how tempting it was to simply stay there, and pushed herself up.

Connor shook his head, all *who, me?* "Cheating? We're *talking.*"

She shot him a skeptical look, not buying his wide-eyed-innocent routine for one minute. That he would even try it with a mouth like his was almost too much to bear. "Sure we are. Talking about our views on education. A topic we have remarkably similar beliefs on."

Another wry smile twisted his lips. "So I'd like our kids to live at home, attending private school. And you agree. What's the problem?"

"Mmm-hmm. And before schooling, extreme-adventure sports. Funny topic to spring up out of the blue. And so co-incidental you would be of the same mind regarding risks of that nature being off the table once a child enters the picture."

"I told you, we have a tremendous amount in common."

"Yeah, and you've worked it all into this 'casual' conversation over the last couple hours—"

"Come on, now, sweetheart, I've worked a lot of things into this conversation."

"—conveniently omitting anything we disagreed on."

Connor's mouth kicked up another degree, his eyes heating in the way she'd found so startling at first, but was now beginning to look for. "Have I mentioned how sexy those smarts of yours are?"

An unbidden belly flip had her glancing away before Connor could see how his words affected her. "I bust you for trying to play me, and this is your response?"

"Yes." The crook of his finger found her chin, and he pulled her back to his gaze. "But that doesn't make what we've talked about any less true. I'm a motivated guy, set on making sure I don't let something important slip through my fingers. I want you to know what I know."

She let out an even breath, hating the way everything Connor said made sense. Clicked, as if it was locking into some waiting place within her.

It was crazy to think, even for a second, about buying into this.

She'd sworn she wouldn't do it again. Wouldn't take another risk. And this…this was a risk unlike any she'd faced before. But staring into Connor's deep brown eyes, all she could think was, what if this time the reward was worth it?

A knock sounded from the front door, and Connor broke the eye contact to check his watch and then push up from the couch. "Got to be your dress."

A moment later a gleaming brass cart was parked in the entry and Connor was verifying the appointment for a stylist to do Megan's hair and makeup. She'd tried to stop him, but he'd dismissed her protests, calling it a perk of being Mrs. Reed…said she should get used to it. Or at the very least use it while she had it.

Fair enough. She'd given in. And now she had to admit she was looking forward to letting someone else work on her hair. In all honesty, her plate felt a little full already with the business of this marriage on it. And the herculean task of making her hair look good just wasn't something she had room for.

The door shut, and Connor, all tapered cut and balanced perfection, was closing in again. The skin along her shoulders began to tingle in reckless anticipation of that back-to-hard-chest-and-stomach stance he seemed to favor. And then he was there, running a thumb down the column of her neck. "Would you feel better if I shared a few points of dissent?"

Casting a glance over her shoulder, she saw his eyes were serious. And so close.

"Yes, I would."

Looking back at the dress before she turned around completely and did something monumentally stupid—which, considering her marital status, was really saying a lot—she pulled open the thin, protective plastic. Stroked her fingers over the silver, above-the-knee sheath.

Connor cleared his throat. "Camp."

She shot another look back. "What?"

"I don't like the idea of sending the kids away for extended periods of time."

"But camp's a treat. Once they're old enough, of course. They have so many incredible programs out there. Nature camps. Space camps—"

"Yeah, arts, football, gymnastics, and everything else a little boy or girl could be interested in." Shoving a hand through the dark silk of his hair, he let out a sigh. "I still don't like the idea, but I've given on the point already."

Her brows lifted along with the corners of her mouth as she turned to face him completely. "Wow. Any other small victories I should know about?"

"Christmas at home. Every year. All of us. Period."

She let out a small gasp, her hand moving to her heart in genuine shock. "You fought against…Christmas?"

Those dark eyes softened, crinkling at the corners. "Please wipe the 'he hates puppies' look off your face. I didn't want to count out a trip somewhere exotic. But your arguments were compelling, so it was a compromise easy to make."

Wow, he was so—

Wait.

Her eyes narrowed on him. "And now you're showing me how *reasonable* you are with all your willing concessions. Do you ever stop?"

Yes, she was fully aware of just how *unreasonable* her response to this man giving her exactly what she'd asked for was. But based on the twisted smile playing on his lips, Connor didn't seem to mind.

"Not until I get what I want."

She was getting lost in his eyes, feeling herself drawn closer with every minute they spent together. "And you want me."

Connor leaned in, closing the distance between them until the heat of his body was licking over hers. She swayed, suddenly breathless. The palm of his left hand flattened against her spine.

"I've got you." His voice was a low rumble against her ear, the contact between them almost a kiss before he stepped back and handed her the dress. "What I want is to keep you."

CHAPTER SEVEN

WITH HER HAIR AND MAKEUP already done, Connor had barely gotten his arms through the sleeves of his tuxedo shirt before Megan was stepping out of the master bath again. This time decked out in the metallic-silver bridesmaid dress that left nearly the full length of her toned legs on perfect display.

Damn.

Megan shifted under his scrutiny, smoothing her hands over her hips with downward strokes probably intended to eke out a few millimeters of additional coverage.

Not happening.

"I had nothing to do with picking out this dress."

As if he needed her to tell him. If Megan had been picking, he imagined she'd have selected something deceptively conservative. Like the dress she'd been wearing the night before. At first glance it had looked modest enough, but when he let his eyes linger for even a moment, the seductive hints had time to make an impact. The cut of the back, the line of the waist. The cling and fall, emphasizing all the right curves. Megan had an eye for what flattered her, but she managed it in a stylish, understated way. Something he liked.

Well, hell. He liked this dress too. But it was a different sort of appreciation happening here.

"Let me guess. Tina?" he asked, thinking it had to be she of the GOT SPERM T-shirt behind this kind of flash.

Megan smirked. "You'd think. But believe it or not, this was all Jodie. Something about the dress being a gift to us single girls."

"Bridesmaid's gift?"

"Jodie was convinced these dresses would give us the pick of the casino."

Connor let out a bark of laughter. "Well, she's got that right. And might I mention how utterly pleased I am you've decided to bring me along tonight. Especially considering the hard time I'd have had letting you out of my sight otherwise."

A wash of pink tinged Megan's cheeks as the smallest smile played at her lips. "Are you the jealous type?"

"Let's call it possessive." Her lids lifted, and seeing the pleasure in her eyes at his statement, he added, "But only when something is very important to me."

Pearly-white teeth pressed into Megan's lush little bottom lip as she turned away, fidgeting with the studs and links he'd set out on the polished mahogany dresser top. Her hair wound up the way it was, she couldn't hide the pretty color suffusing the skin along her neck and ears. And he couldn't fight the rush of pure masculine satisfaction at having driven it there.

After arranging everything into a neat row, Megan turned back to him. Her cheeks showing only the barest hint of her remaining blush. "I should get my shoes on. And you…"

She bent a little, reaching for the shoes set neatly at the wall. Stood, shifted and tried again. Pulled at the hem riding higher with each attempt.

Wow. Thank you, Jodie.

Flustered, Megan cleared her throat. Clearly working to maintain her poise.

"You should finish getting dressed yourself." She waved at his open shirt, her eyes lingering even as she turned her head. "We've got to get going pretty quickly."

"Mmm-hmm," he said again, making a mental note, once this better-than-a-late-night-cable-show was over and they left the villa, not to let Megan bend over for anything.

Catching on to his level of distraction, Megan shot him a

scathing glare...one that quickly dissolved into laughter. "This is ridiculous. Stop staring so I can get my shoes!"

Then, eyes to the ceiling, she muttered something adorably mild about men and Jodie and wishing she had a parka.

"Okay, low of me," he conceded, not even trying to make it believable. "I'm sorry."

"Right." She laughed, only, the sultry sound of it died on her lips as he stepped close, catching her hips in his hands, giving in to the temptation to flex his fingers...just once.

Megan's eyes went wide at the undeniably intimate contact, and he waited, gauging her response.

When she didn't push him away, he backed her toward the edge of the bed. "Why don't you sit, and I'll help you with the shoes."

Megan perched at the edge of the bed, still reeling from the feel of Connor's hands sliding over her hips, moving the fabric against her skin as he guided her to where he wanted her to be. She shouldn't have allowed it. Should have done more than stare up at him helplessly. But something inside her wouldn't react to Connor as a stranger.

Her body remembered him...even if her mind did not.

She wanted him. This sexy barefoot man, dressed in black tuxedo pants and a crisp, white shirt hanging dangerously open as he teased her. And for the first time, she understood the kind of mind-numbing allure that led women to make the worst decisions of their lives. And smile about it after.

Connor swept up her shoes with a finger through the straps and then knelt in front of her to lift her foot. "Do they hurt after all the walking last night?" he asked, running his thumb around her heel and then up through her arch.

She stared, too caught up in the intimacy of the scene and how shockingly good it felt to respond with more than the barest shake of her head.

"Good." Eyes locked with hers, he slipped the point of her shoe over her toes, gently fitting the heel and running a lazy circle around her ankle with his thumb. She watched, breathless, as his large hands deftly worked the delicate glass-beaded strap through its buckle.

So unbelievably sexy.

It was unreal.

It was…a fairy tale. Which was bad.

This man was telling her their marriage was based on the kind of up-front honesty and pragmatic realism that kept expectations attainable. And yet, everything about him—his incredible looks, his wealth, his knack for saying exactly what she needed to hear and, most of all, his romantic overtures—screamed *too good to be true*.

So what was she doing buying into the charade?

Letting herself see them years from now, chatting as they dressed together for some coming event.

Connor's finger slipped beneath the buckled strap. "Okay?"

"Perfect." Like everything else he'd shown her. Only, nothing and no one were actually perfect.

Connor's mouth pulled into a rueful slant. "You make *perfect* sound like it's not such a good thing. And like you aren't talking about your shoe."

But she was talking about the shoe, only not the way it fit.

"You're telling me this marriage between us is going to work because we aren't bringing any fairy-tale expectations into it. But here you are, down on one knee, fitting a glass slipper on my foot. Everything you do and say is like some fantasy come to life…which makes it hard to know what reality is actually going to feel like."

Connor gave her a thoughtful nod and set down her bejeweled foot. "I admit, I'm making every effort to sweep you off your feet. I want you to fall for me."

He picked up her other foot, giving it the same attention as the first. "But if it puts your mind to rest, I'm pretty sure Prince Charming wasn't using the old shoe excuse just to get his hands on his wife's leg."

Buckles complete, he let his hands skim up over her calves, stroking a light path behind her knees as he went on. "What's more, based on the target audience for those stories, I'd really hope he wasn't entertaining the kind of thoughts running through my mind as I watched you wrestling your short skirt. Because there was nothing PG about where my head was at."

"Really?"

A nod. "Strictly X stuff. I promise."

"Connor." His name was a plea on her lips, and the moment it sounded, the humor in his eyes faded and the lines of his face hardened.

"We're good together, Megan. It's not about glass slippers or fairy tales or love at any sight. It's not about private schools or mutual goals or any of the other things we've talked about today. It's about you and me fitting together. It's about this feeling of rightness you told me about last night. The one I've had since I met you. And I keep seeing signs of it today. Tell me. Tell me you feel it too."

"I feel it." The connection was there. Undeniable between them.

But whether *feeling* right together for one day was the same as actually *being* right together through the rest of their lives...

"I just don't know—" The words died in her throat at the sight of the burning heat staring down at her. The desire blazing in his eyes. Desire for her.

The same desire firing through her body, spilling hot through her center and filling her mind with a smoky haze. Suddenly she wanted those big hands everywhere on her. She didn't want to worry about good judgment or long-term consequences. She simply wanted this man, whose promises sounded too good to be true, to deliver on the one in his eyes.

"Connor," she whispered, drawing her leg slowly in, and the man with it. "You make me want…"

God, she couldn't say it. Couldn't even think it. All her rational thought was tangled up in the rising awareness between them, the slow glide of his touch over her skin, the need simmering between them.

And then he was off the floor, one hand moving from her leg to brace on the mattress beside her hip. The other climbing to the outside of her shoulder, so all she could do was lie back, staring into his eyes as his large body moved over her own. His knee replaced his left hand at her hip, and she was surrounded.

He was so close she could feel the heat radiating off his body, the wash of his breath against her jaw, the tickle of his open shirt grazing her arms. Decadent. Intimate. Too seductive to resist. Her fingers closed around the draping fabric, pulling him toward her until only the barest space remained.

She pulled again. A subtle nudge. Then a stronger tug, but all it earned her was another one of those devastating half smiles and the slow shake of Connor's head as he reached into his pocket and withdrew her ring.

Braced on one arm and his knees above her, Connor slid his free hand up her left arm, rolling the glinting diamond band along the path of her skin until he held it poised above the tip of her ring finger, so close she could feel an almost magnetic pull from the wanting.

It would be so easy to give in. Give him what he wanted. What, on some level, she wanted too.

Let him slide that platinum band over her finger, and say yes to what would inevitably feel good in the moment, but had the potential to devastate if she wasn't careful.

Forcing the air in her lungs to move again, she managed a single word. "Wait."

Connor's smile quirked suggestively. "Nervous? I promise I'll be gentle. I've done this before."

Her eyes closed as she once again found herself relieved by his sense of humor and ability to lighten the mood without undermining the seriousness of what was at stake.

Finding more breath, she whispered, "We can't. Not yet."

"Why not? We're already married." His voice dropped lower as he lightly teased the diamond band around the tip of her finger. "I can tell you want it."

Yes, right then, she did. But wearing his ring meant giving up her plans. Giving up the security of a future she could control completely. Giving up a promise she'd made to herself... for the chance of something so much more.

Connor was poised above her, his sharp gaze studying her every minuscule reaction. Hesitation. Blink, blush and tremor.

Tentatively, she placed her free hand against the center of his chest. His bare skin was shades darker than her own. Hot. Firm. Tempting her toward reckless action just to ensure she had more time to enjoy it.

But that simply wasn't who she was. If he knew her at all, he would understand.

"I'm not ready. I'm not sure I can give you what you're asking for."

A nod. Then, "Wear it anyway. You're still my wife for now. Why not try the whole package on for size and see how it feels?"

Her gaze drifted over to the band of diamonds so close to sliding home. Each flawless stone throwing off light in all directions. It was exquisite.

Nothing could compete with this ring.

Swallowing once, she peered back up at Connor, who waited above her, the possessive intent in his eyes making her ache to give in. But she couldn't do it.

"It's probably better if I don't." Trying to match his lighter tone, she curled her fingers into her palm and dodged, "And about this whole being-married thing. I was thinking we might not mention it. Let everyone think I'm just a cheap floozy rather than the honest woman you've made me."

CHAPTER EIGHT

CONNOR SWALLOWED, his body going still. "You don't want them to know."

Guileless eyes met his. "I'd prefer they don't."

And then she was wiggling out from beneath him. Crawling off the bed from one side as he backed off from the other, returning the ring to his pocket.

Megan stood in front of the bureau mirror frowning at the few hairs out of place from their brief roll in the sack. They had to leave soon, and considering he'd actually hired someone in to sculpt her hair into perfection, it made sense she'd be trying to fix her look.

But suddenly all he could see was a woman concerned with her image, and for the first time he wondered if he didn't really know her after all.

He shook his head. It couldn't be right.

"I thought you didn't lie."

It was the quality in her he appreciated above all others. It was *important* to him.

One brow shot high as she turned to meet his eyes. "I don't. But that doesn't mean I walk around regurgitating every personal detail of my existence without prompt. I'd prefer you not bring it up, because seriously, no one is going to ask."

A lie of omission. Well, that was irony.

He knew all about them. Had been one for the first decade of his life and had sworn never to be one again. And yet here he was, married to a woman making a dirty little secret of him from the start.

Freud would have a field day with this.

Okay, so it wasn't as though he'd discovered Megan stowing the ring in her car's ashtray while she hit the bars. They'd been married for less than twenty-four hours, and she wasn't even certain she wanted to wait another twenty-four before filing for divorce. But still, her not wanting people to know rubbed him in all the wrong places. Partly because one of the first things to attract him about her was the way she owned her life. Her actions. She wasn't making excuses or apologies or even taking the easy way out of an explanation. In the few hours he'd known her before he talked her into changing the plan for both their lives, she'd made him believe in who she was. How she lived. And this—this secret didn't fit with that.

Which made him wonder about some of the other things he'd believed.

"I told you honesty was important to me. We talked about it *today*." And same as last night, she'd agreed about the critical importance of trust in any marriage, but especially one not based on love.

"Connor…" Megan's voice had taken a stern edge, as though she was the one who didn't like what was being said. "This is my cousin, and while we aren't spectacularly close, if I show up with your ring on, no one is going to pay attention to Gail's wedding at all. It wouldn't be fair to her. I'm sorry, but I hope you can respect my feelings."

Connor's head snapped up, the lead boulder in his gut evaporating under her words.

"You aren't trying to hide something you're embarrassed about?"

Her head tilted slightly, as if she wasn't quite sure what she was hearing. "You mean because you're such an unattractive, insufferable dog who's probably going to fleece me for everything I'm worth…and I wasn't smart enough to chew my arm off for a clean escape?"

The laughter was back, bolstered by more relief than he'd thought he could experience. "Something like that."

Megan gave a tiny smile before turning thoughtful. Then, "I suppose, if I'm being totally honest, I am a little embarrassed about it. I mean, I made one of the biggest decisions of my life during a night when I'd drunk so much I don't even remember doing it. But I'm not under any delusions about keeping our marriage under wraps. Everyone at this wedding is going to know about us—approximately two seconds after I talk to my mother. Which is why I haven't called her yet."

"What if we decide to divorce? You could sweep it under the rug."

Megan laughed. "Maybe you could, but not me. Even knowing she can't keep a confidence to save her life, I don't keep secrets from my mother. I'll tell her what's happened as soon as I get home. And then the minute I hang up…" Megan's eyes closed, and she drew in a slow breath. "Believe me. I'll be hearing about this for the rest of my life. Regardless of the outcome."

Connor offered a hand to Megan. "You okay with that?"

Megan wagged her head a little, eyes on the ceiling. "It's my life. So yes. I'm good with it."

Damn, he liked the things that came out of this woman's mouth. He liked the way she thought. The way she cared. The way she lived. The way she stood by the choices she believed in. And despite his initial reaction to her not wearing his ring, he liked the way she could see past her own situation to consider the feelings of those around her.

That strength of character was what he wanted for his family.

"And with me?" he asked. "If I promise not to bring up the wedding, are you still good with me?"

Megan's eyes were soft, steady as she met his. "I'm good with you too."

The wedding went off without a hitch. Gail and Roy tied the knot in a chapel not so different, according to Connor, from the one where they'd been married the night before. The vows were made, the rings exchanged and then the marriage was sealed with a kiss. It was beautiful, despite Jodie and Tina making jokes at Megan's expense throughout the ceremony, laughingly suggesting in her lack of experience she'd managed to botch her one-night stand by dragging it into the next day.

She'd been prepared for the barrage of teasing. Had warned Connor about it. But what she hadn't expected was how protective her new husband was. And the way he managed to sabotage most every joke the quibbling duo attempted. Still, the girls were nothing if not persistent.

"So, really, Connor, what are you doing here?" Jodie asked, straining to be heard over the nightclub music booming around them. "I mean, sure, Megan reeled you in last night, but aren't you ready to rip the hook out and take off yet?"

Whether she'd been going for flirtation or just a joke, the question was typically tactless, and Megan reminded herself white-chocolate martinis weren't a solution. Not since the idea of them alone had her stomach ready to revolt.

Connor stretched his arm across the back of Megan's chair, the warmth of it permeating the tuxedo jacket he'd wrapped her up in as soon as the ceremony ended. "Not at all. Megan's incredible and I see this relationship going the distance."

Tina leaned forward, putting her best assets on display. "Relationship?"

A slow heat began to build in Megan's cheeks as all eyes shifted to where Connor's thumb ran a lazy pattern against her shoulder. He'd been attentive without being overly demonstrative throughout the evening, obviously making an effort to respect her wishes and keep their marriage under wraps at least until the ink dried on Gail's matching certificate. But this line of questioning could lead them toward the truth in a hurry if something didn't change.

Tina's shrewd eyes darted between them twice, before she stepped back with a cool laugh. "Oh, Megan, tell me you didn't?"

Her heart sank. Somehow Tina had figured it out. Gail, who was waiting as expectantly as everyone else, would never forgive her.

"Tell me you didn't go and make another *friend*?" The last word fell with such disgust it took Megan a second to realize she hadn't been discovered. She didn't need to feel ashamed for hijacking her cousin's wedding. Relief washed over her in a wave, buoying her mood enough she couldn't contain the smile stretching across her face.

"What are you talking about?" Connor asked, casually enough. Only, something about his voice sounded off, and as she turned to face him, she didn't like the look of his half smile at all.

"Nothing. It's nothing, Connor," she said, hoping he'd recognize the plea in her eyes for him to leave it. The plea and the promise that she'd explain later when they weren't within glowering distance of Gail's wedding party. "I'd love another tonic. Any chance you'd come to the bar with me?"

After a beat, the smile turned more genuine and Connor stood, offering her his hand. "How about a dance first."

Before she could mutter a protest, he had her flush against his chest and was deftly leading her with his hands, thighs, chest and hips into the midst of the clubgoers. Moving in a way that was all easy rhythm and physical confidence. Nothing *friendly* about it.

Within a few minutes, she'd returned to the state that teetered between laughter and lust and was totally unique to her experience with Connor, leaving Tina and Jodie and all their barbs a distant memory.

Connor signed off on the open-bar bill for their group and then grabbed the tall tonic and ice Megan had requested, eyeing their table like a man about to face the gallows. Megan was still in the ladies' room, but something told him waiting for her outside the door would smack of stalker. So rather, he made his way to the table prepared to deflect the pointed questions about his bank accounts, Reed Industries' worth and whether Megan had managed to snag any of his sperm.

He was ready to get out of there. First, because his wife's laugh, which was all kinds of sexy abandon, was proving to be a temptation he couldn't resist much longer, and second, because Tina and Jodie, and even Gail, were grating hard. Pushing buttons he hadn't known he had. Megan's ability to let it roll off her back gave him the sense she'd had too much practice. And he didn't like it.

As it turned out, Gail had kicked off her shoes and propped her feet on one vacant chair, leaving the only other available between Tina and Jodie, whose antics had vacillated between mildly annoying and downright nasty.

No, thanks.

Roy and his two groomsmen were huddled in the same kind of quiet conversation they'd been engaged in through the rest of the evening—excepting the ceremony, of course—the monosyllabic, extended-silence kind.

Opting to stand off at the side, he watched the dance floor while he waited for Megan.

A cackle of laughter had the muscles of his spine tightening unpleasantly. And then Gail's chiding reprimand. "You two are terrible!"

He didn't want to know. Shouldn't even have been able to hear over the music.

A less-than-delicate snort from Tina. "Please, it's pathetic." *But their voices.*

And Jodie. "She can't stop collecting these guys."

That brought his head around. They hadn't noticed him standing behind them, and again they were talking about his wife. The woman who'd fought with him in an effort to respect this day.

"I don't know who she thinks she's kidding with this one. There's no way—"

"No way," chimed in Tina.

"—he's anything more than the next 'friend,' trying to do her some sort of favor. Keep us off her back probably."

Gail held up a hand between them. Good. Her cousin, showing some loyalty. Only, then she started talking and his vision went red.

* * *

Megan's steps faltered as she approached the table.

"...keep wondering with all these 'buddies' is if she's *so great to talk with*, then what exactly is *bad enough* to drive these guys away?"

Megan's breath caught in her throat as Gail sloppily speculated on her life with Connor standing directly behind her.

He'd heard.

She knew by his utter lack of reaction. The stillness in a form that was so much energy.

Jodie nodded sagely as Tina glanced up and, catching Megan's eyes, let out a snort of laughter.

Closing her eyes, she drew several deep breaths.

They'd already put in their time. They could leave.

Maybe he wouldn't say anything and they could just forget it.

When Megan opened her eyes, Connor was already around the table, no doubt as ready to make a break for it as she was. More. Gail wasn't even his relative.

Or...well, not by blood anyway. Lucky.

And then he was at her side, sliding a hand around her waist as he pulled her close. Closer. And closer still until her eyes went wide as his marauding hand slid across her bottom in a slow, blatant caress to rest at the very top of her thigh. Face burrowed into the side of her neck, he drew a long breath, teasing his nose along the sensitive stretch of skin behind her ear.

He was making a point. Letting them see what she'd asked him to rein in for the sake of Gail's special day. Really, she couldn't hold it against him. In fact, it sort of made him her own personal hero.

Letting her pull back enough for decency, Connor smiled down at her. "What do you think about wrapping it up here?"

Tina's chin pulled back and Jodie rolled her eyes. Gail scrunched up her nose and stuck out her bottom lip. "No. You've got to stay. Bride's prerogative and all. It's my day, so park it."

Connor's menacing half smile slanted over his lips as he looked at the table. All nonchalance, with one hand still resting dangerously low on her hip, the other tucked casually in his pocket.

"Bride's prerogative," he murmured. "Definitely."

She should have seen it coming, should have known. But it wasn't until he'd caught her hand that she saw what he was holding.

The floor dropped out from under her.

"Megan," he said with a doting smile and a steely glint in his eyes. "I know you wanted to wait to announce our news, but I honestly can't. Not. Another. Second."

She was too stunned to react when he slid that gorgeous glittering band over her finger, raising their joined hands for everyone to see. "I know it was fast, but there wasn't a chance in hell I was letting this woman get away."

Gail was the first one to pick her jaw up off the floor, her watery eyes now darting between the ring she wore and Megan's. "You got married," she gasped. "At my wedding?"

Megan started fumbling for something to say, for an apology maybe, though it didn't really seem right. She opened her mouth, only to have the air squeezed out of her lungs by Connor's arms wrapping snug around her. "No, of course not," he assured with all the sensitivity of an assassin. "We got married first. This morning."

Tina and Jodie were both shaking their heads as if understanding was impossible.

"I know it's early, but I think we've waited long enough to get back to our honeymoon. So if you'll excuse us…" And with everyone watching, Megan found herself swept off her feet, tucked into Connor's arms. "Drinks are on me tonight. Congratulations."

CHAPTER NINE

"WHAT IN THE HELL do you think you're doing?" Megan demanded from the far side of the elevator where she stood, hands on hips, eyes boring into him like little embers of hell.

Connor snapped the picture from his phone then slipped the device back into his tux pocket before it ended up incinerated beneath his wife's fiery glare, or more likely crushed beneath the spike of her sexy glass slipper.

"Documenting our first fight."

For a moment, all the red-hot rage directed his way turned to utter shock, leaving her sputtering in a way he couldn't deny he was getting a serious kick out of. But in a blink, she rocketed back to fury, leaning into the space between them, her voice going lethally low. "I can't *believe* you did that."

"Come on, it's something for the scrapbook. You'll thank me later."

"You know good and well I'm not talking about a picture."

Yeah, he did. The way he knew taking a snap of her when she was this cranked up was probably a move just short of suicide, but like his decision to break his promise to her back in the club, it was one he wouldn't regret.

"We had a deal," she hissed, her eyes darting between him and the elevator's digital display. "But maybe you forgot. Or perhaps our agreement didn't suit your needs at the time, so you *just changed your mind.*"

The car slowed, sounding a low chime to alert them they'd arrived at their floor. The doors soundlessly opened and Megan turned forward—her face a mask of calm, belied only by the rapid pulse at her neck. Placing his hand at the small of her back, they stepped out into the main floor.

"Definitely the latter," he answered quietly at her ear.

A taunt, almost daring her to lose her cool in the midst of all these people. But not Megan. She kept it together, impressing him more and more. Confirming once again how well suited she was to being his wife. Not that he'd make a habit of goading her in public or out of it. He didn't expect much fighting, but it was important to know how she would handle it.

From there, they walked silently through the hotel, before arriving at their private villa.

He was more than ready to go toe-to-toe with her on this point, regardless of what kind of mad she had on. That scene at the nightclub was beyond unacceptable.

The second they were inside, Megan spun on him. *"You promised me."*

He had. But circumstances weren't what he'd expected, requiring a judgment call, and he'd made one. Firming up his stance, he crossed his arms.

"Did you hear what they said?" he demanded, giving his own mad its head. "I wasn't going to let those catty, backbiting—"

Her hand cut through the air. "I don't care what they said. All that matters to me is what *you* said. *Your* word. What it's worth. What I can believe."

He held her stare, not backing down. *"You can believe* I took you to be my wife. To honor, respect and *protect*, for all the days of our life."

Megan blinked up at him, suddenly at a loss for words. "Those were our vows?"

"They were mine. And I meant them. I'm not the kind of husband to twiddle my thumbs while my wife is maligned. I would have liked to accommodate you tonight, Megan. I fully intended to. But in a choice between breaking my vow to protect my wife and breaking my vow to protect your cousin's 'special day,' you can bet I'll be putting you first every time."

"Oh." She swallowed past the knot of emotion in her throat, trying to force it back down. Trying not to allow a few simple words the power to leave her vulnerable.

Then after a moment, Connor closed the distance between them, pulling her into his chest. "I'm sorry I had to break my promise to you. But I meant what I said about taking care of you. I won't stand by while someone hurts you."

"I could have handled it." She'd been doing it her whole life.

"Why should you?"

"Gail deserved to have her wedding day." And more than that, because he'd agreed to let her!

"Yes, but so did you." Connor caught her face in his hands, tipping it back so she was looking up at him. "Just because you don't remember doesn't mean it doesn't count."

Everything he said sounded so right. Tempted her to trust. To leap. But the void she was looking out over was simply too great to ignore.

Searching his eyes, she asked the question that was the crux of her fears and reluctance. "What if you change your mind?"

"That's the point, Megan. I won't.

"Commitment—" he rubbed the bridge of his nose as he let out a thoughtful sigh "—it's very important to me. I'm not looking to fill some temporary position, Megan. I want a wife who will stand by me for the duration." Only, then something in his expression shifted. His eyes went distant for a beat before snapping back to hers. Sharper. More intense. "Maybe if you had more time…"

"You mean date?" she asked, knowing she wouldn't go along with it. No more waiting around to see whether something panned out. No more false hopes and years of indecision—

"No," he said with a hard shake of his head, confirming they were in agreement on the no dating. Connor leaned into her space, putting his face before hers so the sincerity in his eyes was front and center. "Understand this, Megan. You're my wife and I want to keep it that way. But I realize everything hasn't fallen into place for you the way it did last night and I'm asking for a big leap. Still, I'm confident, with a little time, it will.

So I propose a trial period. Give me three months. If you don't think we suit, I give you a divorce and you return to the life you had planned. In the meantime, we start as we mean to go on. You live with me…as my wife."

Her throat felt dry, her heart pounding too fast.

It was crazy. What he was suggesting… "You'd introduce me to your friends and business associates? What if I wasn't happy and wanted to leave?"

"You go. Megan, I'm asking you to give our marriage a shot, not to lock yourself in some prison you can't get out of. Granted, I don't believe you'd leave without giving us a chance. Not once you'd made a commitment—one you remember making, that is. Besides, you're not going to want to leave."

He made it sound so simple. She'd been so tempted, time and again throughout the day—but the doubts. They simply weighed too much.

"I've finally found a way to be happy, Connor. I know you think because love isn't a factor that this arrangement you're suggesting comes without risk, but it doesn't. Not for me. I can't put my faith in someone else again. And that's what you're asking me to do. It—it hurts too much to be let down. I'm sorry."

"You don't think the reward would be worth the risk?"

"I don't know. And maybe that in itself should tell us both something," she whispered.

"Yeah, it does. It tells me instead of waiting, hoping you'd remember or come around, expecting you to see the big picture when I hadn't given you all of the pieces, I should have done this."

And before she could blink, he'd pulled her into a kiss.

Megan was flush to his body. Her hands trapped between them, where they'd come up in a stunted defense that stopped before it really began—stopped at the strange familiarity of this intimacy she couldn't quite remember—stopped at the foreign heat inexplicably swirling like a whirlpool through her center, pulling deeper, concentrating with every back-and-forth pass of his mouth over hers.

No wonder she'd blocked it out.

Connor's kiss was even better than she'd imagined. So good, she felt the resistant determination slipping from her body even as she grasped after it. But it was gone, having taken the edge of aggression in the dark depths of Connor's eyes with it. The hands at her shoulders snaked around her waist and into her hair. The pressure against her lips increased and she opened to him.

Afraid to miss even a second, she couldn't blink and her eyes remained locked with his, anticipating the taste and texture of him mixed with her own.

Only, rather than take his fill, Connor barely breached her mouth, skimming the inner swell of her bottom lip with a slow, agonizing lick so compelling it temporarily overwhelmed even the instinct to breathe.

Using the hand wound loose in her hair to angle her head, he deepened the kiss. Enticing her into a return of action—the tentative flick of her tongue against his.

It was all the invitation he needed, and hands tightening at her hip and hair, Connor's low growl of satisfaction slipped through her lips an instant before the firm thrust and retreat of his tongue. The penetrating claim wringing a response too strong, too immediate, too intense to deny. And then she was clutching at him, pressing close even as he pulled her closer still.

It wasn't enough.

Not for either of them.

Connor grasped her bottom in a firm, kneading caress. Then the back of her thigh, pulling it up along the outside of his leg. Rocking into her so she felt the steely length of him against her belly and the hard press of solid muscle between her legs.

From somewhere in the back of her mind, she was vaguely aware of all the reasons this was such a bad idea…only, she didn't care.

Couldn't stop.

Another deep thrust, and then Connor's devouring mouth moved down to her jaw, her neck. Licking, sucking, pulling at the tender spot until she'd thrown her head back, and her hands restlessly worked between them, grasping at the panels of his shirt. Trying to get a hold enough to rip it open.

"Megan, Megan," he groaned, the hot wash of his breath as intoxicating as the friction of his lips. "Baby, it's going to be so good. Tell me you want this."

"Yes," she moaned. "Yes, yes, yes, please. I want you."

His knee pressed higher between her legs, raising her skirt as he rocked the thick slab of his thigh against her intimate flesh in a way that had tendrils of pleasure sliding through her center.

Flicking a teasing lick over the corner of her mouth, he murmured, "Tell me, yes…tell me you'll be my wife."

This wasn't the time for that discussion. This wasn't the time for talking at all. "Later. Please, we'll talk more about it later."

His hips dipped lower, giving her a fleeting taste of the thick ridge of his erection.

Once.

Oh, God…so hot.

Twice.

Her fingers knotted in his hair as liquid heat spilled through her belly.

And then again.

Her breath rushed out on a gasp at the sharp, needy spasm deep within her.

"Tell me you're coming home with me tomorrow."

"Connor, please," she begged, her body on fire.

"You don't even know how much I like the sound of that," he whispered against her parted lips. "How much I want to hear it against my ear as I move inside you…pushing in deep…"

A whimper escaped her at the erotic images sliding through her with the rough stroke of his voice.

"…taking you higher and higher…until you shatter in my arms."

"Yes…" She was about to shatter already.

"Yes, what, Megan?" he asked, trailing his fingertips from the back of her knee to the curve of her bottom and back. "You know what I want to hear."

CHAPTER TEN

WAIT. WHAT? "Are you...blackmailing me with...sex?"

"I don't know." His hips pulled back a fraction of an inch. "Would it work?"

It would.

Even knowing the game he played, Megan was a hairbreadth from promising anything Connor asked for—if it meant he'd finish what he started.

Only, somehow in the past seconds, her stalled-out mind had sputtered to life again. Weakly turning over the events unfolding around her. Events that would shape the rest of her life.

"No," she choked out, forcing her hands to be still. Her eyes to open and meet the burning black of Connor's stare.

"Damn."

She could see the indecision in his eyes...the debate whether to try again. Try harder.

A tremor of hope slipped through her belly at the thought. One she ruthlessly pushed aside.

"What is this?" she asked, waving a hand between them.

He shook his head, an almost bewildered look on his cocky face. "It's hot."

It was more than hot. "It's distracting. I can't think."

"Good, agree to give me three months."

But before she could even contemplate giving him three minutes, his mouth was over hers again, his tongue sliding between her lips in slow, seductive thrusts. Once again tempting her reservations to abandon their posts.

Heart racing, breath ragged, she shook her head, forcing her hands to center at Connor's chest and then giving him a small push. She couldn't agree to anything. Whatever state she'd been in last night, at this moment, the impairment of her judgment was at record level.

"Megan," he murmured, watching her from beneath heavy lids.

Oh, hell, that look. She swallowed, taking a step back. And then another. She needed to get away. Needed space to breathe. To think.

"Come on, baby. Don't run away. Let's sit on the couch and talk."

Her gaze shot to the couch. Within a blink, it had become fodder for more scenarios than her experience could justify—a den of seduction, rife with erotic potential.

She *had* been reading a lot lately.

"I'll keep my hands to myself," came another low, rumbling assurance, pulling her focus back to Connor. Standing where she'd left him, the shirt she'd been trying to free him of spread wide to reveal the hard muscles banding his abdomen and the perfect discs of his nipples.

Her mouth watered as another couchside scenario accosted her.

"Sure you will." Fine, maybe he would. Maybe it wasn't *his hands* she was worried about.

"Don't believe me? You could always tie my hands." Connor grasped one end of the tie hanging loose at his open neck, let it twist around his finger as he held it out in offering. His wicked smile pushing new limits. "Unless you'd prefer—"

"No!" Okay, it definitely wasn't his hands she was worried about. And with what she was thinking, she wasn't sure she'd ever be able to sit on any couch again, let alone that one.

She forced her feet to move one after the other until she'd cleared the stairs and made the master suite again. Arms crossed, she gripped the hem of her dress and pulled it over her head. Stepped into the shower and jerked the tap to cold, bracing for the crush of clarity she prayed the icy deluge would bring.

"Agghgh!" she half shrieked as arctic needles fired against her overheated skin, coating her body with the cold wash of reason returned.

She'd been about to agree to…anything.

Marriage.

Moving across the country.

And God help her, even with the chill of reality raining down over her…all she could think about was the way his kiss had all but consumed her.

A low groan of reluctant need slipped past her lips, and she positioned her face beneath the pounding spray, waiting for the cold to beat its way through her thick skull and to snuff the smoky thoughts in her mind and the fire blazing through her veins.

"Damn, Megan. I like it when you make those sounds."

The lock. She hadn't even thought about it.

Blinking the running water from her face, she turned to look out the clear glass of the shower stall to see Connor leaning against the wall across the room. His half smile was at full strength, seductive and hungry.

"What are you doing in there, sweetheart?"

"Trying to clear my head."

One brow arched and he pushed off the wall, his predatory gaze sliding over her body.

Why wasn't she embarrassed by his obvious perusal? Not that there was anywhere to hide. The clear glass was more a display case than any kind of shelter from searching eyes. And yet, his eyes on her felt natural. Easy.

Not at all the way she'd felt with other men, but then, she'd been working outside the norm from the word go that morning. She should stop making the comparisons.

"Hmm. Clarity looks good on you. Maybe I could use some too."

This time it was Megan's mouth that tipped. *Definitely.* This guy needed to have the fire inside him doused. "You think?"

Connor's hands were on his half-open fly, finishing the job she'd started down in the entryway. And then he was stepping out of his tuxedo pants, leaving them in a heap on the floor as he took a step toward the shower.

Megan's mouth dropped open as she realized just exactly what she'd been inviting.

Was her brain ever going to work right again?

His hands moved to the black boxer briefs straining atop the force of his erection. Those went next, and then he was completely, mouthwateringly naked. His body more beautiful than her fantasies could have imagined. And he was closing the distance between them. Coming for her. Opening the glass door, his eyes blazing hot enough to make her body burn even under—

"What the—?" he barked out as he hopped into the far corner of the shower.

Megan knew she probably shouldn't have laughed, but there was something decidedly satisfying in, for once, not being the one caught off guard. And the stunned confusion etched across the frozen mask of Connor's face was simply too irresistible.

The rapidly thawing mask of confusion.

"You did that on purpose," he charged, maintaining his position beyond the stream of water.

"You said you wanted the clarity," she answered, her body going alert as his focus narrowed on her breasts and then lower. They were both naked. Standing at opposite ends of the oversize stall. The second Connor grabbed for her, she darted out the door, laughing. "Who was I to stop you?"

A deep growl sounded behind her as she reached for the plush warmth of the robe folded over the lip of the tub. Wrapping up, she turned back to the shower and froze. Hands flat against the wall above the tap, muscles flexed and straining, Connor, braced beneath the spray as the cold beat over his body. Then with a shake of his head, he focused on her where she stood beyond the glass.

"I'll be honest, this doesn't work as well as I'd expected it to."

"My thoughts exactly," she answered, half mesmerized by the picture before her.

"Megan, I'm trying really hard to stay where I am right now, but if you don't walk out that door, I'm going to walk out this one and put you against it."

Her mouth fell open.

First the couch. Now the door. It was as if he had seductive superpowers with his ability to infuse the most mundane household objects with deviant potential.

"Or maybe that's what you're waiting for." The promise in his voice was what had her feet moving past the threshold, where she dared one glance back at Connor, who stood watching her, his expression dark, smile wiped clean from his face.

Connor's palm hit the tile with a wet smack as he swore under his breath.

Tempted as she was, she wouldn't take the risk.

Grabbing the soap, he scoured his body with rough strokes, using the task to give himself the time he needed to work through his options.

But damn it, none of them were going to give him what he wanted. Megan coming home with him.

Sure, he was fairly certain, even though it went against her general morals, if he offered Megan no strings, he'd have her beneath him before the water dried from his body. But he didn't want a single night with her. And he wasn't after the dog-and-pony show of dating either. Even with someone like Megan, he didn't want to sink another year into a relationship lacking the authenticity of people who knew they were in it for more than a three- or four-hour window at a stretch. He didn't want to see her at her best. Primped and prepared for some night of romance. He didn't want to be waiting for the *real* to start.

He wanted the *real* right now.

And he'd had it. Until it spilled through his fingers like an overturned cocktail.

Now, no matter how he tried to show her what it had been like, tell her what he'd learned, make her feel the insanity of the connection between them…it wasn't the same. Wasn't enough.

She was going to fly away tomorrow. And nothing he did was going to stop her.

Jerking the tap off, he rubbed the water from his eyes and shook out his hair.

Then, wrapping a towel around his hips, he readied himself for the goodbye he was certain awaited on the other side of the door. Or more likely down in the living room. But definitely not on the couch.

Enough pussyfooting around.

He swung open the bathroom door, determined to face the music like a man—and rooted to his spot, stunned by the sight of Megan, swimming in her giant robe, feet tucked beneath her in the wingback at the far corner of the master suite.

"Okay," she said, nervously wringing her hands. "I'll be your wife."

Megan was talking, but damned if he'd understood a word she said after *I'll be your wife.* In a heartbeat he'd crossed the room and had her in his arms. Her mouth was still moving when his crushed down, silencing the words he hadn't been able to follow. She could tell him later, when the adrenaline rush deafening him to everything but the roar of victory quieted inside his head. Until then, he'd keep her mouth busy with something more productive than talk.

Hands splayed over his chest, she pulled back from him, laughing even as he tried to follow her retreat. "Wait," she pleaded, her hands moving from his chest to frame his jaw. "Wait, Connor. We need to get a few things straight before we go any further."

Walking them back to the bed, he shook his head. "Later. Postnuptial agreement, whatever, we'll work it out. Tomorrow."

"No, that's not what—" Then, twisting her head around, she looked behind her. "No, Connor. I'm serious. Not the bed—"

Only, he was already tipping Megan back onto it. "I know you liked the door idea, but give the bed a chance. You won't be disappointed."

And then his mouth was on hers again, his hand following the smooth line of her thigh to her bare hip. And hell, yes, she was arching into him, moaning around the thrust of his tongue, clutching at his shoulders and then his hair. Opening wider to him and following the retreat of his tongue with the light flick of her own.

She was so sexy. She was *his*.

And he was going to taste every…single…inch of her tonight.

His mouth was on her neck, his tongue sliding over the rapid beat of her pulse when Megan's muffled curse, followed by an urgent wriggle and squirm, had him pulling back to meet her eyes.

"Damn it."

Her face screwed up into a knot of acute frustration, making Connor pull back even more as, baffled, he watched her scoot from the bed.

"*Now*, Connor. We need to talk now. Because I can't agree to everything. We need some ground rules."

"Ground rules." He didn't like the sound of that. "Such as?"

Tightening the belt on her robe, she shifted her weight and squinted at him. "No sex."

Connor's teeth ground down as he drew a long breath through his nose. "You mean…tonight?"

But even as he asked, he knew the answer.

"No. I'm talking about at all. Through the three trial months."

Forcing himself to laugh instead of swear, he shook his head. "Forget it, Megan. This is a real marriage we're trying on, and sex is a healthy, normal part of it."

"It's too distracting," she protested. "I couldn't even think straight when you and I were—" her hand waved back and forth through the air between them "—on the bed. And I'm talking about changing the plans for the rest of my life. I *need* to be able to think."

His brow furrowed. "You'll have plenty of time to think, sweetheart. How about I promise not to 'distract' you when we're discussing something important?"

"Yeah, I'm not sure your concession is going to be enough. When we're together…even kissing…Connor, I can't think enough to tell you to stop when my future is on the line."

Okay, grinning like a fool probably wasn't sending the best

message, but damn, he liked what he was hearing. "You seemed to manage it pretty well…and more than once."

"Barely!"

"Have I mentioned how happy I am you married me?"

"Connor, I'm serious—"

"I'm serious too," he said, following her off the bed and taking her shoulders in his hands. "As far as getting pregnant goes, obviously we'll wait until you're confident this is the life you want. But sex? Not a chance. I'm going to seduce you, Megan."

"I'll say no," she whispered, her eyes already drifting to his mouth.

"Fair warning—" his thumb moved to the pale pink line where her bottom lip became skin "—if you do, I'll stop."

She nodded, closing her eyes when the motion caused him to stroke across that bit of sensitive flesh. So pretty.

"I know you will."

Her eyes opened, and this time she looked him over from damp head to precariously situated towel to toe and back again, as though steeling herself against temptation.

This was his wife!

The muscles in her throat moved up and down as she swallowed. Twice. Then those gorgeous blue pools blinked up at him, determination doing its downright best to put in a showing.

"I can resist you."

Connor gave in to the slow grin pushing at his lips. "You can try."

CHAPTER ELEVEN

"ARE YOU OUT OF YOUR ever-loving mind?" Jeff demanded, his outrage reaching through the phone as clearly as if the man himself had crawled through the line to grab him and shake.

"Would you believe out of my mind, over the moon and totally in love?" Connor asked, shouldering his carry-on as he left the airport newsstand.

"No" was Jeff's flat, less-than-amused reply.

"Yeah, well, you're right." Sidestepping a couple locked in a passionate embrace, he scanned the gates and checked his watch. "I'm perfectly sane. Grounded, with my feet planted firmly in reality, and married to a gorgeous, sexy, intelligent woman who happens to be everything I'm looking for in a wife."

"Wow, I didn't realize you were looking for a gold-digging brainwasher, Connor, or I'd have pointed out the throngs of them throwing themselves at your feet for the last decade. What the hell happened, man. Did she drug you?"

Connor's jaw tightened, his teeth grinding down.

He'd known what people would think. The conclusions they'd draw. And he'd told himself he didn't care. That neither of them would. Hell, Megan wasn't afraid to fly in the face of convention any more than he was. But just as at the wedding, that protective instinct had him ready to throw down over those disparaging comments.

"Not even close. In fact, I suppose the case could be made *I* actually drugged *her*."

There she was. Back from the coffee bar, a tray loaded with

a couple of roadies and a pastry bag in one hand, a laptop back-pack hanging from the other. He slowed his steps, preferring to get this cleared up out of earshot.

"Um…Connor, what are you talking about?"

"I let her drink too much and she ended up blacking out most of the night."

"Let me guess," came Jeff's dry reply. "She remembered the part about getting married, though."

"Yeah, but unfortunately she didn't remember *why* she'd thought it was such a great idea at the time. Took some effort on my part to remind her. Even now, she's still on the fence, but she's willing to give it a chance. We're on our way to Denver to pack her things."

"You're serious?"

He wasn't sure he'd ever heard Jeff's voice squeak that way, and the sound of it pushed the smile he'd started this call with back to his lips.

"As a heart attack. You'll have to take my word for it, but, Jeff, I *know* her. And I *like* her a hell of a lot."

Then because he simply couldn't pass on the opportunity to goad an old friend when the opportunity was right there, he added, "Back on the horse, like you said."

"Speaking of… Does she know about Caro?"

"She does. I told her the first night." He cleared his throat and looked out over the tarmac. "Then again yesterday." He'd been damn lucky she'd asked him about any serious relation-ships during their refresher course in *Know Thy Mate*. Caroline had been the dead-last thing on his mind, and something told him it wouldn't exactly have fostered the trust they were build-ing if he hadn't gotten that tidbit on the table. And even now, he realized there were details he should fill in. Specifics that didn't actually change anything, but—hell, Megan's capitula-tion in giving this marriage a try had been a close thing. Too close. He wasn't willing to risk some unfortunate chronology putting her off, at least not until they were on more solid ground.

"Can't believe you didn't introduce us yesterday. I want to

meet this woman…now that I know she didn't drag you down the aisle at knifepoint," Jeff clarified.

Connor grinned and started walking again, raising a hand when Megan turned his way, her too-wide smile doing too many things to him at once.

"Soon. For now, I'm ready to get her home."

"Good to hear it. But I want details. Start at the beginning."

"You'd been gone about thirty seconds when the 'gymnast' shows up at the table, with this whopper of a line."

"The gymnast? *Dude!*"

Megan met him halfway and, apparently having overheard the last bit, arched an amused brow. Leaning toward the phone, she piped in, "I'm not a gymnast."

Connor ducked and dropped a quick kiss at her temple, relishing the faint blush in her cheeks. "Only, she's not a gymnast, and it's not actually a line…"

Megan woke to the steady *thud, thud* of Connor's heart beneath her ear, the constant weight of his arm around her waist and the whirl of a mind anxious to put sleep behind it.

After two nonstop days in Denver, they'd packed the bulk of her apartment, leaving only the barest essentials behind. Laughter and fun like she'd never known had punctuated intense negotiations, strict limits and hard deadlines as a plan for the next three months came together. Sleeping arrangements, travel and social obligations, their respective professional commitments and myriad other details of this life they were embarking on had to be addressed. With so much to do, and so many decisions to make…it had been after midnight when Connor finally carried her over the threshold of his spacious San Diego home and about five minutes after that when they'd collapsed into bed.

Now Megan was blinking the sleep from her eyes, a silly grin curving her lips as the phrase "Today is the first day of the rest of your life" came to mind. Squinting around the unfamiliar room, she located a clock at the far corner and winced at the realization *today* was beginning at the ungodly hour of four.

Megan made a stealthy escape from the bed and padded

down the stairs, flipping on one light after another as she tried to familiarize herself with a house not yet her home, searching for clues about the man she'd married along the way. What she'd discovered was an immaculately decorated showplace, where each room had a central piece of artwork around which everything else flowed. Horses in charcoal tore across an open plain in the massive study, a bronze figurine capturing the essence of a weary rider atop his mount was the central focus in a reading room, and aged leather behind glass in the living room revealed her husband had the heart of a cowboy.

Such a contrast to the clean lines and neat cut of his made-to-measure everything else. At least everything she'd seen so far. But perhaps that had just been Vegas.

There was so much left to learn.

Her mother's parting words from their previous morning's conversation whispered to her.

"You're going to have to step up your game if you want to hang on to this one…"

She shook her head. Some advice.

There was no game. There never had been.

She knew better, thanks to the lessons learned at her mother's knee.

Turning from the relic of the Old West, her gaze caught on the floor-to-ceiling glass doors making up the southwest wall. The inky black of the early hours had faded to blue and the landscape around them had begun to take shape. Palms stretched like dark cutouts against the morning sky and elusive streaks of white rushed the shores.

Slowly she stepped forward, wanting to put her mother's words and the memories they spurred behind her. Lose herself in the beauty revealed by the approach of the rising sun. Only, the past had already taken hold. All the "daddies" who'd walked through her life. The great guys Gloria Scott had been willing to do anything—*be anyone*—to keep ahold of. The wild changes to her mother's personality and personal goals heralding the arrival of each new man. Megan's own determination not to let this one get too close—no matter how nice or fun he was—because it wouldn't last. It never lasted. The tug at her little girl's nerves once things started to slip. The sidelong looks, the downward pull of a mouth. The hope that maybe she was wrong. That maybe if she was good enough, if she tried hard enough, this one wouldn't leave.

But they all did.

Eugene, Charlie, Pete, Rubin, Zeke, Jose and Dwayne. Seven husbands come and gone, and still her mom hadn't figured it out. A person couldn't *make* something last if it wasn't meant to, like a person couldn't *be* someone they weren't. And trying only prolonged the inevitable.

Some were easier to let go. And some—she let out a heavy sigh as the memory of sun-crinkled eyes winking at her from across a worn dock squeezed her heart—the echoes of their absence were so deeply ingrained in her psyche they touched every relationship she'd ever attempted.

Her fingers trailed the wood frame of the sliders as a thread of anxious tension stitched through Megan's belly. In spite of her determination not to, was she just repeating her mother's mistakes?

She'd married a man she'd known for less than a day. A man who'd been so sold on the woman he met that first night—a night she couldn't remember—he was determined not to let her get away. Sure, Connor thought he knew her. But what if he was wrong? What if she hadn't been herself and he was so caught up in the hard-won victory he was after that he simply hadn't realized it yet?

How long before he saw past the illusion of who he wanted her to be—and actually saw *her*?

Would it be within the span of this trial or would it be after she'd finally let herself believe—

"You're up early."

Megan spun around to find Connor watching her from the hall, a pair of light cotton gray pajama bottoms hanging dangerously low on his trim hips. The bare expanse of his cut chest was emphasized by the casual way he'd leaned one arm at the edge of the open frame doorway.

"So are you."

God, he was gorgeous with his mess of silky hair standing every which way and a day's growth roughing up the perfection of his square-cut jaw, giving him a sort of roguish look to match the smile and eyes.

"My bed got lonely," he offered with a wink that did something crazy to her insides and reminded her of how impossible it was not to get caught up in this man's convictions when they were together.

He believed in them. Was so ready to take that headlong dive into their future. Made it seem so simple.

Just jump.

When he looked at her the way he was right then, it made her want to jump too. Made her want everything he was offering. But wanting something didn't necessarily mean it was right. She had to keep her head.

"Lonely."

He grinned. "Yeah, well, I also figured you might like a tour of your new home. Some coffee maybe?"

She let out an involuntary moan. "Coffee, yes, please."

Laughing, he walked over and caught her hand. "My ego's demanding the next time you make that noise, it's not going to be because of coffee. Come on."

In the kitchen, she rifled through the freezer as Connor got the pot brewing.

"I'm not much of a cook, in case I didn't mention it already, but frozen waffles I can do," she offered over her shoulder.

Connor closed in behind her, one arm reaching past to swing the freezer door shut. "In a minute."

Her heart skipped a beat and her belly fluttered.

"Connor," she warned, taking a step in retreat.

"Relax, sweetheart," he soothed, catching her hips and backing her to the neat square kitchen table, then popping her up to sit atop. "All I'm after is my previously agreed-upon good-morning kiss."

Their compromise on physical intimacy.

It had been a point of contention between them, with Megan

determined not to let seduction sway her thinking about the marriage, and Connor wanting—well, everything. In the end, neither of them had been interested in the kind of precedent three months of strictly platonic set—trial or not. So they'd settled on a daily kiss count of four, with good-morning, have-a-good-day, welcome-home and good-night kisses to be granted at the corresponding times.

Four. She could totally handle four kisses.

Her body warmed at the knowledge it was time to pay the piper.

Parting her knees, he stepped between them. Leaned in close. Closer. And closer still until he'd braced one hand on the hardwood behind her and wrapped the other around her waist, leaving Megan no choice but to cling to his shoulders.

"One kiss, Connor," she whispered, already feeling drugged by the sleepy bedroom scent of him.

"One kiss. Any way I want to take it."

Breathless, she stared up into his eyes. "And you want it on the breakfast table."

Letting out a low groan, Connor ran the bridge of his nose along the line of her jaw to below her ear. "God, yes. But I'll settle for the kiss if it's all you're ready to give me."

"Just the kiss." She'd tried to keep the pleading quality from her tone, but she wanted to be reminded of the chemistry. The magic. What this was leading to if everything worked out. Or maybe all she wanted was Connor's mouth on hers again.

That cocky smile cranked another notch, Connor's lids dropping slumberously low. "We'll see."

And then she had it. The first soft rub of his lips against hers. The gentle, coaxing hint of the hot demand to come.

God, she wanted this to last.

CHAPTER TWELVE

"No sex?" Jeff coughed through the line.

Hands tightening on the wheel, knuckles going white, Connor hadn't missed the undertones of amusement, no matter how his friend tried to cover it.

Glad someone thought it was funny.

"Yeah, I can't believe it either. But Megan…" He took a slow breath, glancing out over the cliffs down to the ocean beyond before returning his attention to the road in front of him. He'd been so sure he had her with the daily make-out quota, because when they kissed—he slid a finger into his collar, freed the button and loosened his tie—they *really* kissed. But true to her word, Megan held strong. "She doesn't want her judgment clouded while she figures things out."

"Right. I get it. Blow-your-mind bedroom antics have a tendency to confuse priorities. Give meaning to the meaningless. Make things seem 'special' when really they aren't. Smart."

Connor ground down his molars, not exactly sure what response he'd wanted from Jeff…but certain it wasn't this.

"So aside from the fact that your fresh-from-the-chapel wife finds you totally resistible, how's the *rest* of married life treating you?"

"Good. No surprises." Not really, anyway. "Megan's more reserved than she came across our first night. And she's somewhat preoccupied with making sure I know what I'm getting into. You know, listing faults in the name of full disclosure because she doesn't want to risk me stumbling over some deal breaker once she's committed."

After a few seconds' pause, the joking tone was gone. "Deal breakers?"

"Relax," Connor assured. "Minor stuff. Quirks mostly."

After all, he couldn't care less if she wasn't a stellar cook or had a tendency to go overboard when she picked up a new hobby. But he sure as hell cared whether the woman he married was going to be straight with him. And every time they were together, she showed him she was.

Even so, he wanted her confidence back. The faith she'd put in herself and him when she'd spoken her vows. But every time she revealed some other fault, waiting a beat to see how he'd handle the news, whether it would shake him, he was reminded how that faith had been wrung out of her like a bar rag.

Didn't matter. She'd see soon enough. And until then…well, he really couldn't complain. She was strong. Smart. She knew how to protect herself.

"She makes me laugh. And she's exceptionally easy to be with. Easy to talk to." Easy to look at and easy to think about. Maybe even a little too easy on that last count.

But it was to be expected.

Megan was a challenge. And though he'd gotten her to give their marriage a chance, he knew she wasn't sold. Which meant she was an unfinished project. A deal hovering on the brink of closure. Damn it, she was an itch yet to be scratched. He wanted her, and until he knew she was securely his, she'd be occupying more of his mind than he would typically allot to a relationship.

"Man, I'm glad you found a woman you can talk to. I know you'd always figured on a marriage that was more of a merger. And after Caro—"

"Look, I'm about home." Connor slowed at the driveway, waiting for the security gate and garage to open. "Time to wear down the wife."

"Got it." Jeff laughed, not taking the abrupt end to the conversation personally. If he had something to say, he'd make sure he got another chance to say it. "And good luck... Sounds like you're going to need it."

Connor cut the call and jumped out of the car, a slow grin spreading to his lips as his mind latched on to the last sight he'd had of his wife before he left for work. He knew she wouldn't look like the sexy kitten she'd been that morning, purring under the kiss he'd pressed against her lips before she'd been quite awake. Sleep mussed and warm. The silky pajamas she'd been wearing shaping over her nipples and riding high toward her ribs.

Small wonder she'd been on his mind the past eleven hours.

She'd be dressed by now. Probably all neat and tidy. Still, he couldn't quite kick the salacious happenings taking place in the not-so-far-back of his mind. Silky, sleep-mussed happenings wrapped up in a welcome-home, I've-been-aching-for-you-all-day kind of kiss.

Yeah, fat chance.

Closing the door behind him, he called down the hall with a facetious "Honey, I'm home."

The silence echoed back to him as he dropped his keys on the glass-topped table and kept walking toward the stairs. The second floor was dark and empty, with only a single dim bulb illuminated at the top of the flight. The third floor too. His brow furrowed as he checked his phone for messages. None.

It wasn't as if returning to an empty house was a new experience for him, but with Megan living there, he'd expected... something different.

Not that he was disappointed. He'd wanted an independent woman who wouldn't make him feel guilty about the schedule he kept or as if her life was tied to his.

Wish granted!

Only walking through the empty house that had never felt lonely to him before, he had to concede a week into their marriage that he hadn't anticipated getting his wish would suck quite this way.

Midway down the darkened hall, Connor paused, just outside Megan's office door. A sliver of light leaked through the seam, and from within came the quiet yet distinct sound of keys tapping.

She was here.

Turning the knob, Connor opened the door to Megan's sanctuary...and discovered his silk-clad morning fantasy staring hard at the monitor as her fingers assaulted the keyboard in front of her.

The sexiness of her sleep-rumpled look had gone mildly stale throughout the day, and yet Connor couldn't take his eyes off her. She was intense, focused. And bobbing her lovely head ever so slightly to the beat of whatever she had pumping into her ears through those hot-pink little earbuds.

Never in a million years would he have expected to come home to a scene like this if he'd married Caro. She'd have been polished and primped. Attentive in the distant way he'd become so familiar with. Making small talk, much as they did with strangers through a cocktail party.

And he'd never have really known—in all honesty, would never have really cared—where her head was at.

Not like this, he thought with a bemused smile. Right now, he knew exactly where Megan's head was. Deep in her work. The project she'd been waiting on must finally have come in.

Standing unnoticed in the doorway, he considered his alternatives.

He could walk across the room and take advantage of her distraction. Pull her blond mess to the side and start with her neck, close his mouth over the spectacularly sensitive spot behind her ear and work his way forward from there...

Or he could go order some dinner—because based on what he was seeing, he'd bet food hadn't even crossed her mind. And when he took his kiss...he wanted Megan paying attention.

Running a hand over the back of his neck, he turned away.

"Connor?"

Her voice was overloud and she was staring at him, looking adorably confused.

He tapped his ear and she pulled the bud from her own.

"Hey, gorgeous. How was your day?"

He'd meant the compliment, but Megan seemed to have taken it tongue in cheek—her face blanching as her hands went to her hair and then those silky pajamas that told more secrets than they kept.

Only, then the most interesting thing happened. That flash of embarrassment faded and something that looked a lot like challenge took its place. "I get caught up in my work...I lose track. It can be irritating for some people."

Ah, more with the disclosures. Whatever it took.

"You near a good stopping point if I call in Chinese?" he asked, sensing the time to wrap things up would put her in a better place to break for the night. It was how it would be with him.

"You wouldn't mind?" Her eyes shot back to his, infinitely softer than they'd been only seconds before.

"I better not—tables'll be turned soon enough." No question. "I'll order and grab a quick shower. Meet me downstairs when you're ready."

At her slight frown, Connor stopped. "Something wrong?"

"You don't want your kiss?"

"Oh, I want it," he assured, giving in to the grin hovering around his lips. "But not until I've got your undivided attention. So wrap it up."

The door closed and Megan stared at her computer, relieved by Connor's easy acceptance of her distraction and yet unable to shake the doubts. The sense that if it wasn't this that opened Connor's eyes to a future he didn't want, then it would be something else. Eventually.

She didn't want to think that way. There was so much *right* between them, and yet, a part of her couldn't buy in. A part of her saw the calm mask Connor wore when she showed him something he, by all rights, ought to dislike—and wondered what lay hidden beneath.

Sure, getting tied up with work this evening wasn't such a big deal. But it didn't seem to matter what she said or did. As if no bad habit or personal shortcoming even registered. As if maybe Connor was so determined to prove how perfectly suited for this marriage they were that he'd turn a blind eye to anything that didn't fit.... Until one day he wouldn't be able to do it anymore.

What happened then?

God, she wanted to believe. But with so much at stake, she needed Connor to acknowledge more than some illusion of perfection. She needed to know he was really seeing her.

CHAPTER THIRTEEN

"SHE MADE YOU WHAT?" Jeff choked through the line.

Connor shook his head at Megan's latest attempt to confront him with a reality she expected him to reject. *Her latest failed attempt.*

"Creamed tuna on mashed potatoes. With peas." Canned, boxed and frozen. He knew because she'd left the containers in plain view on the counter. "Apparently it's one of those old family favorites she just has to have once in a while."

"No. Way."

The last time he'd heard that kind of awe in Jeff's voice, the man had just watched a supermodel bungee off the Verzasca Dam in Ticino, Switzerland, tossing him a wink and blown kiss before taking air.

"Damn, she's serious about shaking you."

Connor bristled, reining in the growl currently threatening his cool. "If she's so serious she ought to come up with something more substantial than dinner. Like I'm going to bolt because she served me less than five-star cuisine. *Come on.*"

It was an insult to both of them.

"You ate it?"

"Of course I ate it," he scoffed, surprised Jeff would even ask. "She made it for me."

And he'd finished every bite, as if it was manna from heaven.

Then giving in to a reluctant chuckle, he added, "But I have to admit that gelatinous puddle—*which even Megan didn't eat,* by the way—was without question the worst thing I've ever shoveled into my mouth."

"Dude."

Half an hour later, thoughts of tests and frustrations had been put aside. Connor strode into the kitchen, working his tie and collar open, stare locked on the delectable curve of Megan's backside, showcased in a pair of clingy yoga pants as she— oh, hell—checked what looked like a lasagna in the oven...but smelled, wow, more than a shade off.

Not. Again.

"Hey, gorgeous," he said, announcing his presence a second before sliding his hands over the sweet curve of her hips. He needed a reminder as to why he was going to choke down the coming atrocity. An incentive of sorts.

With his hands coasting over her hips and waist, she swung the steel door closed and started to turn as he said, "How about my welcome-home— Gah!"

Connor's head jerked back as he was hit with the one-two punch of Megan's smiling face covered in some kind of bottom-of-the-vegetable-drawer-looking half-dry paste...and the accompanying rotting stink of it.

"Your kiss?" She laughed, patting him gently on the chest and then casting him a mischievous wink as she stepped out of his hold. "Sorry to surprise you with the swamp-thing mask, but I do one weekly," she offered with a little shrug.

"Weekly." God, he couldn't even imagine coming face-to-face with this odor on a regular basis. Daring a closer look, he leaned in and ran his finger along one tacky cheek. "What's it do?"

Megan shrugged. "Um...well, it tightens your pores. And re-moves impurities. Keeps the skin looking smoother. Younger. More healthy."

Hmm. Half the time he was with her she wasn't wearing any makeup, and she was *beautiful*. Her skin flawless with those pale freckles sprinkled around it. Maybe it was the mask?

"Interesting." Then waving his hand in front of his face, he asked, "So what other beauty secrets should I be looking forward to?"

He'd never asked any of the other women he'd dated about their mysterious feminine rituals, but then, he'd never been curious before. And of course, he'd never been this up close and personal to one either.

Arms crossed, she gave him a scrutinizing look. After a beat, "Waxing."

"Really." His gaze drifted down the line of her body, curiosity on the rise about every potentially smooth, bare strip of skin.

This time it was Megan circling a hand round her face, her all-challenge smile gone full tilt. "Really."

Confusion first. Then understanding. His chin snapped back. "Really?"

Megan arched a delicate brow at him. "Why, it doesn't bother you, does it?"

He might have mistaken her look as playful—if not for the glint of steel in her eyes.

His good humor and amused intrigue shut down.

Another test.

Three weeks and he hadn't proven a damn thing to her. Hadn't made the slightest headway in easing her concerns. And it was starting to chafe. Pull and rub against the seams of who he was—to the point where something had to give.

But not him.

"I know what you're doing, Megan."

She stared at him a beat. Bracing.

Good idea. She was going to need it, because he had a point to make.

He started toward her, letting his mind peel away the layers of defense she'd erected. The mask, the tests, until the only thing he saw was the woman who'd stared up at him that first night. "I know what I want, Megan."

She was backed against the counter, the breath rushing past her lips in a way that called to his most primitive self.

"And if you think the threat of some smelly mask or not-quite-so-sexy waxing ritual is going to keep me from getting it…" He stroked the shell of her ear, tucked a few wayward strands behind as he took the caress down the line of her neck.

He leaned farther into her space and let the edge back into his voice. "…you've got another think coming."

Wide eyes within a flaking mask of putrid green held with his.

Ready not only to meet her challenge, but raise hers as well—Connor closed in, breathing solely through his mouth. "I'll have my kiss now."

Okay, that hadn't gone the way she'd intended it. Not by a long shot.

Breathless and trembling with unfulfilled desire, T-shirt bunched around one elbow, Megan stared down at herself draped across the polished granite of the center island in utter disbelief as Connor coolly strode out of the kitchen. *Whistling to himself!*

As though he'd claimed some victory instead of crawling off this countertop himself, covered in disgusting flecks of algae mask, his tailor-made shirt missing half its buttons and the tent in his suit pants threatening irreparable damage to his fly.

She'd resisted him!

Granted, it had taken her a while to come to her senses. And possibly only then because in the midst of that tempest of passion, she'd opened her eyes to catch her green-faced reflection in the gleaming metal of a countertop bowl. But still, after a few breathless attempts, she'd managed his name. And a few minutes later, she'd even unhooked her ankles from the small of his back and said no.

Like she meant it. Sort of.

Connor had delivered one last, soul-searing kiss and then… dismounted.

Whistling.

Pfft.

So this revolting mask—that even she could barely stand but used religiously because, despite the stink, nothing worked like it—wasn't enough to throw Connor off his game. In truth, she hadn't really expected it to be.

The man she'd married was no lightweight. He was goal driven. Unafraid of confrontation, hard work or the pungent scent of swamp.

Megan swallowed hard.

She wanted him. But every time she found herself confronted with his unflappable, easy confidence—his smooth sell and I-don't-back-down stare—she couldn't stop the thoughts slithering through her mind.

He held too much sway, made all the right promises and left her feeling more vulnerable than she ever had before. Connor wouldn't acknowledge anything out of line with his goal. He wouldn't respond in any believable way. Which terrified her. Because by refusing to acknowledge who *she really was*, and curbing his every response, he was actually preventing her from seeing *the real him*, as well.

But she couldn't make herself walk away. Because for every too-easily-dismissed fault, there were a hundred instances of sincerity. Moments too pure, too intense, to be anything but genuine.

God, she had to be careful.

Megan couldn't believe it had come to this.

She knew which waffles Connor liked. Not only did she know which waffles he liked—she *cared* about which waffles he liked. And even worse—she'd spent the past ten minutes standing in the open door of the frozen-breakfast section determined to find waffles even better. So she could be the one to offer the best damn toaster waffle her husband had ever wrapped his tongue around.

Oh, this was bad. Very bad.

And totally embarrassing, now that she stopped to think about it. They were waffles, for crying out loud.

Feeling suddenly conspicuous, she glanced down the aisle half expecting to find a crowd of snickering onlookers taking bets on which brand she'd opt for, only, instead her focus caught on a head of short salt-and-pepper curls topping a face she hadn't seen in the two decades that had weathered it.

Her breath leaked out of her in a thin, chilled wisp. "Pete."

She blinked, stepping forward before she'd even thought to curb the impulse. It couldn't be him. In all the years, it was never actually him. But this time…she could swear it was.

Heart pounding, she felt a bubble of laughter rising in her chest. Did she hug him? Shake his hand? Tell him that even now she could feel the way she'd missed him all those years ago.

He had to live around here. Though, the way he loved to travel, maybe he was just passing through. Either way, she was already reaching for him when he said, "Say, Sprout, whadiya think about chocolate with peanut butter and marshmallows?"

She stopped, too confused to make sense of the words she was hearing.

Only, then he glanced over at her and let out a bark of surprised laughter as he took a quick step back.

"Oh, heck, pardon me, young lady. For a minute I thought you were my daughter." His eyes crinkled around the edges. "Serves me right, not looking at who I'm talking to."

Just then, a heavily pregnant woman rounded the corner rubbing her belly with one hand as she scanned her grocery list. "No marshmallows, Dad, but I'm down with the peanut butter."

Pete gave her a nod and reached into the case to grab another carton. He dropped it into his cart and then looked back at Megan expectantly.

Because she was staring. And he had no idea who she was.

Of course he didn't. Though he looked so much the same it hurt her heart to see him, she'd been a little girl the last time he saw her. "Pete, I'm Megan Scott. I mean I was Megan Scott. I got married. It's Megan Reed now."

Heat burned through her cheeks as she realized how much it pleased her to be able to tell him that she'd married. To think that she might be able to introduce him to Connor. They'd get along. She knew they would. It hadn't really struck her until just that second, but there were actually a number of similarities between them.

Only, then her racing thoughts ground to a halt and all that excited energy died as the furrow between Pete's eyes dug deep.

"Megan...*Scott*?" He glanced over his shoulder at his daughter, standing a few feet off wearing a pleasant smile on her face, and then snapped his fingers, looking back at Megan. "From the bank over on First?"

CHAPTER FOURTEEN

HE'D BEEN LOOKING for a fight, that much Connor could admit. Pulling around the corner to the house, he'd felt the gathering tension through his back and neck, the same kind of jacked pulse he got before walking into a major negotiation. The fact that his system was ramping for conflict in anticipation of seeing his wife only made it worse.

There hadn't been any new "tests," but the emotional distance, the guarded looks and speculation when she thought he wasn't looking—and hell, sometimes even when she knew he was—had only increased. Something was coming.

Only, then he'd pulled through the security gate and seen the open garage, Megan's car parked and her still in the driver's seat. A quiet alarm began to sound in the back of his mind as he cut the engine and jumped out. All that jacked-up ready-to-go morphed into protective instinct.

This wasn't right.

Rounding the car, he came up to her window and stopped short at the sight of tear-streaked cheeks and a bleak stare. And for the first time since they'd met, he saw something other than how strong Megan was. Beneath all that toughness was something fragile. Something she didn't show to the world but here and now she couldn't hide from him.

His gut knotted hard as the first question slammed through his head.

Had he done this to her? Pushed her too far? Asked too much? Broken her?

Heart pounding, he forced himself to knock on the glass instead of ripping the door off its hinges to get to her. Find out what happened, if he was to blame. Make sure Megan wasn't hurt. *Physically.*

She jumped in her seat as he opened the door, her eyes darting around the interior of the car before landing on him. The arms that had been hanging limply in her lap jerked up, and then she was wiping at her cheeks, mumbling some kind of unintelligible apology as she emerged from her daze.

Resting a staying hand on her shoulder, Connor crouched beside her seat, searching for clues in a face his wife was rapidly trying to clear. Only, with each sweep of her thumbs, another tear slipped free.

"Megan, what's going on, honey?"

She sucked in a shaky breath, swallowed and then bowed her head. "It's so stupid. I'm sorry. I shouldn't be like this. I just… saw someone I used to know."

Connor's muscles bunched. It wasn't him, then, making her cry—and the relief he felt over that was immense. But it was nothing compared to the outrage pouring through him that someone else had done this to his wife.

Someone she used to know.

"Barry?" The idiot who'd run off and married another woman when he'd been making plans with Megan. The one he'd believed wasn't important enough to merit this kind of sorrow. Did the guy have some kind of hold over her heart Connor hadn't realized?

Was he in California to get Megan back?

She shook her head, valiantly trying to force a smile to lips that couldn't bear the weight of it. "No. His name is Pete. And for about a year, a very long time ago, he was my dad."

Her dad.

Connor was at a loss. He knew Megan had been raised by her mother, a serial bride who didn't have much of a track record when it came to keeping husbands. Megan never talked about any of the guys her mother had married, and he'd gotten the sense they hadn't been of particular importance in her life. Only, now he was wondering just exactly how off base he'd been.

"What happened?"

"He didn't remember me." Megan winced and closed her eyes. When she opened them again, she was blinking fast. Giving her head one of those thought-jarring shakes. As though she was physically trying to throw off the emotion. She wanted to be strong. And hell, he admired her for it. But as the tears continued to fall, the heartbreak in her eyes was unmistakable. And damn it, he'd seen that kind of pain before. Knew the kind of soul-deep wound it stemmed from. Feared it.

The kind where a person's whole heart was tied up in the hope of something they understood they couldn't have. The kind another person couldn't fix or fill or make up for…could only pray they were strong enough to withstand.

She was strong.

"Sweetheart, I'm sorry."

"It was so long ago. I don't know how I expected he would remember me, but I was practically ready to throw my arms around—" Her voice broke, and she glanced away.

Damn. Megan looked so lost and vulnerable, he couldn't stand it. Needed to do something. Ground her in some way.

Taking her hand, he stroked a thumb over her knuckles. "Let's go inside."

She nodded and he stepped back, helping her from the car. Her eyes shifted toward the house, and he half expected her to simply draw herself up and walk away. Retreat to a place he couldn't reach her.

Only, then she closed her eyes and *turned into him*, pressing her face against the center of his chest, so there was nothing to do but wrap his arms around her trembling shoulders and hold her close. Stare down in disbelief as Megan clung to him.

Pulling her in closer, he laid his cheek against the silky strands at the top of her head and stroked a hand over her back.

"It's okay, sweetheart. I've got you," he promised, rocked by the depth of meaning behind his words. He wanted to protect her in a way he'd never experienced before. And that she wanted his protection and comfort—could accept it—was profoundly satisfying.

"I told him my name and he couldn't place it. I mentioned my mom and the connection clicked. But it was…so awkward."

Connor ushered Megan inside and up to their room where they lay in bed together with her head resting in the crook of his arm. They spoke in hushed tones, watching the shadows fill in around them as the light faded and the quiet of night replaced the cacophony of day.

"They were all good guys," Megan whispered in response to the question he'd just asked, her breath warming the spot above his heart still damp from her tears. "That was the thing. Mom never picked jerks we could only pray would take off sooner rather than later. They were all nice men we hoped would stay, even though deep down I knew they wouldn't."

"There were seven?"

"Seven she married."

Which meant there were more she hadn't.

He couldn't imagine what it would be like for a little girl to have a revolving door of father figures passing through her life that way, or how her mother could have let it go on. But he knew all about women who couldn't control their hearts—even for the sake of their children. Even for the sake of themselves. At least Megan's mother had been resilient enough to bounce back. Move on.

"When she brought Pete home, I barely even spoke to him. It was terrible, but I think it had only been a couple of months since the one before had left, and I didn't want to—care, I guess. Only, Pete was sort of relentless. He wanted to win me over—do everything to make this new family work. So he told jokes and stories. Took me fishing. Talked to me and actually listened to what I said. He made me feel…special. Like I was more than just the kid who came with the woman he'd married. Like I was his friend too. Thinking back on it now, though, I wonder if maybe it wasn't more a case of me being the perfect project for finding common ground with a wife with whom he otherwise didn't share much."

Connor tightened his hold around Megan's shoulders, giving her whatever time she needed to go on.

"When he left I thought it would be…different. I thought he might stop back so he could say goodbye to me. Maybe call to tell me he missed me or that he was sorry he had to go. But he didn't and I figured it was because of my mom's rule about severing ties. Still, he'd said he loved me, so I kept waiting and hoping. And maybe I never stopped, because when I saw him at the store this afternoon, I was so— Oh, God, Connor, I was such a fool."

"No, Megan. Not you." That she even thought so— Connor silently cursed this Pete and Megan's mother both for what they'd put her through. For not recognizing the impact their careless actions would have. The guy told Megan he loved her. He made her believe it and then walked away. A little girl whose tender heart had already been bruised time and again.

And the worst of it—the part that churned in Connor's gut— was the knowledge that in no small way, he owed Gloria Scott and this string of faithless men a debt of gratitude. If their repeated abuse hadn't broken her ability to trust in love enough to surrender to it, this woman never would have settled for this partnership he had to offer her. She'd have found someone years ago to love her the way she deserved and they'd be married with a half-dozen kids in tow.

He might not be able to give her a storybook romance with love everlasting, but he'd make damn sure she had everything else. He'd be constant. The man she could count on. They'd get past this trial, and time would show her. She'd see.

Megan woke on a gasp, her eyes flying wide as she jolted upright. She scanned the empty bed and room around her. Tried to get a hold on the reality that was now, even as the nightmare she'd been fleeing pressed at her mind.

She'd been running, lost in the kind of fog only the dream-world could conjure. Searching for Connor, knowing it was a mistake, but unable to stop herself.

And then he was there. His arms warm around her, his hushed nonsense a confusing comfort at her ear.

She looked up to ask him what he meant, and it was Pete's face speaking with Connor's voice. "Don't worry, I'm going to win you over."

Desperately she looked around and, again finding Connor across the void, called out to him.

He smiled, the lines at the corners of his eyes etching deeper as she watched. "I don't remember you."

Throwing back the covers, she pushed the nightmare away. Told herself it was just her head processing the mess yesterday had been. Except instead of settling down, the panic she'd experienced in her sleep was on the rise.

She needed to find Connor. Needed to—

"Hey, you're awake."

She spun toward the door where he'd come to stop with that same casual arm slung up around the top of the frame. Jeans and a soft T-shirt tempted her with hints of the powerful body hidden beneath. But it was the ever-elusive half smile that held her, making her feel the coming loss deep in the center of her chest.

She swallowed, watching as Connor's easy posture went straight and the smile slid away with all the warmth that had been in his eyes.

His voice was hard when he spoke. "No."

"Connor, I'm sorry." Wringing her hands, she took a tentative step in his direction. "I can't do this."

"Bull," he fired back, the spark of temper igniting his outrage so completely it was as though the tinder had been set, waiting in place. "You haven't even tried!"

"That's not true. I have. I've been trying for a month. But it's no use. I'm not settling into a life I feel like I can keep. I don't—" She broke off, shifting her gaze from the accusation in his.

God, she didn't want him looking at her that way…she didn't want to deserve it.

"You don't *what*, Megan? If this is it, then let's just own it all. Say it."

Fists balling at her sides, she fought back the pain rising in her chest and did as he asked. "I don't trust you."

"Of course not. I've been honest, up-front and straightforward with you from the word go." Connor pushed off the wall, raking a savage hand through his hair. "Yeah, I wouldn't trust me either."

Megan watched in despair as he stormed from one end of the room to the other and back, his outrage blasting her like gale-force winds.

"It's not you," she swore. "It's me."

Shooting her a condemning look, he let out a harsh laugh. "Is that so? Not a single thing I could do, huh?"

"No." He'd already done too much. Been too perfect. Too perfect to believe he was real.

Connor crossed his arms and stared down at her. "You never wanted to be convinced. From the start you've been looking for any excuse you can find to justify walking away before you had to risk…anything."

Her mouth dropped open. It wasn't true. She just—she—

She was suddenly angry. Really angry.

At herself. At Connor. At Pete and her mother and every event that had brought her to this horrible moment.

"How am I supposed to risk everything on someone who isn't real!"

"What the hell are you talking about?"

"You don't react to anything, Connor! You don't get mad. You don't get frustrated. No matter what I throw at you, no matter what I say, it's like all you're focused on is the goal at the finish line. Secure the wife and nothing else matters. I never see anything but your unflappable calm and easy charm. You're always so *reasonable*. Always with the *rational* approach. The *perfect* solution to any problem. And it's impossible to believe, because *no one* is that perfect, Connor. That's why I can't trust you. That's why I have to leave!"

CHAPTER FIFTEEN

CONNOR STARED DOWN at his wife, absorbing this final revelation.

He'd been vowing to give her everything he had, but... *nothing would be enough.*

He'd thought there couldn't be anything worse than the helpless sense of failure and inadequacy that marked the first thirteen years of his life. When no good grade, lost tooth or scored goal was enough to push the heartbreak from his mother's eyes—not when every milestone achieved was simply a reminder of the man who was missing them all. When Connor's dependence—his very existence—hadn't weighed heavily enough to compete with the bottle of sleeping pills she'd taken to end the pain. But now, to realize he'd simply exchanged one woman with a hurt he couldn't touch for another with a doubt he couldn't overcome... *Damn it*, what was he doing? What kind of messed-up psychosis kept him coming back to this impossible place—when he'd spent his entire adult life actively working to avoid it?

He should let her go.

Except then he thought about the desolate look in Megan's eyes the night before. That instant when he'd been sure she would turn away...but instead she'd clung to him and cried against his chest. Took his comfort. His strength.

And woke up the next morning ready to run.

To hell with this.

"You want to see a reaction, Megan? You want something real?" He stalked slowly toward her, letting the anger pulse off him in waves. "I'm furious. Only, I sure as hell didn't get this way because my wife took the time to cook me a dinner. In fact, it's not any of that trivial nonsense you've been shoving at me. Because—truth?—on the scale of significance, that stuff doesn't even register. What has me pushed past the boiling point...what has me really, really *upset* is learning the woman I thought was so incredibly strong I married her on the spot...is actually a *quitter* who runs from challenge, a *coward* too afraid to even try, a *liar* who makes promises she won't keep and a *cynic* too bitter to believe what's right in front of her face. Is that real enough for you?"

Megan's lips parted on a gasp, her eyes blinking time and again, as though she couldn't quite believe what she'd just seen. What he'd said. Then, barely a whisper, "You're wrong."

Connor shook his head, wishing he were.

"I don't think so. But I'll tell you what I am...mad as hell. *At you.* Right now. More angry than I've ever been at a woman I was in a relationship with. But—and this is the important part, baby, so listen up—*I'm not the one ready to leave.* I'm the one trying to get you mad enough to fight back. To throw down your gloves, get up in my face and prove me wrong. I want you to stay because what we could have is worth fighting for. And if that's not *real* enough, damn it, I want you to stay for this too—" Grabbing her shoulders, he pulled her into a hard, searing kiss.

It was too brief. Didn't satisfy more than the most base claim. And when he pulled back, ire still surging hot through his veins, he met Megan's eyes, daring her next response.

She stared up at him through air thick with tension, her expression stunned, hands resting at his chest and abdomen.

"You're *really* angry."

"Incensed," he assured, not just trying to sweet-talk her, but meaning it completely.

"And you still want me." Her fingers closed around the fabric of his T-shirt. "Us." Her pupils shot wide and the breath trembling past her lips whispered of unfulfilled desire. "This."

Heat licked across the space between them, burning away his restraint until there was nothing left but the single soul-deep truth that had been at the heart of it from the start. "Beyond reason or rationale."

And then there was only the hard press of one body against the next. Megan's mouth opened beneath the crush of his own. Her hands grappling to get higher, to wind tight in his hair, as he flattened her against the wall, hoisting her legs around his hips.

This was the kiss from that first night. This was the reality-shattering, blood-burning, hungry demand for more that had him ready to walk over coals to get it.

This was the woman he married.

Then, without breaking the contact of their lips, Megan told him what he'd been aching to hear. "I'm not a coward and I'm not a liar."

The sweet taste of her claim rushed over his tongue, and he returned it with his own guttural demand. "Prove it."

Another kiss and this time her tongue rubbed against his, soft and wet and so damn eager it stoked their desire to fever pitch.

Megan's restless hands stole down his back, grasping at the cotton of his shirt and tugging it high as Connor braced her against the wall, reaching overhead fast to the bunched fabric and jerking it off. Swooping in to the kiss he couldn't get enough of, Connor stopped at the barrier of Megan's delicate fingers between their lips.

Pulling them free so only that scant half inch remained, she spoke again. "I'm not a quitter."

He caught the back of her head with his palm and held her still to search those beautiful blue eyes. "Then stay, Megan. Stay and give us the chance we deserve."

Megan's arms linked tight around his neck.

"I'm sorry," she whispered urgently against his ear. "You were right about what I've been doing. Focusing on what could go wrong instead of appreciating what's right. I thought if I showed you the worst of who I was—" She broke off, shaking her head before looking back at him imploringly. "I've been trying to play it so smart, but all I've been is stupid and scared."

His hands moved to her waist, holding her tight as though

she weren't already holding him. As though he couldn't quite believe…she was actually fighting for them.

"Megan, tell me what you want." He could give it to her. Whatever she needed. Anything.

Her eyes, so wide and honest and deep, searched his and then darkened as they dropped to his mouth, lingered there for one agonizing beat. "I want *you*."

Megan's head fell to the side as Connor devoured her neck, his mouth moving over her with a carnal intensity he'd shielded her from through every previous encounter they'd shared. All this time she'd been so sure he was giving her seduction his best effort, when in truth he'd been the one holding back.

This…she never would have been able to resist.

Standing in her panties at the edge of the bed, Connor wearing only those sexy boxers that made her mouth water, she trembled at the feel of her palms sliding over the terrain of his bare chest. The hard ridges of his abdomen ticking tight beneath her fingertips.

His body was so perfect she didn't know where to touch first, what to taste.

All of him.

That was what she wanted.

What she needed.

"I'm going to make love to you, Megan." His palms coasted over the lines of her body, leaving a path of warm friction sensitized in their wake. "With my hands…"

God, his touch was so good.

"…with my mouth…" His lips closed over the sensitive hollow at her collarbone, the gentle suction making her groan and squirm.

"Please."

"…with my body…"

And then he was guiding her to the bed, his broad chest meeting hers in one teasing kiss of flesh before he held himself above her. His mouth blazed a trail of heat and need from her neck down to her breast.

"So beautiful, Megan," he murmured, his lips brushing back and forth over the straining bud of her nipple before circling it with the firm point of his tongue and then licking, slowly, lower.

Over her ribs.

Around the small well of her navel.

Across the slight jut of her hip bone.

And then along the scalloped edge of her panties.

All the while she watched, held rapt by the vision of this gorgeous man indulging in his free rein over her body.

His hands coasted over her hips, knees, calves, touching her reverently as though in truth he meant to cover every inch of skin. Fingers sliding around her ankles and then back up, it wasn't until he'd reached her knees she realized the strategic shift of his arms from the outside of her legs to the inside, and even as she watched, he was coaxing her knees farther apart, opening her to him as he dropped kisses down the lacy V at the center of her panties, teasing her through the fabric with the warm wash of his breath...the press of his kiss.

"Oh, God, Connor," she moaned at the firm stroke of his tongue over the silky panel covering her.

Running his lips back and forth across the damp of her panties, he groaned. "I love it when you say my name right."

She gave in to a breathless laugh at his words, but then lost hold of the thought at the next wet stroke of his tongue.

A needy ache was building low in her belly, a tension without limit.

Fingers moving into the strands of his hair, she tried to urge him upward. "I want—"

Catching her wrists, he guided them back to their previous position above her. Holding her there for a beat that said *stay* more clearly than the voiced word itself.

Connor's fingers curled around her panties to peel them from her hips and slip them off her legs. His eyes, dark with hunger and glinting with determination, were mesmerizing as they met hers.

"I'm going to kiss you like this, sweetheart...the way I've wanted to from the start. Long and slow and deep..." he said, the sensual threat of his wicked half smile doing things even his touch hadn't accomplished.

Then, with a look so devilish she shivered, he added, "And French."

"Connor!" she gasped at the first wet velvet rub of his tongue. But the only reply was another hot lick. Her hands flew to his hair, his shoulders, the bed beside her hips, grasping and desperate beneath the most exquisite openmouthed kiss she'd ever experienced.

It was thorough. Spectacular. Her body was on fire around the slow thrusts, the curling licks and languorous strokes of his tongue. Then he was touching her at the same time. Circling his thumb at her opening and then slowly, firmly pressing inside as his kiss concentrated on the throbbing center of her need.

"Oh, God!" she cried out at the feel of him both inside her body and out.

It had been so long since she'd had a man's attention this way, but never had it been like this.

Need coiled low in her belly, each deliberate thrust of Connor's thumb intensifying the sensation until her hips were rising to meet him. Her pleasure cresting.

Her breath broke into ragged pants.

She was almost there. Sinking her teeth into the swell of her bottom lip to keep from screaming, Megan gripped the bedspread beneath her.

"Let go, Megan. I want to hear you." Another deliberate lick through the center of her, this one spiraling around that point of need so primed she didn't know if she could bear the exquisite pleasure the contact brought her.

Cries of need and desperation ripped past her lips, echoed around the walls of the room and rained down over them. Letting go with Connor like this was too good, too intense. So much more than she'd known was possible.

The pressure building within her touched every cell in her body, rubbed against the confines of her form and pushed steadily at the places she never expected it to reach. Places she

thought far deeper, more tender and too forbidden for any man
to find. Places she hadn't even known existed herself.

Her head thrashed, the sounds escaping her little more than
incoherent pleas.

And then Connor closed his lips around that singular spot
and gently sucked.

Starbursts exploded behind her eyes and she shattered.
Her mind went blank and her body spasmed hard around and
beneath Connor's touch as her thighs gripped his shoulders
through wave after wave of release.

It was endless. Satisfaction like she'd never known. Loving
like she'd never had. And yet it wasn't enough. Her body, so
sated with pleasure, continued to ache. Everything inside her
pulling toward the man who defied all logic.

Reaching out, she cupped Connor's hard jaw as he leaned
over her, sliding his hand under her bottom to lift and reposi-
tion her at the center of the bed.

A moment later he'd rolled on a condom. Then, poised at her
opening, he shifted his hips, penetrating her with the thick head
of his erection. Gasping at the first shallow thrust stretching
her wide, she clutched at his powerful shoulders.

He felt so good.

Connor rocked back, then eased forward again, setting a
rhythm that took him incrementally deeper with each stroke
until finally he was buried to the hilt within her, joining them
as completely as two bodies could be.

Looking down into her eyes, he vowed, "No more holding
back, Megan. Neither of us. I want it all."

So full she could barely breathe, she gasped the single word
echoing through her heart, "Anything."

His mouth descended on hers, searing her with a hot kiss
before breaking away. "Everything, Megan."

Megan opened her eyes to the sight of one large masculine
hand engulfing her smaller one, both tucked close to her face.
Hard muscle and powerful strength warmed her back and tan-

gled with her limbs as steady breaths caressed the bare skin of her shoulder.

It was heaven.

And she'd almost thrown it away.

The heavy arm thrown over her side tightened, alerting her that Connor was awake. Turning to face him, she was struck by the intimacy of their heads sharing a single pillow as the late-morning sun spilled across the bed.

Looking into the too-symmetrical perfection of her husband's face, she asked, "Are you still mad at me?"

Connor rolled onto his back, but kept his face turned to hers so she saw when his half smile tipped the balance. "No. I'm not much of a grudge holder. Or much of a fighter, for that matter. If you really want to know, this is the first time I've ever fought with a woman."

"Ever?" she asked, not quite sure what to make of that. "Are you that easygoing?"

He swallowed and looked up to the ceiling. "Yes and no."

Then, looking back to her, he clarified. "It's true that little stuff doesn't bother me much. I mean, there are things to get upset about and things that just don't matter so much. But before you...I was never invested in a relationship like this."

"It's that different with us?"

"Yeah. So how about you, Megan—still scared?"

This time it was Megan who looked to the ceiling.

"Yes. But you're worth the risk."

Pulling her hand up so it rested on his chest, Connor played with her ring a moment, the look on his face telling her there was more on his mind. Something that perhaps wasn't so easy to say.

He frowned and his focus on her ring intensified, as though looking at it was somehow an anchor against his thoughts. Then, after a moment, he cleared his throat. "I get it, you know. What scares you about this. Us. Me.

"You don't want to end up putting your faith in a guy like your mom married—who's going to make you promises and then walk away. You don't want to *let* yourself get hurt that way again. And the fact that you're trusting me— Megan, I swear, I'm not going to let you down."

"I know," she whispered, sensing Connor's growing tension, but unsure what was driving it. "Connor, what's going on?"

He cleared his throat again and then turned to face her. Those dark eyes, achingly open to her. "I want you to know that I understand where you're coming from because I know how it feels to be left behind. To let yourself need someone and have them leave."

There was a long pause while Megan wondered if he was going to say any more. In the end she couldn't bear it any longer. "Why, Connor?"

"I think…I think I've I told you about my mother," he started.

Megan's heart began to thump. "She died when you were young."

A nod. "What I didn't tell you… What I don't tell…anyone is that she took her own life."

Megan sat up in the bed, tucking her knees beneath her as her hand flattened against Connor's heart. "Oh, Connor. I'm so, so sorry."

Patting her hand, he gave her an appreciative nod and pulled her back down against his chest. "Thank you, sweetheart. She'd been very unhappy for a long time. And eventually, it was too much for her."

"But you were only thirteen."

Her stomach knotted. Suddenly, so many pieces fell into place. Connor's bond with Jeff. His resentment toward a man who didn't deserve the title *father*. Why he understood how difficult it was for her to trust.

There were a lot of ways a person could be left. And her husband had firsthand experience with one of the worst.

"I've had a long time to come to terms with it. And like I said, I don't really talk about it. But you're putting your faith in me. Trusting me. And you deserve to know that I understand what that means."

Throat tight, she nodded against his chest. He was talking

about her trusting him, but in that moment, all Megan could see was the trust Connor had just put in her.

She was going to be worthy of it.

CHAPTER SIXTEEN

THE HOT SPRAY OF THE SHOWER blasted his face as, hands against the marble wall, Connor tried to pry his thoughts from under the duvet and the sexy little nymph he'd left buried beneath it. Five was too early to wake her with the kind of kiss on his mind. Especially since *she'd woken him* around two with a custom version of her own.

God help him, she was incredible.

Even better, *insatiable*.

And the level of compatibility between them—undiluted by vanilla vodka and unfettered by the doubts Megan had finally found her way around this past week—was off the charts. Beyond expectation.

He'd known she was smart. Had been impressed by her ability to intelligently discuss nearly any topic to come up, add her own unique perspective, find the humor in related connections. But now that she'd relaxed into the trial, she'd truly opened up… and that brain of hers *blew his mind*.

Megan made him want more than he'd imagined he could with a wife. And because of who she was—how she was—he could relax and enjoy…without worrying about leading her on.

Because his sweet, sharp, smoking-hot wife had the very same limitations he did.

Neither one of them fell in love.

Like neither one of them wanted anything more than exactly what they had.

Okay, that wasn't quite true. Connor wanted more.

He wanted this trial behind them and any lingering doubts that kept Megan from putting it there assuaged.

He wanted her pregnant.

At the idea alone, he groaned. Megan growing big and round with his baby. So damn hot.

Okay, the DNA portion of this merger and acquisition had to wait, but the rest...

Water streaming down his face, he shot a look toward the room they shared. She *had* woken him first. In his book, turnabout was fair play. His hand was already on the knob for the tap, when he remembered Megan had to work today.

Like he had to work today.

One of them at least should get more than three hours of sleep...eventually.

Wisps of cool air slipped through the steam an instant before Megan's slender arms wrapped around his waist, and her breasts, warm and hard-tipped, pillowed against his back.

"Good morning, Mr. Reed," she murmured, pausing for a decadent little lick over his spine. "Thought you could sneak out without my good-morning kiss?"

He turned, taking her in his arms so the water would reach her, as well.

She was sleep ruffled, sexy and soft. Her bare, wet skin a temptation he wondered if he'd ever be able to resist.

"Not a chance." Sinking into a slow, deep kiss, his body hardened and his mind blanked of anything beyond all the creative ways he could get her to say his name in the next hour.

Work could wait.

"One night in Las Vegas? And you knew?" came the delighted question from Georgette Houston, her bright eyes darting eagerly from Megan to Connor and back again.

Nearly six weeks into a marriage based, at least in part, on Connor's desire to have a fundraiser-ready wife on hand to balance the social against his business, and this intimate dinner squeezed in before Connor's trip to Ontario and her looming deadline was their first night out with another couple. Larry and

Georgette Houston. Both in their mid-fifties and both treating Connor and Megan more like family than a longtime business associate with a deal to pitch and his tagalong wife.

Megan opened her mouth to answer, happy to share the sanitized version of their meeting—as it had been told to her, anyway—when Connor beat her to the punch, a goofy grin hanging on his one-sided smile.

"Neither one of us was looking for romance, but we ended up talking, and talking, and talking some more. One thing led to another and...well, here we are." Connor leaned in, his arm stretched across the back of Megan's chair in the kind of comfortably possessive posture that sent butterflies skirting around her stomach. "Larry can tell you, when an opportunity as spectacular as this one presents itself, I'm not one to risk losing it. I wasn't letting Megan out of my sight until I'd secured a date for the rest of our lives."

Georgette's hand fluttered to her chest as she sighed over the romance of it all.

Larry exchanged a good-humored look with Connor, muttering something about getting the point loud and clear, and promising to have a look at the numbers Connor was sending over to him the next day.

The dinner continued for another few hours, the conversation easy and entertaining. Megan could tell Connor respected the older man and truly enjoyed his company. The laughter around their table was rich and warm, and by the end of the evening, she felt as though she had two new friends.

Friends she hoped to keep for a lifetime, because a lifetime was what she was looking at with Connor. What she wanted. What she was thanking her lucky stars for granting her the second chance to have.

Letting down her defenses had been one of the most difficult things she'd ever done. But forced to see what her fears were making of her—she'd had to try.

And once Connor had teased that trust from the tight hold of her fist...handing it over had been incredible. A heady, addictive thing. A release she'd never allowed herself to truly experience before.

And she felt…free.

Safe.

As if maybe fairy tales came in varieties she hadn't known existed. And this one was hers.

As the men collected their coats, Georgette took Megan's hands in her own, squeezing warmly.

"I can't tell you how thrilled we are Connor found you. He had such a rough start with that father of his. He's earned the happiness you two obviously share."

"Thank you, Georgette."

The older woman shook her head, a little crease forming between her eyes. "To think how close you came to missing each other."

Megan's head cocked to the side. They'd agreed not to share the part of their "love story" where she'd woken up without a memory and tried to leave, so she didn't know exactly what Georgette was referring to. "Because of the short window of opportunity in Vegas?"

The smile at Georgette's lips faltered, her gaze shifting to Connor and back. It was only the smallest slip, really, before a wide, reassuring and yet somewhat less sincere smile replaced it. "Of course."

Pulling her in for a hug, Georgette whispered, "I've never seen him look at anyone the way he looks at you. You're special."

This time it was Megan's brow furrowing, her mind churning over that instant of hesitation and the words that were setting off quiet alarms in the back of her mind. As Georgette released her, Megan opened her mouth to ask…and then stopped. She was being paranoid. *Cynical.* Looking for nonexistent problems behind words that shouldn't have been anything but the most beautiful reassurance. So instead she replied with a heartfelt truth.

"He makes me feel that way."

And then Larry was wrapping Georgette in her coat, and the

goodbyes, well-wishes and promises for another dinner were filling the space around them and the night out was at its end.

Only, one look at Connor, at that half smile she had no trouble reading at all, and she knew—for them—the night was just beginning.

Connor kicked the hotel door closed and, toeing off his shoes, dropped into the unwelcoming cushions of the couch with a groan. It was official. Megan had spoiled him completely.

He'd gotten hooked on the wind-down of their nightly conversations. On the company of a woman whose mind kept him guessing and eager for more.

And now, for the first time in as long as business travel had been a part of his life, he was keenly aware of what he was missing at home.

It sucked.

Yeah, he still got off on the negotiations, bouts of hardball and the pursuit of his goals. But here at the end of the day... something was missing.

Eyes glued to the monitor in front of her, Megan tried to focus on her last line of code. Only, something inside her balked, grinding a mental heel into the ground of her concentration.

She needed a break. Some food.

The rattle and clink of coins spilling from a slot machine—Connor's latest text tone—had her lips curving and the lethargy weighing her down evaporating into thin air.

11:37 p.m....CONNOR: You up?

Delighted, she responded, asking how the meetings had gone. She'd missed him like crazy. No matter how much she'd told herself to rein it in, she hadn't been able to. And now—

The front bell sounded. Was he back? Here to surprise her?

She sped downstairs, hoping to find Connor waiting. Only, as she reached the first floor, her phone rang again. Answering, she swung the door open and felt her heart flip in her chest.

"Oh, my God, I love you," she gasped, blinking back tears.

The delivery guy nodded. "I get that a lot, actually."

Amused, Connor asked through the line, "You two need a moment alone, or you ready for dinner?"

Twenty minutes and half a sausage-and-mushroom thin-crust later, Megan was curled into the living room couch, phone to her ear as she watched the flames flicker in the gas fireplace.

She could hear the rustle of fabric through the phone, the weary groan—and more than anything, she wished she was there. "I'm glad you called."

"I've gotten kind of used to catching up at the end of the night. I like it."

Megan closed her eyes, snuggling into the sound of Connor's voice. "Yeah, I do too."

"So this marriage thing…it's working out for you?"

A smile played at the corner of her lips. "Yes, Connor. You've proven yourself to be quite the provider."

"That's not— Okay, good."

Megan's eyes were open wide then, something in her heart snared on the broken edge of what he'd been about to say. "It's working out for me. Like you said it would." Her voice quieted. "Even better, maybe."

A part of her expected some kind of cocky response. But instead, a long breath sounded from across the miles. "For me too."

CHAPTER SEVENTEEN

"I'm TELLING YOU, it's a done deal." Connor spun his chair away from his desk, letting his gaze run the familiar lines of downtown San Diego from his top-floor corner office.

"Yeah?" Jeff asked. "Trial's over? You guys starting production on Connor 2.0?"

He nodded. "Any day now."

Hell, probably tonight, based on the way Megan had lured him back into bed that morning. Twice.

Fortunately his first meeting hadn't been until ten, because nothing would have kept him from taking delivery of the naughty promises in his wife's eyes when he'd leaned over the bed to kiss her goodbye and she'd taken hold of his tie and tugged him down on top of her. Or after he'd showered and come back out of the bathroom to find she'd slipped into his suit shirt, buttoning only two buttons and leaving the necktie in a loose knot to trail down the seductive valley between her breasts.

Her game of dress up had cost him a good hour...and the tie, he thought with a satisfied grin.

"That's what I hear. Amazed you kept the lid on it as long as you did, but these last couple weeks—I can't go anywhere without somebody's wife bringing up your marriage."

Connor's eyes narrowed, tension winding up the base of his skull. "And?"

"And there's all the usual speculation you'd expect under the circumstances. Caro. The quick turn between. But then the people who've actually been out with you—Clausens, Stalicks,

Houstons—they're telling everyone it's the real deal. They've never seen you this way."

"Me?"

"Apparently you're in love. Everyone can see it. Brings a tear to my eye."

Pushing a short laugh past the uncomfortable knot in his throat, he deflected, "You're watching *Steel Magnolias* again, aren't you?"

"Always with the jokes."

"I'm a guy. That's how it works. Stop by after knitting club some night and I'll explain."

Jeff let out an amused snort. "Just for that, I'm learning. And someone's going to have a very special Christmas coming up."

This time it was Connor laughing, because it was entirely possible he was going to find some handcrafted atrocity in his stocking this year. "Jeff, I'm not denying there's something incredible between us. But neither Megan nor I are under the misconception it's love. Everyone else? Hell, people see what they want to and make assumptions based on what they expect. I'd rather they assume we're in love than suggest something less flattering."

"I get it. And look, I was just curious if something had changed."

"Hell, no," he clarified in no uncertain terms. "That total annihilation of boundaries isn't a game I'm into. Megan and I have a deal, and love isn't a part of it, thank God."

Even if he took his parents out of the equation, Connor had seen it too many times before with his friends, with his business associates. Love changed things. Expectations. Relationships stopped working within the framework they were established, and suddenly everything turned fluid—became a constantly changing playing field based on emotions that had come off the chain. There was no more reason. Just a vulnerability that—best case—was mutual.

"No worries, Megan and I both know the score. I made sure up front. You know I wouldn't let her get hurt." Then for a little sport, threw in, "So go find your own wife and stop worrying about mine."

"Yeah, but who says it's *your wife* I'm worried about."

Another night of champagne toasts and charitable endeavors behind them, Megan stood before the mirror in her dressing room, trying to wrestle the clasp on the sapphire necklace Connor had given her the night before. The stones, warm from her skin, winked and glittered beneath the lights, begging her to leave them on.

Her hands fell away from the clasp as Connor stepped into view behind her. His hands smoothed outward over the terrain of her shoulders, then, following the cut of the back of her dress, met again at her spine where he unhooked the top catch.

Working the zipper down the length of her back, he dropped a kiss atop one bare shoulder and then moved to the other side to do the same. "So…I was thinking about our honeymoon."

The stiff fabric of her midnight gown fell forward, gaping in the kind of provocative way Megan had never associated with herself, until now.

"What about it?" she asked, trying to concentrate on what Connor was saying, though all she seemed to register was the play of his thumbs over her newly exposed skin.

His hands slid over her waist between the loose fabric of her dress and skimmed around the front. Wide palms and strong fingers explored her hips and belly before smoothing back up to capture her breasts in his palms.

"I was thinking I ought to take you on a real one." A gentle suction pulled at the skin behind her ear as his words pulled at the tender place inside her. "You don't remember our wedding. Or our courtship…brief as it was. I want to give you a honeymoon to remember."

A memory to keep.

Hot emotion rose fast from the well she'd thought dry, pushing itself past her lips in a gasp and her eyes in a flutter of salty drops she blinked away as quickly as they came. Turning in Connor's arms, she caught his face between her palms and kissed him. Felt her dress pool to the floor as his hands molded to her bottom, pulling her close and lifting her until they aligned in all the right places.

Her legs wound at his waist as Connor carried her to the bedroom, his mouth making devilish work of the skin across her chest, along her neck and behind her ears. His tongue making promises his body would soon deliver.

How could it be like this with him? How had she ever lived without him? She pushed the questions aside, knowing she wouldn't ever have to again.

Connor wasn't going to leave her. He wasn't going to change his mind.

He'd made a commitment to her different from any of the promises she'd heard in the past. He'd shown her what kind of man he was. Made sure she understood what his word meant. She knew, with him in her life, she finally had someone to count on.

She could let go of all the defenses and anxieties with him.

She could trust him. With everything she had. For as long as they both should live.

An echo of those words whispered through her mind as her back met the soft resistance of their bed. Connor's flushed face and suspiciously disheveled hair—almost as if someone had spent a good amount of time working their fingers through it—flashed through her mind. The look in his eyes… It was like nothing she'd seen before. It was relief and awe and humor and victory and desire all there for her to see. All there, focused on her. As he said the words *For as long as we both shall live*…

Not a fantasy. Not her imagination.

Memory.

Reality.

A night she'd thought lost to her forever.

There in his eyes had been the answer to a riddle she'd struggled to solve. An answer she'd found her way to through a different path, but now… God, the way he'd looked at her. The confidence she'd felt looking back at him… It was the kind of confidence that lasted forever.

It was why she'd been able to make a decision in one night, which had taken her nearly two months to come to after.

"I don't need a honeymoon," she whispered, her fingers sifting through the silk of his hair as Connor worked down the line of her body.

"Sure you do." His tongue flicked at the hollow of her navel, briefly blanking her mind of anything beyond the wet, teasing contact. "Turks and Caicos, Tahiti, Venice, Niagara Falls?" He kissed lower, carefully catching the edge of her lacy panties between his teeth before slipping his fingers beneath and gently sweeping them down her hips and off her legs.

The playful glint in Connor's eyes was gone as he stood at the foot of the bed, staring down at her where she lay, waiting for him. She was bare of everything except the exquisite necklace at her throat and the matching slender heels at her feet.

Propped up on her elbows, she gave in to the wicked impulse to tease, sliding one knee against the other as she watched him work the buttons of his shirt with a determination she'd never witnessed before.

He'd made it to the fourth button when she straightened her leg and, using the peep front of her heel, caught the leather strap of his belt and tugged. His eyes, a dark blaze, flickered to meet hers just as she sank her teeth into the swell of her bottom lip.

For an instant, everything came to a stop. "You're a fantasy, Megan."

And then the rest of the buttons came loose in a quick series of pops as he ripped the shirt open.

Wide shoulders jerked free from between the lapels of the now-ruined shirt. The belt was gone next and then Connor was on the bed, crawling up her body even as his hand slid under her bottom and pulled her down to meet him.

Connor had to have her.

His wife didn't flaunt it for everyone to see—thank God— but she was the sexiest thing he'd ever laid eyes on.

If he'd had an ounce more patience, he would have gotten the damn pants off before he'd gotten on top of her. Only, the business with the belt and the lip biting about did him in. He needed contact. Now. Needed to feel those gorgeous heels at his back and the soft cradle of her thighs around him. He needed the wet sanctuary of her mouth and the sharp tug of her fingers in his hair.

Again he pulled her against him, rocking into the sweet spot between her legs. Torturing himself with the layers remaining between them because he couldn't make himself break away from the too-necessary contact.

Only then Megan snaked her hands in to work his fly—a look of utter concentration in her eyes as she caught the waist of his tuxedo pants and boxers with her heels and pushed them down his body.

When she'd gotten them as far as she could, he kicked them free and met her eyes. "Impressive."

The smile on her face was priceless, as if she'd accomplished the greatest feat imaginable…or the most critical task at least… by divesting him of his pants—hands-free.

The pink tip of her tongue wet her bottom lip as she held his gaze.

"I've got mad skills," she stated breathlessly.

"So you do." The smile curving his lips might have seemed out of place in the midst of this kind of sexual urgency, except fun always seemed to find a place when they were together.

Megan's eyes went to his mouth and then her fingertips drifted to the same place, feathering softly over his lips. "Beautiful."

Women had been complimenting his looks for most of his adult life, but never had such a simple statement had such a profound effect. Looking down into her eyes, he wanted to get lost in them. Wondered how he hadn't had to fight off a thousand men in Vegas to get to her himself.

And then he realized. This look he wanted to lose himself in forever… It was for him. Only for him.

He needed to be inside her. Needed it the way he needed his next breath. More, even.

Pushing to his knees, he leaned over toward the nightstand beside the bed and reached for the drawer—only to have Megan's hand follow the line of his arm and wrap around his wrist, urging him to stop.

His eyes went back to hers. "Condoms, sweetheart."

"Wait." Holding his gaze, her palm drifted down his chest, stilling over his heart. "Just you, Connor. Nothing between us." She swallowed, took a slow breath. "I don't need any more time to decide. To know."

Connor blinked. This was it.

What he'd been waiting for.

She was his. Finally.

She was...*crying*?

The hot surge of satisfaction beating its way through his veins froze as he stared at the still-shimmering smudge beneath her eye. The single glittering bead of betraying emotion caught in the dark points of her lashes. Lashes framing those gorgeous, trusting eyes that were staring up at him with—with so damn much—

"Megan," he croaked, then muttered a curse, closing his eyes when the pliant, sexy body beneath him went tense.

No. No, it wasn't love. She'd told him herself that she didn't fall in love.

Neither of them did.

What he was seeing was affection. The affection he'd been working for, cultivating from day one with the intent of securing her commitment. Only suddenly seeing it shining up at him from those trusting eyes, as his wife offered him the very thing he'd been striving for, granting him the unfettered access to her body that would cement them together forever—he recognized it for what it was.

Too much.

She wasn't supposed to look at him like that. As if she was entrusting him with a piece of her soul. Making herself vulnerable in a way he couldn't abide.

"I thought you wanted this," she said, all the breathless pleasure of only moments ago replaced with uncertainty, hurt and confusion.

"I do. You know I do…only…" Damn it, he couldn't believe he was going to say this. Couldn't believe he had to. Forcing a laugh he didn't feel, he burrowed his face against the soft shell of her ear. "You've been drinking champagne tonight… and after what happened with the wedding…I think we ought to make our most important decisions over coffee and toast."

"But—"

"Shh." Catching the slender arms that had sought to stop him scant moments ago, Connor pushed them above Megan's head and held her wrists in the loose clasp of one hand as he reached for the nightstand drawer.

A moment later, he was buried inside the tight sheath of Megan's body…working to convince them both to forget about the barriers—both physical and emotional—he'd put between them.

CHAPTER EIGHTEEN

THOUGH CONNOR HAD MADE a playground of her body, pleasuring her time and again until she didn't have the strength to do more than melt into the warmth of his body—as the minutes drifted by with the night shadows, the hours with the darkness, sleep didn't come.

She'd offered him what he'd been asking for. What he said he wanted.

She'd offered him *herself.* Their future.

And he'd turned her down.

No. It wasn't rejection. That was what she'd come to through those sleepless hours. It was protection.

Connor felt he'd failed her the night they married, and he wouldn't risk letting her make a decision as monumental as this if there was any chance her judgment might be impaired.

It wasn't rejection at all. It was a good thing.

It was further evidence of the kind of caring she was learning she could count on from the man she married.

A smile curved her lips as she heard his rapid descent down the stairs. There were definitely worse things than having a man committed to her well-being.

Checking her reflection in the microwave door, she pushed a few wayward strands of hair behind her ear, then smoothed her hands over her abdomen, desperate to calm the butterflies within.

With the coffee carafe in hand, she stepped over to the intimate nook and then poured two mugs.

A second later, Connor rounded the corner, immaculately dressed, every hair in place. He flashed her a smile and grabbed a triangle of toast from the plate she'd set.

"Perfect, I'm running late."

Before she could do more than open her mouth, he'd dropped a kiss on her cheek and thrown back half the coffee.

Taking the mug with him, he paused at the doorway, his eyes flickering to the carafe in her hand and the half-eaten toast in his.

Connor met her eyes and she saw the recognition there. The heart that had been too stunned to beat suddenly picked up, warming the chill within her chest.

"Toast and coffee," she offered with a small smile.

Connor set down his mug at the counter, his expression reserved. "Megan, you've got to believe me when I tell you how honored I am you feel like you're ready to make this commitment. And I want it. I do."

Except he didn't. She could see it in the lines of his face. Hear it in the strain of his voice. Feel it in the sinking pit within her belly.

"I don't understand." The words had passed her lips, pleading and broken before she'd had the chance to consider them. Hold them back in an effort to protect her pride. "It sounds like you're telling me no. Like—"

Like all the fear and worry she'd reasoned herself out of the night before had been more justified than she'd allowed herself to believe.

Connor crossed to her, taking her shoulders in his hands. "I want it. But the more I consider the situation, the more important I believe it is you take the full term of the trial to decide."

She searched his eyes, refusing to give in to the tears stinging her own. "You were so certain before. You didn't have a single doubt."

"For myself, I don't, Megan. But for you— Hell. I know how well you'll fit into my life. I'm not entirely sure you've had enough opportunity to see how I'll fit into yours."

She shook her head. "How can you say that? I've had two months—"

"The first one didn't count. Take two more. Be sure." He dropped a kiss on her forehead and then set her back, changing the subject as though they'd been talking about the weather. "I've got meetings late tonight and first thing tomorrow, so don't wait up. I'll probably crash at the office."

And then he was gone.

Connor's fists clenched, his knuckles turning white atop the dark mahogany of his office desk as the image of Megan's stricken face once again flooded his consciousness.

Damn it, he'd known better. But he'd been so hell-bent on convincing her to commit, to see he was the man she wanted, he'd in essence become a man he wasn't. And those tears—that overflowing well of emotion in her eyes—were all the evidence he needed to know the whole married courtship had gotten out of hand.

A quick knock sounded a moment before his secretary's head popped past his office door. "Excuse me, Connor, but the conference call with Zurich is starting in five minutes. Did you need me to send those files…?"

She'd let the words trail off rather than actually saying what they both knew. Those files he'd been working on and had promised to have to her a half hour before. Those files he still hadn't finished.

Damn it. This wasn't the guy he was.

He needed to get his head on straight. He needed to get some perspective. And he needed to make sure the man he was giving Megan was the man she'd be spending the rest of her life with.

He was confident she'd still want the marriage.

Even after a readjustment in expectations, there was no way her plan could compete with his.

But first things first. The office. That was how it had always been. How it always would be.

"Stella, see if they can push back a half hour. I'll get the files to you in twenty. My apologies for the inconvenience. Yours and theirs."

Time to get his focus back where it belonged.

The front door sounded with the muffled thud Megan had been pretending not to listen for since the previous morning. Connor had told her he wasn't coming home, but a part of her had been hoping.

Waiting.

Trying not to think of all the sleepless nights she'd spent as a little girl, weighing every creak and groan, listening for a return that wouldn't come. Because despite Connor's abrupt change of heart regarding moving forward with their marriage, she knew he was coming back.

He wasn't walking away. He wasn't leaving her.

This wasn't the same kind of blindside. Startling, yes, but not devastating.

He was looking out for her. Taking the extra time to ensure they didn't face the same doubts that had been a part of their first month together.

And now Connor was home. Back. Hanging his coat in the closet and dropping his keys on the table, offering the same greeting he did every night.

"Hello, Mrs. Reed."

Relief surged through her as she closed the distance between them, offering the kiss that had become a part of their routine from nearly the first. Everything was fine. Nothing had changed.

She wanted to bury her head in the front of Connor's shirt, press her forehead against the hollow at the center of his chest and give in to the emotion threatening to overwhelm her. She wanted his arms around her, his reassurance hot against her ear. She wanted all his sensible reason, soothing the wild insecurity that had plagued her since the minute he'd walked out the door.

Only, insecurity was a part of her she couldn't stand. It was something she didn't want in this life she was building, and so rather than collapsing against the man she'd literally been aching for, she satisfied herself with the sight of his easy smile. With smoothing the shoulder of his shirt as she asked how his day had been. If he'd slept all right at the office apartment. With his assurance that he'd been fine—had spent so many nights there it felt as much like home as this apartment.

Then ducking down into his messenger-style briefcase, he pulled out a manila folder, flashing the same smile he'd had walking in the door. The one that had her attention snared, but didn't last long enough for her to identify why.

Maybe he was tired, regardless of what he'd said about the comfort of the apartment.

"Got time to talk honeymoons?" he asked, heading past her to the living room.

A relieved laugh burst from her lungs as she followed, giddy elation bubbling up within her.

Nothing had changed.

She was the one who should have gotten more sleep.

Settling into the couch, Connor flipped open the folder and then started sorting the brochures within.

Megan tucked her feet beneath her. "So I see you have some ideas."

Only, then she saw what they were...Zurich, Munich, Taiwan.

"Not so much of a secluded-beach guy, huh?" she asked, a numbness creeping over her with the awareness of what these locales signified.

Connor shrugged, stacking the brochures in piles and then revising the order. "I like the beach fine, but what I'm thinking is it makes more sense to kill two birds with one stone."

Kill two birds...? She looked at the piles again.

"I need to get out to each of these locations for business in the next month..." Connor left the rest of the sentence to hang as his hand smoothed over her shoulder. "Hey. I know we were talking about making it some romantic-fantasy thing, but after the meetings I had yesterday and today, it's time to get my head out of the clouds and back to reality. I'm happy to take you on a trip. But practically speaking, one of these places is going to get us the most mileage. I'll get my meetings taken care of, while you take in the sights. Hit a few tours. Do some shopping."

That creeping numbness began to melt off beneath the heat of her rising temper. What in the—?

He'd been the one to suggest the honeymoon. The romantic destinations. But of course, that had been before she'd offered herself up on a platter. Megan stared back at that easy smile and indulgent expression, feeling for the first time as if the man in front of her was a stranger.

...time to get back to reality...

Was that what this was? Some kind of warning before she committed? Connor's way of making sure she understood this life ahead of them wasn't always going to be sunshine and roses?

"Hey, if you're dying for some beach time, though, you could take a trip to Hawaii. Or maybe hit a spa somewhere. Take a girlfriend with you."

She held up a staying hand. "I get it, Connor."

The honeymoon was over. And she was about to see a side of her husband he hadn't shown her before.

CHAPTER NINETEEN

DONE UP IN ANOTHER DESIGNER gown, Megan sat tucked into the back corner of the limousine, watching the lights and windows pass in a blur. Eyes shifting to the opposite seat, she noted Connor sorting through the work he'd brought along when they'd picked him up from his office a few minutes ago.

He'd greeted her with a kiss—chaste as it was—compliments on her gown and hair. A question about her day.

And yet nothing about it seemed real.

Yes, he listened to her answers, cataloging the information for later use. But the connection they'd shared from the start— that invisible something weighting every comment, every question, every small smile or subtle glance with meaning and value and *more*—had evaporated with her offer of what he'd sworn up and down he wanted.

Of course, Connor was still pleasant. Still charming. Still available to answer her questions or provide an hour or so of company at the end of the night. But the interaction was a mere shadow of what it had been in the weeks before.

Her husband had become the list of attributes he'd provided that first day they spent together.

Had this been what he'd meant their marriage to be from the start? The romance, the laughter, the intensity of the connection between them…was it all simply Connor reeling her in? Securing her affection and interest so she'd consider his proposition?

She couldn't believe it, couldn't understand why he would

have tried so hard to give her a taste of something she wasn't going to be able to keep.

Unless it was some sort of test. Connor ensuring she understood just exactly what she was committing to give up?

No, he wouldn't be so cruel. She *knew* him, and he would never intentionally do something to hurt her that way.

Besides, the kind of connection between them couldn't be faked. It wasn't something to manufacture. And it hadn't been one-sided.

So what was this?

Her eyes drifted across the car. Connor's focus was fixed on the spreadsheets in front of him. His flawless features intense. And yet nothing like the way he'd looked at her.

Was it possible he'd been as deeply affected by the unexpected connection between them as she and it was just too much...too soon? He simply hadn't had a chance to get comfortable with it and had forced a step back?

Maybe all he needed was time.

And maybe she was a self-deluding fool. But she'd told Connor once he was worth the risk, and having tasted how sweet it could be between them, she still believed that.

Yes, the idea of the man she married turning off his emotions so suddenly, so completely, was terrifying...but she couldn't accept Connor was capable of such callous indifference.

Maybe all he needed was time to adjust. Time and a little space to get his head around what was happening with his heart. And then that undeniable connection would do the rest.

She could wait. For him...for them, she would be the wife he wanted, until he realized what it was he needed. Yes. They were worth it.

Megan turned toward the window, blinking back the tears that had come with her revelation and the certain soul-deep knowledge everything was going to be fine.

Suddenly she felt so much lighter.

Moments later, the car pulled up outside the gold hotel awning. Connor set his documents aside, touching a finger to the phone at his ear. "We're at the hotel, so the rest of this is going to have to wait. You around tonight?"

His eyes flashed to hers, checking to see how she'd take the news he was scheduling a midnight meeting with one of his managers.

She offered an easy smile, then pulled a small compact from her beaded clutch and shifted her attention to a reflection she couldn't care less about. Same glossy lips and matte-finished face.

The only change was her understanding of what had happened to her marriage through the past week…and how she intended to go on from there.

Together.

She could wait for Connor. Because they were worth it.

Connor let out a short cough a long minute later. "Yeah, sorry, still here. Tonight, then. Talk to you in a few hours."

Returning the mirror to her bag, she smiled up at Connor, refusing to acknowledge the slight furrow in his brow or the way his eyes had narrowed on her.

Sensing something different, maybe?

A surge of confidence pushed through her veins at the reminder of their connection, the depth of their awareness. Everything was going to work out.

"Ready?" she asked as the door swung open and the chilly night air slipped around them.

Connor stepped from the car, leaning back in to take her hand. "Always."

She was flawless.

By now Connor should have gotten used to how smoothly Megan fit into the fabric of his life.

She'd had the entire table eating out of her hand within minutes of their arrival. Her engaging smile and seemingly limitless font of information. The authenticity he'd found so appealing, a magnet to everyone around them.

Amazing.

He'd been concerned he'd blown it, letting things get too out of hand emotionally between them—worried there might not be any coming back from that point. But after a few days of testing this more accurate representation of the life they would have together, she'd decided. Tonight in the car...he'd seen it. Acceptance.

He'd been stunned and relieved. Hell, had he been relieved. Because he didn't want to give her up. Didn't want to lose her. Now he just needed to keep his head on straight so he didn't screw this up.

A round of laughter sounded from the group where Megan stood, the musical quality of hers standing out to his ear above the rest. Threatening to pull at the place he'd called off-limits.

Slender fingers fanned wide at her neck as, head tipped back, she enjoyed whatever story Lenny was sharing with his audience.

Beautiful.

When her eyes opened again, he turned away.

He'd about exhausted the second chances he was going to get with this woman, so no more letting go and building unrealistic expectations he wouldn't be able to deliver on. Wouldn't want to deliver on.

"So it's true?"

Connor's head jerked around toward the source of that well-cultured East Coast accent. Even in accusation, the modulated delivery was as polished as if she'd been inquiring after a great-aunt's health.

Caro.

Instinct had him ready to check whether Megan could see them, but he tamped the need down.

If she happened to be looking his way, he'd attract less attention by simply exchanging a few pleasantries before moving on. Moving out.

That was what he would do.

Collect Megan and take her out of there.

She was aware of his previous engagement to Caro and knew their parting had been a recent thing.

Of course, the specifics... He'd shared them the night they

met. Intended to share them after, as well. But first, he'd been fighting so hard to win her over. And then everything had been too good to chance ruining. And this past week, he hadn't wanted to add one more thing.

There hadn't been any urgency because he hadn't expected Caro to turn up. Only, here she was, standing two feet away, peering up at him with eyes revealing nothing of her true feelings. Her smile in place—the one he'd seen every single time they'd shared space through the duration of their relationship. Smooth. Polished.

"Caro, I hadn't heard you were back in town. How have you been?"

"How have I been, Connor?" A cool voice, a pleasant smile. "Humiliated."

His gut knotted. He should have gotten in touch with her. Told her himself.

"You shouldn't feel that way," he said. Then, hoping to ease the sting, added, "Everyone knows you left me. You broke our relationship off—"

"Our *engagement*. You were going to marry me."

He nodded, a gathering tension spreading through his shoulders. Along his spine.

"Yes. You broke off our engagement," he conceded, keeping his voice as low as she'd managed to keep hers. Even so, he could feel the burn of eyes on them. Could sense the attention this few minutes' exchange had garnered. A quick scan of the area by their table showed Megan had moved.

Good.

He'd wrap this up and then get her out of there. With Caro back in town, he needed to tell Megan everything. She might not love the timing of how it had all played out, but she'd understood that first night. He had to believe she would understand now.

Caro's voice took on a sharper edge than he'd ever heard from her, assuring even more attention turning on them. "How could you do this to me?"

He met her eyes, sincere in his apology. "I never intended

for you to be hurt. We ended the relationship and you left. Went back east—"

"Because I wanted *more from you*. I wanted you to realize what we had. What you were giving up. I've been waiting—" She broke off, the emotion in her voice spilling over into her eyes.

"You said you wanted something you knew we didn't have. Something that wasn't between us. You never implied—"

"I thought you needed to figure it out on your own. That given enough time, you would realize you wanted more than an 'understanding.' I thought you would come after me."

No. It wasn't possible. Caro couldn't be standing in the middle of this ballroom with tears spilling down her cheeks. Not this woman he'd never seen with a hair out of place, who'd never raised her voice or been anything but the most polished, lovely, impenetrable piece of porcelain beauty in his presence.

He didn't want to be the cause of her pain. Had never wanted that. "Caro, when I met Megan…"

He knew how it looked. Knew he would probably never be able to make her understand.

"Did you fall in love with her?" The words snapped past her lips with a sort of biting accusation he never would have expected. But she was hurt, and the truth was he didn't know her that well. Had never wanted to look beyond the social-elite exterior she'd shown him. "No. I'm guessing not. Just another handy assembly of qualifications falling into your lap a mere thirteen days after you suggested Bali for our honeymoon, is that about it? Too convenient to pass up. An opportunity not to be missed.

"I knew you were cold, Connor. But even for you… Does she have any idea? Probably not, considering how fast you married her. I'm guessing it won't be too long, though, before she sees through the smile and charm, your attention, affection—sees how you can turn it on and off at the flick of a switch. Walk away without a backward glance. Or maybe she doesn't care. Maybe it's the pretty packaging and size of your checkbook that matters."

Connor felt the burn of anger mingling with his guilt. He knew Caroline had been hurt, and he was truly sorry for it. If the barbs she was throwing had been directed at him alone, he would have taken them. But they weren't.

"Caro," he said, lowering his voice as he leaned closer to her. "Don't do this. People are watching."

She scanned the crowd around them, straightened her spine, and then met his eyes with bitter satisfaction shining in her own. "Yes. They are."

And just like that, he knew.

Straightening away from the woman who might have been his wife, he found Megan standing stock-still at the edge of the crowd surrounding them. She appeared frozen in place. Caught midstep on her way toward him. One hand half-extended, her mouth hanging in a mockery of the gentle smile she always wore.

"Megan," he said, taking a step toward her. "Let's get our coats."

Megan's eyes followed his approach. One blink. Two.

From behind him, soothing words sounded as a number of women moved in to try to defuse the situation with Caroline—only, she wasn't through yet.

Voice rising above the din, she called, "I was going to offer your new wife the advice I wish someone had given me—not to fall in love with you. But by the look on her face, it's already too late."

Damn it! "Enough, Caro."

Megan's lips parted on an intake of breath that may have been the precursor to a response or refutation…only, then they closed with a tiny shake of her head and a helpless smile.

His hand settled at the curve of her hip, his body moving in close enough to shield her from prying eyes. "We'll talk at home."

CHAPTER TWENTY

MEGAN WALKED THROUGH to the living room, her steps clipped and graceless, her mind a riot of fragmented thoughts, confusion and unwelcome emotion.

The door closed behind her.

The lock fell and Connor's approach echoed through the marble entry.

Dropping her wrap over the back of the couch, she stared across at the wall of glass—and the black void of the Pacific beyond—wishing she were anywhere else but there.

"I know…" A muffled curse sounded as Connor's hand ran over his mouth in the reflection. "I know you weren't…prepared for that."

Megan shook her head.

No. Not even a little bit.

"I feel like a fool," she admitted, figuring one of them should offer up the whole truth.

Connor closed the distance between them, circling his arms around her belly and pulling her into the solid heat of him. "Don't. If anyone was a fool tonight, it was me and Caroline. I still can't believe— Hell, Megan, you have to understand I never expected this from her. If I had—"

"What?" she demanded, pulling free of his arms to face him. "Bothered to tell me the truth? Shared the more damning details…so I'd have a chance to be prepared if they ever came up?"

Connor's expression hardened. "I never lied to you."

"Please. Thirteen days? And what about the wanting different things. The realization you weren't right for each other. You made it sound like a loss of interest, when in fact it was the very opposite. She'd *fallen in love* with you!"

"I didn't know— Damn it, she said—"

"Forget what she said, Connor! Anyone looking at her could see how she felt. Like apparently anyone looking at me can see the way I feel. She certainly did."

His mouth snapped shut, his eyes losing the blaze of conflict altogether as his head began a slow shake of denial. "Megan. No—"

"Relax, Connor. I already know I made a mistake."

"Megan—" Connor raked a hand through his hair, grabbed a fistful of it at the base of his skull and then shook out his hands.

What could he say?

Damn it, the look on Megan's face earlier that night. She'd been trying so hard to compose herself, to keep it together, but the hurt he'd seen in her eyes... It went hand in hand with the watery emotion he'd seen the night she'd offered her commitment. It was everything he'd wanted to avoid. Everything *he'd told her to avoid.*

"What happened with Caroline was over before you and I even met."

"I heard. By thirteen days."

"Yes. Not that it should have mattered if it was thirteen hours," he retorted. "This marriage is an arrangement between like-minded parties. It's a partnership, not a love affair. I never lied to you or kept anything of importance from you."

She looked at him then, almost stunned, as if she didn't recognize him.

He didn't like it. Not at all. She knew him already, understood him. What was happening tonight didn't change anything.

"No. You didn't. I'm the one who wasn't honest."

"What the hell are you talking about?" he snapped.

"Don't worry, Connor. The only person I lied to was myself."

He should have let her go, but when she turned to walk away, he couldn't stop himself from reaching for her arm. "This doesn't change anything, Megan. All the reasons we make sense are still the same."

Her eyes went to the spot where his hand circled the bare skin of her arm. "Have you stopped to consider, Connor, that you've been so fixated on showing me all the reasons this marriage could work, you haven't really let yourself see the reasons it might not?"

"No," he said more harshly than he'd intended. Then, grasping for the understanding he knew she deserved, he tried again. "Megan, you're upset. Hurt. Embarrassed. I get it. But you're too smart to let one night dictate your future."

"You're right. I am too smart to let a single night of discomfort get in the way of something real. Of course, we're not talking about a single night, just like we aren't talking about something real. So don't even pretend we are."

Stiffening, he took a step back. "Say it."

Say it so he could start working her back from this place he wasn't going to let them go.

Her shoulders squared. "I can't be the wife you want."

Too late. "You already are."

"Then maybe it's not me at all. Maybe it's you. Maybe you aren't the husband I want."

His hand slid from her arm, all the arguments he'd been ready to throw at her suddenly abandoning him.

They were too right together. They made too much sense.

It was all this damn emotion he'd made it a point to avoid his whole life mucking everything up.

What they needed was some perspective.

"Let's not do anything rash, okay? You need some space. Why don't I get a suit and head to the office. I've got a call tonight anyway. I'll stay there. You think. And then tomorrow night we'll talk."

Megan's desolate gaze returned to his, and after a pause, she offered him a single nod.

They would be fine.

Megan was a practical woman. Realistic, Connor reassured

himself as he grabbed a suit from his closet and packed a quick bag. She needed some space to get over her hurt. And then tomorrow—damage control.

Change of plan. He couldn't afford the distance he'd been putting between them right now. So he'd close in again. Just a little. Just enough.

Bag packed, he shook out his hands and headed downstairs.

Megan was in the kitchen. He knew she wanted away from him, and yet he couldn't stop from following the sounds of the refrigerator door closing, the clink of glass against granite, the quiet gurgle of pouring wine.

Rounding the corner, he found her standing against the counter, her glass sitting untouched beside her as she waited for him.

"Do you have everything?" she asked. Polite. Detached. Exactly the kind of considerate inquiry his ideal wife would offer.

Hollow. Too damn hollow to be coming from the woman he married.

"Almost." He crossed to her in a single stride, pulling her into him and taking what was inevitably intended to be a protest for the opportunity it was.

Upturned face.

Parted lips.

The good-night kiss he couldn't leave without.

Only, Megan's lips were stiff and unyielding. She didn't pull away. It might almost have been better if she had. Instead, she'd allowed the kiss to occur, taking it with the same cool detachment offered in her words.

That wasn't how it was between them, and he might be a jerk for pressing the point tonight, but if he was going to give her the space to think, he wanted to be damn sure he'd left her with something to think about.

He brushed his lips back and forth against hers, knowing she thought to simply ride it out. Tolerate the intimacy. But rather than give up, he pulled her closer, sliding his hand up the silky expanse of her bare back to her neck. Burying his fingers in the soft strands of gold and gently coaxing her back, he deepened the kiss, licking softly into her mouth.

At her teeth, the corner of her mouth, her soft, wet tongue.

She didn't want to respond. Didn't want to give him anything. And still, he could feel the catch of her breath across his lips. The pull of her mouth against his when, on a weak moan, she surrendered.

"Megan," he groaned, holding her tight.

Her tongue rolled softly with his, her mouth drawing at him. Taking. Giving. Until all the cold space was charged with the same current that had been running between them from the very first night—until he knew, even though he was leaving, *this* would stay with her.

When he pulled back, Megan wouldn't look at him, but he could see the red flush of her cheeks.

Her hand fluttered over her lips, and she shook her head, finally meeting his eyes with the glittering rage of her own. "Have you ever stopped yourself from taking more than someone wanted to give?"

Her words shocked him. "That's not—"

But her hand flew up, cutting him off as the first damning tear slid down her cheek—and suddenly there was nothing he could say. No defense. All he could do was watch as she disappeared around the corner in a swirl of dove-gray silk— knowing that lack of will on his part was going to cost him serious ground.

She had no defense against him.

Even seeing him coming. Bracing herself against his advance. Megan hadn't stood a chance.

She'd crumbled beneath the assault of his kiss, praying he'd say something to make her feel better—to convince her things were other than they were—clinging to the very man she desperately needed to leave.

Only, Connor was exactly who she thought he was.

A man who could turn his feelings on and off with the flick of a switch.

A man who could walk away without a backward glance.

A man who could leave one woman and, in the span of a few days, move on to the next.

He was exactly the kind of man she'd sworn never to allow herself to be susceptible to again. And as if she'd been hard-wired to seek out his special brand of abuse, she'd married him within hours of meeting.

The signs had all been there. Warnings left and right. Her mind flashed back to that first night out with Georgette—the awkward moment when the silence all but screamed there was more than she knew. But instead of listening to instinct—she'd actively dismissed the concern.

Because she hadn't wanted to be *cynical*. Ha!

What she hadn't wanted was to face the truth.

Disgusted, Megan slapped a layer of tape across the top of the box. Bit the cap off her marker pen and scrawled the address of her apartment in Denver at the top.

Then, stacking the box with the other two, she looked around her at the house she'd thought would be her home. She'd spent the night breaking down the life she'd begun to build there. Dividing her belongings into two categories. Her life. And her life with Connor.

It was only the belongings from the former she would keep. And of those, there was only a handful she could pack herself and still catch her flight. The rest she would coordinate with Connor once she was back in her own space.

She didn't have any fantasies about being able to leave and wash her hands of him forever.

They were married, after all.

Legally bound.

They would need to talk. But not here. Not today.

Guilt burned through her as she thought of Connor returning to find her gone.

He'd be livid. Feel betrayed.

But Connor had become too proficient at manipulating her. And as evidenced by his infuriating kiss, she was simply too weak to resist. Which meant this was the only way.

She couldn't afford to stay in a situation where her will had become a casualty of Connor's desires.

She'd built her life around doing the smart thing. Being practical. Responsible.

It was one of the things that had drawn Connor to her in the first place.

But around him, she didn't make the smart decision. She didn't do the right thing.

When it came to her husband, she threw caution to the wind and gambled on the feel-good. Telling herself she knew what she was doing…even when she had no idea.

It wasn't the life she wanted for herself. And it wasn't the life she wanted for the child she planned to have. She owed them both more.

Which was why she was leaving. Before Connor had a chance to change her mind.

Gone. Nine in the morning and already she was gone. The house quiet and still beneath the rusty sound of Connor's breath sawing in and out of his lungs.

Goddamn it.

He'd thought she would wait. Thought her conscientious core of respect and sensitivity would be enough to ensure she wouldn't leave without talking to him. Telling him to his face it was over.

At least, trying to.

But as sensitive and respectful as Megan was, beneath all that softness, she was *smart*. Too smart to give him the chance to talk her out of anything.

So she'd worked through the night. Packing only what she could take with her. Organizing the rest for his convenience.

He wanted to topple every damn piece of furniture in the place.

He couldn't freaking believe she'd actually done it.

She wasn't supposed to leave. She was supposed to calm down enough that he could talk sense to her. Remind her of the kind of life they could have together.

But instead, she'd caught some red-eye out, leaving him to find the life he'd planned for them dismantled into piles and labeled in her hand.

To hell with that.

Hands curling into fists at his sides, he stormed out of the dark office that still smelled like sunshine.

It wasn't over.

She might have left, but it wasn't as though she was out of reach. The only reason she would have gone without talking to him was that she'd been afraid he'd be able to coerce her to stay if they'd been face-to-face.

He was going to prove her right.

Go after her. Make her see reason. Make her come back. Forget about some halfhearted kiss that stopped nearly before it began. He'd seduce her. Completely. Start with his mouth and tongue. Back her against the wall because it drove her completely wild— and yeah, he wasn't above using his body to exploit the weaknesses of hers.

And once he had her mindless, breath breaking against his ear, her hands clutching at his hair, her pleas filling the space around her, he'd use that leverage—

"You can't leave me. I won't let you go..."

The echo of those decades-old words from a man he hated to the woman who hadn't been able to resist them had his steps grinding to a stop, the blood burning through his veins running cold.

He was just like him.

No matter how Connor swore he wouldn't let him be, that bastard was a part of his DNA.

How many times had his mother tried to leave his father? Tried to break things off and start a life separate from the man who would never make her properly part of his?

He thought about that morning so many years ago. The too-small, too-still shape of her curled in on herself in the middle of her bed. The knowledge, even before he reached out to try to wake her—

What would it have meant for them if his father had respected her wishes and let her start living her own life without him?

Could she have pulled herself together? Found the will to just…live?

Opening the fist he'd had clenched since he'd torn through the house and found Megan gone, he stared down at the band of diamonds in his palm.

This was the second time she'd returned it to him.

The second time he'd completely ignored what she wanted.

Raking his hands through his hair, he balled them at the back of his skull and stared out the windows at the ocean beyond.

He wasn't his father. He'd spent his life proving it to himself and anyone who dared connect the Reed name. He'd stood at the door of his father's office that last day and turned down his money. His job. His grudging recognition.

Told him he wouldn't accept any of it. The only thing he would take were the memories of how this man had ruined his mother's too-short life with his selfishness.

And those only because, try as he might, he couldn't make himself forget.

An awful pain settled deep within him. He had to let Megan go.

It would be better for them both.

Forcing his breathing to level out, he turned around and walked back to her suite of rooms.

Once this space was cleared of her things, he'd be fine. Move on, just as he always did.

Even if *always* had *never* been like this.

CHAPTER TWENTY-ONE

MEGAN HAD THOUGHT the phone call with Connor two nights earlier uncomfortable.

Yes, she'd expected they would need to talk, say the things her absence had already announced, work out the return of her belongings and discuss a divorce. And they had. But what she hadn't expected was the call to go the way it had.

So very easily. Peaceably. Politely.

Connor's casually conversational tone—

"Do you have a lawyer already or can I get one for you?"

"Sounds like the earliest the shippers can get there is Friday. Going to be okay until then?"

"You sure you don't want any of these clothes? This blue dress was dynamite on you."

—working her over in a way no amount of hostility, accusation or railing could have accomplished. It had nearly killed her to leave, but the hurt of knowing how little her departure had affected him was so much worse. He'd turned off all emotion… in a single day. Been so unaffected, the call had unfolded more like friendly chitchat than the first step in the end of a marriage.

Back at the house, he'd been ready to "talk" her out of leaving, but he'd still been in the fight at that point. Once she'd gone and the loss was confirmed…it was as if he'd simply shrugged it off. And she'd been wrecked to have all her suspicions so quickly confirmed.

But, as brutal as having her heart crushed again was, the fresh pain of it was exactly what she'd needed to alleviate her doubts about artificial insemination and her choice to forgo relationships in the future.

She would never doubt again.

So the call, as uncomfortable as it was, had been worth it.

Or so she'd thought right up until sixty seconds ago, when she'd opened the door expecting to find the shippers on her stoop, but instead faced Connor smiling that aggravating smile at her.

"Hey, gorgeous, got something these guys can prop the security door open with. Shouldn't take too long—"

"What are you doing here?" she snapped, too shocked to soften her demand.

A careless shrug. "Didn't know if you had anyone to help, and figured it would go more smoothly with a second body. You know, make sure there weren't any problems."

Throat thick with emotion she didn't want to face, emotion she needed to put aside, she shook her head. "Connor, you shouldn't have come here. I left because—"

"Call it marital privilege." His smile stayed exactly as it was, but his eyes were hard as they scanned the guys unloading one box after another from the truck. "I'm still your husband, so might as well work it while I've got it."

Marital privilege—who was he kidding?

She wanted to argue with him, tell him how much his showing up on her doorstep—when she'd left in the earliest hours of the morning to avoid seeing him again—infuriated her. But Connor wasn't stupid. He'd known exactly how much this would upset her, and he'd chosen to come regardless because Connor always did what Connor wanted.

"Anyway, I'm here," he said, reaching over her head and wrapping his hand around the security door she'd been holding on to for dear life. "So, what do you say we haul this stuff up to your apartment and get these guys out of here?"

She nodded, trying to ignore the way his casual work shirt stretched across the broad expanse of his chest, or how when he'd leaned in to take hold of the door she hadn't yet relinquished, it put him close enough for the too-good scent of his soap and skin to tease her.

Unable to resist, she drew a deep breath through her nose and held his delicious scent within her. Savoring it as she savored the memories it spurred. Memories of late nights, bare skin and pleasure that engaged her every sense.

She'd fallen so far. So fast.

Connor's free hand closed over her waist, and she looked up into those dark brown eyes. It was a mistake. She shouldn't be this close. Shouldn't have allowed herself to be snared by the one lure sure to catch her.

The hand at her waist coasted over the small of her back, shooting sparks of sensation across her skin, sparks that threatened to reignite a flame.

"Megan," Connor said, urging her closer to all his heat.

She knew she should push away. Being this close meant getting burned, but— "Watch out, sweetheart, the guys need to get by."

Her head swung around to the first mover, who was edging around her, a box marked OFFICE in his arms.

"Thanks, ma'am."

She nodded, embarrassment blazing in her cheeks as she tried to step back from Connor's hold and into the door. Only, he held her firm, until she had no choice but to meet his eyes again. This time she kept her head.

"Let me go so I can tell him where to put everything." So she could breathe and think and stand a chance at remembering all the reasons she needed to keep her distance from this man who wreaked havoc on her judgment.

His thumb slid in the smallest caress against the base of her spine, and then his attention shifted back to the men and the truck and the return of Megan's life to what it had been before she'd met him.

What the hell was he doing there? He'd decided to let Megan go.

Had spent the entire damn day she left getting himself to a

place where that possessive part of him all about *keeping her* was tamped down enough for him to be able to call. Talk to her *without trying to talk her into anything*. Make sure she'd made it back to Denver and was okay.

He'd done it.

Worked out a few logistics regarding the return of her things and hung up patting himself on the back for finally doing the right thing.

And then he'd gone to bed and stared at the ceiling until he finally gave up and drove into work. Where he'd spent the next eighteen hours.

When the shipping crew arrived, he'd supervised the packing of Megan's belongings. Figuring once they were out of the house—the constant in-his-face reminder of what he'd wanted and what he'd lost removed—he'd be able to relax. The vise around his lungs would ease up. The persistent knot in his gut would finally loosen. But as the last box left the house, he'd found himself following behind. Checking the truck, grilling the guy in charge about how long it would take to arrive. What precautions were in place to ensure her belongings would be in the same shape when they'd arrived as when they left. If the men who'd done the loading were the same ones who would be unloading. How long he'd been working with them.

When he realized no amount of reassurance would be enough, he decided to fly out and meet the truck in Denver.

Make sure the movers delivered her things and got out of her apartment without a hitch.

Simple. No ulterior motives involved.

Yeah, sure, fantasies about getting her beneath him, on top of him, wrapped so sweet and tight and hot around him had been running through his head on a thirty-second loop. But did he have plans to act on those fantasies?

No.

At least, he hadn't until she'd peered up at him from so temptingly close. Those eyes that had been filled with ire when she saw him waiting at her door going soft and warm as he'd gotten her out of the way of the mover.

Fine. He still wouldn't act. Her looking up at him the way she did, when he knew for damn sure she didn't want anything, spoke volumes about the sway he held with her. Too much.

And the emotion in her eyes? Yeah, no stroke to his ego had ever compared…but he still didn't want a relationship with that kind of emotion. That kind of responsibility. What he wanted was Megan wanting him…but not needing him. Not vulnerable to him. Sure as hell not trying to leave him over and over again…and simply failing.

Screw that.

No. He'd make sure she was okay and then he'd be able to take off without looking back.

With the last box delivered, Connor signed the paperwork, tipped the guys and then closed Megan's door.

Her apartment felt smaller than he remembered it. But then, there were boxes stacked in the center of each of the four rooms, eating up space. She hadn't brought everything to San Diego. Not the furniture. But her keepsakes. Books. Knickknacks.

Things he'd laughed about seeing as she unpacked them, but now wondered if he'd miss having them gone.

Opening one odd-shaped box, Megan withdrew a lamp with a beaded shade, and he found himself watching intently as she returned it to the place it had previously occupied, curious about how her life fit together without him in it.

Setting the lamp on the small table beside a reading chair, she plugged the cord into the outlet and stepped back, an unreadable expression on her face.

He couldn't tell whether she was happy to see it returned or not.

She turned to him, and he knew what was coming next. Wasn't ready for it and so cut her off before she could say goodbye.

"Which room do you want to start with?" he asked, jamming his hands deep into his jeans pockets so she wouldn't see his fists, and plastering an easy smile on his face.

"Connor, thank you for getting my things returned so quickly, but I can handle the rest."

"I'm here," he said, aware his voice had lowered. Taken a stern tone. "I'll help. Let the office know I'll be out a day or two—"

"What?" she gasped.

"We'll order some pizza, pick up a bottle of wine for tonight. Throw in a movie." He'd make it casual. Not intimidating. No demands. No pressure. Not really.

"A pizza? Are you out of your mind or are you intentionally being cruel?" She was vibrating with tension now, and suddenly Connor was right there with her.

"I'm trying to help. I want—"

"It's not about what you want, Connor! How can you not get this? I can't be friends with you!"

And then he was in her face, his hands wrapped tight around her upper arms, as he bellowed back, "I don't want to be god-damn friends, Megan!"

She blinked, as shocked by the break in his reserve as he was.

"What do you want?" she asked too quietly for the way they were locked together.

Seconds passed and then finally the breath he'd been fighting to contain shot past his throat with the only answer he had.

"I want you. I want what we were supposed to have. I want the wife and the partner I found in Vegas. I want you to admit I can give you more than you can have alone."

"It won't work."

"Why not?"

"Because—" she held up her hands helplessly, too much pain and emotion shining in her eyes to be anything other than what came next "—I love you, Connor."

It wasn't a surprise after what she'd said before moving out, or at least it shouldn't have been. He'd seen the evidence in her eyes. In her hurt. In a million little things he'd given up trying to deny. But hearing the actual words on those lips he couldn't get enough of—they hit him like a sucker punch, knocking the wind from him and leaving him stunned.

Megan walked to her door and held it open, her eyes on the floor ahead of her feet. "Please, just go."

CHAPTER TWENTY-TWO

MEGAN BACKED UP her files and then stared at her monitor. Too many sleepless nights and the desperate need to distract herself had the latest phase of her project complete well ahead of schedule.

What was she going to do now to stave off those unwelcome thoughts? The insidious whispers slipping too fast through her mind?

...good morning, Mrs. Reed... I'll take my kiss now...

Some days she gave in to them, losing herself in the memories. The pleasure she'd found in those moments. Other days, like today, she fought against them, not wanting the pain that came with the understanding of what she'd lost.

The monitor blurred.

More tears. How long would it take before she cried the last? At the sharp ache in her heart, she wondered if it would be ever.

The trill of her phone sounded. And, closing her eyes to wipe the last of her tears from evidence, she reached for the handset, welcoming whatever distraction waited on the other end.

Maybe a credit offer?

A survey?

Whoever the poor sucker was on the other end of the line, they were going to be earning their check today. She'd keep them busy for the next hour and a half at least.

"Megan Scott," she answered, still having to force it past her lips.

A pause, and she assumed it was some automated system

registering the pickup and kicking her over to a live person. Only, then—"Scott? I realize it's been a while since we spoke, but I'd have thought someone would have notified me if I'd gotten divorced."

Connor.

How was it possible for a person's heart to leap and fall all at once?

"It may not be official yet, but it will be."

"Right. Sure." He cleared his throat. "So I was over in New York a few days, but I'd been meaning to check in once you'd had a chance to get your things unpacked. Make sure there wasn't any damage. You got everything?"

A reasonable inquiry. Connor took his responsibilities and commitments seriously. That was all this was. Taking a steadying breath, she answered equally reasonably, "Everything was in perfect order. Thank you again for your help."

"Glad to hear it. You'll let me know if you realize anything is missing."

"I don't think there is."

"Terrific. So now that you're settled back in, what are your plans?"

Megan stared at the phone a moment. How could he ask? "Connor, you know what my plans are. After everything that's happened...nothing's changed." Nothing except her heart was broken into a thousand pieces and every time she heard Connor's voice, so casual and inquiring, it broke into a thousand more. "I—I really need you to let me go. I think it's better if our lawyers handle the communication from here."

You know what my plans are...

The words pounded through Connor's skull as relentlessly as a jackhammer, over and over again, until now, hours after Megan had ended the call, he felt the reverberation of them through every cell in his body.

He'd known from the start Megan had a path laid out for her future. A family without the complications of a marriage or a man. And he'd been fine with it. Because he believed it would never come to pass.

He was supposed to have time. Time to win her back. Time to figure a work-around Megan wouldn't be able to resist.

She'd fallen in love with him. Which meant she was capable of the one thing that, previously lacking, had led her to consider artificial insemination.

She'd fallen in love with him. So she was supposed to believe it would happen with someone else. Eventually. And wait.

Only now she was going to go through with it.

Nothing's changed...

Uh-huh. Not one damn thing. Except he was physically sick to his stomach thinking about Megan with another man's child. Thinking about that unbreakable connection, that intimacy of union—even if the donor never knew she existed, the idea alone was enough to put him into a near rage.

And what about all the months to come? Her relationship with her mom was tenuous at best. Who was going to be there to help her through the tough times? The times when she was sick, weak, hungry...or scared.

Hell. He hated that almost more than he hated the idea of some piece of another man mingling with the very essence of who she was.

His mother hadn't talked a lot about what it was like raising him on her own. She hadn't wanted him to feel like a burden. But he could remember a night when she'd been crying, talking to his father. Asking him if he'd any idea what it was like for her—waking up in labor by herself. Not understanding what was happening. Having to get to the hospital and spend all those hours waiting for a man who had made promise after promise, but never came to her. A man who let her deliver his child, scared and alone, while he'd hosted a Christmas party with his wife.

Megan wouldn't even have the hope someone might come.

Damn it, why couldn't she just let him be with her?

Pushing out of his chair, he walked over to the bar and poured a glass of scotch, threw it back in the hopes the burn would dull the gut-wrenching ache with all the what-ifs and why-couldn'ts constantly swirling around Megan's name in his belly.

It didn't help. So he poured another, figuring if he couldn't kill the pain in his gut, maybe he'd at least be able to numb the pounding in his head.

An hour later, he was thinking more clearly than he ever had before. Pushing the empty bottle aside, he reached for his phone.

"I need you..."

Connor woke with what felt like the better half of a landfill in his eyes and the near certainty that somehow through the course of the night he'd ended up on a cruise—the gentle rock and loll of the space around him doing things he didn't entirely love to his stomach. Only, then the mattress beneath him sagged with a shift of weight that wasn't his own.

Not. Alone.

Elation ripped through him as he tried to pry his eyelids open, experienced a stab of pain at the intrusion of light and clamped them closed again.

It didn't matter.

If he wasn't alone, then somehow, someway, he'd gotten Megan back into his bed. God bless whatever he'd been drinking last night.

Blindly reaching across the sheets, he encircled the first warmth he encountered and pulled it close. Or tried to, except—

"I don't know what you heard," said the octaves-too-low voice from considerably too close, "but I'm not that kind of girl."

Jeff.

This time Connor wrenched his eyes open, forcing them to withstand the searing pain of daylight and the utterly confusing sight of his hand wrapped around Jeff's jeans-clad thigh, where it rested atop the comforter on his bed.

His bed.

Not a cruise ship.

So what was with the sudden, violent pitch— Oh, hell!

"Yep. Bucket's right over the side, champ," Jeff stated, using his leg to shove him in the opposite direction. "Knock your-self out."

Thirty minutes later, Connor was showered and dressed. Minty freshness doing its best to disguise the funky aftermath of a night misspent.

What had he been thinking?

Dragging himself into the kitchen, Connor dropped into a chair at the table and hazarded a glance at Jeff, who was cook-ing steak and eggs, a smug smile on his smug face.

"Not to suggest I wasn't thrilled to find you in my bed this morning, but what are you doing here?"

A smug flip of the spatula. Damn him.

"My phone's on the table. There's a voice mail that gets the ball rolling, but I think the texts cover the gist of it pretty well. See for yourself."

The churning mess that was his stomach solidified into a lead ball. Oh, hell. Thumbing through the messages, the lead ball grew with each exchange.

8:42 p.m....REED: Need you to go to Denver w me.
8:46 p.m....JEFF: In meeting. Give me 1 hr.
8:53 p.m....REED: No can do. Want wife back. Going now. Think I cn talk her into it wth sperm.

Hell. Please don't let him have called her.

8:53 p.m....JEFF: R U drinking?
8:55 p.m....REED: Have wht she wants. Solllid plan. Better than hers.
8:56 p.m....JEFF: Leaving now. Wait 4 me.
9:02 p.m....REED: Don't worry botu it.
9:02 p.m....JEFF: WAIT 4 ME
9:04 p.m....JEFF: PICK UP YOUR PHONE
9:57 p.m....JEFF: You should stop for drink @ that bar in ter-minal with the big olives B4 flight
10:22 p.m....REED: Hey, UR at the bar. You look pissed.

Connor looked up at his friend. His very best friend in the entire world. "How did you do it?"

"Luck mostly. And some cash. Called your car service and got a guy ready to block your driveway—just in case. I know you don't drink and drive, but, well, you weren't exactly yourself. When you called for a ride, he was already there. Drove you to the airport, the very long way. Meanwhile, I took the chopper down and picked you up at the bar."

"And you stayed with me…in my bed…to make sure I didn't drown in my own puke?" Pushing a hand through his hair, he shook his head. This was a low like he'd never expected to see.

"Yeah, but mostly to keep you from calling Megan, dumbass. By the way, your phone met with a bit of bad luck when a meat tenderizer fell on it last night. Sorry."

Jeff slid a plate of steak and eggs in front of him and dropped into Megan's chair at the table, diving into a plate of his own. "So what's the deal?" he asked around a bite of eggs.

Nothing's changed…

"She's planning to get pregnant."

"Ah, and you thought you'd help her out. Right. Only, I'm wondering, if she didn't want you to get her pregnant before, then where did you think your swimmers were going to get you last night?"

"If I had to guess, I probably figured I could talk her into reconsidering. Make her see what I could offer her. What she was giving up."

"And that would be the material comforts. Financial security?"

Connor grunted. "At least someone sees it."

"Yeah, I see something. But I'm not sure it's the *same thing* as you."

He wasn't in the mood to decipher hidden meaning or subtle subtexts. "Spit it out."

Jeff shook his head, the lines between his brows drawing together. "Ask yourself this, Connor—what is it that's got your *man*ties in such a twist? I mean, really…what is it about Megan you don't want to lose?"

Connor opened his mouth to answer, ready to explain about how right they were together. How easy it was. Only, suddenly, he could see the past few months with a clarity he'd never had before, and a tension, different than the one he'd already become so intimate with, slid down his spine.

Their marriage had been a train wreck from about the word go.

His bride so soused she woke up the next morning unable to remember his name, let alone why she'd agreed to marry him.

She'd been a hassle from the start. The kind of work he never invested in relationships. She'd taken time. She'd taken romancing. She'd kept him on his toes, kept him working, kept him guessing. She'd infuriated and confused him.

And he'd relished every minute of it.

It didn't make sense.

In retrospect, Megan had basically brought every complication and frustration indicative of the love relationships he claimed to loathe to the table, and had him all but begging her to give him more.

She affected him like no one he'd ever met. And even knowing what kind of chaos she'd delivered upon his life...the idea of not having her in it was killing him.

Staring back at Jeff's smug, smug face, he nodded. "Okay. I think I've got it."

CHAPTER TWENTY-THREE

Six hours later, Connor tore down the stairs, patting his pockets as he went.

Wallet? Check.

Keys? Check.

Ring box? Burning a hole in his jacket pocket. Check.

A rushed glance at his watch and his adrenaline spiked. He could do this.

The flight left in forty minutes and he'd be on that plane even if it meant buying the damn airline to ensure it. And once he got to Denver— His stomach took a dive as a thousand scenarios flooded his mind…only one of which would bring about the happily-ever-after he'd only hours before come to terms with wanting.

Shoving all outcomes but that one from his mind, he grasped the knob from the front door and—

Ticket! He hadn't printed the damn thing out, and after his phone's tragic demise, he needed the paper.

Internet station in the kitchen!

Sprinting down the hall, he almost bit it skidding around the corner.

He needed to get there.

Needed to be with his wife.

Needed to tell her it could work between them. And not because of the reasons he'd been laying on her from the start, but because of all the reasons he'd figured out once she left. All the things he realized he couldn't bear to live without.

Flipping open the computer, the black screen flashed to life, bringing up a background with a picture of the two of them at a charity dinner from the month before.

They were laughing. His fingers playing with a bit of her hair as they stared into each other's eyes.

And the way he was looking at her...how the hell had he missed it?

He'd have to wait for the plane to figure it out. There wasn't time now.

Bringing up the browser, he distractedly noted Megan's email was still open from the last time she'd used the machine. About to open a new tab for the airline, he paused as one of the bold-faced messages caught his eye and the preview shattered his plans.

It was from the sperm bank, dated five days prior.

Subject: Per your inquiry, Donor #43409089RS1 available for immediate pickup.

Megan had brought this on herself.

Blinking down at her tablet, perched on the pass-through counter dividing her kitchen and living room, she sat, a silent observer to the video chat that was Gail, Jodie and Tina's rally of support.

"Oh, and you're really surprised he got away?"

What had she been thinking?

"Shut it. You saw the way he looked at her during the reception."

"Shut it? Nice talk, Tina."

Well, she'd been hoping a triple dose of misery in the form of this fingernails-down-a-blackboard bickering might distract her from the misery that had begun in her heart and then slowly, steadily spread until it had overtaken every part of her being.

No such luck.

Where was a white-chocolate martini when she needed one? A white-chocolate martini of birdbath proportions with a garden hose–size Crazy Straw to expedite consumption.

"Are you joking?" Tina leaned around Gail to scowl at Jodie.

Not that she'd be able to drink it, even if one materialized out of thin air. The thought alone had her belly kicking up rebellion enough she had to close her eyes and draw several deep breaths through her nose.

Besides, God only knew what kind of mess she'd wake up in if she followed the cocktail path to avoidance again. A mess of sheets and covers...and Connor's legs tangled with her own?

No.

She wasn't supposed to want that. Had to stop wanting that. Or at the very least, stop fantasizing about ways in which to make it happen.

"You want nice talk? How about—"

"Girls," Gail cut in. *"This is about Megan. Her life is beyond tatters. Again. Another failed relationship. This time a marriage. Granted, we all know about the hasty courtship and may have had our own theories about the probability of success—"*

Jodie gasped, hand flying up to not quite cover the smile riding her lips. *"Gail!"*

But Megan's cousin simply ducked her head a pinch, holding out her hands as if to say, *We were all thinking it.*

At which point the three began a rapid-fire exchange rife with theories, speculations, the more pathetic bullet points from Megan's romantic past, a tangent about Jodie buying a pair of shoes out from under Tina, something about a sweater in high school...a boy from middle school...the Laura Ingalls Wilder books from first grade...

She might have cut them off, but the sad truth was she simply didn't care. That instant of weakness with the forbidden fantasies had opened the door to something worse—something far more devastating.

Memories. Broken bits and pieces of what had actually been. Connor...*I love it when you get my name right... I've got you. What I want is to keep you... Everything, Megan... So this marriage thing...it's working out for you? You're a fantasy... I don't want to be goddamn friends...*

Oh, it hurt so bad.

"Great, Jodie. See what you did—she's crying—"

"Me?"

"Oh, no, Megan, honey, don't cry. So maybe the whole love thing isn't for you. So what? Think about something happy."

"Yes! Think about your little sperm-bank baby!"

Megan shook her head and wiped her thumbs beneath her eyes, hating her apparent inability to keep the tears at bay.

"I'm fine. I'll be fine." Someday. Maybe. "I just need a drink."

Pushing up from the stool where she'd been seated, she circled around to the sink and poured a glass of water. Thought of the way Connor had so often shown up in her office with a cold drink or some healthy snack. The way he'd been so thoughtful and attentive to her, most of all when she'd managed to forget to be attentive to herself.

He'd been aware of her on a level no one ever had before.

But it hadn't been love.

How ironic that her inability to fall in love had been the destruction of every other relationship she'd had. And actually finding it, the destruction with Connor.

Why now?

Why couldn't she have been the wife he needed her to be?

Three swift knocks sounded at her door, thankfully drawing her out of that downward spiral of self-destructive thought.

Her eyes swung to the door, her heart tripping in her chest until she realized the security door hadn't buzzed. Mrs. Gandle from 2C had probably signed for another package.

Chastising herself for that stupid surge of hope, she walked to the door and swung it open—

"Connor?" she choked out, shaking her head in disbelief at the scowling man standing at her door, a plastic shopping bag hanging from one hand.

"No security chain?" he demanded, his outrage potent and possessive. "First some little old lady downstairs holds the door open for me, letting me march right in, and then you open the door without even checking who's out here? Megan, this is a decent neighborhood, but what the hell?"

She shook her head, too stunned to register anything beyond the fact that Connor was here.

He'd come back.

Again.

Connor shoved his free hand through his hair, acutely aware of the ass he was making of himself and yet unable to walk away as he should.

"What are you doing here?" she asked, her words barely a whisper.

He opened his mouth to answer, but then all he could do was stare. Soaking in the sight of her smattering of freckles and gorgeous mouth he hadn't seen smile for too damn long.

Her face seemed thinner and he didn't like the shadows beneath her eyes, and yet no one had ever been so beautiful as she was right then.

Clearing his throat, he looked down into the eyes that had been haunting him for weeks, and then to the hand that had come to rest defensively across her belly.

"Why did I wait so long?" he asked himself, keenly aware of the futility of the question.

Megan blinked, confusion and hurt and a thousand other things shining too bright in those beautiful eyes. And then resolve. "You need to stop this, Connor. What you're doing, calling, showing up. It's—" she swallowed, looking as though even that simple act took monumental effort "—it's hurting me."

He hated knowing it was the truth. Wishing he'd been smart enough from the start to make it so neither one of them would have had to go through this kind of pain. "I'm sorry."

"Then leave," she whispered. A single fat tear spilled over her bottom lid, and his heart twisted with a pain he'd never experienced before. "Please. I can't be what you wanted me to be. I'll never be able to be that for you. Let me go."

"No." He shook his head solemnly. "I tried. I did. But I can't."

"You have to—"

"I'll *never* let you go!" The words had ripped past his throat before he'd had the thought to temper them. But they were the truth.

Megan froze in her spot, her gorgeous mouth parted in mid-protest, brows pulled high together in an expression that was pure, helpless disbelief.

But not elation. Not blissful surrender.

At the first blink, the sign she was breaking out of that stunned state of suspension, he panicked. He hadn't said enough, hadn't explained, couldn't risk her response before he told her everything she needed to know.

So he pulled the lowest trick he had in his arsenal. This was too important to him—*she* was too important to him—to risk playing by the rules. And for the first time in his life, he didn't damn his father for that bit of unscrupulous DNA spiraling through the darkest parts of who he was.

He embraced it.

Stepping forward, he caught Megan with one hand beneath the fall of her hair, silencing any denial she might have made with a kiss bursting with every bit of aching, unfulfilled longing, heartbreak, desire and need he'd suffered since the moment she left. He told her with his lips how he missed her, with his tongue the way of his want. Gentle bites hinted at the hold she had on him.

And when her fingers were wrapped in his shirt, her breath rushing across his lips and cheeks, her eyes again locked with his—he went on. Telling her what he'd only discovered for himself.

"Megan, I never wanted love. I saw what it did to my mother and didn't want any part of it. All my adult life I avoided that kind of intimacy, holding myself at arm's length and making unbreachable boundaries a part of every relationship. It was easy. Until I met you. In the span of a few hours, I'd married you and all the rules I lived by were a thing of the past. I swore up and down we'd have the kind of controlled marriage where no one could get hurt, but I couldn't even control myself. Nothing halfway was enough with you. I made every excuse in the book, but I couldn't admit what was really going on."

"Connor…" His name passed her lips on a breath that barely dared to take voice.

"I said I didn't want to be your friend, but it's not true. I want to be your friend and your lover and your husband and the father to your children—" He broke off, swallowing past a well of regret without limit. "I know you're going to tell me it's too late, but Megan, it's not."

He dropped to one knee. Watching her eyes go wide, he held up the gallon of organic whole milk in one hand and, pulling the box from his pocket with the other, flipped open the lid, revealing the two rings nestled together within black velvet. One the diamond-encrusted wedding band she'd returned to him twice already but he couldn't accept she didn't want. The other a solitaire as weighty as the promise it conveyed. "I will love this baby like it's my own. It will never know a single minute of doubt because I swear to love it as much as I love you."

Megan's breath sucked in at his confession. His revelation. His freedom.

"You don't remember my first proposal, but I'm hoping this one will stick. Megan, I love you. And I'm asking you to let me give you a lifetime of what you've shown me matters most. Laughter, love, late-night conversations. I'm asking you to be my wife in the most conventional, traditional and time-tested meaning of the word, for as long as we both shall live."

Heart slamming, breath held, he waited as his world hung in the balance.

CHAPTER TWENTY-FOUR

THIS COULDN'T BE HAPPENING. It wasn't real. It wasn't possible.

This was a nervous breakdown in action. It had to be. Something she should have seen coming…except the gallon of milk was the sort of surreal her brain typically didn't conjure.

Which meant… "Oh, my God."

Her breath left on a quiet sob and she reached for him, pulling at his shirt until he stood. Taking the milk from him, she set it on the secretary table with a small shake of her head.

"I'm not pregnant, Connor."

He stared into her eyes a long moment, the muscles of his throat working as though he was trying to make words that wouldn't come. And then he pulled her into his arms, his big body wrapping around her as ragged breath sounded against the top of her head.

Relief, powerful enough to overwhelm a man as strong as Connor, washed over her. It was humbling to witness.

"Your email was still open on the kitchen laptop," he said, his words glass-and-gravel rough. "I saw the message about a requested donor being ready for pickup."

Megan flattened her hand against his chest, the only reassurance she could offer within the decadent confines of Connor's hold. "That message was in response to an inquiry I'd made months ago. Before we met. I wasn't ready to move forward with those plans."

They were still married, for one. And the way she felt about Connor… She couldn't begin something so important with her heart still torn to shreds. She'd assumed her plans would be on hold for at least another year or two.

Releasing his python grip on her, Connor gently cupped her jaw as he tipped her face to his.

"I don't care." The steady calm of his words in direct contrast to the burning intensity in his eyes.

Her brow lifted in question.

"I want you anyway. Even if I don't get a baby in the bargain."

A soft laugh pushed past her lips. How did he do it? Make her laugh when her world was up in the air?

"You want me anyway?"

A nod. "I love you, Megan. I didn't think it was something I had in me, but that was because I'd never experienced it before I met you."

He loved her.

Connor searched her eyes, one corner of his mouth curling into a wolfish smile as the hands at her jaw slipped into her hair. Gently he urged her head back and lowered his mouth for a soft, sinking kiss that tasted like every promise she'd never allowed herself to dream of asking for. Then, fitting his lips more firmly over hers, he slid his tongue past her teeth to stroke against her tongue, once, twice, again and again, until her hands were locked in the fabric of his shirt and she was clinging to him with everything she had.

Never breaking the kiss, his hands began a slow roam over the contours of her body, following the curve of her waist and the lines of her arms. Threading through her fingers and making the world around her spin, until she was grounded by the unyielding resistance of the door to her apartment at her back. The seductive press of her wrists against the solid panels, and the mind-jumbling weight of Connor's body in full delicious contact with her own.

"I love you," he whispered against her lips.

"Oh, my God, yes."

Both of them froze at the punctured illusion they were the only two people on the planet. In the room.

"Shhhh!"

Connor's chin pulled back as he looked down into her rapidly heating face.

"I'm sorry—I forgot." How could she have forgotten?

Together they turned toward the source of the invasive words, to where her abandoned tablet sat on the pass-through counter, three eager-eyed, utterly shameless faces filling the screen.

Connor straightened, pushing back from her to walk to the electronic device. "Sorry, girls, show's over."

"No, wait!"

"Heya, Connor, nice moves."

"Dang it, Jodie! See what you di—"

Flipping the cover closed, he severed the connection and turned to face her.

She shouldn't have laughed. Really.

"Funny, is it?" he asked, a smile on his face.

"Accident," she swore, holding her hands up. "I was distracted."

"So it would seem," Connor replied, nodding toward her still-raised left hand.

Her gaze followed his to the fourth finger of her left hand, where her wedding ring glinted beside the new ring that had been nestled in black velvet when she'd last seen it.

"Sneaky," she whispered, barely able to push the word past the well of emotion at seeing her wedding band returned to her hand.

"I was hoping seeing them on your finger might help me get the answer I'm waiting for."

"I love you, Connor. And I want everything you're offering. I want to be your wife and the mother to your children. But—"

He stepped forward, all that cocky confidence falling away. "But?"

She smoothed her hand over the stubble-rough edge of his jaw before letting it drift to the buttons of his shirt. "But what would you say about waiting on the baby. Maybe taking a few months or a year—"

"A trial?" he asked, nodding quickly. Determination and

resolve pushing past the disappointment and hurt that flashed across his face. "Anything to make you feel safe. Confident."

Slipping the first button free, she shook her head. "No. I don't need any trial."

He searched her eyes. "Then what?"

"Maybe for a while, all I want is you."

"Yeah?"

Working the next button free, she nodded. "After all, we've got the rest of our lives together. Now, Mr. Reed, I'm ready for my I-love-you kiss."

That half smile pushed hard at Connor's gorgeous lips until it spread, encompassing his whole mouth and then his face.

"Gladly, Mrs. Reed," he answered, emotion making his voice gruff as he took her in his arms and dipped her back. "I love you."

And then he gave her a kiss that was meant to be the first of its kind, but tasted so familiar there was no denying those undercurrents of love had been there all the time…just waiting to be recognized. This one, though, her husband delivered wholly. Without reservation. Without limit.

It was a promise of forever…and she believed.

* * * * *

THE HEIR'S CHOSEN BRIDE
MARION LENNOX

Marion Lennox has written over a hundred romance novels and is published in over a hundred countries and thirty languages. Her international awards include the prestigious RITA® Award (twice) and the *RT Book Reviews* Career Achievement Award "for a body of work which makes us laugh and teaches us about love". Marion adores her family, her kayak, her dog and lying on the beach with a book someone else has written. Heaven.

CHAPTER ONE

Information required on whereabouts of Dougal Douglas (or direct descendant), brother to Lord Angus Douglas, Earl of Loganaich. Contact solicitors Baird and O'Shannasy, Dolphin Bay, Australia, for information to your advantage.

'MR DOUGLAS, you're an earl.'

Hamish groaned. He was hours behind schedule. The Harrington Trust Committee was arriving in thirty minutes and his perky secretary-in-training was driving him nuts.

'Just sort the mail.'

'But this letter says you're an earl. You gotta read it.'

'Like I read e-mails from Nigeria offering to share millions. All I need to do is send my bank account details. Jodie, you know better.'

'Of course I do,' she told him indignantly. Honestly, he was being a twit.

But she forgave him. Who wouldn't? Hamish Douglas was the cutest boss she'd ever worked for. Jodie had been delighted when Marjorie had retired and she'd been given the chance to take her place. At thirty-three, Hamish was tall, dark and drop-dead gorgeous. He had ruffled black curls, which fought back when he tried to control them. He had deep brown twinkly eyes and the most fantastic smile…

When he smiled. Which wasn't often. Hamish might be one

of the most brilliant young futures brokers in Manhattan, but he didn't seem to enjoy life.

Maybe he'd smile when he realised he really was an earl.

'This one's different,' she told him. 'Honest, Mr Douglas, you need to look. If you're who these people think you are then you've inherited a significant estate. A significant estate in lawyer speak...I bet that means a fortune.'

'I've inherited nothing. It's a scam.'

'What's a scam? Is Jodie bothering you with nuisance mail?'

Uh-oh. Jodie had been rising, but as soon as the door opened she sat straight back down. Marcia Vinel was Hamish's fiancée. Trouble. Jodie had overheard Marcia on at least two occasions advising Hamish to get rid of her.

'She's a temp from the typing pool. Surely you can do better.'

'But I like her,' Hamish had replied, much to Jodie's delight. 'She's smart, intuitive and organised—and she makes me laugh.'

'Your secretary's not here to make you laugh,' Marcia had retorted.

No, Jodie thought, shoving the offending letter into the tray marked PENDING. Life's too serious to laugh. Life's about making money.

'What's the letter?' Marcia said, with a sideways glance at Jodie to say she didn't appreciate Jodie knowing anything about Hamish that she herself didn't. 'Is it a scam?'

Jodie knew when to turn into a good secretary. She tugged on her headset, paid attention to her keyboard and didn't answer. 'What's the letter?' Marcia said again, this time directly to Hamish.

'It's some sort of con,' Hamish said wearily. 'And Jodie's not bothering me any more than anyone else is. Hell, Marcia, I have work to do.'

'I came to tell you the Harrington delegation's been delayed,' Marcia told him. 'Their flight's two hours late from London. Relax.'

He did, but not much. That meant rescheduling and...

'I'll rearrange your appointments.' Jodie emerged from her headset and he cast her a look of gratitude. 'Only I do think you should read the letter.' She mightn't like Marcia, she decided, but at least Marcia would make Hamish look at it.

He went back to frowning. 'Jodie, get real. Letters saying I'm an earl and I've inherited a fortune are the stuff of a kid's fantasy.'

'But it doesn't say send bank account details. It says contact a solicitor. That sounds fusty rather than scammy. Real.'

'Let me see,' Marcia decreed, and put out an imperious hand. Marcia was a corporate lawyer working for the same company as Hamish. She was the brains, he was the money, some people said—but Hamish had earned his money with his wits, and there was a fair bit of cross-over.

The two were a team. Jodie handed it over.

There was silence while Marcia read. The letter was on the official notepaper of an Australian legal firm. It looked real, Jodie thought defiantly. She wasn't wasting her boss's time.

And Marcia didn't think so either. She finished reading and set the letter down with an odd look on her face.

'Hamish, do you have an uncle called Angus Douglas? In Australia?'

'No.' He frowned. 'Or...I don't think so.'

'Surely you know your uncles,' Jodie said, and got a frown from Marcia for her pains. She subsided but she didn't replace her headset.

'My father migrated from Scotland when he was little more than a kid,' Hamish told Marcia. 'There was some sort of family row—I don't know what. He never told my mother anything about his family and he died when I was three.'

'You never enquired?' Marcia demanded, astounded, as if such disinterest was inexcusable.

'About what?'

'About his background. Whether he was wealthy?'

'He certainly wasn't wealthy. He migrated just after the war when every man and his dog was on the move from Europe. He married my mother and they had nothing.' He hesitated. 'All I know...'

'All you know is what?' said Marcia, still staring at the letter.

'While I was at college my roommate was doing a history major. I went through some shipping lists he was using, just to see if I could find him. I did. Apparently my father left Glasgow in 1947 on the *Maybelline*. There was no other Douglas on the passenger list so I assumed he was alone.'

'Maybe he had a brother who migrated as well,' Marcia said thoughtfully. 'Maybe his brother went to Australia instead. Honey, this letter says someone called Angus Douglas, Earl of Loganaich, died six weeks ago in Australia and they're looking for relations of Dougal Douglas. Your father was Dougal, wasn't he?'

Hamish's face stilled.

'What?' Marcia said, and Jodie watched her face change. She knew that look. She'd seen it when Marcia was closing on a corporate deal. The look said she could smell money.

'There probably aren't that many Dougal Douglases,' Hamish said slowly. 'But…my father's address on the shipping manifest was Loganaich. I'd never heard of the place. I looked it up, and it's tiny. I thought some day I might go find it, but…'

'But you got busy,' Marcia said, approving. He certainly had. Hamish had been one of the youngest graduates ever to gain a first-class commerce-law degree from Harvard. After that had come his appointment with one of the most prestigious broking firms in New York, and he'd whizzed up the corporate ladder with the speed of light. At thirty-three, Hamish was a full partner and a millionaire a couple times over. There'd been no time in his fast-moving history for a leisurely stroll around Scotland. 'Hamish, this means you really might have inherited.'

'This is cool.' Jodie beamed, forgetting her dislike of Marcia as imagination took flight. 'The letter says they're not sure whether they have the right person, but it does fit. It says your father was one of three brothers who left Scotland in 1947. The oldest two went to Australia and your dad came here.'

'He can read it for himself,' Marcia snapped and handed it over to Hamish.

'It'll be a scam.'

'Read it,' Marcia snapped.

And Jodie thought, Whoa, don't do that, lady. If Hamish was my guy I wouldn't talk like that.

But Hamish didn't notice. 'It's probably nothing,' he said at last, but dismissal had made way for uncertainty. 'But with the Loganaich connection… Maybe we should check.'

'I'll make enquiries about this law firm,' Marcia said. 'I'll get onto it straight away.'

'There's no need…'

'There certainly is,' Jodie breathed. 'Oh, Mr Douglas, the letter says you're an earl and you've inherited a castle and everything. How ace would that be? A Scottish earl. You might get to wear a kilt.'

'No one's seeing my knees,' Hamish said. He grinned—and then the phone rang and a fax came through that he'd been waiting for and he went back to work.

Castles and titles had to wait.

'They think they've found him.'

Susie Douglas, née McMahon, was sitting on a rug before the fire in the great hall of Loganaich-Castle-the-Second, playing with her baby. Rose Douglas was fourteen months old. She'd been tumbling with her aunt's dog, Boris, but now baby and dog had settled into a sleepy, snuggly pile, and the women were free to talk.

'The lawyers have been scouring America,' Susie told her twin. 'Now they think they've found the new earl. As soon as he comes, I…I think I'll go home.'

'But you can't.' Kirsty stared at her twin with horror. 'This is your home.'

'It's been great,' Susie said, staring round the fantastically decorated walls with affection. The two suits of armour guarding the hallway were wonderful all by themselves. She talked to them all the time. *Good morning, Eric. Good morning, Ernst.* 'But I can't live here for ever. It doesn't belong to me. I agreed to stay until Angus died, and now he has.' She took a deep breath. 'I've been marking time for too long, Kirsty, love. Eric and Ernst belong to someone else. It's time I moved on.'

'You mustn't.' Yet there was a part of Kirsty that knew Susie was right. This moment had been inevitable.

Susie had come so far… After the death of her husband, Rory, Susie had fallen apart, suffering from crippling depression as well as the injuries she'd received in the crash that had killed her husband. In desperation Kirsty had brought her to Australia to meet Rory's uncle. Lord Angus Douglas, Earl of Loganaich. It had been a grand title for a wonderful old man. In the earl they'd found a true friend, and in his outlandish castle Susie had recovered. She'd given birth to her daughter and she'd started to look forward again.

To home?

Susie's home was in America. Her landscaping business was in America. Now Angus was dead there was nothing keeping her here.

But while Susie had been recovering. Kirsty, her twin, had been falling in love with the local doctor. Kirsty and Jake now had a rambling house on the edge of town, kids, hens, dog—the whole domestic catastrophe. Kirsty's home was solidly here.

'I don't want you to go,' Kirsty whispered. 'Angus should have left this place to you.'

'He couldn't.'

'I don't see why not.'

'This castle was built with entailed money,' Susie explained. 'After the original Scottish castle burned down, the family trust made money available for rebuilding. Angus managed to arrange it so he rebuilt the castle here in Australia, but he still couldn't leave it away from the true line of the peerage. If I'd had a son it'd be different, but now it goes to a nephew no one knows. It belongs to a Hamish Douglas. An American.'

She said 'an American' in a tone of such disgust that Kirsty burst out laughing. 'You sound as if Americans are some sort of experimental bug,' she said. 'Just remember you are one, Susie Douglas.'

'I hardly feel American any more,' Susie said, sighing. Rose rolled sleepily off Boris, and Susie scooped her baby daughter up to hug her. 'I have my own little Australian.'

'Half American, half Scottish, born in Australia. But she belongs here.'

'You see, I'm not sure any more,' Susie said, sighing again. 'Angus has left me enough to buy a little house and live happily ever after here. But I need to work and there's not a lot of landscape gardening to be had in Dolphin Bay.'

'There's me,' Kirsty said defensively, and Susie smiled.

'You know that counts for a lot. But not everything. I need a job, Kirsty. Rory's been dead for almost two years. My injuries from the crash are almost completely resolved. I loved caring for Angus, but without him the castle seems empty. The only thing keeping me occupied is the upkeep on the castle and the garden, and once the new earl arrives…'

'When is he arriving?'

'I don't know,' Susie told her. 'But the lawyers say they've found him and told him he's inherited. If you were told you'd inherited a title and a fortune, wouldn't you hotfoot it over here?'

Kirsty gave a bleak little smile at that. So much sorrow had gone into this fortune, this title…

'I guess I would,' she admitted.

'Once he arrives there's nothing for me to do,' Susie told her, twirling the curls of her almost sleeping daughter.

'Maybe he won't come,' Kirsty said, trying not to sound desperate. She wanted her sister to stay so much. 'Or maybe he'll want you to stay as caretaker.'

'And leave it earning nothing? What would you do if you inherited this place?' Susie asked.

'Sell it as a hotel,' Kirsty said bluntly, and though she added a grimace it was no less than the truth. Angus had built this place when his castle back in Scotland had burned to the ground. The old man's whim had led him to rebuild here, in this magic place where the climate was so much kinder than Scotland's. But now…the castle seemed straight out of a fairy tale. It was far too big for a family. Angus had known it could be sold as a hotel, and his intention was surely about to be realised.

'It feels like a home,' Kirsty added stubbornly, and Susie laughed.

'Right. Fourteen bedrooms, six bathrooms, a banquet hall, a ballroom and me and Rose. Even if you and Jake and the kids and Boris came to live with us, we'd have three bedrooms apiece. It's crazy to think of staying.'

'But you can't go back,' Kirsty said again, and her twin's face grew solemn.

'I think I must.'

'At least stay and meet the new earl. Maybe he'll have some ideas rather than selling. Maybe he could employ you to make the garden better.'

'We both know that's a pipe dream.'

'But you will stay until he gets here. That's what Angus would have wanted.'

'I miss Angus so much,' Susie said softly, and her twin moved across to give her a swift hug.

'Oh, love. Of course you do.'

'The new laird might not even grow pumpkins,' Susie said sadly, and Kirsty had to smile.

'Unforgivable sin!'

'We've got the biggest this year,' Susie said, brightening. 'Did I tell you, the night before Angus died I snuck into Ben Boyce's yard and measured his. It's a tiddler in comparison. Angus died knowing he would definitely win this year's trophy.'

'There you go,' Kirsty said stoutly. 'The new earl just has to collect his pumpkin and take over where Angus left off.'

'The lawyers say he's some sort of financier. An American financier valuing a prize pumpkin…you have to be kidding.'

'I'm not kidding,' Kirsty said. 'You'll see. He'll come and he'll fall for the place and want a caretaker and landscape gardener extraordinaire, and pumpkin pie for dinner for the rest of his life.'

'He won't.'

'At least wait and see,' Kirsty begged. 'Please, Susie. You must give him a chance.'

* * *

'Holiday?' Hamish glared at his secretary in stupefaction. 'You are joking.'

'I'm not joking. Your holiday starts next week—sir. Oh, by the way, I'm quitting.'

'You're not making sense.' Hamish was late for a meeting. He'd been gathering his notes when his unconventional secretary had burst in to tell him her news.

'You're having three weeks' holiday starting next week,' Jodie repeated patiently. 'And I'm quitting.'

He gazed at her as he'd gaze at someone with two heads.

'You can't quit,' he said weakly, and she grinned.

'Yes, I can. I'm only a temp. I came here two years ago on a two-week agency placing, and no one's given me a contract.'

'But people don't just leave—'

'Well, why would they when the money's brilliant?' Jodie acknowledged. 'But have you noticed that people *do* leave this firm? They start taking time off because they can't cope. They're constantly tired. They forget things. They stop being efficient and then they're bumped. So all I'm doing is leaving before I'm bumped. Why do you think Marjorie retired so young? Listening to you and the girlfriend made me think…'

'Me and Marcia?'

'You and Marcia. She's as pleased as could be about your new title—she can't wait to get married so she'll be Lady Marcia Douglas—but as for agreeing you don't have time to go see a castle…'

'It's a fake castle,' he said faintly.

'A castle is a castle and it sounds cool,' Jodie declared. 'Just because it's not six hundred years old doesn't mean it's not a real one. And Marcia's idea of putting it on the market without seeing it is ridiculous. Anyway, I was talking to Nick, and he said—'

'Nick?'

'My partner,' she said with exaggerated patience. 'The man I share my life with. He's a woodworker. He was a social worker with disadvantaged kids, but the work just wore him out. He loved it but it exhausted him. He's almost as cute as you, and I talk about him all the time. Not that you listen.'

Hamish blinked. He hesitated and glanced at his watch. Then he carefully laid his papers on the desk in front of him. Jodie was a great, if unconventional, secretary, and it'd be more efficient to spend a few minutes now persuading her to stay rather than training someone new—

'Don't do this to me,' Jodie begged. 'You're scheduling me into your morning and I don't intend to be scheduled. I'm working on changing your life here. Not the next half-hour.'

'Pardon?'

'You see nothing but work,' she told him. 'The typing-pool gossip is that you've been blighted in love. That explains Marcia but it's none of my business. All I know is that you're blinkered. You've been given the most fantastic opportunity and you're throwing it away.'

Hamish sat down. 'This is—'

'Impertinent,' she told him, and beamed. 'I know. But someone needs to tell you. Nick's been given a contract to rebuild the choir stalls at a gorgeous old church up in New England. We're both going to move. That's why I need to quit. So then I thought if I was quitting I should try to save you first. Nick agrees. Spending your whole life making money is awful. Owning a castle and not visiting it before you sell it is madness. So I've cancelled every one of your appointments for the next three weeks, starting the minute you've finished with the Harrington committee. I haven't just crossed them out of your diary but I've contacted everyone and rescheduled. Job's done. As of next week I'm out of here, and if you have the brains I credit you with, so will you be.'

'I can't.'

'Yes, you can,' she told him. 'Your Lordship.'

'Jodie…'

'Yes?' She was beaming, as if she'd just played Santa Claus. 'I've booked flights for you. From JFK to Sydney, and there's a hire car waiting so you can drive straight down to Dolphin Bay. If you want to take Marcia they're holding two seats, but I told them you'd probably cancel one.'

'Marcia won't come.'

'No, but you will,' she told him. 'You've been in this job for nearly ten years, and no one can remember you taking a holiday. Oh, sure, you've been away but it's always been on some financial wheeler dealer arrangement. Dealing with Swiss bankers with a little skiing on the side. A week on a corporate yacht with financiers and oilmen. Not a sniff of time spent lying on the beach doing nothing. Isn't it about time you had a look at life before you marry Marcia and...?' She paused and bit back what she'd been about to say. 'And settle down?'

'I can't,' he said again, but suddenly he wasn't so sure.

'I've cleared it with all the partners. Everyone knows you're going and they know why. You've inherited a castle. Everyone's asking for postcards. So you're going to look pretty dumb sitting round this office for the next three weeks doing nothing. Or telling everyone that I've lied about you needing a holiday and you're not taking one, yah, boo, sucks.'

'Pardon?' he said again, and her grin widened.

'That's not stockbroker talk,' she told him. 'It's street talk. Real talk. Which I've figured you need. If you're going to go from share-broking to aristocracy maybe you need a small wedge of real life in between.'

'Look, you dumb worm, if you don't get out of there you'll be concrete.'

Susie's hair was escaping from her elastic band and drifting into her eyes. She flipped it back with the back of her hand, and a trickle of muddy water slid down her face. Excellent.

This was her very favourite occupation. Digging in mud. Susie was making a path from the kitchen door to the conservatory. The gravel path had sunk and she needed to pour concrete before she laid pavers, but first she had to dig. She'd soaked the soil to make it soft, and it was now oozing satisfactorily between her fingers as she rescued worms. Rose was sleeping soundly just through the window. The sun was shining on her face and she was feeling great.

She needed to get these worms out of the mud or they'd be cactus.

'I'm just taking you to the compost,' she told them, in her best worm-reassuring tone. 'The compost is worm heaven. Ooh, you're a nice fat one…'

A hand landed on her shoulder.

She was wearing headphones and had heard nothing. She yelped, hauled her headphones off, staggered to her feet and backed away. Fast.

A stranger was watching her with an expression of bemusement.

He might be bemused but so was she. The stranger looked like he'd just strolled off the deck of a cruising yacht. An expensive yacht. He was elegantly casual, wearing cream chinos and a white polo top with a discreet logo on the breast. He was too far away now to tell what the logo was, but she bet it was some expensive country club. A fawn loafer jacket slung elegantly over one shoulder.

He was wearing cream suede shoes.

Cream shoes. Here.

She looked past the clothes with an effort—and there was surely something to see beside the clothes. The stranger was tall, lean and athletic. Deep black hair. Good skin, good smile…

Great smile.

She'd left the outer gate open. There was a small black sedan parked in the forecourt, with a hire-car company insignia on the side. She'd been so intent on her worms that he'd crept up on her unawares.

He could have been an axe murderer, she thought, a little bit breathless. She should have locked the gate.

But…maybe she was expecting him? This had to be who she thought he was. The new earl.

Maybe she should have organised some sort of guard of honour. A twelve-gun salute.

'You're the gardener?' he asked, and she tried to wipe mud away with more mud as she smiled back. She was all the welcome committee there was, so she ought to try her best.

A spade salute?

'I am the gardener,' she agreed. 'Plus the rest. General

dogsbody and bottle-washer for Loganaich Castle. What can I do for you?'

But his gaze had been caught. Solidly distracted. He was staring at a huge golden ball to the side of the garden. A vast ball of bright orange, about two yards wide.

'What is that?' he said faintly.

She beamed. 'A pumpkin. Her name's Priscilla. Isn't she the best?'

'I don't believe it.'

'You'd better. She's a Dills Atlantic Giant. We decided on replacing Queensland Blues this year—we spent ages on the Internet finding the really huge suckers—and went for Dills instead. Of course, they're not quite as good to eat. Actually, they're cattle feed, but who's worrying?'

'Not me,' he said faintly.

'The only problem is we need a team of bodybuilders to move her. Our main competitor has moved to Dills as well, but he doesn't have the expertise. We'll walk away with the award for Dolphin Bay's biggest pumpkin this year, no worries.'

'No worries,' he repeated, dazed.

'That's Australian for "no problem",' she explained kindly. 'Or you could say, "She'll be right, mate."'

This conversation was going nowhere. He tried to get a grip. 'Is anyone home? In there?' He waved vaguely in the direction of the castle.

'I'm home. Me and Rose.'

'Rose?'

'My daughter. Are you—'

'I'm Hamish Douglas. I'm looking for a Susie Douglas.'

'Oh.'

He really was the new earl.

There was a moment's charged silence. She wasn't what he'd expected, she thought, but, then, he wasn't what she'd expected either.

She'd thought he'd look like Rory.

He didn't look like any of the Douglases she'd met, she decided. He was leaner, finer boned, finer...tuned? He was a

Porsche compared to Rory's Land Rover, she decided, limping across to greet him properly. She still had residual stiffness from the accident in which Rory had been killed, and it was worse when she'd been kneeling.

But the pain was nothing to what it had been, and she smiled as she held out her hand in greeting. Then, as she looked at his face and realised there was a problem, her smile broadened. She wiped her hands on the seat of her overalls and tried again.

'Susie Douglas would be me,' she told him, gripping his reluctant hand and shaking. 'Hi.'

'Hi,' he said, and looked at his hand.

'It's almost clean,' she told him, letting a trace of indignation enter her voice as she realised what he was looking at. 'And it's good, clean dirt. Only a trace wormy.'

'Wormy?'

'Earthworms,' she said, exasperated. This wasn't looking good in terms of long-term relationship. In terms of long-term caring for this garden. 'Worms that make pumpkins grow as big as Priscilla here. Not the kind that go straight to your liver and grow till they come out your eyeballs.'

'Um…fine.' He was starting to sound confounded.

'I'm transferring them to the compost,' she told him, deciding she'd best be patient. 'I'm laying concrete pavers to the conservatory, and how awful would it be to be an earthworm encased in concrete? Do you want to see the conservatory?'

'Um…sure.'

'I might as well show you while we're out here,' she told him. 'You've inherited all this pile, and the conservatory's brilliant. It was falling into disrepair when I arrived, but I've built it up. It's almost like the old orangeries they have in grand English houses.'

'You're American,' he said on a note of discovery. 'But you're…'

'I'm the castle relic,' she told him. 'Hang on a minute. I need to check something.'

She limped across to the closest window, hoisted herself up and peered through to where Rose snoozed in her cot.

'Nope. Still fine.'

'What's fine?' he asked, more and more bemused.

'Rose. My daughter.' She gestured to the headphones now lying abandoned in the mud. 'You thought I was listening to hip-hop while I worked? I was listening to the sounds of my daughter sleeping. Much more reassuring.' She turning and starting to walk toward the conservatory. 'Relics are what they used to call us in the old days,' she said over her shoulder. 'They're the women left behind when their lords died.'

'And your lord was…'

'Rory,' she told him. 'Your cousin. He was Scottish-Australian but he met me in the States.'

'I don't know anything about my cousins.' She was limping toward a glass-panelled building on the north side of the house, moving so fast he had to lengthen his stride to keep up with her.

'You don't know anything about the family?'

'I didn't know anyone existed until I got the lawyer's letter.'

'Saying you were an earl.' She chuckled. 'How cool. It's like Cinderella. You should have been destitute, living in a garret.' She glanced over her shoulder, eyeing him appraisingly. 'But they tell me you're some sort of financier in Manhattan. I guess you weren't in any garret.'

'It was a pretty upmarket garret,' he admitted. They reached the conservatory doors, and she swung them wide so he could appreciate the vista. 'Wow!'

'It is wow,' she said, approving.

It certainly was. The conservatory was as big as three or four huge living rooms and it was almost thirty feet high. It looked almost a cathedral, he thought, dazed. The beams were vast and blackened with glass panels set between. Hundreds of glass panels.

'The beams came from St Mary's Cathedral just south of Sydney,' Susie told him. 'St Mary's burned down just after the war when Angus was building this place. He couldn't resist. He had all the usable timbers trucked here. For the last few years he didn't have enough energy to keep it up, but since I've been here I've been restoring it. I love it.'

He knew she did. He could hear it in her voice.

She didn't look like any relic he'd met before.

Susie was wearing men's overalls, liberally dirt-stained. She was shortish, slim, with an open, friendly face. She had clear, brown enquiring eyes, and her auburn curls were caught back in a ponytail that threatened to unravel at any minute. A long white scar ran across her forehead—hardly noticeable except that it accentuated the lines of strain around her eyes. She was still young but her face had seen...life?

Her husband had been murdered, he remembered. That's what the lawyers had told him. Back in New York it had seemed a fantastic tale but suddenly it was real. Bleakly real.

'Do you know about the family?' she asked, as if she'd guessed his thoughts and knew he needed an explanation.

'Very little,' he told her. 'I'd like to hear more. Angus was the last earl. He died childless. Your husband, Rory, was his eldest nephew, and he and the second nephew, Kenneth, are both dead. I'm the youngest nephew. I never knew Angus, I certainly didn't know about the title, and I'm still trying to figure things out. Am I right so far?'

'Pretty much.'

'Angus and my father and another brother—Rory and Kenneth's father—left Scotland just after the war?'

'Apparently the family castle was a dark and gloomy pile on the west coast of Scotland,' she told him. 'The castle was hit by an incendiary bomb during the war and it burned to the ground. As far as I can gather, no one grieved very much. The boys had been brought up in an atmosphere that was almost poisonous. Angus inherited everything, the others nothing, and the estate was entailed in such a way that he couldn't do anything about it. After the fire they decided to leave. Angus said your father was the first to go. He boarded a boat to America and Angus never heard from him again.'

'And Angus and...what was the other brother called—David?'

'Angus was in the air force and he was injured toward the end of the war. While he was recuperating he met Deirdre. She was a nurse and her family had been killed in the London Blitz, so when he was discharged they decided to make their home in Australia. David followed.' She hesitated. 'The relationship was hard, and the resentment followed through to the sons.'

'I don't understand.'

'A situation where the eldest son gets everything and others get nothing is asking for trouble.' She walked forward and lifted a ripening cumquat into her hands. She touched it gently and then let it go again, releasing it so it swung on its branch like a beautiful mobile. There were hundreds of cumquats, Hamish thought, still dazzled by the beauty of the place.

Did one eat cumquats? He'd only ever seen them as decorator items in the foyers of five-star hotels.

'Angus rebuilt his castle here,' she said. 'It was a mad thing to do, but it gave the men of this town a job when things were desperate. Maybe it wasn't as crazy as it sounds. He and Deirdre didn't have children but David had two. Rory and Kenneth. I married Rory.'

'They told me that Kenneth murdered Rory,' he said flatly. It had to be talked about, he decided, so why not now?

She pushed her cumquat so it swung again and something in her face tightened, but she didn't falter from answering. 'There was such hate,' she said softly. 'Angus said his brothers hated him from the start, and Kenneth obviously felt the same about Rory. Rory travelled to the States to get away from it. He met me and he didn't even tell me about the family fortune. But, of course, it was still entailed. Rory was still going to inherit and Kenneth wanted it. Enough...enough to kill. Then, when he was...found out...he killed himself.'

'Which is where I come in,' he said softly, trying to deflect the anguish she couldn't disguise.

She took a deep breath. 'Which is where you come in,' she said and turned to face him. 'Welcome to Loganaich Castle, my lord,' she said simply. 'I hope you'll deal with your inheritance with Angus's dignity. And I hope the hate stops now.'

'I hope you'll help me.'

'I'm going home,' she told him. 'I've had enough of...of

whatever is here. It's your inheritance. Rory and Angus have left me enough money to keep me more than comfortable. I'm leaving you to it.'

CHAPTER TWO

THIS was where he took over, Hamish thought. This was where he said, *Thank you very much, can I have the keys?*

The whole thing was preposterous. He should never have let Jodie insinuate her crazy ideas into his mind.

The thought of being left alone with his very own castle was almost scary.

'Let's not do anything hasty,' he told Susie. 'I'll get a bed for the night in town, and we'll sit down and work things out in the morning.'

'You're not staying here?' she asked, startled.

'This has been your home,' he said. 'I'm not kicking you out.'

'We do have fourteen bedrooms.'

He hesitated. 'How do you know I'm not like Kenneth?'

She met his gaze and held. 'You're not like Kenneth. I can see.' She bit her lip and turned back to concentrate on her cumquat. 'Bitterness leaves its mark.'

'It's not fair that I inherit—'

'Angus and Rory between them left me all I need, thank you very much,' she said, and there was now a trace of anger in her voice. 'No one owes me anything. I'm not due for anything, and I don't care about fairness or unfairness in terms of inheritance. Thinking like that has to stop. I have a profession and I'll return to it. To kill for money…'

'But if your baby had been a boy he would have inherited,' he said softly. 'It's unjust.'

'You think that bothers me?'

'I'm sure it doesn't.'

'Fine,' she said flatly. 'So that's settled. You needn't worry. The escutcheon is firmly fixed in the male line, so there's no point in me stabbing you in the middle of the night or putting arsenic in your porridge.'

'Toast,' he said. 'I don't eat porridge.'

She blinked. This conversation was crazy.

But maybe that was the way to go. She'd had enough of being serious. 'You don't eat porridge?' she demanded, mock horrified. 'What sort of a laird are you?'

'I'm not a laird.'

'Oh, yes, you are,' she said, starting to smile. 'Or you probably are. Fancy clothes or not, you have definite laird potential.'

'I thought I was an earl?'

'You're that, too,' she told him. 'And of course you'll stay that as long as you live. But being laird is a much bigger responsibility.'

'I don't even know what a laird is.'

'The term's not used so much any more,' she said. 'It means a landed proprietor. But it's more than that. It's one who holds the dignity of an estate. Angus was absolutely a laird. I'm not sure what sort of laird Rory would have made. Kenneth would never have been one. But you, Hamish Douglas? Will you make a laird?'

'That sounds like a challenge,' he said, and she jutted her chin a little and met his look head on.

'Maybe it is.'

He hesitated, not sure where to take this. Not at all sure that she wasn't just a little crazy herself. 'Maybe I'd best stay in town,' he said. 'I'll come back in the morning to organise things.'

'There's not much to organise,' she told him. 'But you need to stay here. There's only the Black Stump pub, and Thursday is darts night. There's no sleep to be had in the Black Stump before three in the morning. Anyway, if anyone moves out it should be me. It's your home now. Not mine.'

'But you will stay,' he said urgently. 'I need to learn about the place.'

'What do you intend to do with it?'

There was only one answer to that. 'Sell.'

Her face stilled. 'Can you do that?'

'I've checked.' Actually, Marcia had checked. 'If I put the money into trust, then, yes.' The capital needed to stay intact but the interest alone—plus the rent rolls from the land in Scotland—would keep him wealthy even without his own money.

'You don't need me to help you sell it,' she snapped, and then bit her lip. 'I'm sorry. I know selling seems sensible but…but…'

She took a deep breath, and suddenly her voice was laced with emotion—and pain. 'I'll stay tonight. Tomorrow I'll pack and go stay with my sister until I can arrange a flight home.'

'Susie, there's no need—'

'There is a need,' she said, and suddenly her voice sounded almost desperate.

'But why?'

'Because I keep falling in love,' she snapped, the desperation intensifying. 'I fell so far into love with Rory that his death broke my heart. I fell for Angus. And now I've fallen for your stupid castle, for your dumb suits of armour—they're called Eric and Ernst, by the way, and they like people chatting to them—for your stupid compost system, which is second to none in the entire history of the western world—I've even fallen for your worms. I keep breaking my heart and I'm not going to do it any more. I'm going home to the States and I'm going back to landscape gardening and Rose and I are going to live happily ever after. Now, if you'll excuse me, I need to finish my work. Bring your gear in. You can have any bedroom you like upstairs. The whole top floor is yours. Rose and I are downstairs. But I need to do some fast digging before Rose wakes from her nap. Dinner's at seven and there's plenty to spare. I'll see you in the kitchen.'

And without another word she brushed past him, out of the conservatory and back into the brilliant autumn sunshine. She grabbed her spade she'd left leaning against the fence and headed off the way they'd come. Her back was stiff and set—her spade was over her shoulder like a soldier carrying a gun—she looked the picture of determination.

But he wasn't fooled.

He'd seen the glimmer of unshed tears as she'd turned away—and as she reached the garden gate she started, stiffly, to run.

'Kirsty, he's here. The new owner.'

Susie had been crying. Kirsty could hear it in her voice, and her heart stilled.

'Sweetheart, is he horrid? Is he another Kenneth? I'll be right there.'

'I don't need you to come.' There was an audible sniff.

'Then what's wrong?'

'He's going to sell.'

Susie's sister paused. She'd known this would happen. It was inevitable. But somehow…somehow she'd hoped…

Susie had come so far. Dreadfully injured in the engineered car crash which had killed her husband, Susie had drifted into a depression so deep it had been almost crippling. But with this place, with her love for the old earl, with her love for the wonderful castle garden and her enchantment with her baby daughter, she'd been hauled back from the brink. For the last few months she'd been back to the old Susie, laughing, bossy, full of plans…

Angus's death had been expected, a peaceful end to a long and happy life, but Kirsty knew that her twin hadn't accepted it yet. Hadn't moved on.

Kirsty was a doctor, and she'd seen this before. Loving and caring for someone to the end, watching them fade but never really coming to terms with the reality that the end meant the end.

'So…' she said at last, cautiously, and Susie hiccuped back a sob.

'I'm going home. Back to the States. Tomorrow.'

'Um… I suspect you won't be able to get travel papers for Rose by tomorrow.'

'I have a passport for her already. There are only a couple of last-minute documents I need to organise. Can I come and stay with you and Jake until then?'

'Sure,' Kirsty said uneasily, mentally organising her house

to accommodate guests. They were extending the back of the house to make a bigger bedroom for the twins—and for the new little one she hadn't quite got round to telling her sister about—but they'd squash in somehow. 'But why? What's he like?'

'He's gorgeous.'

Silence.

'I…see.' Kirsty turned thoughtful. 'So why do you want to come and stay at our house? Don't you trust yourself?'

'It's not like that.'

'No?'

'No,' Susie snapped. 'It's just… He's not like Rory and he's not like Angus and I can't bear him to be here. Just—owning everything. He doesn't even know about compost. I said we had the best compost system in the world and he looked at me like I was talking Swahili.'

'Normal, in fact.'

'He's not normal. He wears cream suede shoes.'

'Right.'

'Don't laugh at me, Kirsty Cameron.'

'When have I ever laughed at you?'

'All the time. Can I come and stay?'

'Not tonight. Tomorrow I'll air one of the new rooms and see if I can get the paint fumes out. You can surely bear to stay with him one night. Or…would you like me to come and stay with you?'

'No. I mean…well, he offered to stay at the pub so he must be safe enough. I said he could stay.'

'Would you like to borrow Boris?'

'Fat lot of good Boris would be as a guard dog.'

'He's looked after us before,' Kirsty said with dignity. OK, Boris was a lanky, misbred, over-boisterous dog, but he'd proved a godsend in the past.

Faint laughter returned to her sister's voice at that. 'He did. He's wonderful. But I'm fine. I'll feed Lord Hamish Douglas and give him a bed tonight and then I'll leave him to his own devices.' The smile died from her words. 'Oh, but, Kirsty, to see him sell the castle…I don't see how I can bear it.'

* * *

The castle was stunning.

While Susie finished her gardening Hamish took the opportunity to explore. And he was stunned.

It was an amazing, over-the-top mixture of grandeur and kitsch. The old earl hadn't stinted when it came to building a castle as a castle ought to be built—to last five hundred years or more. But into his grand building he'd put furnishings that were anything but grand. Hamish had an Aunt Molly who'd love this stuff. He thought of Molly as he winced at the truly horrible plastic chandeliers hung along the passageways, at the plastic plants in plastic urns, at the cheap gilt Louis XIV tables and chairs, and at the settees with bright gold crocodile legs. It was so awful it was brilliant.

Then he opened the bathroom door and Queen Victoria gazed down at him in blatant disapproval from behind an aspidistra. He burst out laughing but he closed the door fast. A man couldn't do what a man had to do under that gaze. He'd have to find another bathroom or head to the pub.

More exploring.

He found another bathroom, this one fitted with a chandelier so large it almost edged out the door. The portrait here was of Henry the Eighth. OK. He could live with Henry. He found five empty bedrooms and chose one with a vast four-poster bed and a view of the ocean that took his breath away.

He decided staying here was possible.

Susie was still digging in the garden below. He watched her for a minute—and went back to thinking. Staying here was fraught with difficulties.

What had she said? She'd fallen in love with a castle, a compost bin, the worms she was digging out of the mud right now.

She'd cried.

The set look of her shoulders said she might still be crying.

He didn't do tears.

The smile he'd had on his face since he'd met Queen Victoria faded. He put Susie's emotion carefully away from him.

He sorted his gear, hanging shirts neatly, jackets neatly,

lining up shoes. He had enough clothes to last him a week. Otherwise he'd have to find a laundry.

Marcia called him a control freak. Marcia was right.

Almost involuntarily, he crossed to the window again. Susie was digging with almost ferocious intensity, taking out her pain on the mud. He saw her pause and wipe her overalled arm across her eyes.

She was crying.

He should stay at the pub. Darts or not.

That was dumb. Fleeing emotion? What sort of laird did that make him?

He owned this pile. He was Lord Hamish Douglas. Ridiculous! If his mother knew what was happening she'd cry, too, he thought, and then winced.

Too many tears!

For the first part of his life tears had been all he'd known. When he'd been three his father had suicided. That was his first memory. Too many women, too many tears, endless sobbing…

The tears hadn't stopped. His mother had held her husband's death to her heart—over his head—for the rest of her life. She held it still.

Her voice came back to him in all its pathos.

'Wash your knees, Hamish. Your father would hate it if he saw his son with grubby knees. Oh, I can't bear it that he can't be here to see.'

Tears.

'Do your homework, Hamish. Oh, if you fail…'

Tears.

Or, as he'd shown no signs of failing, 'Your father would be so proud…' And the sobbing would continue. Endlessly. His mother, her friends, his aunts.

There'd been tears every day of his life until he'd broken away, fiercely, among floods of recriminations—and more tears—and made his own life. He'd taken a job in Manhattan, far away from his Californian home. Far from the tears.

He hated the crying—the endless emotion. Hated it! His job now was an oasis of calm, where emotions were the last thing he needed. Marcia was cool, calm and self-contained. Nary a tear. That was his life.

He shouldn't have come, he thought. This title thing was ridiculous. He'd never use it. Marcia thought it was great and if she wanted to use the 'Lady' bit then that was fine by him.

Marcia would never cry.

He'd call her, he decided, retrieving his cell phone. Manhattan was sixteen hours behind here. Four in the afternoon here made it midnight back home. Marcia would be in bed, reading the long-winded legal briefs she read as avidly as some read crime novels.

She answered on the first ring. 'Hamish. Fabulous. You're there, then. Should I address you as Lord Douglas?'

'Cut it out, Marcia,' he said uncomfortably, and she backed off in an instant. That was the great thing about Marcia. She never intruded on his personal space.

'I'm sorry. Did you have a good journey?'

'Fine, thank you.'

There was a moment's pause. Marcia was expecting him to say something else, he knew, but he was still watching Susie under his window. Susie was digging as if her life depended on it.

'What's it like?' Marcia said eventually, all patience. 'The castle?'

'Crazy. Queen Victoria's in my bathroom.'

'Who?'

'Queen Vic. It's OK. I've changed to one with Henry the Eighth.'

'What are you talking about?'

'Portraits in the bathroom. The place is full of kitsch. Queen Victoria is a trifle…distracting.'

'Oh.' She sounded annoyed. 'For heaven's sake, Hamish, just take it down.'

That'd be sensible, he thought. He'd take all the portraits down. He'd send them to his Aunty Molly. As soon as Susie left.

'Was there anyone there to meet you?'

'Rory Douglas's widow. The lawyer told us about Rory Douglas.'

'He did,' she said, and he could hear her leafing through documents till she found what she wanted. 'I've got the letter here. He was murdered by his brother, which is why you inherited. What's she like?'

'Emotional.'

'A lachrymose widow,' she said with instant sympathy. 'My poor Hamish, how awful. Will she be hard to move?'

'What do you mean?'

'If she's been living there…she's not a tenant for life or anything, is she? You can still sell?'

'She offered to move out tonight.'

'That's great!'

'I can hardly kick her out tonight,' he said and heard her regroup.

'Well, of course not. Will you need to use some of the inheritance to resettle her, do you think? Does she have somewhere to go?'

'She's American. She's coming home.'

'Not entirely silly, then,' Marcia said with approval. 'She has plans. What about you? How long do you think it'll take to put the place on the market?'

'I'll paint a "For Sale" sign on the gate tomorrow.'

'Be serious,' she told him. 'Hamish, this is a lot of money. If the place is full of kitsch you'd best clean it out so it doesn't put potential buyers off. Will it sell as a potential hotel?'

That much he knew. 'Yes.'

'Then there are specialist realtors. International hotel dealers. I'll get back to you with names.'

'Fine.'

Was it fine?

Of course it was fine. What Marcia suggested was sensible.

He thought about posting Queen Victoria to his Aunt Molly.

He watched Susie.

'Steak and chips.'

Hamish had only partly opened the kitchen door when Susie's voice announced the menu. He blinked, gazing around the room in something approaching awe. This room was built to feed an army. It had huge overhead beams, a wonderful flag-stoned floor, an efficient gas range, as well as an old-fashioned slow combustion stove.

'How do you like your steak?' she demanded.

She was being brisk. She wasn't crying. Emotion had been put on the backburner, and she was being fiercely efficient.

'Medium rare,' he said, and she smiled.

'Great.' Then her smile faded, just a little. 'Medium rare, eh?'

'Is that a problem?'

'It might be,' she said cautiously. 'It depends.'

'On what?'

'On how it turns out. I was planning on beans on toast before you arrived. Much more dependable.'

'You know where you are with a bean,' he agreed, and she looked at him with suspicion.

'Don't you give me a hard time. Kirsty's bad enough.'

'Kirsty?'

'My sister. She and her husband are the local doctors. Kirsty said I have to give you something good to celebrate your first night here. She dropped off the steaks a few minutes ago. She would have stayed to meet you but she has evening clinic and was in a rush. But she left Boris, just in case you turn nasty.'

Boris was—apparently—a nondescript, brownish dog of the Heinz variety who was currently lying under a high chair. A toddler—a little girl about a year old—was waving a rusk above the dog's head, and the dog had immolated himself, upside down, all legs in the air, waiting with eternal patience for the rusk to drop.

The dog hadn't so much as looked up as Hamish had entered. Every fibre of his being was tuned to the rusk. Some guard dog!

'What will Boris do if I turn nasty?' he asked, and Susie grinned.

'He'll think of something. He's a very resourceful dog.' She produced a frying-pan and then looked doubtfully at the steaks.

The steaks lay in all their glory on a plate by the stove. They looked magnificent.

'How are you planning on cooking them?' Hamish asked.

'I'll fry them,' she said with a vague attempt at confidence. 'That doesn't sound too difficult.'

'You're cooking chips?'

'They're oven fries,' she confessed. 'Kirsty brought them as well. You put them in the oven, you set the timer for twenty minutes and you take them out again. Even I can't mess that up. Probably.'

She was making a huge effort to be cheerful, he thought, and he'd try to join her.

'Tell me you're not responsible for Queen Victoria,' he said and she grinned. She had a great grin, he thought. He was reminded suddenly of Jodie.

Jodie would love Loganaich Castle.

'Aunty Deirdre is responsible for Queen Vic,' Susie told him. 'Angus gave her carte blanche to decorate the castle as she saw fit—but he also gave her a very small budget. I think she did great.'

'She surely did,' he said faintly. Susie brushed past him on her way to the fridge and he started feeling even more disoriented. She'd showered since he'd last seen her. Or since he'd last smelt her. She was wearing clean jeans and a soft pink T-shirt, tucked in. Her hair was still in a ponytail but it was almost controlled now. And she smelt like citrus. Fresh and lemony. Nice.

'Mama,' the little girl said. 'Mama.'

'Sweetheart,' Susie said, and that was enough to slam reality home. His mother always called him 'sweetheart' when she was trying to manipulate him.

He stopped thinking how nice she smelt, and thought instead how great it was that he had his Marcia and his whole life controlled, and he'd never have to cope with this sort of messy tearful existence.

Susie was carrying a tub of dripping to the stove. She scooped out a tablespoon or more into the frying pan. Then looked at it. Dubiously.

'What are you doing?' he said faintly, and she raised her eyebrows as if he'd said something stupid.

'Cooking.'

'Deep frying or shallow frying?'

'Is there a difference?

He sighed. 'Yes. But with that amount of fat in the pan you're doing neither. The chips are already in the oven?'

'Yes.'

'How long have they been in?'

'Five minutes.'

'How do you have your steak?'

'Any way I can get it.'

'Then you'll have it medium rare as well, and I have five minutes before I start cooking. Can you find me an apron?'

'You're kidding.'

'No.'

'Gee,' she said, stunned, but willing not only to hand over cooking but to be admiring while she was at it. 'You really can cook?'

'I can cook steak.'

'Would you like to make a salad, too?' Her voice said she knew she was pushing her luck. It was almost teasing. 'I can mix up chopped lettuce and tomato but anything else is problematic.'

He sighed. 'I can make a salad. But I do need an apron.'

'An apron,' she said, as if she'd never heard of such a thing.

'Something to cover—'

'I know what an apron is,' she said with dignity. She looked down at her faded, work-worn clothes. 'I just never use one. But I'll bet that Deirdre was an apron lady.'

She turned and searched a capacious drawer by the door. 'Hey!' She held up something that took Hamish's breath away. Bright pink with purple roses, bib and skirt, the garment had flounces all round the edge and a huge pink ribbon at the back. 'Good old Deirdre,' Susie said in satisfaction. 'I knew she wouldn't let me down. You'll look great in this.'

Yeah, right. He could just see the next front page of the *Financial Review*. There were guys back home who'd kill to see this, and he was well known enough to hit the social pages of the tabloids.

He eyed Susie in suspicion. Mobile phones could also be cameras. If you wore an apron like this, you trusted no one.

'You have a washing machine?' he demanded, trying not to sound desperate.

'I have a washing machine.'

'Then I'll make do without the apron.' Some things were no-brainers. 'Just this once.'

'That's big of you,' she told him, laying the frills aside with regret. 'Why are you tipping out the dripping?'

'That was half an inch of fat, and if you thing I'm spoiling my first Australian steak, you have another think coming.'

'Ooh,' she said in mock admiration. 'Bossy as well as a good cook.'

'Watch your fries,' he told her, disconcerted.

'Hey, we'll get on fine,' she said happily. 'You can cook. I can't. A marriage made in heaven.'

Then she realised what she'd said and she blushed. The blush started from her eyes and moved out, and he thought, She's lovely. She's just gorgeous.

Rose chortled from her high chair and Hamish allowed himself to be distracted. He needed to be distracted. Whew!

Rose was a chubby toddler, dressed only in a nappy and a grubby T-shirt reading MY AUNTY WENT TO NEW YORK AND ALL SHE BROUGHT ME WAS ONE LOUSY T-SHIRT. She had flame-coloured curls, just like her mother, and huge green eyes that gazed at him as if expecting to be vastly entertained.

It was very disconcerting to be gazed at like that. He'd never been gazed at like that.

In truth, Hamish had never met a toddler.

This situation was getting out of hand.

Rosie chortled again, raised her hand and lifted her rusk. It fell. On the floor beneath, on his back, Boris did a fast, curving slide so his mouth was right where it needed to be. The rusk disappeared without a trace.

Rose and her mother—and Hamish—all gazed at Boris. Boris gazed back up at Rose in adoration, and then opened his mouth wide again.

Hamish laughed.

Susie stared.

'What?' he said, disconcerted, and she flushed and turned away.

'N-nothing.'

'Something.'

'It's just… For a minute…' She took a deep breath. 'The Douglas men,' she said. 'Angus and Rory had the same laugh. Low and rumbly and nice. And it's here again. In this kitchen. Where it belongs.'

For a moment neither of them spoke. Did she know what power she had to move him? he wondered.

He'd never known his father. Oh, he had a vague memory of someone being there, a grey, silent, ghost-like presence, but that was all. He'd seen faded photographs of a man who didn't look like him. He had no connection at all.

And suddenly he did.

He didn't do emotion.

'I'm hardly a Douglas,' he said, more sharply than he'd intended. 'My father died when I was three, and I've had no contact with anyone but my mother's family.'

'But you *are* a Douglas.'

'In name only.'

'You don't want to be a Douglas?'

Not if it means all this emotion, he thought, but he didn't say it.

'Move over,' he told her instead. 'It's time to put the steak on. Four minutes either side, which gives me time to whip up a salad. But there's no time for idle chat.'

'You don't do idle chat?'

'No.'

'I'll concentrate on my chips, then,' she told him, and proceeded to sit on the floor, flick on the oven light and watch. Which was distracting all on its own. 'I know when to butt out where I'm not wanted.'

'I didn't mean to be rude.'

'Neither did I,' she told him. 'But maybe that's the way we

have to be. You don't want to be a Douglas. I can't bear to be near one. So let's get tonight over with and then we can both move on in the direction we intend to go.'

CHAPTER THREE

She woke to singing.

She must be dreaming, she decided, and closed her eyes but a moment later she opened them again.

"'I'll be true to the song I sing. And live and die a pirate king.'"

It was a rich, deep baritone, wafting in from the window out to the garden. Straight out of Gilbert and Sullivan.

Hamish?

It was early. Too early. She'd had trouble getting to sleep. Rosie was still soundly sleeping and she didn't have to get up yet. She didn't want to get up yet.

She closed her eyes.

"'It is, it is a glorious thing, to be a pirate king.'"

She opened one eye and looked at her clock.

Six a.m.

The man was mad, she decided. Singing in the vegetable garden at six in the morning.

It was a great voice.

OK, she'd just look. She rolled out of bed, crawled across the floor under the level of the sill, then raised herself cautiously so she was just peeking…

He was digging her path. *Her* path!

The window was open and the curtains were drawn. Before she'd even thought logically, she'd shoved her hands on the sill and swung herself out. 'What do you think you're doing?'

Hamish paused in mid-dig. He was wearing shorts. And boots.

Nothing else.

This wasn't a stockbroker's body, Susie thought as he set down his spade and decided what to say. The man had a serious six-pack. He was tanned and muscled—as if he'd spent half his life on a farm rather than in a stockbroker's office.

He had great legs.

Oh, for heaven's sake…

'Whose boots are they?' she demanded, and then thought, What a ridiculous question to ask. But the boots were decrepit—surely not carefully brought over from New York.

'I found them in the wet room,' he told her, looking like he was trying not smile. 'There's a whole pile. I figured if I inherited the castle with contents included, then at least one lot of boots must be mine. They're a size or two big but I'm wearing two pairs of socks. What do you think? Will I take Manhattan by storm?' He raised a knee to hold up a boot for inspection.

Boris had been supervising the path-digging lying down. Now the big dog rose, put out a tongue and licked the specified boot. Just tasting…

It was such a ridiculous statement—such a ridiculous situation—that Susie started to giggle.

Then she suddenly thought about what she was wearing and stopped giggling. Maybe she should hop right back in through the window.

But he'd already noticed. 'Nice elephants,' he said politely.

And she thought, Yep, the window was a good idea. She was wearing a pair of short—very short—boxer-type pyjama bottoms and a top that matched. Purple satin with yellow and crimson elephants.

There was a story behind these elephants. Susie's two little step-nieces had wanted pyjamas with elephants on them. Harriet from the post office had been in Sydney for a week to visit an ailing sister and had thus been commissioned to find pyjama material with elephants. What she'd found had been royal purple satin with yellow and red elephants—the lot going much cheaper by the roll. Harriet had been so pleased that she'd bought the entire roll, and every second person in Dolphin Bay was now sporting elephant-covered nightwear.

'They're home-made,' Susie managed. 'I know the seamstress.' She managed a smile and Hamish thought—not for the first time—what a lovely smile she had. 'She'll make you some too if you like.'

'No, thank you,' he said hurriedly, and she grinned.

'You could really take New York by storm with these.'

'I don't think Manhattan is ready for those pyjamas.'

There was a silence. She was trying not to look at his six-pack. He looked like he was trying not to look at her pyjamas.

'What are you doing?' she asked, as much to break the silence as anything. Though it was obvious.

The garden was in the full fruit of late autumn. The fruit trees were laden. The lavender hedge was alive with early-morning bees, everything was neat and shipshape, and the only discordant note was the path she'd started digging. She'd dug the first twenty yards. Twenty yards had taken her two days.

Hamish had dug another fifteen.

'I assume you wanted the rest dug,' he told her.

She bit her lip. 'I did. It's just…'

'I've put the soil in the compost area,' he told her, guessing her qualms. 'I've left it separate so you can mix it as you want.'

One question answered.

'And the worms are in the yellow bucket,' he told her, answering her second.

He was laughing at her! He'd done what represented over a day's work. She should be grateful. She was grateful! But he was laughing.

'Worms are important,' she said defensively, and he nodded.

'I've always thought so. But not the kind that come out of your eyeballs.'

'There's no need to mock.'

'I'm not mocking.'

More silence.

'You don't get muscles like those sitting behind a desk,' she said tentatively. She felt she shouldn't mention those muscles—but she was unable to stop looking at them.

'I work out.'

'You use a gym?'

'There's a gym in the building where I live.'

Of course. More silence while she tried again not to concentrate on muscles.

Oh, OK, she'd look. Guys looked at good-looking women all the time. She could do a little payback.

'So I'm not doing the wrong thing?' he prompted when the silence got a bit stretched—and she hauled her thoughts together and tried to think what she ought to be saying. What she should be looking at.

'Of—of course you're not. I'm very grateful.'

'What are you planning on doing once you've dug?'

'I have a pile of pavers under the lemon tree.' She pointed. 'There.'

He looked. And winced. 'They look like they weigh a ton. You were going to lay them yourself?'

'Of course I was.'

'But you've been injured,' he said. 'The lawyer told me—'

'I'm fine.'

'You limp.'

'I don't limp much. I'm fine.' She took a deep breath, moving on. 'Not that it matters. They're your pavers now.'

'Susie, do you have to leave so soon?'

'I…'

'I'm here for three weeks,' he said urgently. 'I had a phone call this morning from the States. That's why I'm up early. A combination of jet-lag and a phone call at four. The best way to sell this place—'

Do I want to hear this? Susie thought, but she hardly had a choice.

'—is via a realtor who specialises in selling exclusive country hotels. He comes, assesses potential, and if he likes what he sees then he'll put this place on his list of vendors and promote the place internationally. He'll be in Australia next week. Marcia thinks I should persuade you to stay till then.'

Marcia? Susie wondered, but she didn't ask.

'Why do you want me to stay?'

'You know the history of the place. The agent holds that important. If people come to an exclusive location they want the personal touch. They'll want to know about Angus and the family and the castle back in Scotland. All its history.'

'I'll write it out for you.'

'I'll sell the place for more if you're here to give a guided tour,' Hamish said flatly. 'Widow of the incumbent earl's heir...'

'If you think you're going to play on Rory's murder to get your *atmosphere*—'

'I didn't say that.'

'You didn't need to,' she told him, and glowered.

'But will you stay? I'll pay you.'

'Why will you pay me?'

'Well...' He considered. 'You could still pave the garden.' He eyed her, assessing and guessing her weakness. 'You would like to get this path finished.'

'I would,' she admitted, and bit her lip.

'Then I'm happy to pay landscape gardening hourly rates. Think about it,' he said—and went right back to digging. Leaving her to think about it.

Which slightly discomposed her. She'd expected more...argument?

Staying on here was dumb, she thought. More than dumb. She looked at Hamish's broad, bare back and she thought that staying could be unsettling. Would be unsettling. She hadn't looked at another man since Rory had died and, of course, she never would, but there was that about Hamish which made her very solid foundations seem just a little shaky round the edges.

She didn't want her foundations shaken. Her world had been shaken quite enough for one lifetime.

So she should go. Immediately.

But then...

She and Rose had lived here for over a year. She'd started

packing after Angus had died, but her efforts had been desultory to say the least. She needed to get organised. Today's deadline might not be actually feasible.

She thought about it for a bit more. She watched Hamish dig some more. He'd have blisters, she decided, seeing him almost inconspicuously shift the spade in his hands. She knew what he was doing. She'd done it herself often and often. He was finding unblistered skin to work with.

He was strong and willing but he wasn't accustomed to this sort of work. He was a Manhattan money-maker.

The locals would hate the idea of the new laird being such a man.

But that started more ideas forming. Hamish was asking a favour of her. Maybe she could ask one of him. Angus's death had left such a void. Maybe they could have a laird one last time, she thought. Maybe…

'I'll do it, but not for payment,' she called out, and he looked up, surprised, as if he hadn't expected to see her still to be there.

'You'll stay?'

'Yes.' She grinned. 'I'll even cook.'

'More fries?'

'I can do toast, too. And porridge if you're game.'

He smiled at that, and she thought, Yep, there it was again. The Douglas chuckle and the Douglas smile in a body that wasn't a Douglas body at all. It was a body she knew nothing about and wanted to know nothing about.

She had to get those foundations steady.

'I look forward to meeting your toast, but not your porridge, Mrs Douglas,' he told her formally, and she managed to smile back and then thought maybe smiling wasn't such a good idea. He didn't have enough clothes on. She didn't have enough clothes on. It was too early in the morning.

He was a Douglas!

'Tomorrow's the Dolphin Bay Harvest Thanksgiving fête,' she told him as he started digging again. 'We need a laird.'

'Pardon?' He bent to separate some worms and then dug a couple more spadefuls.

'The laird opens the fête. It's traditional. No one's doing it tomorrow because everyone's still mourning Angus. But not having anyone there will be awful. Maybe we should do it in stages. Maybe we could use you tomorrow as the last of the Douglases.'

His spade paused in mid air—and then kept digging. 'You know, I might not be the last of the Douglases,' he said cautiously. 'The Douglas clan appear to be quite prolific. In fact, if I give you the phone book you might find almost as many Douglases as Smiths, Greens and Nguyens.'

'No, but as far as I know you're the only Lord Douglas in this neck of the woods.'

'Which leaves me…where?'

'Opening the fête tomorrow.'

Another pause in the digging. Another resumption. 'Which involves what exactly?'

'Saying a few words. Just "I now declare this fête open". After the bagpipes stop.'

'Bagpipes,' he said, even more cautiously, and Susie thought the man wasn't as silly as he looked. Actually, he didn't look the least bit silly.

And he'd guessed where she was headed. She could see the suspicion growing and she almost giggled.

'It's a very nice kilt,' she said.

He set down his spade and turned to her in all seriousness.

'Don't ask it of me, Susie. I have knobbly knees.'

She did giggle then. 'I can see them from here. They're very nice knees.'

'I only show them to other Douglases.'

'Me, you mean.'

'You and my mother.'

'Not…Marcia?'

'Marcia has the sense not to look,' he told her. 'I'd never have exposed them to you but you woke unreasonably early. Normally I have huge signs out. CAUTION: EXPOSED KNEES. So that lets me out of fête opening.'

'Then I'm off to pack.'

'Susie, this is a business trip,' he said, and there was suddenly more than a trace of desperation in his voice. 'I'm not an earl. I'm not Lord Douglas. In this day and age it doesn't make any sense. I won't use the title. I'll sell the castle and I'll get back to my ordinary life.'

'You sound afraid,' she said, and he cast her a look that said she wasn't far off the mark.

'That's dumb. Why would I be afraid?'

'It's not so scary, standing in a kilt and saying a few words.'

'People will expect—'

'They'll expect nothing,' she said softly. 'The people here loved Uncle Angus. He was their laird. You won't know the story but this castle saved the town. After the war the men depended on the schools of couta to make their living—great long fish you catch by trawling in relatively shallow water. But some disease—worms, actually—hit the couta, and the men didn't have boats big enough for deep-sea fishing. Everyone was starting to leave. It was either leave or starve. But then along came Angus. He saw this place, fell in love with it and realised the only thing that could keep it going was another industry. So he persuaded the guardians of his family trust—your family trust—to let him rebuild his castle here. The men worked on the castle while they gradually rebuilt the fishing fleet. The people here loved Angus to bits and his death has caused real heartache. You wearing a kilt tomorrow—no, it won't bring Angus back, but maybe it'll fill a void that for many may seem unbearable.'

Emotion, Hamish thought. More emotion. But Susie's chin was tilted upward. She was defiant rather than lachrymose, throwing him a dare.

Open a fête…

It was a dumb, emotional thing to do. It had no foundation in logic and he should run a mile.

'Why are you digging my path?' she asked.

'I was bored.'

'What are you going to do until this assessor gets here?'

'I'll go through the castle books.' I'll get rid of some kitsch, he thought, but he didn't say it. Marcia was researching a place where he could hire some decent antiques to make the place look firstclass.

Maybe Queen Vic could stay…

Queen Vic was in a plastic gilt frame. She'd been a cheap print and was a bit frayed around the edges. Keeping Queen Vic would be a dumb, emotional decision and he needed to stay tight here.

'The castle books are in the hands of the executors,' Susie told him. 'Mr O'Shannasy's the local solicitor but his office is always closed Fridays. That means you can't start work until Monday. Which leaves the weekend free for fair opening.'

'I have a path to dig.'

'It's my path,' she said, almost belligerently, and then stopped. 'I mean…'

No emotion. 'It's your path until you leave,' he said hurriedly.

'Which is today unless you open the fête.'

'Why is it so important?'

'I just don't want the stage to be empty.'

'It's a sentimental gesture.'

'What's wrong with that?'

'I'm a businessman.'

'You can be a businessman again when you leave here. Be Lord Douglas for a bit. It's your title. Enjoy it.'

'I would have thought lords enjoy themselves by…I don't know, holding lavish banquets. Driving Lamborghinis.'

'You can have porridge and toast for breakfast. We'll put marmalade on top of the toast, banana on top of the porridge, and call it a banquet. And I'll drive you to the fête in Angus's old Ford. It has four wheels, same as a Lamborghini. What's your problem?'

'I don't have a kilt,' he said, backed against a figurative wall but still fighting.

'No.' Her face grew thoughtful. 'And Angus's would be too small. He was a much shorter man.' She hesitated. He saw the telltale wash of emotion cross her face and he flinched. But she had hold of herself again. 'My husband used to come here often before…before he went overseas and we were married. Angus had a kilt made for him from the family tartan. You're almost the same size.'

Great. He'd go to a fête wearing the kilt of this woman's dead husband.

But she'd read his expression.

'I'm not asking for sympathy here,' she told him, and there was suddenly anger flooding her voice. 'You can stop looking as if you're expecting me to burst into tears and tell you you're just like my Rory.'

'I never…'

He had.

'I don't need you,' she snapped.

'Of course you don't need me.'

'It's just the town…so many of the old people…they'll come tomorrow, and Angus has only been dead for a few weeks, and they'll see the empty stage and it'll stay with them and spoil their fête. If you get up in your kilt and open the thing and wander round for a bit and don't tell people you're selling, just say you're not exactly sure what's happening, then the locals will have a splendid talking point instead of a focus for grief. The fête was threatening to be dismal. You have it in your power to retrieve things.'

'I don't want—'

'You want what's right for the castle,' she snapped. 'You want the best monetary outcome. You told me yourself you can get that if I stay on until the assessor comes. So use your head and not your heart, Hamish Douglas. Where's the sense in refusing?'

She had a point. But…

'I don't think I want to,' he said weakly, and she cast him a look that contained pure triumph. She had him and she knew it.

'I'll go look out the kilt,' she told him. 'You're skinnier than Rory. We may need to adjust it. And quit the digging. You have more blisters than you need already. Breakfast in half an hour?'

'Er…yes.'

'The first of your many banquets here, my lord,' she told him. She grinned—and went to find her lord a kilt.

* * *

'He's like a fish out of water.'

Actually, he was in water. Hamish was in the shower. His bathroom was right above Susie's and as she'd dialled her sister's number he'd started singing. The Pirate King was being given another airing, and a good one. 'He's here to make money out of the place,' she told Kirsty. 'He's going to sell. I should hate him but…' She hesitated. 'It's like he's some big New York financier but there's someone else underneath.'

'Someone nice?'

'He sings,' Susie explained, and held the receiver out so Kirsty could hear.

'Um…great,' Kirsty said, back on the line after a moment's bemused listening. 'There's lots of testosterone in that there baritone. Are you interested?'

Some questions were dumb. 'Why would I be interested?' Susie demanded. 'Anyway, I'm just ringing to tell you that you can come and take your dog back. I'm quite safe. And he's agreed to open the fête tomorrow.'

'He's agreed…' There was a moment's stunned silence and then something that sounded like a sniff from the other end of the line. 'He's opening the fête? Wearing the Douglas tartan?'

'Wearing the Douglas tartan.'

'Oh, Susie…'

'You won't weep on him, will you?' Susie asked, becoming nervous, and Kirsty sniffed again.

'No, but everyone else will.'

'They'd better not. He'll run.'

'Once he's opened the fête he can run all he wants,' Kirsty said directly. 'That empty stage was going to seem awful. But for the opening to go to another Douglas… It'll almost seem like a happy ending.'

'Yeah, well it's not,' Susie said, suddenly breathless. 'Or…well, I guess it is an ending and it's better than it might be. This'll be something like closure.'

'But he's really nice?' Kirsty demanded, and Susie flushed. She was Kirsty's twin and she knew where her sister's thoughts were headed, often before Kirsty did. She knew where they were headed now, and she had no wish to go there.

'My daughter is attempting to climb onto the back of your dog,' she told her sister with what she hoped was dignity. 'I need to go.'

And she replaced the receiver on any more conjecture.

Things were formal at breakfast. Hamish was dressed again as he might dress for a casual stroll down Fifth Avenue. Understated. Expensive. Cool.

Susie had dressed in shorts and a T-shirt which stayed pristine until she gave Rose her first piece of toast and Rose gave it back. She was therefore decorated with a raspberry streak centre front. Not so cool.

No matter. There was a small glitch when Hamish refused porridge. Susie thought this was one of the few things she could cook—and what sort of a Douglas was he if he didn't eat porridge?—but she finally decided magnanimously to overlook it. They ate their toast with only social pleasantries expressed between mouthfuls.

Hamish appeared not to notice Rosie and Boris doing their best to make him laugh. He didn't comment on Susie's raspberry streak. He appeared to have switched into another mode, one where he was polite and courteous but otherwise remote.

Fine. She could handle this, she decided.

A non-porridge-eating Douglas.

They finished eating. Susie wiped off her small daughter. Then, somewhat at a loss, she offered a full tour and her offer was accepted.

This was good, Susie thought as she led the way through the castle. She carried Rose, Boris following behind as she opened room after room and explained the contents. Formality would get them through the next few days. It was only when Hamish stopped being polite and grinned that her insides started doing funny things.

'This is bedroom number seven…'

'I saw this yesterday,' Hamish said politely. 'All by myself.'

'You looked through the bedrooms by yourself?'

'I was choosing one. You told me I could. Any on the first floor.'

'They're your bedrooms,' she said, and flushed. 'Am I boring you?'

'It's a very nice castle.'

'I'm boring you.'

'What about the beach?' he asked. The sea was right out every north-facing window, tantalising with its sapphire shimmer.

'There's a track just over the road,' she told him. 'When the place is turned into a hotel you may need to build an inclinator. It's a bit steep.'

'But the track leads to the beach.'

'Yes.'

'A swimmable beach?'

'Very much so.'

'You're going to offer to show me?'

'You can find it yourself. You can scarcely miss it. Head north and when it feels wet you've reached the sea.'

'Do Boris and Rose like the sea?'

'I… Yes.' Keep it formal. Keep it formal.

'I'll go and see it by myself, then, shall I?'

'If you like.' Keep quiet, dummy.

'It's safe for swimming?'

'It's great for swimming.'

'I'll get changed then,' he said. 'I'll be back for lunch.'

Keep quiet. Keep quiet…

She couldn't keep quiet.

'I can't get down to the beach by myself,' she said, sense disappearing and desperation taking over.

This had been the hardest part of living here with Rose. With her weak legs, the track was too steep to negotiate carrying a baby, and to live so close and not have access almost killed her. She could only go to the beach when someone was there to help carry Rose. 'Not with…' Say it, she told herself. Say it. 'I—I have a b-bad leg,' she stammered.

He paused. He looked at her.

Formality took a slight backward step.

'You can't get down to the beach?'

'Not carrying Rose.'

'But you like the beach?'

'I love the beach. So does Boris and so does Rose. We all love it.'

'So if I carried Rose…'

To hell with formality. 'We could all go,' she said, enthusiasm taking over. 'I could pack a hamper. We could take an umbrella and a rug for Rose to snooze on when she gets tired.'

'How long are we staying?' he demanded, startled.

'Hours and hours,' she said happily. 'If I'm leaving this place for good in a few days, then I need all the sea I can get. When this place is a luxury hotel it'll be beyond my reach for the rest of my life.'

'So all I have to do is carry Rose.'

'And the hamper. And the picnic basket and rug. You may have to take two trips.'

'You're a manipulator.'

'The beach is worth it.'

CHAPTER FOUR

HE CARRIED the hamper, the beach umbrella and the rug down to the beach and left them there. Boris accompanied him, bounding down the track with the air of a dog about to meet canine heaven. When Hamish returned for the next load, Boris bounded up again, panting with expectancy, seeming as anxious as Susie was that his pseudo-mistress wasn't left behind. Susie was waiting, dressed in a pale lemon sarong, her arms full of Rose and Rose's necessities.

'Hamish will take us to the sea,' Susie told Rose, handing her over, and the little girl beamed, leaned over and wrapped her arms around Hamish's neck.

He froze. The feel of a baby's arms felt…weird. Really weird.

Hamish had never held a baby in his life and he'd expected it—her—to cry or at least hold herself rigid. Instead of which she clung happily to his neck and started crooning, 'Ee, ee, ee…'

'She hasn't quite got the hang of S,' Susie told him, and Rose giggled as if her mother had just made a wonderful joke.

'You're OK to get down yourself?' he asked, and Susie's smile turned to a glower in an instant.

'I've got down under worse conditions than this. Some I'll tell you about it. You take Rose and I'll follow.'

So he did, but he carried Rose slowly, not wanting to get too far ahead of Rose's mother, aware that the climb was a struggle for Susie and she hurt more than she admitted. He thought suddenly that what he really wanted to do was scoop her up in his arms and carry her down, but even if he hadn't been carrying her child he knew that she'd swipe away any such effort.

But finally they reached the sand. Boris was off chasing seagulls. The little cove was deserted. Susie lifted Rose from his arms and started undressing her—and Hamish had time to look around him and take stock.

He'd never seen a beach like this. It was a cove, sheltered from rough seas or winds by two rocky outcrops reaching three or four hundred yards from either side of the beach. The little cove was maybe two or three hundred yards long—no more. The sand was soft, golden and sun-warmed. There were two vast eucalypts somehow emerging from the base of the cliffs to throw dappled shade if you wanted to be in the shade. There were rock pools toward the end of the cove. The waves at one end of the cove were high enough to form low surf, but at the more sheltered end there were no waves at all. Here the water sloped out gently, making the sea a nursery pool to beat the finest nursery pool anyone could ever imagine.

'You see why I cracked and asked for help?' Susie asked. She was kneeling on the rug, removing Rosie's nappy and plastering her with sunblock. 'I can't bear not to be down here.'

'Why did you have to crack before you asked?'

She hesitated. 'I don't like to ask for help.'

'It's more than that, isn't it?' he said. 'You're afraid of me?'

'No. I…'

'What did my cousin do to you?'

'It's not that.'

'Tell me.'

She flinched. Carefully she replaced the tube of sunblock in her holdall and then set her naked daughter on the sand. Rose started crawling determinedly toward Boris. Seeing Boris was chasing gulls in circles, here was an occupation that was going to take some time.

Hamish waited, giving Susie space. Finally she sat back on her heels and gazed out to sea.

'They were both your cousins,' she whispered. 'Kenneth

and Rory. Kenneth killed Rory so he'd inherit all this—and when he discovered I was pregnant he tried to kill me as well. He hauled me and my twin, Kirsty, onto a boat right here in this cove and tried to drive us onto rocks.' She shivered but then gave a tentative smile. 'But we're tough. No one messes with the McMahon twins.'

'You're a twin?'

'Yep. And proud of it. Kirsty fell for the local doctor and they married last year. She now has two little stepdaughters and is fast becoming a local.'

'But you want to go home?'

'My life is in the States. It's time to get on with it. You either get on with life or you die,' she said simply. 'I was a mess for a while, but I've come out the other side.'

'So why are you afraid of me?'

'I'm not afraid.'

'I think you are.'

'Rose needs a swim,' she said, almost angrily. 'It's too good a day to mess with by talking about what's past.'

'I agree,' he told her. 'I could use a swim, too.'

'The wave end is better for swimming,' she told him. 'Rose and I use the end without waves.'

'Different ends. Now, how did I know you were going to say that?'

'Just swim,' she snapped. 'Enough with the psychoanalysis. This might be the last time I swim in this place and I intend to enjoy it.'

Susie spent the next hour in the shallows and she was aware of Hamish every single minute. She took Rosie up to her knees in water, then sat with the little girl on her lap while the wavelets washed over them. Rosie splashed and cooed and giggled and Susie giggled with her—but still she watched Hamish.

He was a strong swimmer, she decided. He used a clean, efficient stroke that said he'd been properly trained and he wasn't out of practice. He took no chances in an unknown environment, not going deeper than chest depth but stroking strongly from one end of the cove to the other and back again. When he wearied of swimming he bodysurfed, catching the white breakers with an ease that said he'd done this, too.

He was glorying in the water, in the sun and in the day just as much as she was, she thought. She watched his lithe body slicing through the water with something akin to jealousy. He looked free. He was free to live in this place if he wanted.

He didn't want. He intended to make money from it and leave.

Finally Rose started wearying. She curled into her mother's lap and snuggled and Susie struggled upright and carried her daughter up the beach to dry her off and give her lunch. She fed Rose and gave her a bottle.

While she fed her daughter Hamish still didn't come near. Instead he threw driftwood over and over into the waves for Boris. Boris would take as much of this as anyone would give him, and Hamish gave him a lot, but as Rose snuggled down and closed her eyes in satisfied sleep, Hamish came jogging up the beach to join them.

He looked fantastic, Susie thought. Wide shoulders tapering to narrow hips, not an ounce of spare flesh on him, his tanned skin coated in a fine mist of sand, his black curls flopping forward making him look almost endearing…

Cut it out! she told herself urgently. Get your hormones back where they belong.

'There are sandwiches here,' she managed. 'Rose and I have eaten. Would you like some?'

'Food!' He fell to his knees like a man who hadn't seen food for a week and as he bit into her sandwiches Susie had another of those…moments. Watching him enjoy the food she'd prepared… There was nothing sexy about it at all, she told herself crossly, but she knew that she lied.

'You swim well,' she told him, and if she sounded stiff and formal there wasn't a blind thing she could do about it.

'I was raised in California,' he told her. 'I'm an original beach bum. I've never seen a beach as good as this, though.'

'You're still tanned.'

'I have a penthouse with a sunroof. And a heated pool.'

Oh, of course.

'You're just a paddler?' he asked, polite as well.

She thought, Drat him. How dared he put her in this state of she didn't know what?

'I like swimming.'

'You weren't swimming,' he pointed out, and she flushed.

'Right, like I can swim when I have an attached fourteen-month-old.'

'You'd like to swim?' he asked, and she bit back another angry retort.

'I'm fine.'

'Rose is asleep. You could swim now.'

'I don't like leaving Rose on the beach by herself.'

'She's not by herself,' he said gently. 'She's with me.'

So she was. Her baby was soundly asleep. She wouldn't wake for a couple of hours. Hamish was offering her freedom, and she'd really, really like a swim.

But something was holding her back. Not distrust, exactly. More…

She couldn't put a finger on it.

'You can trust me,' he said, forcing her to try.

'I know.'

'You'll be able to see her all the time you're swimming. Go on, Susie, you know you'd love to.'

She would.

'What's stopping you?'

'Nothing.'

'Swim,' he told her. 'Or I'll lift you up and hurl you into the waves with my bare hands.'

'I'd like to see you try.'

'I wouldn't,' he confessed. 'I might have inherited a title, but Big Bad Sir Brian Blipping Villagers On the Head is a far cry from a wimpish stockbroker who values his back.'

It was only Hamish who was making her nervous. Swimming didn't.

Susie did this often, whenever Kirsty brought her twins over.

They'd take turns to play childminder while the other took off into deep water and gloried in the freedom the water allowed.

It did allow freedom. The car accident that had killed Rory had damaged Susie's spine. Slowly, slowly she was recovering from the damage it had caused but she wasn't free to walk and run as she'd like. Stiffness and residual pain held her back.

But in the water...

She'd always been better than Kirsty in the water. She'd captained her junior-high waterpolo team. She'd been selected to play for the state, and only the fact that her life had got busy had stopped her going further. But for Susie swimming was an extension of breathing.

Now she walked stiffly into the water, stood for one lovely, lingering, anticipatory moment—and then knifed forward into an oncoming wave.

Gorgeous. Just gorgeous. The moment she was through the breaker she felt her other life kick in, the life she'd known before the accident, before Rory's death, before motherhood. She was a girl again, free, her body whole and healthy and ready for whatever the day should bring.

It almost gave her the courage to face the future.

She turned to the beach and Hamish was watching. Even from here she could see that he was tense. He was sitting on the sand with Boris beside him. His arm was draped over the dog. Rosie was curled up close by, sound asleep in the shade, but Hamish was still in the sun. He should be lying on the sun-warmed sand and snoozing, she thought, but he was bolt upright, watching.

He was playing lifeguard, she thought suddenly, recognising his tension for what it was. If she got into trouble he'd be down here in a minute, surging to her rescue.

She waved. He waved back but the tension didn't ease.

She grinned—and then the smile died.

She liked it, she realised. She liked it a lot that he was playing lifeguard for her.

Who'd play lifeguard for her when she went back to the States?

You won't need a lifeguard, she told herself fiercely. You'll be fine. Don't even think that you might still need someone. You've been depressed before and you're not getting depressed again.

She turned to face the other end of the cove. She put her head down—and she swam.

Hamish watched as Susie limped down to the shoreline and was…astonished. She was beautiful, he thought. Gorgeous.

But she was also damaged. She was wearing a bikini that showed off every lovely curve, but it also revealed a wide, jagged scar across the small of her back. Was this the back injury that caused her limp?

She'd lost a husband. She was raising a baby on her own.

He was kicking her out of her castle.

Something inside his gut clenched as he watched her walk into the waves. Emotional decisions were not appropriate here, he told himself fiercely. This castle was worth a small fortune— no, a large fortune—and to keep a woman and a baby here in perpetuity was ridiculous. The lawyers had told him she'd been well provided for, and she'd reiterated that herself. She could go back to America and get on with whatever life she'd had before she'd met this Rory character and been dragged into this make-believe fantasy of titles and castles and…emotion.

He continued to watch as she stood, thigh deep in the waves, seeming to simply soak in the sun. She gazed about her as if taking in the sheer beauty of the cove, though she must have seen it so many times.

She stilled, then knifed forward into the oncoming wave and he forgot about the beauty of the cove.

She simply disappeared. Her dive into the wave produced nary a splash. Her body became a streamlined torpedo, slicing down and under, and it was as if she'd never been there.

She didn't surface.

He was standing up, startling Boris who'd had his ears resting on his knees. Boris barked, expecting adventure, but Hamish had his eyes shaded. He was moving forward, trying to see…

She surfaced finally fifty yards from where she'd gone

under. One breath, a slight turn and then down under again, and he was searching once more.

Where…where…?

Twenty yards this time, only twenty yards and she was moving along the cove rather than out to sea. Another breath, hardly perceptible—the break of her head above water could hardly be seen—and then under again, swift and sure, like a sleek young seal, surfacing to breathe but all economy of effort underwater.

He'd never seen anything like it. He thought he was a good swimmer, but she was magnificent.

He'd run a few steps in those first panicked seconds and Boris was bouncing around his legs, barking, expecting excitement. He lifted a piece of driftwood and threw it into the shallows, pretending to any unseen onlooker that he'd stood specifically to do this. That he hadn't panicked. That the sight of Susie moving with such economy of action—with such beauty—didn't have the power to move him.

Only, of course, it did have the power to move him. He felt…

He didn't know how he felt.

Boris came streaming back up the beach, hauling his driftwood for another throw. The stick was laid at his feet and the big dog shook, sending a spray of sand and sea, hauling Hamish's thoughts back to reality. To at least some semblance of normality.

'I'm going back to babysitting,' he told Boris. 'I'm not watching.'

Boris put his head on the side and gazed at him in mute enquiry.

'Well, I'm hardly a lifesaver,' he muttered, sitting on the beach, hugging the dog and staring out to sea. 'She can swim better than I can. There's nothing I can do for your mistress, boy, except sit with her sleeping baby and give her a few more moments' freedom.'

She waved from behind the breakers and he waved back.

Freedom…

She was glorying in her freedom, he thought, and suddenly he remembered his office back in Manhattan. It was a magnificent office. He had plate-glass windows that looked all the way to the Statue of Liberty in New York Harbor.

There was still plate glass between him and the sea.

'It's just because you've never had a holiday that you're thinking like this,' he told himself, suddenly angry. 'Get over it. Cut it out with the emotion, Douglas. You know where that gets you, and you don't want to go there.'

He lay back on the sand and closed his eyes.

Then he half opened one. Then he shrugged and sat up.

He'd just watch.

It had been a fabulous swim.

Susie came out of the water laughing with delight, pleasure and sheer wellbeing. OK, she was leaving this place, but its memories would stay with her for ever and one of them was this day. She shook herself like Boris, holding her hands out and wiggling her whole body so a spray of water went everywhere. Boris, who'd bounded down the beach to meet her, backed off as the water hit him, and she laughed with delight at her neat reversal of roles.

She looked up the beach and Hamish was watching her. She switched back. She'd had her time out.

Back to being the castle relic.

She walked up the beach and he rose to meet her, holding out her towel. She hesitated for a moment, just because the gesture seemed curiously intimate.

Which was dumb. It meant nothing. How many times had Kirsty done the same thing? She took the towel and retired behind it, enveloping her whole face so she didn't have to look at him.

'Best beach in the world,' he said softly, and she let her towel drop to her shoulders and tried to smile.

'It is.'

'You'll hate leaving it.'

'I will. But I've had it for over a year. It's time for someone else to enjoy it.' Her smile became a little more determined. 'Or many someones. All the people who'll come to your hotel.'

'It's the sensible thing to do, to sell it.'

'It is.'

'You will be all right?'

'I'll be fine,' she told him, determined. 'Thank you for looking after Rose.'

'I've never babysat before.'

'Never?'

'No.'

'No family?'

'No brothers or sisters. An older cousin who was a creep.'

'I think that'd be awful,' she said. 'Being an only kid. Being a twin was wonderful.'

He thought about that, and looked down at her sleeping baby. Another only kid? 'Rose...'

'I'll surround her with kids,' she said, determined. How was she going to do that? She didn't have a clue.

She was going home to juggle baby, career, life.

She was not going to let it get her down.

'Your sister's here?'

'Yes.'

'She has kids.'

'Yes.'

'Why don't you stay here?'

'And be dependent on Kirsty for the rest of my life? No, thanks very much.'

'Independence can be hard.'

'I suspect you're a master of it,' she said. 'I'm just learning but I'll manage.'

'Susie...' he began—and then paused as the sound of a motor cut the stillness. He turned to watch a dinghy putt-putt around the cove. It was a simple, two-person craft with a small motor that would have been dangerous on a day that was any less calm than this. But it was calm and the two people in the boat looked inordinately pleased with themselves. A middle-aged couple—the man in a loud Hawaiian shirt and the woman in a swimsuit that had even more gardenias on than her husband's shirt—were heading straight for them.

As they came within earshot the man stood up in the boat, rocked precariously and yelled.

'Ahoy. Can we land on this beach? Are there rocks?'

'No rocks,' Susie yelled back, relieved her tete-a-tete was over.

They cruised towards the shore, a bit too fast. Neither got out of the boat until it hit sand. Then they sat in the rocking boat, removed their sandals with care and put their toes into the water as if expecting piranhas.

No piranhas.

'Ooh, it's lovely, Albert,' the lady said. 'It's not too cold at all.' She turned to them and beamed a welcome. 'Hi.'

They were Americans. The place was starting to be overrun with Americans, Susie thought. 'Hi,' she replied, while Hamish said nothing at all.

'We just wanted to take your picture,' the woman told her, beaming still. 'That's right, isn't it, Albert? We brought the boat round from Dolphin Bay harbour and I saw you through the fieldglasses with your baby asleep and your puppy, and you all look beautiful. I bet that dog's got dingo in him, I said. And I said to Albert, I'd like to take their picture, because you remind me so much of what we were at that age. And now life's an adventure and it's wonderful but I just thought…seeing you two…' Her beam faded a little. 'You don't mind, do you?' she asked, suddenly anxious that she might have offended the natives. 'If you give me your name and address I'll send you a copy. Albert is a lovely photographer.'

Albert looked bashful, but combined beam and bashful very nicely.

'We're only in Australia for a week,' the woman went on. 'For five of those days Albert has a conference but I said I wasn't going home before I'd met some real Australians. So I got a pin and closed my eyes and stuck it in a map of places we could get to from Sydney and here we are. And I know you aren't aboriginal or anything, but you so look like you belong. Anyway, can we take your picture?'

'Um,' Susie said with a sideways glance at the silent Hamish. 'What do you think…luv?'

He grinned. Her drawl had been an attempt to sound Australian but she hadn't quite managed it.

'Geez, darl, I dunno why not,' he drawled, and his accent was so much better than hers that she almost laughed out loud. 'We could do with one of them photo thingies to show the kiddies when they grow up.'

She choked. Albert suddenly looked suspicious.

'They might already have a camera, Honey.'

'We'd be very pleased to have our picture taken,' Susie said. This was such a glorious morning, she was determined that everyone could enjoy it. She glared at Hamish. 'What my…what he meant was that'd it'd be an honour to have a picture taken by an American.'

'That's all right, then,' Honey said, obviously thinking the same thing. 'Can you cuddle? I don't suppose you want to pick the baby up?'

'She's just gone to sleep,' Susie said. Enough was enough. But then she grinned and leaned down, hoisted the wet and sand-coated dog up and thrust him into Hamish's arms. 'There you go, darl,' she said. 'You cuddle the dingo.'

The dingo stuck his nose into Hamish's face and slurped.

'Gee,' Hamish managed. 'Thanks…darl.'

'Just stand behind the baby,' Honey urged. 'So we can get you all in the shot.'

They did, bemused.

'Put your arm round her,' Albert urged.

'It's all I can do to hold the dingo,' Hamish muttered. Boris was wiggling like the crazy mutt he was. Ecstatic.

'I'll hold the back half,' Susie said and did that, catching Boris's legs.

The dog was now upside down, his front end held by Hamish and his back half held by Susie.

'Now cuddle your wife,' Albert said,

'She's not—'

'Cuddle me, darl,' Susie said sweetly. 'You know you want to.'

He cuddled her. He stood on the sun-warmed beach, with a dog in his arms, with Rose curled up asleep at his feet, with a woman pressed against him and with his arm around her, and he smiled at the camera as if he meant it.

It was like an out-of-body experience, he thought. If Marcia could see him now she'd think he must have an identical twin. This was nothing like he was. The self-contained Hamish Douglas was a world away. He should be in his office now, with his hair slicked down, wearing a suit and tie, in charge of his world.

Instead…

Susie was leaning against him. She was still cool to the touch after her swim. He'd been getting hot on the beach and the cool of her body against his was great.

Not just the cool. The smell of her. The feel of her…

She curved right where she ought to curve. His arm held her close and she used her free arm to tug him even closer. The feel of her fingers on his hip, the strength of her tugging him close….

Whew.

He smiled at the camera but it was all he could do to manage it.

He needed to go home, he thought. He needed to put this place on the market and get out of here.

Why was he terrified?

A vision of his mother came back, his mother late at night, coming into his room, putting her head on his bed and sobbing her heart out.

'I never should have loved. If I'd known it'd hurt like this, I never, never would have loved him. Oh, God, Hamish, the pain…'

He withdrew. His arm dropped and Susie felt it and moved aside in an instant. It had been play-acting, he knew. She hadn't meant to hold him, to curve against him as if she belonged.

'Where shall we send the pictures?' Honey asked, aware as they moved apart that the photo session was definitely over. There was something in their body language that told her there was no way she'd get them back together again. 'Do you have a permanent address? Somewhere we can send a letter?'

Susie gazed at her blankly.

'These people think we're dole bludgers, sleeping in the back of a clapped-out ute,' Hamish said, and managed a grin at his mastery of the language. And the knowledge that went with it. Ute—short for utility vehicle—a pick-up truck. And dole bludger? He'd heard the term on the plane. They'd been flying over the coast and the man in the seat beside him had waved to the beach below.

'There's a major social security problem in Australia,' he'd told Hamish. 'The weather's so good and the surf's so good there's an army of kids who refuse to work. They go on social security—the dole—and spend their life surfing. Go up and down the coast looking for good surf, sleeping in the back of utes. Bloody dole bludgers'll be the ruination of this country.'

And it was too much for Susie. He saw the mischief lurking in her eyes and the laughter threatening to explode, and he opened his mouth to stop her but it was too late.

'We're no dole bludgers,' she told them, in a tone of offended virtue. 'And in truth we're not husband and wife. I'll have you know that this…' she pointed to Hamish as she'd point to some mummified Egyptian remains '…is Lord Hamish Douglas, Earl of Loganaich. His address, of course, is Loganaich Castle, Dolphin Bay. And me… I'm the castle relic. And gardener and dogsbody besides.' She motioned to Rose at her feet. 'There's always a baby in these sorts of situations,' she told them. 'But it's probably wiser not to ask any more questions.'

'You realise they'll still think we're dole bludgers,' Hamish said, when he could get a grip on his laughter and was attempting to get a grip on reality. The couple were putt-putting back out of the cove, with Albert pausing to take one more shot before they rounded the headland and disappeared from view.

'Yeah, we're high on dope. I'll probably get a visit from Social Security.' Susie chuckled. 'I should have told them I was an Arabian princess. We would have just as much chance at belief.'

'But we've made their morning,' Hamish said. The tension he felt as he'd held Susie was dissipating, changing to something different. Shared pleasure in the pure ridiculousness of the moment. Laughter. It was a laughter he hadn't felt before.

He felt…free. 'They've got more local colour than they bargained for.'

'What's the bet they go into the post office when they go back?'

'The post office?'

'Harriet's the postmistress and she has a huge sign out the front advertising information. Collecting and imparting information is a passion. If they go in and say they've met a crazy beach bum who calls himself a lord, they'll get told exactly what's what and they'll be back here for more pictures.'

'We'll retire behind our castle walls and pull up the drawbridge.'

'If only it were that easy,' Susie said, and the laughter slipped a little. 'I… Maybe we should go up now. I want to get some paving done this afternoon.'

'I need to do some cataloguing.'

'Cataloguing?'

'Marcia says I should make lists of contents.'

'Sure.' She eyed him with more than a little disquiet. 'What will you do with Ernst and Eric?'

'Who?'

'Suits of armour.'

'Um…' He'd seen them. Of course he'd seen them. One could hardly miss them. 'I might give them to a welfare shop,' he ventured. 'If I can find a welfare shop that'll take them.'

'I'll buy them.'

'Why on earth,' he said cautiously, 'would you want two imitation suits of armour that stand eight feet high and are enough to scare the socks off anyone who comes near?'

'When I go home I won't have Boris,' she said with dignity. 'I need Eric and Ernst. Besides, they're excellent conversationalists. We've reached consensus on most important political points but the ramifications of the Kyoto agreement in developing countries still needs some fine tuning.'

He stared at her.

Then he burst out laughing.

She looked affronted. 'You can't think the ramifications of such an agreement are a laughing matter?'

'No,' he said at once, wiping the grin off his face. 'They're very serious indeed. Only last week I was telling my potted palm—'

'There's no need to mock.'

'I'm not mocking. But Ernst and Eric are yours,' he told her. 'Absolutely. Who am I to separate a woman from her political sparring partners? How are you going to get them home?'

'I guess they won't let me take them on the plane?'

'You could see if you could get them diplomatic passports. I could make a few phone calls. Eric and Ernst, born in China and holding views that are decidedly left-wing...or I assume they're left-wing?'

'It's dangerous to assume anything about Ernst and Eric,' she said in a voice that was none too steady.

'I won't. I'll approach the situation with diplomatic caution. But we'll do our best, Susie Douglas. When you leave for America I'd very much like to see Ernst on one side of you on the plane and Eric on the other.'

'Eric is a vegetarian,' she said with such promptness that he blinked. 'And Ernst hates sitting over a wing.'

He choked. She was standing in front of him, all earnestness, the sun glinting on her gorgeous hair, the laughter in her eyes conflicting with the prim schoolteacher voice and he felt...he felt...

'I'll see what I can do,' he managed. 'But meanwhile I think we should pack up for the day. I think I've had a bit too much sun.'

CHAPTER FIVE

THEY were formal for the rest of the day. Formal to the point of avoiding each other. Hamish did a bit of cataloguing but there wasn't much point cataloguing imitation chandeliers. Susie did a bit of packing but her heart wasn't in that either.

They met briefly for dinner. 'Soup and toast,' Susie decreed, and Hamish didn't argue. He ate his soup and toast, and then later, when Susie had gone to bed, he ate more toast. Tomorrow he'd have to go on a forage into town and find some decent food, he decided. Then he remembered the next day was the day of the fête and he felt so faint-hearted that he stopped feeling hungry and went back to bed and stared at the ceiling for a while.

He was right out of his comfort zone. Jodie had told him this was a holiday. Weren't holidays meant to make you feel rested?

The sounds of the sea were wafting in his open window but the rest of the world was silent. After the buzzing background hum of Manhattan this seemed like another world. It was so silent it sounded...noisy? The absence of traffic sounds was like white noise.

He lay and listened and decided he was homesick for Manhattan. For his black and grey penthouse, his austere bathroom without kings or queens watching from gilt frames, for his traffic noise...

For Marcia? Of course for Marcia.

Who was he kidding? He wasn't homesick. He didn't know what he was. Finally he drifted into sleep where Marcia and

Jodie and Susie all jostled for position. Marcia was silently, scornfully watching. Jodie was standing with hands on hips, daring him to be different. Susie was laughing.

But while he watched, Susie's laughter turned to tears and he woke in a cold sweat.

And Susie was no longer in his dream. She was standing in the open doorway and she was neither laughing or crying.

She was holding a kilt.

'Behold your valet, my lord,' she told him. 'Your kilt and all your other various appendages await your noble personage.'

He sat up fast. Then he remembered he wasn't wearing pyjamas. He grabbed his sheet—and he blinked at the apparition in the doorway.

Susie was dressed in tartan.

She wasn't wearing a kilt. She was wearing royal blue Capri pants, stretching neatly around every delicious curve, and a gorgeous little top, in the same tartan as the kilt she was holding out for him to wear. Her hair was tied up in some complex knot on top, and it was caught up in a tartan ribbon.

'What are you staring at?' she asked.

'The tartan…'

'You might be the head of the clan but I'm a Douglas, too.'

This woman was his family, he thought, dazed.

Move on. Family was a scary thought. His eyes fell to the kilt she was holding out.

'I'm not wearing that.'

'You promised,' she said with something akin to forcefulness. 'You can't back out now, your Lordship. I've promised as well.'

'You've promised?'

'Well, you promised first. You said you would, and now I've telephoned the organisers and they've told everyone you're coming. They've trucked in the Barram pipe band with an extra piper this year, 'cos last time the piper had a wee bit too much whisky on the bus on the way here and didn't perform to expectation. So there's two pipers to pipe you on stage, your Lordship, and a whole pipe band besides, and the Brownies are doing a guard of honour especially.'

'The Brownies?' To say he was hornswoggled was an understatement. 'What on earth are Brownies?'

'Scary little brown persons,' she said. 'You must have heard of them. They sell cookies and do bob-a-job, only now it's two dollars and you have to sign forms in triplicate saying they can't hurt themselves when they shine your shoes.'

'I'm lost,' he complained, and she grinned.

'Fine. Stay that way. Ask no questions, just smile and wave like the Queen Mum. You want me to help you to dress?'

'No!'

'Only offering. I thought you might have trouble with your sporran.'

'An earl,' he said with cautious dignity, 'especially the ninth Earl of Loganaich of the mighty clan Douglas, can surely manage his own sporran.'

'Tricky things, sporrans.'

'Not to us earls.'

'Well, then,' she said cheerfully. She walked across and dumped a kilt, what looked like a small mountain of spare tartan fabric, tassles and toggles, a purse of some description and a beret with a feather on his bedside chair. Boris followed behind, looking interested.

'There you go, your Lordship,' she said happily. 'Everything you need to look shipshape. Come on, Boris.'

'Boris can help,' he said graciously, and her grin widened.

'I'll leave you with your valet, then, shall I, my lord? Porridge in the kitchen in thirty minutes?'

'Toast.'

'If you're wearing a sporran you need porridge.'

'Toast,' he said in something akin to desperation. 'As the leader of your clan I demand toast.'

She chuckled. 'Ooh, I love a forceful man…in a kilt.'

'Susie…'

She got her features back under control with difficulty. She was back to a grin only. 'Your wish is my command,' she said. 'Sir.' He got a sharp salute, clicked heels and she was gone, leaving him alone with his valet.

'Boris...' he said cautiously, eyeing his pile of tartan as if it might bite. 'What do you think a sporran might be?'

It took him a while. It took him close to an hour, really, but if he was going to do this thing he might as well do it right. By the time he had every pleat in place, every toggle where it was supposed to be toggling, and the feather in his cap at just the right angle he felt like he'd done a full day's work. He gazed in the mirror and thought he had done a good day's work. He looked unbelievable.

Boris was sitting watching with the patience of all good valets, and when Hamish finally adjusted his cap and looked at the final result the dog gave a deep low woof, as if in appreciation.

'Not bad at all,' Hamish told the dog. 'I wish Jodie could see me now.'

And Marcia?

Marcia couldn't help but be impressed with this, he thought, but it was Jodie he thought of. Jodie would look at him and whistle, and giggle.

Like Susie giggled. Susie and Jodie...

Two unlikely women in his life. Jodie was no longer part of what he did. She was making choir stalls with her Nick. Ridiculous. How could she make any money doing that?

And Susie... In a couple of weeks Susie would be a memory as well and he'd be left with Marcia.

Which was the way he wanted it.

'Porridge!' The yell from below stairs startled him out of his reverie. 'On the table. Now.'

He crossed to the landing. Took a deep breath. Swelled his chest.

'Toast!' he yelled back. 'Woman!'

She emerged from the kitchen and gazed upward. And froze. Her eyes took in his appearance, from the tip of his shoes, his long socks with their tassels, up to the feather...

He felt like blushing.

'Wow,' she said at last on a long note of awed discovery. 'Oh, Hamish, wow. They're going to love you.'

'Who?'

'All the ladies of Dolphin Bay,' she said simply. 'Me, too. What a hunk. Do you have everything in the right place?'

'I think so,' he said, still trying not to blush.

'And you've got the appropriate attire underneath?'

'Don't even go there.' He stepped back from the balustrade—fast—and she chuckled.

'No matter. I've never seen such an impressive Scottish hero—and I've seen *Braveheart*.'

'I'd imagine that those guys might be a bit handier with their weaponry than I am,' he said, still cautious. 'I'm all froth and no substance.'

'You certainly look like substance. Porridge now, sir. Double helping if you like.'

'Susie…'

'Yes, sir?'

'I thought I made myself clear. Toast.'

'There's a bit of a problem,' she confessed. 'If I'd seen your knees before this, I might have concentrated a bit more. Very good at focussing the mind, those knees.'

This was ridiculous. He wanted his kilt lowered.

'So what's happened to my toast?' he managed.

'I burnt two lots,' she confessed. 'I was thinking about Angus. And Priscilla.'

'Priscilla?'

'Angus's pumpkin. She's going to win today. Biggest pumpkin on show. I ended up with only one slice of bread left and Rose wanted that for toast fingers in her egg.' She took a deep breath and fixed him with a look that told him he was going to get a lecture, right now.

'Hamish, you might tell me you belong in New York—you might tell me you're not really an earl—but anyone seeing those knees knows for sure that you've found your home right here. You're the ninth Earl of Loganaich and you just need to forget all those silly ideas of being anyone else, including a toast eater, and learn to like porridge. Now, enough argument. I have a team of men arriving in ten minutes to help load

Priscilla onto the trailer. So—what do they say? Save your breath to cool your porridge—my lord.' She smiled sweetly up at him. 'Come and get it while it's hot.'

It was like an out-of-body experience.

Firstly there was the fairground itself. It was nestled between two hills, with the harbour and the town on one side and bushland on the other. One could stroll around the fairground, walk a short distance to the shops or to the boats, retreat into the bush—as a few young couples showed every sign of doing even this early on—or if it all got too hot one could disappear to the beach for a quick swim.

Susie pulled her little car into the parking lot and Hamish gazed around, stunned. It was a fantastic, colourful mix of everything. Everyone. Grizzled farmers, kids with fairy floss, old ladies in wheelchairs. Gorgeous young things kitted to the nines in full dressage gear ready for the equestrian events. Kids in bathing costumes, obviously torn between beach and fair. A clown on stilts lurching from car to car and using the bonnets of the cars to steady himself.

The clown ended up right by them as they parked, and he lurched a little more, made a rush and hit their trailer. By the time they emerged he was dusting himself and staggering to his feet, pushing himself up against their pumpkin. Priscilla was almost as high as he was.

'You hurt that pumpkin and you're dead meat, Jake Cameron,' Susie told him, clearly unmoved by clowns tumbling into her trailer. 'If there's so much as a blemish on my pumpkin, it's disqualified.'

'Hi, Susie,' the clown said, removing a bulbous nose. 'Great to see you, too.'

'I didn't know you rode stilts.'

'I don't,' Jake said morosely. 'But the kids' schoolteacher asked for volunteers and the twins volunteered me. It's not going to work. The kids have been coaching me for weeks and all that's going to happen is that I break my neck. Who's going to fix me up then, I want to know?'

'Kirsty's really good at broken spines,' Susie said, and grinned. 'Or failing that, she's specially trained in palliative care. If you die you'll die in the best of hands.' She turned to Hamish, who was feeling vaguely better that he wasn't the only ridiculously clad person here. 'Hamish, this is Dr Jake Cameron. Jake's my brother-in-law. Jake and Kirsty are Dolphin Bay's doctors.'

'Hey!' Jake said, holding out a red-gloved, vast-fingered paw. 'You're the new earl. Welcome to Dolphin Bay, mate. You want to find a beer?'

Beer sounded fantastic to Hamish—but Susie's hand was on his arm and she was holding on like he wasn't going anywhere.

'Hamish is due at the opening ceremony in ten minutes.'

'No beer until you've done your duty,' Jake said sympathetically. 'But me... I've been all round the fairground on these damned stilts, risking life and limb at every step. I've added local colour for all I'm worth and I'm done. Off duty. Beer it is.'

'So who looks after the kids when they fall off the Ferris wheel?' Susie demanded.

'Heaven forbid,' Jake said. 'But Kirsty's official medical officer for the day. She's taken the pledge for the next few months so I'm a free man.'

'Jake...' Susie said, and stopped. There was a pause. A pregnant pause. 'She's taken the pledge... Are you saying what I think you're saying?'

Jake replaced his nose. Fast. 'Whoops,' he said, backing off. 'No, I didn't say that. Gotta go. Take care of your earl.'

'I will,' Susie said, but still looking very oddly indeed at her brother-in-law. 'Where's Kirsty?'

'Avoiding you, I suspect,' Jake said. 'See you.' And he took himself off like a man hunted.

'What was that about?' Hamish asked, watching the very speedy retreat of the scarlet and purple patchwork clown.

'Oh, if she is...' Susie said. 'How can I go home?' She caught herself. 'No. I must. Business. Let's get you to the stage.'

'Do I really need to?'

'Of course you need to,' she said, astonished. 'Everyone

plays their part. You're part of this community now, Hamish Douglas, like it or not, and at least we're not asking you to say your speech while you're wearing stilts.'

His speech was astonishing all by itself.

The sensation of being piped onto the stage, of every face in the fairground straining to see him, of a gasp of approval as he finally reached the dais and the sound of the pipes fell away...

Susie was right, he thought, appreciating the drama of the situation. If Angus had done this for the last forty years, this small ceremony would be sorely missed—and how much worse it would be because Angus was dead.

Times changed. The time of having a laird in Castle Douglas was over, and people had to accept it, but at least he could do as Susie suggested now. He could play his part.

Speech. He had to make a speech. Not a 'take over the company' sort of speech, not now, but something with, God help him, emotion.

Just this once.

And in the end, the words came.

'I can't replace my Uncle Angus,' he told the crowd, tentative at first but growing surer as he saw by their smiles that just standing up here in the right tartan was enough to plug the void. 'I can't replace Lord Angus Douglas, Earl of Loganaich. I don't want to. But the house of Douglas has been associated with Dolphin Bay for so long that the connection will never die. As long as Castle Loganaich stands, we'll remember the link between castle and town. We'll remember the friendship, the love, the good times and the bad. Lord Angus's death was a low point but he lived a full life with his beloved Deirdre, both of them surrounded by this town full of their friends.' He hesitated.

'Plus the odd monarch in the bathrooms,' he added, and there was a ripple of delighted laugher. Most people here had at least heard of Queen Vic.

But Hamish hadn't yet finished. He was on a roll. Maybe he could be a lord after all. 'Angus's legacy remains in the laughter and the camaraderie I'm seeing here,' he told them. 'Angus would want—Angus would insist—that life goes on and that everyone here enjoy themselves to the full. So I, Hamish Douglas, ninth Earl of Loganaich, make this my first public decree. That this fair is officially open and that everyone here proceed to have a very good time. And after the pumpkin judging… As Lord Douglas, I decree that everyone here take home a slab of pumpkin so I don't get landed with pumpkin pie for the rest of my life.'

Hooray. He'd done it. There was cheering and more laughter. The pipes started up again and Hamish made his way off the stage to find Susie smiling at him through tears.

'Oh, Hamish, that was wonderful.'

'There's no need to cry,' he said abruptly and turned away. Drat, he was almost teary himself.

His laughter faded. He'd almost been enjoying himself but tears always did this. They snapped him right back to dreary reality. Tears in a situation like this were ridiculous. And now, if Susie not only cried but infected him with it…

No!

'Pumpkin judging,' someone yelled. 'We're waiting on the Douglas pumpkin.'

'Ooh.' Susie's tears were gone in an instant and she turned to a middle-aged lady beside her. 'Harriet, can you take Rose for a bit?' She thrust her baby forward, but Rose obviously knew the lady who Hamish recognised as the postmistress. He'd stopped and asked directions from her when he'd arrived.

'Come on.' Susie was clutching his hand and towing him through the crowd and people were laughing and parting to let them through. 'We've got a date with destiny—right now.'

Their pumpkin won. It was the fair's biggest pumpkin, with trophy and certificate to prove it. The second biggest was entered by a withered old man who didn't seem the least bit upset about losing.

Or maybe he did. He laughed and cheered with the rest of them when the pumpkins were weighed, but as the trophy was given to a flushed and triumphant Susie, the elderly man turned to Hamish and an errant tear was rolling down his wrinkled cheek.

More tears!

'He knew, dammit,' the old man said, and he reached out and wrung Hamish's hand so hard that it hurt. 'Your uncle was the best mate a man could have. He knew he'd beaten me this year, damn him. He knew he was a winner. I wouldn't have wanted him to go any other way but hell, I miss him.' He sniffed and his wife darted forward and hugged him and led him off to the beer tent.

Susie came down from the dais, clutching her trophy and certificate, and she watched him go and sniffed again.

'I need a hanky,' she said, helpless with her hands full, and Hamish was forced to find his—from his sporran—and then hold her trophy while she blew her nose. Hard.

'I don't want it back,' he said faintly, and she managed a smile through tears.

'I'm sorry. I know guys hate tears. It's only Ben…' She motioned to where the old man was disappearing beerwards.

'He was crying, too,' Hamish said, and if he sounded a bit desperate then he couldn't help it.

'Aunty Susie! Aunty Susie!' There were shrieks from behind them and he turned to see two pigtailed urchins bearing down on them. Two little girls aged about five, each liberally spattered with what looked like a mix of fairy floss and chocolate ice cream, raced up to them with excitement 'Aunty Susie, Mummy's got a baby for you.'

'A baby?' Susie stood stock still and the colour drained from her face. 'I knew it. I knew…'

'What's wrong?' Hamish asked before he could help himself.

'She's pregnant. I knew…'

'Hi.' Coming up behind the twins was a woman who was the mirror image of Susie. The likeness was so extraordinary that he blinked.

'Kirsty, I presume,' he said, because Susie had retired behind his handkerchief again. Oh, for heaven's sake.

'I'm Kirsty.' A cool, firm hand was placed in his. She smiled and her smile was the same as Susie's. Or maybe not. Maybe not quite as lovely?

That was a dumb thing to think. At least this woman wasn't crying.

'Why is Susie crying?' she asked, and he looked exasperated.

'Because her pumpkin won. I think.'

He expected sympathy and mutual confusion. Instead, Kirsty dropped his hand and enveloped Susie in a hug.

'Oh, sweetheart, I'm sorry. He couldn't see...'

'He did see,' Susie said, hiccuping on a sob. 'He knew. I told you. I snuck into Ben's back yard before he died and I measured it and Angus knew his would be the winner. And I bet he can see us now.'

'Then what—?'

'The twins. They said...a baby.'

Kirsty let her arms drop. She looked exasperated. 'They didn't say a baby.'

'They did.'

'They meant a puppy.'

'A puppy?' Susie lowered the handkerchief and looked out cautiously from behind it. Ready to retire again at any minute. 'What do you mean?'

'This.' Kirsty motioned behind her. 'We want our Boris back, but we've decided you need a dog.'

A small boy was bringing up the rear. He was carrying... What was he carrying?

A puppy.

The puppy was just about the weirdest dog Hamish had ever seen. She was brown, white and tubby, with long, floppy ears, Boris's expressive eyes, a stretched-out body with a puddingy tummy, a tail that added another twelve inches in length—and legs that were about three inches long.

'What is it?' Susie asked, cautious to say the least.

'This is our gift to you,' Kirsty said expansively and grinned. 'To stop Rose being an only child.' She motioned to the small boy holding the pup. 'Susie, this is Adam, and Adam's pup. Now she's your pup.'

'What...?'

'She's courtesy of Boris,' she explained, sounding exasperated. 'You know Jake inherited Boris from Miss Pritchard? Jake sort of assumed—as Boris was eight years old and Miss Pritchard was a civically responsible person—that Boris would have been neutered in the long distant past. OK, he should have checked, but he didn't. He didn't really think about it, until Adam's dachshund came into season. We share a back fence and events took their course. Even then we didn't realise until Daisy Dachshund produced one sad pup. Now that she's a few weeks old, the father's obvious.'

'Sad pup?' Susie said warily, while Hamish looked on, much as one might look through a time screen to another world.

'Well, maybe she's not exactly sad, are you, sweetheart?' Kirsty said, lifting the pup from Adam's hands and holding her up for inspection. 'Maybe she's more…loopy. She's just won cutest puppy in show. Pup, meet Susie. Susie, meet pup.'

'Hi, pup,' Susie said, still cautious.

The pup wagged her tail. Her whole body wriggled, like a cute and furry eel.

'Anyway, Jake and I were watching the puppy judging and it suddenly occurred to us that if you're insisting on returning to America you need something to remember us by. And something to guard you. What better than a pup? We talked to Adam's parents and, amazingly, they're delighted. Even Adam's cool with it. I don't think this puppy fits what he thinks of as a real boy's dog. I know there'll be issues with quarantine but the dog-judging people say it's possible to take pups into the US from here, and Jake and I will pay.'

Susie seemed almost overwhelmed. She sniffed. 'Oh, Kirsty…'

'I don't have any more handkerchiefs,' Jake said, desperate.

'You need a truckload when Susie's around,' Kirsty said cheerfully. 'What do you think, Suze?'

'Oh,' Susie said, taking the puppy and holding her close. 'Oh…'

'I think I hear a beer calling,' Hamish said faintly. 'Is Jake in the beer tent?'

Kirsty grinned at him, not unsympathetic. 'We're all a bit

much, aren't we? But your speech… All I had to do was look at you and I got teary.'

'Susie!' Harriet, the postmistress, was making her way determinedly through the crowd toward them, carrying Rose toward her mother. 'I think your daughter needs a nappy change.'

Hamish was backing already but he backed a few more feet at that. Fast. 'I can definitely hear a beer calling,' he muttered.

But Harriet wasn't about to let Hamish escape. 'Ooh, look at you,' she exclaimed, and thrust Rose at her mother, who proceeded to juggle toddler and puppy with aplomb. The elderly postmistress put an arm round Hamish's shoulders and beamed in possessive enthusiasm. She was a big lady, buxom and beaming, with a tight frizzed perm and painted lips that seemed to have a life of their own. 'Look at me,' she crowed. 'Me and Lord Hamish. Take a picture of us, someone, so I can put it up on the post-office wall.'

'I need—'

'Hey, but it shouldn't be me.' Harriet suddenly corrected herself, whisking herself out of his arms and thrusting Susie forward with an air of enormous personal sacrifice. 'It should be you. Oh, Susie, wouldn't that be something? You and the new laird. Two Douglases finally finding their place, side by side.'

Susie choked, but she had no say in the matter. She'd been thrust next to Hamish and cameras were flashing, just the same as they'd been yesterday on the beach, only worse.

Much worse.

Hamish Douglas was suddenly being photographed with Mrs Douglas, Rosie Douglas and dog.

Things were spiralling out of control here, Hamish thought desperately, and a man had to do what a man had to do.

He put Susie—and appendages—carefully away from him and took two more steps back. Two long steps back.

'I need to find Jake,' he said, in tones he hoped were careful and measured and nowhere as hysterical as he felt. 'And then… I think it's wise if I stop all conjecture about me and…me and Susie right now. I'm engaged to a young lady called Marcia Vinel and she's arriving here the day after tomorrow.'

CHAPTER SIX

HAMISH spent the rest of the day being inspected. From every angle. Susie had been right when she'd said his presence would take everyone's mind off their loss. He could not only hear the buzz his presence was making. He could feel it. He was whispered about, talked about, watched….

'I need to get this kilt off,' he told Jake. 'Did I ever wolf-whistle a woman for having great legs? Kill me now. I deserve it. Everyone's staring at my knees.'

'They're staring at the whole package,' Jake said. 'And you can forget any sympathy from this direction. You're not wearing size twenty purple and red shoes. My feet are killing me.'

'Did Susie tell me you were a surgeon in the city before you were married?' Hamish said curiously. 'What on earth made you move here?'

'Life,' Jake said, and Hamish looked out over the fairground and shuddered.

'Not my idea of life.'

'And your idea of life would be…'

'Control,' Hamish said forcefully. 'Knowing what I'm waking up to every morning.'

'I know what I'm waking up to every morning,' Jake said peaceably. 'Chaos. I wouldn't have it any other way.'

'Poles apart,' Hamish said morosely. Then he thought of another issue. 'And what the hell are you about, giving Susie a dog? Hasn't she got enough to cope with? She's got to make her way in America, get a career going. How's she going to handle a dog?'

'The heart expands to fit all comers,' Jake said and grinned. 'I'm a doctor, you know. That's a very medical sort of diagnosis.'

'Sure it does,' Hamish snapped. 'Susie's now been loaded with a mutt who she'll have to love whether she wants to or not.'

'Love isn't the same as provide for,' Jake said, looking at him curiously. 'It's a bit different. Sure, it means more work but to not accept it…'

'You're telling me there are any real advantages in her getting a dog?'

'Kirsty's her twin,' Jake said definitely. 'If Kirsty says she needs a dog, then she needs a dog. She's lonely as hell.'

'Dogs don't fix loneliness.'

'They do a bit,' Jake said. 'Anyway, the dog wasn't my decision, mate. Kirsty thinks it's a good idea and getting between the twins is like dividing the Red Sea. It'd take a force bigger than I have at my disposal. They're inseparable.'

'But Susie's going home.'

'There is that,' Jake said. He surveyed Hamish thoughtfully and Hamish lifted his beer and studied the dregs.

'If you look at me like that for any more than two more seconds I'm walking out of here and I'll keep walking till I reach America,' he said softly, and Jake grinned.

'Fair enough. You've copped a bit of matchmaking, then.'

'Just a bit. The whole fairground had gone into *Wouldn't it be great?* mode.'

'Well, it would be great.'

'Except I like my women self-contained, clever, cool and sassy.'

'Susie's clever and sassy.'

'Four or nothing,' he said, and drained his beer. 'I'm engaged to Marcia. She'll be here the day after tomorrow.'

Jake raised an eyebrow. Sussing him. And grinning. 'First I've heard of it. But it's no business of mine, mate,' he added, pushing himself to his size twenty feet. 'I have two hundred more balloons to disperse before I'm off duty. One more beer and I'll let the whole lot go skyward. Which might not be such a bad thing, if I didn't have three womenfolk who'd give me a hard time for the rest of my life. They'd probably make me blow up two hundred more.'

'Marcia would never give me a hard time over a balloon.'

'Lucky you,' Jake said. 'Or unlucky you. Depending on which way you want to look at it, but I sure as hell know what way I'm looking at it. I'll leave you to your very important phone call.'

'My…?'

'If Marcia's coming in two days, hadn't you better let her know?' Jake suggested. 'If you're arming the battlements it's always a good idea to let the armour know what's required.'

What was it about this place? He'd landed in some chaotic muddle of people who seemed to think they knew him because his name was Douglas. Who seemed to think they knew more about his life than he did.

Which was clearly ridiculous.

But Jake had said he needed to make a phone call—and Jake was right.

Calculation. Midday here. Eight at night there. Fine.

Marcia answered on the first ring. Still at her desk, then.

'Hi,' she said warmly. 'How's the valuation going?'

'I'm a bit distracted,' he told her. He'd emerged from the hubbub of noise within the beer tent, he'd retreated to the side of the marquee but he could still see the colourful chaos that was the fair. 'Our pumpkin just won a major prize.'

There was a moment's silence. Then… 'Well, hooray for our pumpkin. Hamish, are you feeling well?'

'Are you absolutely imperatively busy at the moment?'

'I'm always absolutely imperatively busy.'

'And if you dropped everything and came here…'

'Why would I do that?'

'The widow,' he said, and his desperation must have sounded down the wire because there was laughter.

'Oh, darling, I did wonder. You're the heir and she's the dowager. So there's a bit of matchmaking?'

'Not on our part. I mean…she doesn't want it any more than I do. But the townspeople do, and it'd make it much easier to keep everything on a business footing if you appeared.'

There was a moment's silence. He could imagine her scrolling down the screen of her electronic diary, juggling appointments. Figuring out imperatives.

'I can spare you three days,' she said at last. 'There's a financial review in Hong Kong starting next Friday I was tempted to attend. Hong Kong's almost your time zone so I could get over jet-lag with you. I have no intention of being in Hong Kong if my mind's not totally focussed. There's some heavy stuff going down. Oil futures. It could be really big.'

'So that means…'

'I'll be with you Monday your time. I'll fly out again on Thursday. Will that solve your problems?'

He stared around him. Oil futures in Hong Kong.

One of Jake's twins—Alice?—was walking toward him carrying a hot dog. She was leaving a trail of ketchup in her wake. She was beaming and holding it out to him as if it was a truly amazing gift.

Marcia here?

She had to come. He needed grounding. Fast.

'That'll be great,' he said weakly.

'I'll let you know the arrangements. Is there anything else you need now? I'm in a rush.'

'No.'

'Then 'bye.' Click.

'Marcia's coming,' he told Alice as he accepted her hot dog, and she gave him a dubious smile.

'Is Marcia nice?'

'Very nice.'

'Does she like hot dogs?'

'I guess.'

'My Aunty Susie says you have to come,' she said. 'The wood chopping's about to start and the laird always has first chop.'

'He's a bit of all right.'

The woodchopping had seemed just what Hamish had needed. His hands were still a bit sore from digging but he put that aside. The sight of logs, waiting to be chopped, meant that he could vent his spleen in a way that didn't hurt anyone (except him—pity about the blisters!), didn't involve so much alcohol that he'd regret it the next day and got him away from Susie.

The logs were propped as posts. The woodchoppers were given a truly excellent axe and told to go to it. Hamish did his first ceremonial chop, then watched the champion woodchoppers with something akin to envy. While he watched the woodchoppers, the inhabitants of Dolphin Bay were watching him, talking about him, clapping him on the back—and looking sideways at Susie.

Things were starting to get desperate. His blisters hurt—but would a real earl be deflected by a few blisters? Of course not.

As the novice events started, he stripped to the waist and proceeded to chop.

'There's something about a man in a kilt and nothing else,' Kirsty murmured, and nudged her sister. 'Ooh-er. A fine figure of a man, our new laird.'

'He's not our new laird,' Susie retorted, a trifle breathlessly. 'A new laird wouldn't sell his castle and run.'

'He hasn't sold it yet. There's many a slip…'

'Cut it out, Kirsty.'

'Susie, he's gorgeous.'

'Kirsty, he's engaged to be married.'

'So you have noticed he's gorgeous.'

'I'd have to be blind not to notice he's gorgeous.'

The logs had to be chopped into four. The way it was done was to chop a chunk out, ram a plank into the chunk, stand on the plank and lop the top off. Then lower the plank and start again with a lower chunk. Hamish was on his second level.

Chunks of wood were flying everywhere—there was more enthusiasm than science in his technique. His body was glistening with sweat.

'Kilts are yummy,' Kirsty said thoughtfully. 'I wonder if Jake'd wear one.'

'I'm yummy enough without a kilt.' Jake had come up behind them, and now he put his arms round his wife and hugged. 'How do you improve on just plain irresistible?'

'I liked you better when you were four feet taller,' Susie told him, eyeing her brother-in-law with disfavour. 'And I don't know how it is but the red nose just doesn't cut it.'

'It turns Kirsty on, though,' Jake said smugly, and Kirsty answered by pulling his plastic nose back to the full length of its elastic, holding it thoughtfully for a moment and then letting it go.

'Yep, I like it better on,' she said, and turned back to her sister. 'Now, where were we?'

'Hey.' Jake clutched his nose in pain and Susie giggled. But there was a part of her…

There was a part of her that was really, really jealous of her sister and her husband, she decided. She'd met and fallen for Rory, but she'd had him for such a short time and then he'd been gone. His loss still had the power to hurt so much that she almost couldn't bear it. The sight of her sister and her husband so happy…

Her eyes turned involuntarily back to Hamish. Hamish smashing through his third the level of wood. Hamish concentrating every ounce of energy in getting the log through, pitting his strength against the wood.

She thought of how he'd been yesterday morning, digging her path with just such energy. What was driving him?

What was this Marcia like?

It wasn't her business.

'I'm going home,' she said abruptly. 'Harriet's over under the trees with Rosie and Pup. I'll go and collect them. I think it'd be better if I took Pup home now and settled her into her new home before dinner. Even if that home is temporary,' she added in an undertone but Kirsty heard and winced.

'Susie, do you mind? About the puppy?'

'I love Pup.' She hugged her sister.

'But Hamish…do you mind that he's taking over?'

'Well…' She shrugged. 'I can't not mind, but it doesn't make sense to care too much.'

'If you two got on…'

'We do get on. And no matter how much better we got on, he'd still sell the castle. It's the only sensible thing to do. Can you give him a ride home?'

'Sure,' Jake told her. 'If you really need to go.'

'I really need to go.'

He won.

Hamish stood over his four pieces of chopped logs and gasped until he got his breath back. This was fantastic. Much better than any gym workout. He was standing bare backed, clad only in his kilt and footwear, the sun burning on his skin, the wash of the sea the background roar to the applause of the crowd. His hands were a bit painful—actually, very painful— but what was a bit of pain? It felt like he'd been transformed into another place, another time. Another life.

He'd won.

He turned to where Susie had been standing, and she wasn't there.

'Where…?' he started, and Jake came toward him and wrung his hand.

'Well done, mate.'

'Ouch,' Hamish muttered, and hauled his hand back. 'Where's Susie?'

'Gone home.'

Right. Suddenly his hands were really, really painful.

This was dumb—but it didn't feel fantastic any more.

Hamish didn't come home for dinner and Susie didn't care. She didn't, she didn't, she didn't. She'd eaten far too much rubbish at the fair to worry about dinner—a piece of the inevitable toast was fine. She fed the puppy the mix Adam's mother had thoughtfully packed. She popped her to sleep in the wet room, and then as the puppy complained she carted her back to the kitchen, sat in the rocker in front of the fire and cuddled her.

'I'm calling you Taffy,' she said. 'I know I had sixty-three other suggestions but they can't tell me what to call my very own puppy.'

Taffy looked up at her in sleepy agreement, curled into her lap and proceeded to go to sleep.

Susie rocked on.

'Me and a puppy and a baby,' she whispered. 'I have a house-ful.'

'Where will I go?' she whispered back. 'Where will I take my little family?'

She'd go back to the house she'd shared with Rory. Of course. That was the best thing to do. The simplest.

But the thought of going back to the house she'd shared with Rory…

'It'll be empty, Taf,' she told the puppy, popping her down onto a cushion by the fire. 'Even with you. It's a gorgeous house on the coast. It looks out over the ocean. It's really wild. Rory worked from home and it was great with the two of us there but…but I'm not sure you and Rosie are going to be good enough company.'

As if in answer to her question, Taffy said nothing at all.

Susie rocked on. She'd lit the range more for company than because she needed its warmth, but the gentle crackle and hiss of burning logs was comforting.

Not comforting enough.

'I have to go home.'

'Isn't talking to yourself the first sign of madness?'

She jumped close on a foot. When she came down to earth she was breathless—and cross.

'What do you think you're doing?'

'Coming home,' Hamish said and it was so much an echo of what she'd been thinking that she almost jumped again.

'You scared me.'

'I'm sorry.'

'It's your kitchen,' she said, but she sounded defensive. She took a grip and tried for a lighter note. 'You've had supper?'

But she was still flustered. He didn't look nearly as together as he'd looked that morning. He was still in his kilt but he'd chopped wood; he'd been drinking beer with the men; he'd joined the tug-of-war teams. He looked dishevelled and tired and frayed, like a Scottish lord coming home after a hard day at battle.

'You've got a splodge of toffee apple on your cheek,' she managed, a trifle breathlessly, and he wiped it away with the back of his hand and grinned.

'I've had a very good time.'

'Not like Manhattan, huh?'

'Not the least like Manhattan. I've never had a day like this in my life.'

'Do you want supper?'

'Are you kidding?' He was standing in the doorway looking big and tousled. His long socks were down at his ankles, his legs were bare and there were grass stains on his kilt. And his hair had hay in it. He looked...he looked...

Cut it out, she told herself desperately. Don't look!

'I've been judging the cooking,' he told her, still with that grin that had her heart doing those crazy somersaulting things she didn't understand at all. 'They made me honorary adjudicator, which means I've tasted scones, plum cakes, sponge cakes...you name it, I've tasted it. Some of it was truly excellent.'

'What makes you a judge?'

'It's the kilt,' he told her wisely. 'Anyone wearing a kilt like this has to know a lot about cooking. A lot about everything, really. That's why they have the House of Lords in England.'

'Sorry?'

'If you're a lord then you get to be an automatic Member of Parliament,' he told her. 'I read it somewhere. I haven't figured out whether it applies to me or not, but I guess inheriting earldomship must make me wise in some respects.'

'Like in judging scones.'

'That'd be it,' he told her, and all of a sudden they were

grinning at each other like fools. The atmosphere had changed and it was somehow…

Different.

She hadn't felt like this since Rory had died, she thought, and suddenly she felt breathless. Traitorish?

No. Free. It was like a great grey cloud, which had settled on top of her for the last two years, had lifted and she felt…extraordinary.

'You don't mind that Marcia's coming?' he said, and she caught herself and forced her stupid, floating mind back to earth with a snap.

'Of course I don't. This is your house.'

'I should have told you.'

'There was no need. There's plenty of room. And as I said, I can always move out.'

'I don't want you to move out…yet.'

Good. Great. She thought about it and wondered if she was being entirely sensible.

'I need to go,' she said a trifle uncertainly, rising and moving toward the door.

'To America?'

'Not tonight.' She managed a smile but the frisson of something different was still in the air and she felt strange. This was crazy. This man was engaged to someone called Marcia and she'd have nothing to do with him after she left here. But today… Today he'd made her smile and he'd made everyone here smile, too. She was under no illusions as to how sad a day it would have been for everyone if Hamish hadn't been here, but he'd bounced around the fair having fun, charming old ladies, eating too many scones and toffee apples, looking fabulous in his kilt. He'd given the locals something to talk about, something to smile over, and even when he left in a few weeks, even though he'd sell the castle, today had been a gift.

'Thank you,' she said simply.

'Thank you?'

'For today. Everyone loved having a laird for the day.'

'It was my pleasure.'

'Really?'

'It was,' he said.

And there it was again. Bang. Like in the comics, she thought a little bit helplessly. Wham, bang, zing, splat.

'Good night, my lord,' she said simply, and he put out a hand and took hers. And winced.

The gesture had been a friendly good-night touch, but as she took his hand in hers and felt its warmth, touched his strength, she also felt something else.

'Ouch,' she said, turning his palm over. And then she saw his palm and she repeated the word with feeling. *'Ouch!'*

'It is a bit,' he confessed, but she was no longer listening.

'Oh, Hamish, your hands. You dope. You blistered them with digging and then to use the axe...'

'We earls aren't wusses.'

'You earls are dopes,' she told him. 'I might have known. Angus was just like you. You know, we had to dress his oxygen canister up in tartan so he could go to his last fair without feeling like a wuss.'

'I don't have an oxygen cylinder,' he said, startled, and she shook her head in disgust.

'Not for want of trying. Hamish, these are awful.'

'Don't say that,' she said uneasily. 'I've been trying to ignore them all day.'

'Right. Ignoring them why? Waiting for your hands to drop off?'

'My hands are not going to drop off.'

'There's ten blisters on this hand,' she said, hauling it closer to get a better look. 'And there's a splinter in this one. And another. You great dope. I'll ring Kirsty.'

'Kirsty?'

'My sister,' she said, exasperated. 'This needs medical attention.'

'I'll wash it,' he said, as if granting an enormous concession. 'That'll fix it.'

'It won't fix it.'

'If you tell me how bad it is one more time, I'll cry,' he said, like it was a huge threat, and she blinked and stared up at him in astonishment.

'Really?'

'Um…no.'

'I wouldn't blame you if you did.'

'I won't. I have an aversion to the pastime.'

'Well, don't stick near me, then,' she told him. 'I cry all the time. Just looking at these makes me teary. You great hulking hero.'

'Hero?'

'Axing away with all of these.' She was examining each blister, searching for more splinters, and the thought of him chopping wood, doing it to make the old ladies smile… That's why he'd done it, she thought. She'd thought he'd done it because it had seemed fun but now, looking at these hands, she thought he'd done it because that's what she'd asked him to do. Create a diversion from Angus's death. Give the locals something else to think about it. He'd eaten scones, he'd chopped wood, he'd placed every eye on him and he'd made people smile.

'Please, don't cry.' He sounded so scared that she stared up at him in even more bewilderment. His face was set, and he was backing away. But she had hold of his hand and she wasn't letting him go anywhere. He was a dope but he was a great, gorgeous dope and he'd done this because she'd asked him to. Therefore—at great personal sacrifice—she'd choke back tears and be businesslike.

'I'm not crying,' she said, trying to sound exasperated and not emotional. 'Sit.'

'Sit?'

'I'll clean them and I'll pull the splinters out. And then I'll put on iodine and we'll see how much of a man you are. You don't cry, huh? Iodine on these will be a real truth test. Iodine would make an onion howl all by itself.'

So he sat in the old rocking chair in front of the range, his free hand soaking in a bowl of soapy water she'd rested on his kilted knees while she carefully examined each blister, cleaned it, lifted out tiny shards of wood with a pair of tweezers—and then anointed each one with iodine.

'You should have a bullet to bite on,' she told him, and he looked down at her mop of auburn curls and thought he wasn't even near yelling. He was hardly thinking about pain.

She was intent on his hand. She was so…simple, he thought, but maybe that wasn't the word. She'd changed from the clothes she'd worn at the fair. Now she was wearing a pair of shorts and a faded T-shirt that was a little too tight. Her legs and her feet were bare. She was wearing no makeup. Her hair was falling forward, stopping him seeing what she was doing with his hand but at the same time distracting him nicely.

She smelt of some citrusy soap, he thought. She'd probably showered when she'd come home from the fair. Maybe she and Rosie had bathed together and the vision of her bathing her baby was suddenly….

Whew. It was just as well Marcia was coming, he thought. A man could get himself into dangerous territory here.

And why wouldn't a man want to?

The thought was so far out of left field that he blinked and almost pulled his hand away. She felt the tug and looked up in concern, all huge eyes and tousled hair and…and Susie.

'I'm trying hard not to hurt you.'

'You're not hurting me.'

'Tell me about your job,' she said, turning her attention back to the splinters as if it was important that she look at anything but him. As maybe it was.

'My job?'

'You're a financier.'

'Mmm.'

'You love being a financier?'

'I guess.' Did he? He wasn't sure.

'I've been trying to imagine why,' she told him. 'I get such a kick out of planting something and watching it grow. Do you see schemes through to the end? Like if someone comes to you and says please can I build a bulldozer factory, can I have some money, does it give you the same thrill? That those bulldozers would never have got built if it hadn't been for you?'

'Um…maybe that's banking,' he said uneasily.

'So you don't do any hands-on supplying of money for doing interesting stuff like building bulldozers.'

'No.'

'So what do you finance?'

'I guess most of my work is taken up with futures broking,' he told her.

'Which is…'

'Figuring out what money is going to be worth in the future and buying and selling on that basis.'

She tweaked out another sliver of wood. Thoughtful. 'So you buy and sell money. It seems a bit odd to me but if it makes you happy…'

Did it make him happy? He'd never thought about it. It seemed such an odd concept that he almost didn't understand the question.

The high-powered finance world was where he'd worked all his adult life. All he knew was wheeling and dealing, the adrenalin rush of vast fiscal deals, the knife edge of knowing it was his brains holding everything in place and if he slipped up…

He thought about his mother's reaction when he'd told her that he'd been made a full equity partner. For once she hadn't cried. She'd closed her eyes and when she'd opened them things had changed.

'Now I can stop worrying,' she'd said.

Full equity partner in one of Manhattan's biggest brokerage firms…well, if that was what it had taken to stop the tears, then great. And he was good at his job. It had earned him a lot, and he had no time to think about anything else.

What else was there to think about but work?

The scent of Susie's hair? That was all he could think about now. That and the feel of her fingers carefully working on his hands. Each blister was being tended with care. It was such a strange sensation. An intimate sensation.

Would Marcia ever tend his blisters?

How would he get blisters around Marcia? He wouldn't. His biggest risk was of repetitive strain injury caused by using his Blackberry too much.

A cold damp something hit the edge of his bare leg and he hauled himself from his reverie and stared down.

Pup.

'Whoops,' Susie said, and laid Hamish's hands carefully on his kilted knees and scooped up the pup. 'That's good timing. Taffy, if you've woken up, you go outside straight away. Hamish, don't touch anything. I'll be back.' And she was gone, whisking the pup out into the gathering dusk.

Don't touch anything.

He sat for a bit, not thinking anything, letting his mind go blank. The sensation was almost extraordinary. When had he last done this?

Simply...stopped.

There was always something to do. Always. Reports to read, e-mail to check, constant analysis. If he didn't keep up then others would get ahead or things could slip by him and, hell, what was the use of being in the heap if you weren't on top?

His laptop was up in his bedroom. He'd connected briefly that morning, checking things were OK. He should go up now and see...

It was seven at night. Three in the morning New York time. Not a lot was happening over there right now.

The Japanese market would be online, he decided. The yen had been looking pretty shaky when he'd left. It wouldn't hurt to stay online for a bit and get the feel for...

Susie was out in the garden. With Taffy.

From where he sat he could hear the sea. He could smell the sea.

She'd told him to stay, so he did, sort of. He walked to the kitchen door and watched while she introduced Taffy to the lawn and explained what was required.

As if the dog could understand.

'There's no hurry,' she was saying. 'I understand it's all a bit strange and new, and there's even more strange and new to come, but we can take our time. Me and Rose will be the constants wherever you are, and we'll always be able to find you a patch of grass. There's not a lot else you need to worry about.'

What about the Dow Jones? Hamish thought, glancing at his watch and wondering what the financial markets had done in the past ten hours. He always needed to worry about the Dow Jones.

But maybe not now. Maybe worrying about financial indices here was…ridiculous.

Susie was kneeling on the grass. The dopy pup had rolled over onto her back, and Susie was scratching her tummy. She wriggled in delight, her ungainly body squirming with ecstasy on the still sun-warmed ground.

How was she going to cope? Hamish thought. With a baby. With a puppy. She had a lot to worry about. She should be worrying about it right now!

She wasn't worrying. She lay on the grass herself and the puppy climbed on top of her. The last flickers of light from the tangerine sunset were soft on her face. She was giggling as the puppy tried to lick her cheek. From behind he could hear Rose chirping as she woke from what he presumed was a very late afternoon nap. Susie would never get her daughter to sleep tonight.

But she didn't care, he thought. She had no sense of order. He remembered his mother if dinner was five minutes late. She'd be almost apoplectic with anxiety.

He thought of Marcia if things didn't run to plan. What would Marcia do if he gave her a puppy?

Marcia would give the puppy right back. And as for a baby…

Marcia letting a baby having an afternoon nap at this hour? Marcia having a baby?

The idea was so ridiculous that he grinned and Susie looked over and saw him grinning and said, 'What?'

'What yourself?'

'You're laughing at me.'

'I'm laughing at your puppy. There's a difference. Rose is awake.'

'Goody.' She scrambled to her feet, put the puppy down and made to go indoors. 'She went to sleep on the way home and wouldn't wake up. She'll be so hungry. I almost woke her but then I remembered there's an English comedy show I like on TV late tonight, and it's the best fun watching it with Rose.'

Then as he blinked, trying to reconcile late-night comedy and a fourteen-month-old toddler, she hesitated. As she'd started toward the door Taffy had followed.

'You haven't done what you need to do,' she told the puppy, and pointed to the grass. 'Duty first.'

The puppy looked up at her new mistress with adoration, and wagged her tail.

'Stay here with her while I fetch Rose,' Susie ordered Hamish, and he nodded and put a foot out to stop Taffy following her mistress.

Taffy sat down and howled.

They both looked at Taffy. Taffy looked at both of them, opened her jaws and howled even longer.

'Whoops,' Susie said. 'What have I let myself in for?'

'Give her back,' Hamish told her.

'What?'

'You don't have to keep her.'

She snatched Taffy up and glared. 'What a thing to say. Don't listen, sweetheart. You're mine. We're a family. I don't mind the odd howl. It's an excellent howl and it's all your very own. I wonder if you'll like my TV programme, too.'

This was seriously weird. There were all sorts of things happening inside Hamish that he had no idea what to do with.

'You can't be a family to that…that.'

'That gorgeous pup? I can be a family with whoever I want,' she snapped, hauling herself up to her full five feet four inches and glaring. 'Taffy needs me out here. Can you fetch Rose?'

'What, get her from her cot?'

'That's the plan.'

'Just walk in and pick her up?'

'You earls have great courage,' she said, obviously trying not to sound sarcastic. 'If you pick her up under the armpits and close your palms, it won't even hurt your blisters.'

It wasn't his blisters he was afraid of. 'I can't pick up a baby.'

'Don't be ridiculous. Get in there.'

'Woof,' said Taffy.

He stared at the pair of them and they stared back, challenging.

He could do this. Right. *You earls have great courage…* Right.

He strode into the house, followed the sound of Rosie's increased indignation and pushed open the door to Susie's and Rosie's shared bedroom. And paused in astonishment.

The bed was vast, a great four-poster with mounds of eiderdowns and more mounds of cushions. There were pinks and purples and almost crimsons and gold. It was an amazing bed.

And the walls…

Deirdre's kitsch ornaments had been taken down, and Susie had covered the walls with prints—not expensive artwork but prints she'd obviously ordered because they appealed.

There were all sorts of prints.

Tree ferns taken from strange angles. Waterfalls. Rock formations. That was one wall.

Another wall was the sea—vast curling waves, surfers doing all sorts of incredible twisting turns, shots of foam, a single rock pool, a tiny minnow against a vast pier pile…

The third was people. Grins. People smiling. These weren't people she knew. Ancient Tibetan grandmothers with gap-toothed grins. Old men smiling at each other in friendship. A group of kids in Scout uniform, smiling in unison.

And the last wall was photographs blown up. Susie as a kid, he thought, looking at twins cavorting on a beach. Photographs of a man who was obviously Rory. A couple in love. He looked at them smiling at each other, and felt a twist of…

No. Don't look. You don't need to feel like this.

It was dumb to put such photographs up, he thought. This was as kitsch as Deirdre's efforts.

But then he thought, No, it's not. He thought of his apartment back in Manhattan, and Marcia's, planned by the same minimalist decorator who'd recoil in horror if she saw this. But this sort of worked. It was a huge collage of life, of living, of all Susie held dear.

An indignant yell brought him back to earth. In the centre of the room was that which Susie held dearest. The toddler was beaming as she saw she'd caught his attention. She was holding her hands out and saying, 'Up.'

'Hi,' he said weakly, and she bounced and grinned and held her hands higher.

'Up, up, up.'

He could do this. He put his hands under her arms and gingerly raised her.

She giggled and pointed to the bed. 'Dappy,' she said.

Dappy. He thought about it. Then he realised what she meant. Um, no.

He made to carry her—holding her at arm's length—out the door, out to her mother, but her yell became urgent. He had her agenda wrong.

'Dappy, dappy, dappy.'

You earls have great courage.

'Where are your diapers?' he asked, and she pointed an imperious finger to the pile on a side table. Under the Tibetan grandmas.

'Dappy.'

OK. He set Rose down on the floor but she yelled in indignation. Her routine was obviously to be followed to the letter.

'Bed,' she said, and pointed.

'Give me a break,' he said weakly, but he was a man under orders. He tossed a diaper across to the bed, then lifted Rose and set her down on the eiderdown. She almost disappeared in its vastness.

She giggled and kicked her feet, squirming away from him and burrowing under the cushions. This was obviously a game, played whenever she woke up.

The bed smelt like Susie.

The room smelt like Susie.

Rose lifted a cushion, grinned at him, chortled and pulled

the pillow back over her head again. He considered, then put a finger on the small of her back and tickled.

Shrieks of laughter and she squirmed deeper. Right under the quilt.

He put his head under the quilt and said, 'Boo.'

'Dappy,' she said, and pushed the quilt away, lay flat and waited. 'Boo' was obviously the magic word.

And he performed magic as well. Hamish Douglas, corporate financier, ninth Earl of Loganaich, successfully changed a diaper.

'Like climbing Annapurna One,' he told himself, setting Rose on the floor, carrying the used diaper into the bathroom in triumph and thinking of the world's second most difficult climb. 'A soggy diaper. A soiled diaper represents Everest.'

Then as Rose looked thoughtful he tossed the diaper into the wastebin and dived on the toddler to take her out to her mother before she could send him up his second mountain.

He wasn't ready for Everest yet.

Susie was still waiting for Taffy to perform. She was sitting on a garden seat, watching the dark settle over the garden, simply...waiting.

Hamish delivered her daughter, Rose squirmed down onto the grass and she and Taffy proceeded to investigate each other.

'Aren't you going to make her dinner?' Hamish asked, and Susie smiled down at her puppy and her daughter and shook her head.

'No one's in a hurry.'

It was such a strange concept that Hamish blinked.

'You want a seat?' Susie wriggled sideways, making room on the bench.

Why would he sit down? Just to sit?

'Maybe I'll work on the path.'

'With those hands? Are you out of your mind?'

'We earls have great courage.'

'You earls need a straitjacket if you work with hands like those. Just stop, Hamish. Rest.'

He sat. Gingerly. It felt weird.

'Thank you for today,' she said gently, and he felt even more weird.

'Why…?'

'You've made today happy for a lot of people. Just by being here.'

'Just by exposing my knees?'

'A thing of beauty is a joy for ever,' she said serenely, and he choked.

'Right.'

'Honest, Hamish.' Her hand came out to touch his arm. Lightly resting. There was no pressure but the feel of her fingers on his arm was almost his undoing. That and the warmth of the night, the soft hush of the sea, the weird domesticity of pup and baby playing at their feet…

'You were wonderful,' she said, and suddenly she twisted so she could kiss him. Lightly. It was a kiss of thanks. No more than that. A feather kiss.

Except…it wasn't.

People kissed all the time, Hamish thought. They kissed in greeting, and farewell, or as had just happened, to say thank you. It meant nothing. There was no reason to think that a twenty-thousand-volt electric charge had just cut off every other circuit in his body.

Why?

There was no reason, he thought, dazed.

Or was it because Susie was a thousand light years away from any other woman he'd ever dated? She was a thousand light years from Marcia. In her faded shorts and T-shirt and nothing else, nothing to attract, nothing at all, she smelt…she felt…

Soft and delicious and absolutely, imperatively desirable.

It was just the day, he thought, hauling back in shock and dazed wonder. It had been a day totally out of his experience, and he was floundering here because he'd never met anyone like this before, and there were probably thousands of women who were like this but he'd just never met them, and he was out of his comfort zone, and…

'Hey, Hamish, I'm not planning on jumping you,' Susie said, and he jerked back to reality. To Susie staring at him with eyes that were bemused—and maybe also a little hurt.

'I know. It's just…I'm engaged to Marcia.'

Maybe that had been the wrong thing to say.

'I know you're engaged to Marcia,' she said with asperity. 'You really do think I'm planning on jumping you. Just because I'm a widow.'

'No.'

'You do,' she said, and there was no disguising the anger now. She rose and stood, glaring at him with her hands on her hips, vibrating with fury. 'If your colleague in the next office said goodbye, have a good vacation, and kissed you, what would you have thought?'

'Nothing.' Of course not. It was what had happened. 'Hey, Hamish is off on a vacation, can you believe that? 'Bye, Hamish, take care.' Kiss.

It meant nothing. But he had to stop thinking sideways. Susie was in temper-on mode.

'But because I'm a widow, everyone looks at me like I'm encroaching. Like I'm just planning how to get the next man into my bed. Like I'm every married woman's worst enemy. Even you. It's so unfair. I loved Rory like I've never loved anyone. I'm not in the market for another relationship, and hauling Marcia over here just to protect yourself… Don't think I don't realise what you're doing, Hamish Douglas. There was no inkling from you that Marcia would be coming until everyone looked at us like a couple. Then you started looking like a rabbit caught in headlights. It's just so dumb. Dumb, dumb, dumb.' She swooped down and lifted Rose into her arms.

'Come on, sweetheart. We'll go make you some dinner and leave his Lordship here in solitary splendour. In the knowledge that his virtue can remain intact for his precious Marcia. But know that even if there were a million Marcias—or do I mean if there weren't any?—there's no way I'm interested in you,

Hamish Douglas, Not the least little bit. Not one skerrick. You leave me as cold as a flat, dead fish.'

She turned and wheeled into the house. Hamish was left starting after her.

Taffy looked at up him, doubtful.

'I'd follow,' he told the pup. 'I'm a flat, dead fish.'

Taffy hesitated a bit more but then as Hamish remained unmoving she obviously decided that maybe Hamish was right. Flat, dead fish were a bit unappetising.

He followed Susie.

There was absolute silence. Even the hush of the sea was fading.

Nothing.

A flat, dead fish.

He should go check his e-mail. He should—

There was a groan from the house and Susie's head appeared at the kitchen window.

'Thanks for sending Taffy inside,' she snapped. 'She's done her business in the hallway. Over to you, your Lordship.'

Great. He rose. *We earls have great courage.*

Even flat, dead fish had their uses.

CHAPTER SEVEN

WHAT followed were a couple of very strained days. Susie and Hamish skirted each other with extreme caution.

They spent the mornings at the beach—well, why wouldn't they as the beach was there and gorgeous? Taffy loved it. Rose loved it. Hamish loved it. He admitted that to himself but, hell, it was a strain. Susie was a small indignant puff of offence and she treated the beach as if they'd put a fence down the middle, with strictly segregated His and Hers zones. When he offered to take care of Rose to give her time to swim she accepted graciously—as if she was granting him a favour—but she flounced out to sea and flounced back, and ignored him in the interim.

'I didn't mean to offend you,' he told her.

'You didn't offend me. You merely implied I saw you as husband material. As nothing could be further from the truth, I believe we need to keep things formal.'

Right. Formal.

By the time Marcia arrived on Monday evening he was almost relieved. Anything to break the formality.

Marcia arrived with Jake. Jake had gone up to Sydney for a one-day pain management conference, and as the times fitted perfectly, he'd offered to collect Marcia from the airport and bring her down. So at eight on Monday night Hamish strolled out to the castle forecourt to greet his fiancée.

'Hi, sweetheart,' he said as she emerged from Jake's truck. He hugged her elegantly suited body close and kissed her—so deeply that he caught her by surprise. When the kiss ended she pulled back and looked astonished.

'Wow,' she said, touching her lips like they were bruised. 'It's only been a few days.'

'I've missed you.'

'Is the widow watching?'

The widow. It took him a minute to catch that but realised, of course, Marcia would think he was playing for an audience. Since he'd implied…

'Have you warned Marcia about our Susie?' Jake asked, sounding interested, and Hamish grimaced.

'I haven't told Marcia anything.'

'Only that the whole place is expecting you to marry her,' Marcia said smoothly. 'You might as well say it like it is, sweetheart. Keep things out in the open so there's no misunderstanding.'

'No misunderstanding,' Jake said blankly. 'Right.'

'Um…good trip?' Hamish said, feeling desperate. 'Have you two found lots to talk about?'

'I slept all the way,' Marcia said. She turned to Jake and gave him her loveliest smile, which was only slightly patronising. 'Thank you so much. I'm afraid I was very boring.'

'Not at all,' Jake told her politely. 'I'll leave you to your Hamish, then, shall I?'

'That would be kind.' Peasantry dismissed.

'Right, then,' Jake said, and with a wry grin he folded his long body back into the driver's seat of his battered Land Cruiser, gave a salute of acknowledgement and left.

'That was a bit brusque,' Hamish said, frowning as Jake backed out of the forecourt. 'Did you two not find anything to talk about at all?'

'Honestly, darling, he's a family doctor. I don't even have any bunions to talk about.'

'I guess not.'

Marcia was out of her territory, he thought, suppressing irritation. She wasn't normally this brittle. Maybe she was just better among her own kind.

He was her kind, he remembered. This was the woman he intended marrying. He loved her cool, sophisticated humour. She was so intelligent…

'So where's the widow?' she asked.

'Inside. I'll take you to meet her.'

But she hung back, taking a moment to absorb the whole moonlit scene, the fairy-tale castle, the mountains behind, the fabulous coastline.

'This will sell for a mint,' she breathed. 'Oh, Hamish, imagine this in *Vogue Traveller.* Your own little Scottish castle without all those horrid fogs and bogs and midges of Scotland.'

'There's nothing wrong with Scotland,' he said, and startled himself by how fervent he sounded.

'You've never been to Scotland.'

'No, but I'm a direct descendant…'

She gave a peal of laughter and tucked her hand into his arm. 'You've become the Lord of Loganaich,' she said affectionately. 'My very own earl, defending the land of his forebears. Any minute now you'll be up on the turrets playing your bagpipes.'

He grinned, relaxing a little. 'I do wear a mean kilt.'

'This I have to see.'

'You need to meet Susie first.'

'The widow. OK, let's get the scary part over and then get down to the fun part. This place sounded good on paper but in reality… Wow! Let's figure what this pile is really worth!'

The meeting between Susie and Marcia was not an unqualified success. Susie was in the kitchen, cleaning up. She greeted Marcia with cautious courtesy. Marcia responded in kind—while clinging to Hamish's arm with proprietorial affection—and then Susie excused herself.

'There's steak in the fridge, Hamish, if Marcia's hungry. I'd cook it but—'

'But I do a better steak than you do,' Hamish told her, smiling encouragingly. Wishing she didn't look so tense. Wishing he hadn't told Marcia there was a problem.

Wishing Marcia wasn't clinging quite so close.

'I'll go to bed, then,' Susie said, and Marcia glanced at her watch, astonished.

'It's only eight.'

'Susie's recovering from injuries,' Hamish said, and then wished he hadn't said that as well, as Susie flashed him a look of anger.

'I'm not recovering from injuries. I'm recovered from injuries.'

'You limp,' Marcia pointed out, and Susie glowered a bit and limped her way past them.

'So I do,' she agreed. 'It's my own little idiosyncrasy. But I like it. I'm going to bed to read a good romance novel and I don't intend to recover at all. Hamish, you need to show Marcia through the castle. I'll bet she's interested in your inventory. And when you've finished... Marcia, could you let me know when this hotel assessor's expected, as I need to organise myself to leave? Good night.'

Taffy was snoozing by the stove. Susie scooped her up, glared at the pair of them and left.

'Have I offended her?' Marcia asked, and Hamish sighed.

'I guess... I mean, maybe it wasn't such a good idea to imply there was a problem.'

'What do you mean? Her limp? It's obvious. She can't expect me not to notice.'

That wasn't the problem he'd been talking about. 'Never mind. Are you hungry?'

'Actually, I ate on the way here and I'm very tired. Maybe the widow has a good idea with early bed.' She snuggled back against him. 'Where are we sleeping?'

'I've put you in the bedroom next to mine. Come and I'll show you.'

'Not yours?'

'Um, no. It just seems...'

'A bit mean?' Marcia was struggling to understand. 'Honey, if she really wants you, then the faster she comes to terms with reality the better.'

'It's not like that. It just... Marcia, it seems like this is Susie's home and I'd like it to stay that way until we leave. I think... separate bedrooms.'

She raised a cool eyebrow. 'Well, that's fine with me. I have a date with my laptop. I've missed so much, trying to get here. There won't be a romance novel for me in bed tonight.'

Hamish slept late. Hours late by his standards. He always woke early in New York to find the latest on the Hang Seng before he went to work. As he was always behind his desk by seven, that meant he went to bed in the small hours and he woke in the small hours. He couldn't remember a time when he'd fallen into bed at ten and slept for more than eight hours.

But here... It was the silence of the place, he thought, or that there was no desk waiting and Jodie had cancelled his imperatives.

He woke and it was already seven-thirty. He lay lazily back on his mound of satin pillows and watched the early morning sunbeams flicker through the floating dreamcatcher Deirdre had hung at the window. Jodie had hung a dreamcatcher on the window of his outer office back in Manhattan. He'd asked her what it was and she'd explained the ludicrous concept in detail.

Susie might not think it ludicrous, he thought. Jodie hadn't. Deirdre obviously hadn't.

He needed Marcia to set him right. She'd be up by now. He should go find her.

But his thoughts kept wandering, snagging different ideas like the dreamcatcher was designed to do.

Where was Jodie was right now? he wondered. Was she making choir stalls with her beloved Nick? He'd miss his secretary when he went back.

When he went back. When he left here.

When he left Susie.

Susie was leaving first.

Maybe he could keep in touch with Susie, he thought. Just to check that she was OK. He'd tell Kirsty and Jake that he'd keep an eye on her.

She'd throw such an offer back in his face, he decided. She didn't need anyone to take care of her.

But he rejected that, too. Of course she needed someone. She thought she was strong enough to care for a baby and a dog and a career. She was planning on working as a landscape gardener again, but anyone could see she had physical problems. Her legs would never hold her up.

He could… He could…

He could do nothing. It was none of his business.

More lying on his satin pillows and thinking. He was head of the clan, he thought. Lord of Loganaich. Laird. It behoved him to care for…

For the relic?

The thought of Susie as a relic was so crazy he laughed and threw off his covers and headed for the shower. He was being dumb. He'd go and find Marcia and show her this crazy castle from stem to stern. They'd smile about how ridiculous it was, they'd talk about practicalities and then she'd bring him up to speed on how the office was coping without him. Marcia was just what he needed.

Right.

Marcia was already in the kitchen. As were Susie and Rose and Taffy. Quite a party. Hamish opened the door and they all turned toward him and glared.

Uh-oh.

A more cowardly man would have retreated. There were obviously issues abroad here. Women's issues?

'We have,' Susie said cautiously, as if she wasn't sure she could trust her voice, 'no soy milk. We have a case of bananas but they're the wrong sort of fruit. Cumquats make the wrong sort of juice and the oranges aren't ripe yet. And Marcia doesn't like the idea of eating strawberries that have been lying on mulch. If you'd warned me Marcia was on a low-carb diet I could have got things in.'

'Low carb's easy,' he said, cautious as Susie and with a wary look at his beloved. 'I mean, steak's low carb.'

'Steak for breakfast?' Marcia shook her head in disbelief. 'Honestly, Hamish, just lend me your car keys and I'll go fetch what I need from the supermarket.'

'It's five miles down the road and it doesn't open until nine,' Hamish said. 'Can't you have toast?'

'The locals eat porridge,' Susie said, lifting a pot onto the range. 'I can recommend it.'

'It's hardly low carb,' Marcia retorted.

'Hey, Marcia, it's hardly a hotel yet,' Hamish said uneasily. 'It wouldn't hurt to break your diet for a morning.'

'I'd prefer not to break my diet,' Marcia said, but she smiled, ready to be accommodating. 'It's OK, guys. I'm not hungry.'

'You're too thin,' Susie muttered.

'A woman can never be too thin.'

'Yeah, you'd know,' Susie muttered, and banged her pan on the range. Then she took a grip. 'Sorry. That sort of just came out. I was too thin for a while and it's scary.'

'I have no intention of heading down the eating disorder road,' Marcia said. 'I have too much control.'

'I'm sure you have,' Susie said, but the eyes she turned on Hamish were suddenly bleak. 'I've made a big pot of porridge. Do you want some?'

'Yes, please.' It was the least a man could do in the circumstances, he thought, but then he saw the sudden gleam behind Susie's eyes and thought, Uh-oh.

'A porridge-eating laird,' she said thoughtfully. 'Finally.'

'I'm back on toast tomorrow.'

'I'm sure you are.' There was definitely laughter there now. She was like a chameleon, he thought. Swinging from happy to sad and back again.

He didn't want her to be sad. Had she been too thin? When? After Rory's death? Hell, he hated to think of what she'd been through.

'Have you been working up in your bedroom?' Marcia asked, and he blinked.

'Um…yeah.'

'Did you see the Euro dropped almost two cents against the greenback overnight?'

'And Taffy slept till dawn without howling once,' Susie added. 'It has indeed been a busy night.'

He couldn't keep up with this conversation. He gave up and sat, and Susie placed a bowl of porridge in front of him. He ladled honey on top, and cream, and he sprinkled it with cinnamon, as he'd seen Susie do with hers every morning, while Marcia looked on with distaste.

'Don't look,' he told her. 'Have a coffee.'

'At least there's a decent coffee-maker,' she conceded. 'Though where you get good beans…you know, that'll drive down the price of this place as a hotel. You won't be able to source reasonable foodstuffs.'

'I'm eating my porridge out in the garden,' Susie announced, a little too loudly. She lifted Rose's high chair—with Rose in it—and hoisted it toward the door.

'Let me help,' Hamish said, getting to his feet, but Susie was already outside.

'Thanks, but I'm fine on my own.'

'You will let me help you down to the beach later on?'

She hesitated, and he could see her reluctance to accept help warring with her huge desire to swim.

'Thank you,' she muttered. 'That would be…nice.' She carried Rose further out, then dived back for her porridge.

'Susie…' Marcia started, but Susie was back out the door.

'I can't leave Rose in her high chair alone.'

'I just thought you might be interested…'

'In what?'

'I've been in touch with the hotel assessors,' she said. 'They'll arrive tomorrow. Can you make yourself available?'

Susie hardly paused. She was carrying her bowl of porridge, walking out the door with Taffy following loyally behind.

'Of course,' she said with dignity over her shoulder. 'I promised. And after that I'll go home.'

Marcia took her Blackberry to the beach. 'Hey, there's a signal here,' she announced, and was content. She lay in her gorgeous bikini and communed with her other world.

As he should, too, Hamish thought, but he was busy watching Susie. He'd swum less than usual this morning, coming back to the towels to keep Marcia company—but Marcia didn't need company. She never did. She was going to make an excellent partner, he decided as he sat next to her beautifully salon-tanned body. She was gorgeous, she was clever and she was totally independent.

She was just what he needed.

Susie was at the other end of the beach—of course. She was sitting in the shallows with Rose. Rose was perched on her mother's knees, kicking out at each approaching wave, as if by kicking it she could stop it coming.

Taffy was barking hysterically at incoming waves, barking until the wave was almost on her then putting her tail between her legs and scooting up the beach just in front of the white water. Then she barked in triumph as the wave retreated—only to have it all happen again.

Hamish discovered he was grinning as he watched them.

But they weren't perfect.

Marcia was perfect.

What was he about, making comparisons?

'I'll go over and give Susie a break from childminding so she can have a swim,' he told Marcia, and she raised her eyebrows in amused query.

'You? Look after a baby?'

'I can change a diaper,' he said, almost defiantly, and her smile widened.

'If I were you I'd never put that on your curriculum vitae. It's not the sort of ability that'll get you a job in our world.'

Our world. He looked down at her Blackberry. Right.

'Do you want help childminding?' she asked, and it was time for his brows to hike.

'You're kidding.'

She smiled. 'You're right. I'm kidding. But if it's something I need to do for a smooth transition...'

She'd do whatever it took to build a solid financial future, he thought. Wise woman.

'Go back to your wheeling and dealing,' he told her. 'Babysitting's not an occupation I plan on doing any more in my life, but you're right. By doing it now I'm making things smoother for Susie.'

'Not for you?'

'Only in that...' He paused. Only in that it made Susie happier? Only in that it let Susie have one of her last swims in this place? He couldn't think how to finish his sentence.

'Go do it, Nanny Douglas,' Marcia told him, deciding to be amused. 'And be careful when you stand up. I don't want sand in my keypad.'

Then it was his turn to sit in the shallows and entertain Rose while Taffy barked and Susie swam. Not that Rose needed to be entertained. She'd happily kick waves for the rest of her life, he thought.

Were there waves where she was going?

He didn't know.

He couldn't care.

Susie disappeared as soon as they got back from the beach, retreating to the bedroom with a couple of vast suitcases she'd retrieved from the box room and a carton of garbage bags. They hardly saw her for the rest of the day.

'I'm so pleased she's being sensible,' Marcia told him. 'There was hardly any need for me to come. I don't think she's the least bit interested in you.'

'No.'

'You know, it really is the most beautiful place,' she said. They'd finished a fairly strained dinner—fish and chips that Hamish had gone into Dolphin Bay to fetch, and a bowl of steamed vegetables for Marcia—and now they were sitting on the balcony, looking out at the bay in the fading light. 'It seems a shame to sell it straight away.'

'What else would I do with it?' Hamish said shortly. He'd thought this through. Sure, this was a financial windfall, and realistically he didn't need the interest that he'd get from its sale. He'd thought that maybe he could leave Susie here as indefinite caretaker but he'd known instinctively that she'd refuse such an offer. It was a dumb idea anyway. It'd leave her in limbo, his indefinite pensioner. She needed to move on. 'You surely aren't suggesting we live here?'

'No, but I've been thinking that doing some capital improvements before we put it on the market might get us a better price,' Marcia told him. 'I'll need to talk to the assessor tomorrow but... Come and see what I mean.'

'What—?'

'Just come and see. Why no one's thought of this before this is beyond me.'

She led the way downstairs out to Susie's vegetable garden, with Hamish following feeling bemused. Marcia had only been here for twenty-four hours, yet she already seemed proprietorial. She was leading him though his very own castle.

He shouldn't mind. He didn't. It was just...

It was just that this was Susie's place, he thought, but that was dumb. But when he emerged to the twilight and saw Susie's garden he stopped thinking his idea was dumb and decided that it was right. It certainly seemed Susie's place. Her garden was fabulous.

He had no illusions as to who'd done the work here. For the last twelve months, as Angus's health had slowly deteriorated, Susie must have thrown her heart and soul into caring for this place. Her vegetable garden could feed a small army. If this was turned into a hotel the chef would never have to go near a greengrocer.

But Marcia wasn't interested in the garden. She was striding purposefully toward the conservatory. She pushed open the doors and flicked the light, then swore as the light didn't work. It was dusk and the place was still lovely—smelling of ripening oranges and overripe cumquats and the rich loam that Susie had been using to pot seedlings. The lack of light made it seem more beautiful.

'This is what I brought you to see,' Marcia said, in the same voice she used when she produced a contract that was hugely advantageous to the firm—and to her. 'It's fabulous.'

'It is,' Hamish said, walking forward and touching the same branch of hanging cumquats Susie had touched the first day he'd met her. Was it his imagination or could he sense her here? This place seemed almost an extension of her.

'We need to take the end wall out so we can get machinery in,' Marcia was saying, and he blinked.

'Pardon?'

'It's great. Can't you see it?'

'See what?'

'The view from the end wall is right down to the sea. The tourists this place will attract will spend most of their time right here.'

'Why?'

'A swimming pool,' she said with exaggerated impatience. 'I thought about it this morning while I was at the beach. The beach is lovely but most tourists don't want to spend much time there.'

'Why not?'

'The sand gets into your Blackberry, for one thing,' she said, getting even more exasperated. 'Hamish, when we went to Bermuda last year, did we spend any time at the beach?'

'We were there at a conference.'

'Exactly. We had things to do. There was a beach but did we use it?'

There had been a beach, Hamish remembered. He thought back to an intense four days of business dealings. He remembered watching the sun rise from his hotel room, watching the view, watching people stroll on the beach…and then fitting in a fast fifteen minutes in the hotel pool before breakfast.

'We're the clientele we'll attract,' Marcia said. 'People who appreciate what luxury really is. Anyway, I'm thinking we need to heave out every bit of kitsch before we put this place on the market. And I'm also thinking that we should dig a pool into this building. Honestly, Hamish, buyers have no imagination. Did you see the potential of this place as a swimming pool?'

'No.'

'There you go, then,' she said triumphantly. 'I'll talk it through with the assessor tomorrow but I think you should hold selling off a little longer while we transform this place.'

She hesitated. 'I don't suppose we could persuade the widow to stay as a transitional caretaker.'

'I suspect we don't have a hope.'

She shrugged. 'Well, there's others. Maybe we need someone a bit more level-headed anyway.' There was a beep from her belt and she lifted her Blackberry and peered at the lit screen. 'Charles,' she said in satisfaction. 'He has some figures I need. If you'll excuse me, darling… Walk through to the end and see if I'm right. A swimming pool and a bar with a view to die for. Our tourists wouldn't have to move. I suspect the pool could double our price.'

And she was off, leaving him to his thoughts.

His thoughts…

He didn't have any thoughts, he decided. He was a blank. He fingered his cumquat some more and thought it was a great smell. It was a great place.

A luxury swimming pool? Maybe they'd have a few of these orange trees in tubs round the side…

'You'd really chop down all Angus's orange trees?'

Susie's muted voice was so unexpected that his heart forgot to take a beat. He stilled, trying to think what to say, and she came out of the shadows and stood right before him. Still in the plain faded shorts and T-shirt he was starting to get to know. Still with bare feet. Her hair was tousled and there was a smudge of dirt on her forehead.

'I didn't know you were here,' he managed, when he got his breath back.

'I've been planting out seedlings into bigger pots. I was intending to plant them straight into the vegetable garden but now I'm leaving I'll need to find other homes for them. Am I supposed to apologise?'

He was still discomfited. 'You could have told us you were here.'

'I could have come out of the dark and said I heard every word? That's what I'm doing now. I didn't mean to eavesdrop but what Marcia was saying…it made me feel…' She paused. 'But, of course, it's none of my business.'

'No.' There was no way to dress this up, he decided, shoving his sense of disquiet aside. If he was going to sell this place he couldn't be looking over his shoulder all the time, wondering what Susie was thinking.

'Angus was so proud of his oranges,' she said wistfully, and he braced himself.

'Someone else will be proud of a swimming pool.'

'It sounds like Marcia will be proud.'

'That's right. Though it's a business proposition. She'll be pleased if it means we get a good price for this place.'

'But...' She paused. 'If you sell the castle, doesn't the money go into trust?'

'It does.' He'd looked into this. It was a complex inheritance, where the castle was a part of the entailed estate to be handed down to the inheriting earl. Generation after generation. It had been made complex by the burning of the original castle, meaning the capital had been moved here. The trustees would allow sale, but the proceeds would return to the trust.

But he'd earn interest on a very sizeable sum.

'Will you and Marcia have children?' she asked. 'To inherit?'

'I...' How to answer that? He thought about it and decided he didn't have to. 'I have no idea.'

'It's just...would your son prefer to inherit a castle or a heap of depreciating money?'

'Hell, Susie...'

'But that's easy, isn't it?' she said sadly. 'That's the choice you made and you've made it really fast.'

'What would I do with this place if I kept it?'

'You could think laterally,' she said with sudden asperity. 'Instead of thinking what's the best way to make money from this place. You're not exactly needy.'

'No, but—'

'But you'll chop down these gorgeous orange trees. Do you know, it's five hundred miles to the nearest place you can grow oranges from here? The locals here eat Angus's oranges all winter. We have the best vitamin C intake per capita of any place in the country.'

'Gee,' he said blankly, and she glared at him in the dusk. He couldn't see the glare, he thought, but he could feel it.

'You don't care.'

'Susie, we both need to move on.'

'I am moving on,' she said with irritation. 'You're not moving anywhere, as far as I can see. You're taking your money and bolting back to your safe hole in Manhattan. What is it with you and money? Why is it so important?'

'Money's important to everyone.'

'To provide necessities, yes,' she snapped. 'Even enough to buy the odd luxury when you feel inclined. But Marcia says what you earn is way out of that league.'

'Marcia has no right—'

'And neither do I.' She turned her back on him, lifting a branch of cumquats, heavy with fruit. She started plucking the fruit from the loaded branch, making a pile on the bench beside her. 'OK. I'll butt out of what's not my business.'

'What are you doing?'

'I'm picking your cumquats,' she snapped again. 'What does it look like?'

'What for?' They were hardly edible. He'd tried one yesterday. They looked fabulous, like tiny mandarins, lush and filled with juice, but the first bite had seen him recoil.

'They're great for marmalade.'

'You can't cook.'

'I intend to learn,' she said with dignity. 'I'm leaving here the day after tomorrow and I'm taking some of Angus's cumquat marmalade with me.'

'So you'll learn and do it tomorrow.'

'Why not?'

She was fearless, he thought. A vision of Susie down in the cove was suddenly in his head, a scarred, limping woman, diving full on into the white water and heading for the outer reaches of the cove. Her body strong and sure and determined.

She'd succeed in her landscaping business, he thought. Clients would be lucky to get her. She was so…

So…

He picked a couple cumquats to add to her pile and her body grew stiffer. She had her back to him—he was of no importance to her.

'Thanks, but I can do this myself.'

'You just said you can't cook marmalade.'

'Neither can you.'

'But I have a connection to the Internet. I bet we could find a recipe.'

'So you'll find a recipe,' she said, and then decided maybe she was being a bit grumpy. 'Thank you. I'll do them tomorrow.'

'The assessor's coming tomorrow.'

'I'll do it after I've talked to him. Or he can talk to me while I stir the marmalade.'

'You need to pack tomorrow.'

'I'm almost packed.'

'You need to swim.'

That made her pause. She hesitated. 'I…'

'You do want to swim on your last day?'

'Of course, but—'

'But you also want to make marmalade. So let's make it now.'

The stiffness of her back had lessened and she turned cautiously around. 'Could we?'

'I'd imagine we need lots of sugar and lots of jars.'

'How do you know?'

'Well, the jars are a given,' he said. 'I'd guess we can't eat more than half a pint of marmalade tonight.'

'I suppose not. We will need jars.'

'And my Aunty Molly used to make jam,' he added. 'So I know we need almost as much sugar as fruit.'

'You used to watch your Aunt Molly cook?'

'I did.' He sounded uncomfortable—he knew he did—and he saw her hesitate as if she'd ask more. She stared at him, searching his face in the dim light, looking for…

He didn't know what she was looking for. And, whatever it was, he knew he didn't want her to find it.

Or he thought he didn't want her to find it.

This conversation was too deep for him. Way too deep. His thoughts were starting to become knotted, and untangling them was impossible. Chop them off and get on with it, he thought, suddenly savage, and he tugged a cumquat branch toward him and started plucking.

'If we're to finish before midnight, then we start now,' he said, and she waited—and watched—for a moment longer before deciding to play along.

'Rose didn't have an afternoon nap so she's out for the count,' she said. 'So's Taffy. I guess if I go to bed, all I'll do is dream of uprooted orange trees, so I might as well make marmalade.'

'Susie…'

'I know. There's nothing either of us can do about it.' She shrugged. 'I'm being unfair. It's a very nice offer to teach me to make marmalade. I accept with pleasure. Do you think Marcia would like to help?'

CHAPTER EIGHT

MAKING marmalade was a tricky business. It took sugar, cumquats, jars, a recipe, concentration...

They had everything they needed. Deirdre had obviously decided the pantry stores needed to be filled just like a real castle's would be in case of siege—and as sugar didn't seem to have a use-by date and the castle was slightly younger than siege times, they were set.

They found a hoard of a hundred or so empty jars. Hamish downloaded a recipe from the Internet. They had a couple buckets of cumquats.

Which left concentration.

Concentration was harder.

Susie had to remove pips from every cumquat. Hamish was standing right beside her, pipping his own cumquats. The castle was totally silent. Taffy and Rose were fast asleep. Marcia was in her room, online to the other side of the world.

Weren't you supposed to talk companionably as you cooked? Susie thought. Wasn't that in the manual?

He was so big. So male. He was focussed on each individual cumquat pip as if it was his next million-dollar deal.

He was just...just...

She was so...

So what? He didn't know. She was pipping her cumquats in silence, focussed absolutely on the job in hand. She was holding a cumquat half at arm's length, squinting at it so she wouldn't get hit in the eye by juice as she prodded for the pip. Her tongue was out to the side, just a little bit. Intense concentration.

For marmalade.

She'd make a good futures broker, he thought. She was up to approximately cumquat number ninety and she hadn't faltered. Intelligence. Persistence. Great little tongue. Cute nose. Eyes that were so...

'How many more, do you think?' she asked, and he hauled himself back to cumquat duty with a start.

'I'm thinking we've done enough.'

'Right.' She eyed the rest of the cumquats they'd picked—in a bucket on the floor and as yet unpipped—and shoved them under the bench with her bare toe. Out of sight. Maybe she wouldn't make such a great futures broker. Maybe she'd make a better criminal lawyer.

He started to smile but she was waiting, expectant, and he had to haul his thoughts together and turn to the recipe.

'OK. Put the cumquats and sugar together and cook until done.

'Just like that?'

'That's what it says.'

'No skill at all. I could do this myself.'

'Would you like to?'

She hesitated. 'No. I wouldn't know what to do at the end.'

'It says what to do here.'

'Great. You read and I'll stir,' she said. 'OK?'

So she stirred and he read and he stirred and she read and then they both sat and watched the vast pot of honey-gold marmalade until finally, finally their test drop formed a skin and Hamish announced that it was done.

Their cleaned jars had been sitting in the range for the duration of the cooking, slowly warming. Hamish set the jars out and Susie poured and poured and poured until they had thirty-odd jars of cumquat marmalade lined up on the big kitchen table. They attached lids, they cleaned up their mess and then they turned and looked in satisfaction at what they'd done.

All evening they'd worked almost in silence. It wasn't that they'd meant to be silent or that they were uncomfortable with each other, it was simply that words were unnecessary, Susie thought. Now, as she looked at the golden jars, words were even more unnecessary. What they'd done this evening…

She'd take this home with her. Would she eat it? Maybe, but maybe she'd keep one jar.

How long did marmalade last?

How long did love last?

Where had that come from? Dumb thought. She thought of Rory, of standing beside the man she loved, making her wedding vows. She'd thought it would be for ever.

And now she was standing beside this big, kindly man who was Rory's cousin. What she felt for him was…different.

Of course it was different. How could she love Hamish?

How could she not?

But Hamish's thoughts were on practicalities. 'We'll box them up,' he said softly, looking at the pots with the air of a man who'd done a difficult job to his satisfaction. 'If we send them air freight they'll get there as fast as you will. You'll be able to eat Loganaich Castle Marmalade for breakfast every morning.'

'Will you keep some, too?'

'Sure.' He eyed the bucket under the bench. This was a great new splinter skill. How come he'd never thought of doing such a thing? 'Maybe Marcia and I can make some more. But do you want all these?' he asked, suddenly uncertain. 'If you eat porridge for breakfast, then you'll hardly use thirty pots of marmalade.'

'I only eat porridge while I'm here. I never eat porridge while I'm anywhere else.'

He relaxed. 'Very wise. So if Marcia and I make more marmalade we can send it over.'

'Maybe this is enough.'

'It'll last for a good long time.' He grinned, trying to tease her to smile. He liked it when she smiled. The stress lines around her eyes faded, making her seem younger, more carefree. Which was how she should be. 'Every time you eat it you can think that the cumquat trees haven't lived in vain.'

But that was a mistake. As soon as the words were out he knew that he'd committed an error. Reminding her the cumquat trees were doomed.

'I guess I'll remember they've been knocked down.'

'If you want to be miserable you can think that.'

'I don't want to be miserable.'

'Then don't think about it. Move on, Susie.'

'Stop remembering this place?'

'If it makes you emotional, yes.'

'If I stopped thinking about anything that makes me emotional I'd be in for a pretty barren existence.'

'You stay under control that way.'

'Which is important?'

'Of course it's important.' He moved to adjust a marmalade jar which had dared not be in line with the others. Right. He now had thirty perfectly controlled pots.

But moving hot jam jars was a mistake. The jar he moved cracked, like a mini-explosion in the stillness. Maybe the jam had been too hot. Maybe the jar hadn't been heated up enough. Whatever the reason, there was suddenly jam running over the table, spoiling his careful symmetry.

He moved to shift the nearest jars away from the broken one. He lifted one, then swore as the heat seared through the cloth he'd used to lift it. He dropped it—and it cracked like its neighbour.

'I'd just let them settle this among themselves,' Susie said cautiously, eyeing the mess with trepidation. 'This might be an instance where lack of control just has to be accepted.'

'I never—'

'Hamish, if you lift another jar you're risking all-out calamity. I do want some marmalade to take home.'

He eyed the jars. He looked at his burnt fingers. He looked at the mess. 'But if I shifted these—'

Susie grabbed his arm and tugged him over to the sink. 'Leave it,' she ordered. 'Your poor hands.' She plunged his hand under cold water—which did feel better than trying to pick up more marmalade.

'I'll get some burn cream,' she told him but he shook his head.

'It's minor.'

'Then stay under water for a little longer.'

So he did. The marmalade mess stayed untouched. He stayed…out of control?

She was so close. She was holding his arm, forcing his hand to stay under the water. She was so…

'Susie, I'm really sorry about the trees,' he managed.

'You don't have to be sorry about the trees,' she said stiffly.

'If I didn't think what Marcia said made sense… If I didn't realise that any purchaser will do exactly that, chop them down to make way for a pool…'

'Of course,' she said, and sniffed. 'It's totally sensible.' She sniffed again.

'Susie, don't cry.'

'I'm not crying.'

Of course she was crying. Tears were welling up behind her eyes, threatening to fall at any minute.

'OK, we won't do it,' he said desperately—and she dropped his hand in astonishment.

'What?'

'We won't pull down the orange trees.'

'Just because I cried?' she said cautiously.

'I can't bear to see you—'

'You can't bear to see me cry so you'll do what I want.' She thought about it, and suddenly the tears welled up even more. 'I think I need a slice of your inheritance.'

'Susie…'

'Oh, I do.' Tears were streaming down her face now. 'I really do. And I want you to promise me that you'll wear your kilt every third Monday of the month for the rest of your life.'

He was backing off. 'Don't be ridiculous.'

She wiped her face with the back of her hand, turning off the tears like a tap. There was dangerous mischief glinting behind the tears. 'It's not me who's being ridiculous.'

'You…' He stared at her, stunned. 'You turned on those tears…'

'At will. Neat trick, isn't it?'

'To get what you want?'

'I never cry to get what I want.'

'You just did.'

'Believe it or not, I didn't. If you think I really want you wearing a kilt, driving the women of this world crazy…'

'Then why—?'

'I was teasing, Hamish Douglas. Teasing. You've never heard of the word?'

'By crying.'

'Can we leave the crying alone? It's getting boring.'

This was crazy. She was standing there glaring at him, her eyes still wet, marmalade splashed all over her T-shirt, daring him…daring him…

'I hate you to cry,' he said, sounding dumb, but he didn't know how else to sound.

'So I'm not crying.'

'Susie…'

'What?' she said, almost crossly, and she folded her arms across her breasts and glared.

'You're crazy.'

'Sure. I'm crazy.'

'I want…'

'What do you want, Hamish Douglas?'

What did he want?

The question hung. He glared at her, marmalade-stained and rumpled and angry and not crying, and suddenly…

Suddenly the mist cleared to make way for one dumb plan. There was a myriad of emotions running through his head right now, emotions chasing their respective tails, but the only thing he could think was a stupid, unwise, crazy thought. But once thought, it was not possible to put it aside. It was just there. It had to surface.

It did surface. 'I want to kiss you,' he said.

There was a moment's silence. A long moment's silence. She

appeared to consider, jutting her chin slightly forward, slightly belligerent, taking her time to come up with a response.

And finally she did.

'Well, why don't you?' she said.

What was he doing, wanting to kiss Susie?

Was he mad? He was engaged to Marcia. Marcia could walk in at any minute. Even though she wasn't possessive, to find her fiancé kissing another woman might push her a wee bit far.

Might? It would, he thought wildly, searching frantically for the control he so valued.

But his control was nowhere to be found. For Susie was right in front of him. Battered, bruised and beloved Susie.

Beloved? Where had that word come from?

It was just there. As was Susie. She was right in front of him, ready and waiting to be kissed.

Was she mad? Was she losing her cotton-picking mind? To kiss Hamish... To let him kiss her...

He was engaged to another woman and the day after tomorrow she was leaving here and she'd never see him again in her life.

Which was why...which was why she was proposing to let him kiss her, she decided. For there was a tiny part of her brain that said this was all there was, this moment, this tiny connection that could only last for one fleeting kiss and then be over.

She'd dared him to kiss her. And he'd do just that. Or she certainly hoped he would.

The signs were good.

He had his hands on her waist. He was taking his time, lingering, looking down into her eyes as he drew her against him. He was making sure that he wasn't coercing her. He was making sure that she hadn't made some daft, stupid mistake when she'd agreed to be kissed.

Maybe she had made some daft, stupid mistake but she wasn't admitting it. Not now, when he was so near. So close.

Not when he was so...Hamish.

She was being drawn into him now. She was allowing those

big, capable hands—these lovely, strong and battered hands—to pull her against him. Her breasts were being moulded against the strength of his chest. His hand shifted to cup her chin, tilting her face so her eyes met his.

Things were looking hopeful here. Very hopeful indeed.

He smiled down at her then, a rueful, searching smile that asked more questions than it answered. But there was such tenderness in his look. Such…love?

He was asking a silent question, but she couldn't respond. How could she respond? She gazed helplessly up at him, and the last vestiges of her laughter faded as she felt her heart lurch sideways. As she felt her heart still, and then start to race as it had almost forgotten it could race.

As she fell. As she tumbled deeper and deeper in love with the man before her.

He was engaged to another woman. She tried to think that but she couldn't.

For it simply couldn't matter. This was too important, she thought. Hamish intended to kiss her and all she could do was wait…and hope.

Or raise her face a little more to meet his kiss?

Or she could put her hands on his face and draw him down to her.

Definitely. She'd definitely do that.

She could not think of Marcia. Or Rory. There was no room to think of anything or anyone but Hamish.

And his kiss.

She could drown in this kiss.

What was he doing? Kissing a woman who wasn't Marcia?

He was doing what was right, he decided. He was doing what needed to be done.

He was doing what he'd ached to do from the moment he'd first seen Susie.

Oh, the feel of him. The strength, and yet the tenderness. The certainty and yet the hesitation. His mouth plundered hers, yet she knew that if she pulled back—at the slightest hint of pressure—he'd release her.

For this was no man claiming his rights. He was as unsure as she was, as stunned by the strength of feeling between them, and the feeling was unbelievably erotic.

Hamish.

The wild beating of her heart settled and things slipped into place, things that had been out of kilter with her world for so long. She'd thought when Rory had died that she could never love again—but the heart expanded to fit all needs.

She still loved Rory. She'd love him till the day she died but Hamish was a different man, a different love. Her new, wonderful love.

His lips were on hers and he kissed her as she'd ached to be kissed—but she hadn't known there was this ache within her. His lips were tentative, tasting her, feeling her response, feeling by the faint parting of her lips that he was, oh, so welcome.

Hamish.

Maybe she said his name. She didn't know. But his kiss moved, to her nose, gently teasing. To her eyelids, maybe tasting the salt still left by her tears. Her fake tears, produced to mock, but how could she ever mock this man?

His fingers were raking her hair and the sensation was magic. She moaned a little and kissed him back, finding his mouth and claiming it. Tugging his body hard against hers. Curving into him.

She lifted his hand and led it to her breast. Her body was arching against his. It had been almost two long years since she'd been held by a man. She'd loved one man and she'd thought her body could never fit with another but she was wrong, oh, she was gloriously, wonderfully wrong. Her Hamish.

Marcia was nowhere. Marcia simply didn't exist. But this was no betrayal. Susie was no traitorous vixen searching for another woman's man. This had gone way past that. Hamish belonged to no other woman.

Hamish was simply a part of her.

She locked his arms behind him, then lifted her head to

allow him to kiss her as deeply as he wanted. He was tasting her neck, caressing her shoulders with his tongue, and the sensation was so exquisite she thought she must sob with aching pleasure. He slipped his fingers under the soft fabric of her T-shirt, cupping the smooth contours of her breasts, making her moan softly with love and desire. Her hands were locked about his head now, deepening the kiss, deepening, deepening...

There was such want. She hadn't known how alone she was until tonight, when suddenly she was no longer alone.

This man was her man. She knew it at some primeval level she couldn't begin to understand and didn't want to try. The only place in the world that she should ever be at peace was right here, in this man's arms.

Within the arms of the man she truly loved.

She melted into his kiss with abandon, surrendering to the promise of his body. To the feeling that here in his arms anything was possible. She'd never be lonely. She'd never be alone. With Hamish beside her, she could take on the world.

'Susie,' he whispered, and his voice was as unsteady as she felt. 'Dear God, Susie, we can't.'

'We can't...?'

'Make love.'

She froze at that. She froze and thought about it. And reality came flooding back. Awareness of her surroundings.

Awareness of Marcia?

'You mean we can't make love right here in the marmalade.'

'Well...it'd be a bit sticky.'

'I guess.' She pulled away a little, searching to see his face. He looked dazed. Confused. And a little afraid?

'Hey, there's no need to look scared,' she said, and he shook his head, searching for some sort of reality.

'I'm not scared.'

Reality was slamming back fast. Marcia was just upstairs. Hamish was engaged to be married to Marcia. Susie was on her own. The day after tomorrow she was leaving here. Hamish had never said he wanted her. He never said he needed her, yet here she was, wearing her heart on her sleeve, making herself wantonly available.

It couldn't be wanton to kiss the man she loved.

But he didn't love her. She could see. If his eyes reflected hers they'd be full of love and desire and he'd be moving to hug her, moving to claim her.

Instead of which he was staring at her as if she were some sort of witch, capable of casting a spell.

'I didn't mean…'

It needed only that.

'You didn't mean to kiss me?'

'No. Susie, I'm—'

'Engaged to Marcia.' Somehow she made her voice work. 'Of course. I… Look, it's late and we're overtired and—and it was only a good-night kiss after all.'

Liar, she screamed at herself, but he was nodding, though his eyes said he knew as well as she did that it had been no such thing.

'We can't… Susie, Marcia and I are getting married.'

'Of course. And you and I, we'd be impossible. I'm so emotional.'

'Yes,' he said, and there was almost relief in his voice. 'You cry.'

'I do,' she agreed cordially, feeling like crying now, but there was no way she'd cry. Something being destroyed that had hardly started to be created.

He was still looking at her as if he was afraid. She wanted to scream. She wanted to…

She didn't know what she wanted.

'Of course I cry,' she whispered. 'And you hate crying. I cry all the time, happy and sad, and you can't stand it.' An errant tear rolled down her cheek right then and she wiped it away with anger. He was right—she couldn't even stop crying to save herself.

'I'm not in control,' she admitted. 'Well, that's OK, that's the state of my existence, but for a moment there you weren't in control either. That's what's scaring you, isn't it? You hate it. Well.' She took a long, searing breath, searching frantically for the words to say to finish it. As it had to be finished.

She finally found them, right or not, but the words that had to be said.

'Marcia's upstairs, Hamish. She's your fiancée. She's your future. And I need to check on Taffy. I need to check on Rose. My baby and my puppy. They're my future. And by kissing you I'm just interfering with the way of the world. With the way things have to be from this day forth.'

And before he could say another word she'd turned and fled, out of the kitchen door, back out into the night.

To the vegetable garden? To the conservatory? To the beach?

He couldn't know. There were tears welling in her eyes as she turned away. He couldn't follow.

Should he go to Marcia?

No. He was going to bed. Alone.

CHAPTER NINE

HAMISH went upstairs. He paused by Marcia's door, feeling bad. He knocked lightly and opened the door a crack. Marcia was on the phone, her laptop on her knees, listening intently to the person at the end of the line and staring at her screen. She looked up briefly, saw it was him and blew him a kiss, using the phone instead of fingers.

He wasn't wanted. He closed the door and went to his own room.

Bed.

Sleep?

It was nowhere to be found.

Why had he kissed her? It wasn't as if he could possibly take this any further. It was so unsuitable. Hell, if he married Susie she'd expect...

More than a telephone kiss good-night?

It could never work. He thought of the house he'd grown up in, a house full of hysterical women who had used their emotions to manipulate everyone around them. He'd fought so hard to get away from that. To catapult himself back into it...

Susie wouldn't try to manipulate him.

No, but she couldn't help it. He thought of finishing work and heading home as he usually did, exhausted beyond belief. Collapsing into bed before getting up to do some hard gym work before the next day at the office. How would Susie fit into that?

She'd hate it. He'd hate it. He wouldn't do it.

What would he do instead?

Cut it out, he told himself fiercely into the night. You've spent the last thirty years building up the life you want and to toss it all away for one…one…

It wouldn't be one, he told himself grimly. It'd be more. Susie came with attachments. Rose. Taffy. And more. She'd want more.

And they'd all be emotional. He thought of Taffy sitting on the grass and howling her lungs out because she couldn't get what she wanted.

He grinned.

No. Be serious. Get up and go see what's Marcia working on.

She wouldn't thank him for the interference. She was fiercely independent.

Good. Great.

Life was fine. Go to sleep.

Ha.

He lay for another half-hour or so, listening to the soft hush-hush of the sea. The castle was quiet.

Maybe he could go down and chat to Ernst and Eric.

As if on cue, there was a knock on the door. He didn't have to resort to tin-plated armour, he thought. It'd be Marcia.

'Come in,' he called, and wondered why he felt empty. As though Marcia coming in was going to expose something he didn't want exposed.

But it wasn't Marcia. It was Susie, peering round the door, her face worried in the moonlight.

'Sorry to wake you.'

'You didn't wake me.' He was half out of bed. 'What's wrong?'

'Nothing. I just… Is Taffy here?'

'No.'

'Are you sure?'

'Sure I'm sure.' He frowned. 'My bedroom door was shut when I came upstairs and it's shut now. She couldn't have got in.'

'Oh. Sorry, then.'

'Is she lost?' He was out of bed, crossing the floor, concerned.

'No,' she said, urgently, stopping him in his tracks. 'There's no need for you to come.'

'But if you can't find her…'

'She'll be somewhere sound asleep,' she said. 'This place is too big. We'll find her when she wakes up.'

'But you were looking for her now.'

'I thought I'd take her outside for a piddle before I went to bed. But if she's curled up somewhere I can't find her then I'll have to wait until she wakes up.'

'But…how will you know?'

'I'd imagine Taffy is very good at letting us know where she is when she's hungry,' she said, and he could tell that she was making a huge effort to keep her voice light. Damn, he shouldn't have kissed her. It had brought in all these tensions that he didn't have a clue what to do with. 'You've heard her howl.'

'So I have,' he said. 'But—'

'Go back to bed, Hamish,' she told him.

'Have you checked Marcia's room?'

'Yes. She's been working all the time. She's still working now. I thought… Anyway, if you hear Taffy raising a riot in the wee small hours you'll know what it is. I've warned Marcia.'

'Let me help you find her.'

'No,' she said flatly. 'Please, Hamish, go back to bed.'

'I'd like to help.'

'I don't want you helping.' She hesitated. 'Hamish, I need to be by myself. For the rest of the time I'm here. I'm not sure why what happened tonight happened, but it was dumb and meaningless and I need to back right off. Good night, Hamish.'

She closed the door before he could respond.

He should follow. He could help her search. The thought of Susie searching for her pup in this vast castle left him uneasy.

The thought of Susie doing anything alone left him uneasy.

What had she said? What happened tonight was dumb and meaningless?

Of course it was. They both knew it. Susie was a woman who was controlled by her emotions, and he…well, he knew where emotions belonged.

They didn't belong with Susie!

* * *

'Taffy?'

If Hamish heard, he'd come down and help. He mustn't hear. But where was a little dog out here in this huge garden? And the cliffs so near... Taffy had gone over the road to the beach with them so she knew the way. If she'd tried...

There was only one path down to the beach. If she'd become disoriented and ended up on the rocks...

Should she ask Hamish for help?

No. It was as she'd assured him. The night was calm and still and if Taffy needed anything she only had to howl. She'd be snoozing in some obscure corner, and if Hamish came down and helped her search for a puppy who didn't need finding then they might...they might...

She daren't ask Hamish for help. But she needed to find Taffy. She needed to hug her.

She needed to hug someone.

She was bone weary. She had a huge day tomorrow. She should be in bed right now.

Instead, she was just going to walk over the road to the beginning of the path to the beach. Just to check.

'Taffy?'

Seven a.m. Hamish walked into the kitchen, wanting coffee, and Jake was standing at the kitchen bench. Fully clothed. Pouring coffee.

Maybe it was a guy thing but walking in on a man who was fully dressed and looked ready for business—hard, physical business—when wearing boxer shorts and nothing else made Hamish feel a bit like retreating. Fast. He eyed Jake's workmanlike moleskins and heavy-duty shirt with misgivings.

'Morning?' he said cautiously, and Jake swivelled to stare at him.

This wasn't a stare of 'Ooh, who's wearing ancient boxers?'. It was a stare of active dislike.

'Good of you to join us,' he growled.

Hamish glanced at his watch. Seven was not what you'd call a slovenly hour to wake up.

'Are you here for breakfast?'

'We had breakfast an hour ago.'

'We?'

'The girls and I. Kirsty's taken Rose home with her. Susie's searching the bushland behind the garden. I've come back to make a few phone calls. We'll get some back-up.' His voice was so cold each word was practically an icicle 'I want Susie to get some rest. She's not fit to be searching as she's been doing all night.'

His heart stilled.

'Taffy,' he said. 'Hell, she didn't find Taffy.'

If anything, Jake's expression grew colder. 'She said she told you the pup was lost. I thought she must have been mistaken. To let her stay up all night...'

'She didn't stay up all night.'

'Oh, she didn't?' Jake said. 'Fine.'

Hamish stared at Jake in consternation. Jake stared back, as if Hamish was something lower than pond scum.

'I offered to search with her,' Hamish said desperately. 'She said she was sure the pup was somewhere in the castle. That she'd howl when she woke up. She's good at howling.'

'It's not much use howling when you're outside,' Jake muttered, more to himself than to Hamish. 'There's owls hunting at night. If Taffy's attracted one of them... I'm thinking that's what will have happened.'

'She's not outside,' Hamish said flatly. 'She's in the castle.'

'If she was in the castle she'd be howling by now. She's a ten-week-old pup who hasn't been fed for twelve hours.'

'But she was locked in the wet room. Susie put her there when she put Rose down for the night.'

'I gather Marcia used the wet room as a passage early last night,' Jake said. 'It seems she left the door open.'

Hamish thought back. Marcia in the conservatory, fielding phone calls. Marcia walking back to the house to get notes. She'd never notice a pup...

'Where's Marcia now?'

'On the phone to New York. Where do you think?' Jake's voice said Marcia was right there in the pond with Hamish.

'She hasn't seen the pup?'

'What do you think?

Hamish was already backing out the door, heading for some clothes. 'Why are you here?'

'Susie rang Kirsty at dawn.'

'Over a dog?'

'Dumb, isn't it?' Jake said cordially. 'Only a dog. But Susie loves her.'

Hamish closed his eyes. 'I'll get dressed.'

'Right,' Jake said politely, turning back to the phone. 'I'll add you to the search party, shall I?'

'She'll be dead.' Susie stood in the middle of the cove and stared despairingly along the beach. 'She'll have been taken by an owl or an eagle. It's just dumb to keep looking. Dumb, dumb, dumb.'

'Hey, it's not hopeless,' Kirsty told her. She'd left all the kids with her housekeeper and come straight back. 'We have half Dolphin Cove out searching. Jake says the numbers are up to eighty already.'

'Eighty?' Susie hiccuped on a mix of laughter and a sob. 'For one little puppy.'

'Everyone loves you,' Kirsty said solidly. 'There's people coming from everywhere to look.'

'She'll be dead.'

'We'll keep looking until we find her.'

Hamish couldn't believe it. He'd been out in the bushland behind the castle—three hours of combing the rough gullies and hillside, searching in what seemed an increasingly hopeless case. He'd returned to find the kitchen like a military planning area.

'What'd happen if a child was lost?' he asked in amazement.

Kirsty looked up from the table where she was crossing grid lines off a map and gave him a weary smile.

'More of the same.' She shrugged. 'Much more. OK, it might be over the top but the wind's up, which means the fishing fleet can't get out, so the fishermen don't have anything else to do. And everyone knows Susie's leaving tomorrow. We're upset about it already, without this happening.'

'Where's Susie now?'

'I talked her into having a lie down.' She hesitated. 'You know, Susie's not just devastated because of the puppy.'

He thought about it and decided, yes, Kirsty was right, but he knew where Kirsty was headed and there were places there he didn't want to go.

'She'll miss you, too,' he said, deliberately obtuse, and she gave him a long, thoughtful look that reminded him uncomfortably of her twin.

'As you say.'

'Is Jake out searching?'

'Jake had morning surgery. He had to go.'

So Jake was getting on with business. 'Well, someone has some sense.'

Her face stilled at that. Yes, she really was very like Susie, he thought, and then he thought about what he'd said. Maybe it hadn't been…sensible?

'Sense is a really strange thing,' she said softly. 'Just when you think you have it cornered, it turns into something else. Be careful what you think is sensible, Hamish Douglas. It might just turn around and bite you.'

'Hamish.'

As if on cue, a voice came from the door. He turned and Marcia was standing in the doorway, looking displeased. 'Where have you been?'

'Out searching.' The cell phone in her hand vibrated before he could say any more. She stared at the screen, prioritised and abandoned the caller.

How often was she separated from her phone? Hamish thought, and then he wondered how often he'd been separated from his. Until he'd come here, maybe never.

'You're wanted,' she said briefly, obviously annoyed.

'Susie wants me?'

'By the hotel assessor,' she snapped. 'You knew he was

coming this morning. He's in the drawing room. I've shown him around but he wants to talk to you—and to Susie.'

'I'll come,' he said wearily, raking his hand through his hair. 'But Susie's not to be disturbed.' He turned back to Kirsty. 'Let me know if there's any news.'

Hamish had to focus.

Lachlan Glendinning was the representative of an international realty firm. He'd been valuing a hotel up in Northern Queensland and he'd taken time and considerable trouble to travel to Dolphin Bay. Telling him he couldn't spend time with him because a puppy was missing—especially when Susie had the whole town combing the surrounding estate looking for him—seemed crazy.

But there was no mistaking that outside with the search party was where Hamish wanted to be.

Why? he wondered as he answered Lachlan's endless questions, going over the family history as he knew it. Luckily he'd read many of Angus's family papers so he had the answers to most questions. But his eyes kept straying outside. People were going back and forth under the window. He could see people down on the beach.

'I hear there's a lost dog,' Lachlan said genially. He was smooth and slick and clever, knowing exactly what he was looking for in the real estate market and knowing he'd found it in Loganaich Castle. 'This is quite some community spirit you have here. The town's picturesque, too. I'm thinking we could build this really big.'

'I'm sure you could,' Marcia agreed. She'd abandoned her cell phone and had joined in the conversation with enthusiasm. She and Lachlan spoke the same language.

'I really would like to speak to Mrs Douglas,' Lachlan said regretfully. 'Are you sure there's no way?'

'There's no way.' Hamish rose. 'Marcia, would you like to show Lachlan the grounds? If he's seen all there is here…'

'I've seen enough of the inside,' Lachlan said. 'It's a great interior.' They passed into the hall and he poked at Ernst with his gold-embellished fountain pen. 'Though these guys will have to go. I know where we can get some real ones.'

'Ernst and Eric are coming home with me.'

It was Susie, entering unannounced. Her face was pale and there were the ravages where tears had been, but there were no tears left now. She was dignified and in control, and she introduced herself and took Marcia's place by Lachlan's side as if it was her right.

'I'll show you the garden,' she told him. 'I'm sure Marcia and Hamish have business to attend to.'

'I should go back online,' Marcia agreed, and Susie gave her a bright and brittle smile.

'Of course.'

'I'll go back to the search,' Hamish said softly, but the look she directed at him had no trace of a smile left in it.

'It's no use,' she told him. 'Taffy's dead. She's been out all night. If the nocturnal owls didn't kill her, the wedge-tail eagles will have by now.' She turned to Lachlan. 'I'm sorry I wasn't here to greet you. Marcia says you'll be thinking about converting the conservatory to a swimming pool before any sale is made. You need to see it. I'll take you.'

'Susie, you don't need to think about that,' Hamish said uneasily, and received a flash of anger for his pains.

'I know I don't need to think about it, Lord Douglas,' she snapped, emphasising his title with a short, harsh syllable. 'My plane leaves tomorrow afternoon and after that this is all your business. This castle is in the hands of the heir. That's you. And you're going to sell it and put the money in the bank.'

'Which is the only sensible place for it,' Marcia interspersed.

'It is,' Susie agreed dully. 'Of course it is. So, shall we see the possible site for your luxury swimming pool, Mr Glendinning?'

'Susie, go look for your puppy,' Hamish said desperately, and she looked like she wanted to slap him.

'My puppy is dead.'

Then why wasn't she crying? Hamish thought. She should be crying. He'd know what to do if she cried.

What was he saying? He wanted a woman to cry?

'We'll show Mr Glendinning the conservatory together,' he said, gently now, but her anger was increasing.

'We'll do nothing together.'

'Susie…'

'Let her go,' Marcia said. 'She's got the time, Hamish. Surely you have better things to be doing.'

What? he thought blankly. What?

'I'll go back to the beach.'

'Give it up,' Marcia said wearily. 'Didn't you hear Susie? The creature's dead.'

The creature.

He was supposed to be marrying this woman.

He thought of Taffy last night, sitting plump on her bottom and howling her displeasure.

The creature.

'We have no proof she's dead,' he said, to the room in general. 'If you'll excuse me, I'll keep looking until we're sure.'

And he walked away and left them to it.

Why hadn't she cried?

All that long day Hamish watched Susie move like an automaton. She spent a long time with Lachlan, detailing the castle to his satisfaction. She worked in the kitchen, feeding the searchers. She did a bit more searching herself but her back was obviously paining her. She was limping badly and when Kirsty decreed she should stop, she stopped. She went back to packing, the pile of stuff she was discarding growing higher and higher.

'I'll ship Ernst and Eric over to you,' Hamish said at one stage, and if looks could kill, he'd have been dead right then.

'I've changed my mind. They'd never be at home with me in America. They belong at the foot of the stairs and if you want to shift them…well, that's your business and I don't want to know about it.'

'Susie, stay a little longer,' he urged.

'Why?'

'We don't know about Taffy.'

'We do know about Taffy. Cut it out, Hamish. I'm leaving.'
She wouldn't budge.

At dusk Marcia came to find Hamish. She met him on the way
upstairs to change. He'd been bashing through thick bushland
in an increasingly hopeless search for Taffy, and he was filthy.

'We need to take Lachlan out to dinner,' she said. 'He's
spent the day photographing the castle from every angle—not
that you'd have noticed. Honestly, Hamish, your behaviour has
been less than civil. He's staying at the pub tonight. It'd be
better if we could put him up here, but I dare say you won't ask
the widow to do that.'

'Do you have to call her the widow?'

'You know who I mean.'

'I won't ask Susie to have another guest on her last night,'
Hamish snapped, wondering again how he'd never noticed how
insensitive Marcia was. 'It's bad enough that we're here. Jake and
Kirsty are bringing dinner. Susie needs her family and no one else.'

'Then you and I should at least take him out to dinner. You're
not Susie's family.'

He wasn't. Hamish hesitated. Marcia was right. He should
give Lachlan dinner. And...would Susie want him to be
around tonight?

But Kirsty came through the front door then, carrying a casserole.

'Hi,' she told them. 'Dinner in thirty minutes?'

'We're going out to dinner,' Marcia said, sounding efficient.

'Oh?' Kirsty raised her eyebrows. 'You, too?' she asked
Hamish.

'Um...'

'I shouldn't put pressure on you,' Kirsty told him. 'But it
would be better if you were here tonight.'

'Why?' Marcia demanded. 'Why should Hamish stay?'

Kirsty looked a bit taken aback at that, as if she hadn't
actually expected an argument.

'To leaven the loaf,' she said at last. 'Susie's miserable.
We've searched a two-mile radius and Taffy's nowhere. Taffy

was supposed to be the little bit of Dolphin Bay she was taking away with her. Now there's just Susie and Rose.'

Not even Ernst and Eric, Hamish thought, leaning back on a suit of armour. Welcoming the sharp dig of a halberd in the small of his back.

'Susie will be better off without a pup,' Marcia said sharply. 'The fewer encumbrances, the better.'

Kirsty looked at her thoughtfully. Appraisingly. Then glanced sideways at Hamish, leaning wearily on his halberd.

'You're taking the assessor, Lachlan, out to dinner?' she asked Marcia.

'That's right.'

'Then can I ask that you, Marcia, take Lachlan out to dinner, and you, Hamish, stay here and see if you can cheer Susie up. Wear your kilt or something.'

'I suspect there's not a lot that'll cheer Susie up,' Hamish said.

'No,' she admitted. 'But we can try.'

Hamish hesitated.

Marcia looked at her watch. She tapped her foot. She looked at Hamish and saw indecision. Or maybe…decision. There was one thing that could always be said about Marcia: she was good at sussing which way the wind was blowing. She was excellent at not wearing herself out fighting the inevitable.

'I'll go, then,' she said, visibly annoyed. 'Honestly, Hamish, someone has to keep a business head on their shoulders in this whole debacle.'

'They do,' he agreed, but he was watching Kirsty, seeing Kirsty's disapproval, thinking how very like her twin she was. Was Susie vibrating with the same disapproval?

Probably not, he thought. She'd be in her bedroom, sorting the last things she wanted to take from this place. She'd be thinking of Angus, or of Taffy, or of walking away from her vegetable garden and leaving her wonderful conservatory to be ripped apart. There'd be no room in her distraught mind for disapproval of one dumb would-be earl.

'You're not spending more time looking for the dog?' Marcia was demanding, looking at him as if she didn't know who he was any more. Which, come to think of it, was pretty much exactly how he was feeling about himself. 'Everyone's saying it'll be dead.'

'She'll be dead,' Kirsty said softly, and the look she gave Hamish then was slightly doubtful. 'But we'll give the grounds one more sweep after dinner.'

'Miracles don't happen,' Hamish said flatly, and Kirsty gave him another odd look.

'We'll see. We certainly have enough pumpkins around here for a spell or two to happen.' She shook herself, obviously perturbed that she was getting fanciful. 'OK. I have a full casserole dinner ready to be brought in from the car, provided by the ladies of Dolphin Creek. Any crisis round here, sick baby, lost puppy, can't solve yesterday's crossword, you'll be handed a casserole—so we have, at last count, eleven. Marcia, if you and Lachlan aren't joining us, we'd better start now. We have a lot of eating to do.'

It was a very strained meal. They had eleven casseroles. Between them they ate about half of one, and that was with Kirsty and Jake's twins helping. The two little girls were the only bright company during the meal, but even their chatter was pointed.

'Daddy, why does Aunty Susie have to go back to America?'

'That's where her home is.'

'But her home is here.'

'This castle belongs to Lord Hamish now,' Jake told them gently.

'But everyone says Lord Hamish doesn't want it.'

'Lord Hamish doesn't have to want it,' Susie told the girls, with only a hint of a tremor in her voice. 'It's just the way things are. It's his, and I don't belong here any more.'

'But you're our Auntie Susie,' Alice said tremulously, and Penelope agreed.

'We want you to stay. And you haven't got a puppy to take home now. You'll be really, really lonely.'

'I'll have Rose,' Susie said, her voice strained to breaking point. She rose to fetch the coffeepot from the stove and started to pour. 'Coffee, Hamish?'

'Please.'

'None for me,' Kirsty told her, and Susie stilled. She'd been facing the stove. Now she turned, very, very slowly, to face her twin.

'You always have coffee after dinner.'

'I... Not now.' Kirsty seemed all at once uncomfortable and Susie's face grew even more blank.

'I was right,' she said, and her voice was devoid of all expression. 'At the fair. You deflected me with Taffy and I was so preoccupied I let myself be deflected. You're pregnant.'

'Oh, Susie,' Kirsty said, her face twisting in distress.

'That's lovely news,' Susie managed, and stooped to give her twin a hug. But there was no joy, Hamish thought, watching the tableau in incomprehension. What was going on?

'I so didn't want you to find out.'

'Until when?' Susie turned back to her coffee cups.

'I thought...until you were settled back in America.'

'Won't this make a difference?' Hamish asked, concerned. They both seemed on the edge of tears, but there were no tears. Just rigid control.

'Sure,' Kirsty said coldly. 'Ask Susie to stay because I'm pregnant? How could I do that to her?'

Easy, Hamish thought, remembering his mother and his aunts. He knew exactly how emotional blackmail was done.

'I won't ask for the same reason Susie hasn't asked you not to sell the castle. Not to destroy the greenhouse. I bet she hasn't, has she?'

'No, but—'

'And if I did and you agreed?' Susie said, suddenly fierce. 'How do you think that'd make me feel for the rest of my life? And if Kirsty thought I was staying now just for the baby...she couldn't bear it. That's why she hasn't told me. I don't know where you come from, Hamish Douglas, but we don't do emotional blackmail here.' She swallowed and turned her back on him, facing her sister again. 'You're due when?'

'Not until November. It's early days yet.'

'If I can, I'll come back.'

'Of course you will.'

'To stay?' Hamish said cautiously, and got another glare for his pains.

'To visit. Like normal people do.'

'But you guys are twins,' he said, feeling helpless. 'You should be together.'

'They'll be together for the birth,' Jake said, putting his hand across the table to reach his wife, taking Kirsty's hand in his and holding it firmly and with love. 'If I have to sail across the Atlantic single-handed and haul Susie back here in chains, I promise you'll be together for the birth. I'm covering the expenses and if Susie argues, then she'll see what brothers-in-law are really made of.'

'Oh, Jake,' Susie said, choked.

And Hamish thought, Here at last come the tears. But they didn't. Susie stared at her sister and her brother-in-law for a long moment—and then went back to her coffee-making.

With one mug of hot chocolate for the expectant mother.

CHAPTER TEN

KIRSTY and Jake and assorted kids left soon after. The arrangement was that they were taking Susie to the airport the next day—Jake had organised medical cover for the town from a locum service so both doctors could leave. They took all the kids home with them to give Susie a clear run with her packing.

'We'll be here at eight tomorrow to pick you up,' Kirsty told her twin.

'I'll be ready,' Susie promised.

And Hamish thought once again, Why didn't she cry? She should be crying.

She cried at pumpkins. Why didn't she cry now? Suddenly he thought he wanted her to cry. It'd be OK if she cried, he decided. It was the set, wooden expression on her face that he hated.

He stood in the hall and waited while she waved them off from the front step, and he was waiting for her as she returned.

'What would you like me to do?' he asked softly, and she glanced at him with suspicion.

'Nothing.'

'I'll go down to the beach, then,' he said. 'Just for a last check.'

'Taffy's dead.'

'You don't know that.'

'Yes, I do. I'm not stupid. Ten-week-old puppy in this terrain… I see things how they are, Hamish. Not how I want them to be.'

'You should be able to hope…'

'I gave up on that when I buried Rory,' she said flatly. 'Now, if you don't mind, I have things to do.'

'Can I help you pack?' He should butt out, he thought. He was adding to her distress just by being here. He felt so damned helpless...

'I would appreciate help in Angus's room,' she said, and then looked as if she regretted saying it.

'What needs doing in Angus's room?'

'It's just...' She hesitated. 'I've never cleared it out. I mean, it all belongs to you but I thought...his personal stuff...most of it needs to be thrown away but I don't want Marcia doing it.' The last few words were said in a rush, fiercely, and he thought she'd burst into tears but she didn't. She was pale and almost defiant, tilting her chin as though expecting to meet a fight.

'Marcia's the least sentimental of all of us,' he said mildly and her chin came forward another inch.

'All the more reason why she shouldn't be the one who takes care of it.'

So on a night when she should be doing her own personal packing, when the last vestiges of the search party made vain sweeps of the beach and the hillside looking for Taffy, when Kirsty and Jake cared for the kids so Susie could spend one night alone with her memories, she and Hamish sat on Angus's bedroom floor and sorted...stuff.

Stuff.

Deirdre's stuff and Angus's stuff. The old man hadn't cleared his wife's things, and everything was still there.

The clothes were easy. They'd go to the welfare shops. Hamish could be trusted with that so, with the exception of Angus's kilt and sporran and beret, they were bundled into boxes to be carted away.

But the kilt and beret and sporran... 'I don't know what to do with these,' Susie whispered, holding up a kilt that was far too small for Hamish.

Hamish fingered the fabric, watching the graceful fall of the pleats, thinking of the times Angus must have worn this, the number of fêtes he'd opened in this town, the affection in which he'd been held.

'Is there a local museum?'

'No.'

'A library maybe?'

'Yes…'

'Then why don't we donate it as a display?' he suggested. 'I could donate the cost of a display cabinet. We could put Angus's and Deirdre's photos in it, photos that show them as they were, vibrant and having fun, and set this costume up beside it. Do you think the locals would like it?'

There was a moment's hesitation. Had he said the wrong thing? Would she cry?

She didn't cry. 'That'd be wonderful,' she said in a small voice. 'Can I leave it with you to see that it's done?'

'Of course.'

She nodded, a brisk, businesslike little nod that had him wishing, wishing she'd falter a little, give him room…

Room to what?

'I'm not marrying Marcia,' he said into the stillness, and her head jerked up from the papers she was sorting.

'You're what?'

He hadn't even known he was going to say it. He hadn't even really thought about it.

Or maybe he had.

He'd approached marriage to Marcia as he approached business propositions, he thought. The marriage would be advantageous to both of them. But these last few days had been like the switching on of a lightbulb in a dimly lit room. Suddenly he could see colour where before he'd only seen grey.

Suddenly he'd not only stopped fearing emotion, he was thinking a bit more emotion wouldn't be such a bad thing.

Like Susie crying so he could hug her better?

'Does Marcia know you're not marrying her?' Susie asked. Her head lowered again, and her voice dulled. She was in a grey world of her own right now, he thought, methodically packing stuff into boxes, lifting Angus's papers, checking them, putting unwanted ones in a pile to be burned. Shifting the detritus of a past life. Absorbed in her own misery.

'I'll tell her tonight.'

'I'd appreciate it if you left it until I was gone. She's going to blame me.'

'Why should she blame you?'

There was a twisted smile at that. 'I'm a corrupting influence,' she said dryly. 'I make you leave your Blackberry at home when we go to the beach.'

'That's a good thing, too,' he said stoutly and then watched her for a bit more as she went back to sorting papers. 'Susie, do you have to do this? I can do it after you leave.'

'Angus would want me to. I should have done it before this. I just…I couldn't bear to.' She hesitated. 'Will Marcia be upset, do you think?'

He thought about it. Would Marcia be heartbroken? No. But maybe her pride would be hurt. 'I think maybe I should have told her before I told you,' he said ruefully.

'Yeah, she'd hate that. Well, forget you told me. I'll forget I know.'

'I need you to know,' he said softly, and it was true.

Silence. She bent her head over her sheath of documents. A pile of notepaper, pastel blue.

More silence. Where was he going here? He didn't know.

Five minutes ago he'd been engaged to Marcia. He still could be, he thought, confused. What he'd said didn't have to go out of this room. It wasn't irrevocable.

But it was irrevocable, and the more he thought about it the more irrevocable it seemed. Engaged? He wasn't engaged to Marcia. Engaged meant entwined, linked, connected. He surely wasn't entwined, linked, connected to Marcia.

Tonight he'd watched Kirsty and Jake over the dinner table. He'd seen their eyes meet as they'd shared their distress. And that glance… It had been nothing, but it had meant everything.

He wanted that sort of communication with the woman he married. He didn't want to share a beach-towel with a laptop.

'Go to bed,' he told Susie, softly because he wasn't sure what his head was doing—where his thoughts were taking him. He needed time to think this through.

'These are personal. I need to sort them.'

'I'll pack them up and send them to you.'

'No. You pack the clothes.'

'Susie, you need to pack your own gear. The way you're going you won't get to bed tonight. It's not as if you can sleep on the plane. Rose will be a full-time job.'

'That's not your business,' she snapped.

It wasn't. But, hell, he couldn't bear to see this.

'There's nothing so personal—'

'These are letters,' she cut across his protest, fiercely angry. 'These are personal letters.'

'Then maybe we shouldn't read them at all.'

'No.' Her anger faded a little at that, but the pain seemed to remain. She was kneeling on the floor by Angus's bedside cabinet, papers spread around her. Still in her shorts and T-shirt, with her hair tangled and wisping round her face—the last thing she'd thought of today had been brushing her hair—she looked absurdly young. How could this slip of a girl be a mother? Hamish wondered. How could she be a landscape gardener by herself? Susie against the world?

'Listen to this,' she said softly, and he paused in his folding of sweaters and let himself watch her face again. She was holding herself rigidly under control, he thought, so rigidly that at any minute it seemed she might crack.

'Listen to what?'

'I know…well, maybe I know that we ought to burn these without reading them,' she whispered. 'But Angus knew he was dying, and he left them. So maybe…maybe…'

'What?'

'Maybe he didn't mind us reading them. Maybe he was even proud of them. This is from Deirdre. Way back when she was shopping for the contents of this castle. We're talking forty years back.'

'It's not too personal?'

'You need to know a bit of back-story,' she told him, ignoring his query. 'Angus put a huge amount into this castle, because building it provided an industry for the men of the town in a time of recession. But the locals say he scared himself with how much it cost, and when it came to furnishings he turned into a real scrooge.'

'I can't imagine the Angus I've heard about being tight with his money,' he said, and Susie's face softened in agreement.

'Neither can I. But listen to this. Deirdre's obviously in the city on a buying spree, writing to Angus back home.'

My love, we have children!

Angus, darling, it's one of the great sadnesses of our marriage that we haven't been blessed with babies and we can't adopt. Well, I've found a replacement. No, sweetheart, I haven't picked up a couple of strays, much as I'm always hopeful a couple will come our way. But today I've found Eric and Ernst.

Who are Eric and Ernst? I can hear you say it in increasing trepidation. Irish wolfhounds, maybe? Diggers up of vegetable gardens?

No.

They're warriors. They stand eight feet tall in their gauntleted—is that what you call it?—feet. They're a sort of made-in-Japan imitation suit of armour, real and ready to fight, lifelike right up to the eyes in their visors— white glass eyes with a little black pupil that bobs up and down when you lift the visor up and peer in. I found them in the back of a theatre-prop-cum-junk-shop and they're so neglected. Angus, Ernst is missing a leg! Can you believe that? We'll need to build him a new one. Do you know a leg builder? They're shop soiled and tattered and unloved, and I just looked at them and knew they were destined to stay with us for as long as we live.

Anyway, dearest, kindest Angus, this is to say that we're coming home on Friday and if you were planning on meeting the train in your car can you think again? I talked to the nice man at the railways today and he says he can't guarantee they'll be safe in the goods car so I've bought two extra tickets. Ernst and Eric can sit in the carriage with me. Isn't that the best thing? Can you imagine it? Oh, my dear, I'm so excited. I so want you to meet them. You and me and Eric and Ernst, ready to live happily ever after from this moment forth.

There was a long silence.

It was a ridiculous letter.

Hamish thought of Marcia writing such a letter, and couldn't.

He tried to imagine Susie writing such a letter—and could, very, very easily.

Susie and Deirdre. Twin souls?

There were too many twins. His head was spinning.

'Why couldn't she have children?' he asked at last, trying to sound neutral. 'Surely forty years ago adoption was an option?' He was changing the subject here, and he wasn't quite sure what he was changing it from, but he was starting to feel desperate.

'Deirdre was profoundly deaf,' Susie said softly, rereading the letter with a smile. 'I imagine adoption agencies wouldn't see deafness as a desirable attribute in adoptive couples. From what I know of Deirdre, she might have excluded herself on those grounds.'

That floored him. He sat back on his heels and thought of what he knew of Deirdre.

'I thought she was a nurse during the war.'

'She was.'

'How could she be a nurse if she was deaf?'

'She worked in a rehabilitation hospital. I imagine she would have fought tooth and nail to be useful. Lack of hearing wouldn't have stopped her. From what I've heard of Deirdre, she refused ever to stand still. Half the older generation of this town knows some sort of sign language as everyone wanted to talk to her. They tell me she was irresistible. Angus loved her so much.'

The twin thing slammed back again. Deirdre and Susie, taking on life no matter what life threw at them.

'How could they ever have communicated?'

'Without e-mail?' Susie said dryly. 'It's beyond comprehension, isn't it? But Angus said he woke up one morning in his army hospital; she was standing by his bed and she smiled at him—and he just knew.'

'Love across a crowded room,' he said disparagingly. 'Right.'

'One of the other soldiers had lent him a magazine like *Playboy,*' she continued, ignoring his attempt at sarcasm. 'He'd gone to sleep with Bunny of the Month splayed across his chest. He woke and Deirdre was giggling and he thought, Sod bunnies, this is the one I want.'

Sod bunnies.

Susie was smiling again. When she smiled it was as if the sun came out, Hamish thought, and Angus's words slammed into his consciousness with the force of a high-voltage charge.

This is the one I want.

'I don't suppose…' he said into the stillness, and then paused.

'You don't suppose what?' She was back to sorting, her head down, her curls falling forward, intent on the task at hand.

'I don't suppose you'd like to marry me?'

There was complete and utter silence in the room, and the silence lasted for ever.

What had he said? The words rang round and round in the silence, echoing over and over. He hadn't meant to say them, he thought wildly. They were just suddenly—there.

'Marry,' Susie said at last, and she sounded like she'd been winded. 'You're asking me to marry you.'

'Yes.' He thought about it, wondering what on earth he was saying, but somehow the words still sounded right. His proposal might have been made on the spur of the moment, but that was definitely the gist of what he'd been asking.

'And you're asking me to marry you because?' Susie demanded. She had her breath back now, and was sounding politely bemused. Which was wrong. He didn't want her to sound politely bemused.

'I suspect I'm in love with you,' he managed, and listened

to what he'd said and thought, Yep, that sounds OK, too. He sounded confused—but then he was feeling confused. About some things.

Not marriage. He was sure about this.

'You're engaged to Marcia.'

'I'm not marrying Marcia.'

'Marcia thinks you're marrying Marcia.'

'I've made a mistake,' he said. 'Jodie told me I was making a mistake and I didn't see it. It's only now—'

'Who's Jodie? Another fiancée?'

'Jodie's with Nick. He's a woodcarver.' He thought about the way Jodie had said goodbye to him, the way she'd dared him to take this holiday and move on.

Jodie would be proud of him.

'So you moved on to Marcia?'

'Jodie's my secretary.'

'She's still in your life?'

'Susie, can we get back to the issue at hand?'

'Which is that you'd like to marry me.'

'Yes.' This was dumb, he thought. He was sitting on one side of the room in a tangle of sweaters and socks. She was sitting on the far side of Angus's bed, surrounded by papers. He should be down on one knee on her side of the room. At the very least they should just have had a candlelit dinner—not the Country Women's Association Tuna Surprise.

He thought of the finesse of his proposal to Marcia and the dinner that had preceded it and he almost grinned. But not quite. A survival instinct was kicking in here, telling him that chuckling over cliché engagement settings wasn't quite the thing to do right now.

'Why do you think you love me?' She still had the conversational tone. He'd like to move closer but her words…they were like a defence, he thought. A bit brittle. A bit too casual.

'Susie, I don't want you going back to the States by yourself.'

'I'm not going by myself. I'm going with Rosie.'

'You know what I mean.'

'I'm not sure what you're suggesting here.' She still hadn't moved and neither had he. It was like some crazy, stilted conversation about something that concerned neither of them. 'Are you saying you want me to stay here and you'll stay, too—or are you saying you want me to come back with you?'

He hadn't thought that far ahead. He tried to make his mind work, but there was something akin to fog blanketing everything. Making it impossible to apply logic.

He was terrified, he thought suddenly. He was just plain terrified. Stepping off into some abyss…

'Hey, Hamish, I'm not going to accept,' she said gently. There's no reason to look like that.'

'Like what?'

'Like I'm a cliff edge,' she said gently. 'I won't do that to you.'

'You're no cliff edge.' But he'd been thinking that. How had she known?

'You don't really want to marry me.'

'I do.' This seemed important. If he kept saying it then it'd start to make sense, he decided. It must make sense.

'What would you do with me?' She almost sounded amused. 'Back in Manhattan?'

'You could work. There's all sorts of landscaping jobs.'

'Window-boxes to be planted out. That sort of thing.'

'We'd get a place further out,' he said, starting to sound as dopy as he felt. 'I can commute—or stay in Manhattan during the week and come home at weekends.'

'In the tiny gaps you have from work.'

'At least you wouldn't be alone.'

She let her breath out in a long exhalation. She looked at him then, really looked at him—and then she pushed herself to her feet.

'Hamish, this is crazy. You haven't thought it out. Forget you said it. It's time I went to bed. I'll get up early and see how much of this I can cope with then.'

She was letting him off the hook, he thought, but he didn't want to be off the hook. Sure, he hadn't thought this through, but the essentials were there. He rose with speed, crossing to stand before her, reaching out to grasp her wrists and hold her at arm's length.

'Susie, it could work,' he said urgently.

'Don't be daft.'

'I'm not daft.'

'If you didn't feel sorry for me,' she said softly, 'would you be even thinking of marriage?'

'No, I—'

'That's what I thought,' she said flatly and hauled her arms back.

'No!' His word exploded across the room, frightening in its intensity. He took her hands in his, urgent. 'Susie, it's not like that.'

'It's not?' She swallowed, seemingly as confused as he was. Struggling to figure things out. 'If I wasn't limping, would you be thinking you could possibly let Marcia down?'

'I can't marry Marcia. Not feeling as I do about you.'

'But you're talking about commuting. In the gaps from work. In the same breath as a proposal. To stop me being lonely.' She took a deep breath and carefully, carefully disengaged her hands. 'Hamish, when I was single I loved having my own space. I had lots of friends and loneliness didn't come into it.'

'But you're lonely now.'

'Because I met Rory,' she said softly. 'When he and I were together there wasn't loneliness. How could there be? Sure, there were nights when we were forced to be apart, but our phone bills were enormous and we'd go to sleep talking to each other. Thinking of each other.'

'As you and I—'

'Shut up and let me finish,' she told him, and her voice was almost kindly. 'Because it's important. Rory died and I learned what loneliness is. It's the awful, awful emptiness when people leave.'

'Susie…'

'It gets filled,' she said, almost conversationally. 'Now I'm alone I've gone back a little to how I was. I depend on me for my company. It's taken two years but I've learned to cope. But, you know, Kirsty comes to dinner, and then she leaves and the loneliness closes over me again. I fell for Angus and it was good, but when he died, it was bleakness all over again. Emptiness. You know, there are lots of single people who don't like people staying overnight because the house seems so empty when they're gone. Loneliness happens again and again and what you're offering… Hamish, every time you walked out the door I'd be alone.'

'I'd have to work,' he said, startled, but she shook her head, as if she was sad about his incomprehension.

'Yes, but when you went to work I wouldn't come with you.'

'What the—?'

'In your heart,' Susie whispered. As he stared at her in confusion, she smiled. 'Hamish, you don't understand and maybe if I hadn't had it with Rory then I wouldn't understand either. But Hamish, I've fallen in love with you.'

She'd fallen in love… He reached for her but she took a step back, holding up her hands to ward him off.

'No.'

'No?'

'No,' she said softly. 'If you think that makes a difference…'

'Of course it makes a difference. I've fallen for you, too, Susie.'

'Have you?' she said. 'You've spent your whole life defending yourself, learning not to let anyone close, and you're not about to stop now. You're going to spend our entire married life waiting for me to manipulate you. If I was fool enough to marry you. Which I'm not.'

'I know you won't manipulate me.'

'No, you don't. You don't know anything about me.'

'I know you're the most courageous person I've ever met.'

'That's pity,' she said flatly. 'Not love. If I died tomorrow, would you cry?'

'I don't cry,' he said before he could stop himself, and she stilled.

There was a long, long pause.

'No, she said at last. 'You don't cry.'

'Susie, I'm not emotional.'

'Well, there you go, then,' she said softly. 'Maybe we're a match after all, because neither am I.'

'Are you kidding?'

'You see, that's the problem,' she whispered. 'What you see is on the outside. You're thinking you might marry the outside. But inside…you don't have a clue. You just don't have a clue. And now, if you'll excuse me, I'm going to bed.' She made to push past him but he stepped across the doorway.

'Susie, please, think about it. It'd be sensible.'

'It'd be committing me to loneliness for the rest of my life,' she whispered. 'Even I think I deserve better than that.'

CHAPTER ELEVEN

WAS she mad?

Susie lay and watched the shadows. This was her last night in this castle.

The man she loved had asked her to marry him.

A courageous woman would take him on and train him, she thought desperately into the stillness. Marry him and ask questions later. Have a tantrum or six when he spent fourteen-hour days at the office seven days a week and treated her as being on the outskirts of his life. Which was what would happen. She was under no illusions as to how Hamish saw marriage.

He'd had some sort of epiphany this week, she thought. He'd seen Marcia out of her business zone and seen how sterile the life they proposed was.

So he'd gone for the easy solution. The noble one. Ditch the businesslike fiancée and pick up a ditzy one with a gammy leg and attached child. Give his life a bit of interest and do good along the way.

Problem solved.

She rose and crossed to the window, staring out at the moonlit sky. An owl swooped across the night sky and she thought of Taffy. Taffy...

She'd had her for what? A whole day? And she'd gone, and Susie felt...

Sick.

'This is it,' she whispered into the dark. She wanted Rose

here so she could hug her, so she could tell her baby she was doing the right thing. 'I can't expand my heart any more. The heart expands to fit all comers? Maybe, but how often can it break and stay intact?'

She wanted to cry but the tears wouldn't come. Nothing would come. She should sort a few more things. She should…

Dammit, if it's not packed now I don't want it,' she told the moon fiercely, watching the flight of the owl over the water's edge. 'I've got no more room. I have no more room for anything.'

'Marcia, I can't marry you.'

It was two in the morning. Hamish had been sitting at the kitchen table, waiting for Marcia to come back. Which had taken quite some time. Now she'd burst in the back door, still laughing, and had stopped dead when she'd seen Hamish waiting.

He should have broken it gently, he thought as her laughter stopped. He'd been sitting here for hours, trying to make it right in his head. Nothing made sense any more, but the only absolute that stood out was what he'd just said.

He couldn't marry Marcia. In the end the words had just come.

'What? What have they told you?' Marcia demanded, and he blinked.

'Pardon?'

'Hell, this place! How did they know?'

He blinked again—and then he focussed. She looked rumpled, he thought. There was sand in her hair. A strand of dried seaweed was intertwined with the normally impeccable French knot.

The knot was coming undone. She put a hand up to adjust it, a pin came loose and it tumbled free.

What was going on?

'You've been on the sand dunes?' he ventured cautiously, and she swore and shook her hair looser, causing a shower of sand to fall to the floor.

'God, who'd live in a small town? People have been staring at me since I hit the town boundaries. I might have known.' She glared across the table at him, defiant. 'What do you mean, you can't marry me? You're not getting prudish on me, are you?'

'Prudish?'

'I was bored, OK? There's nothing to do in this godforsaken place and you were stuck with the widow.'

'So…' He was putting two and two together and making six. But maybe six was right. 'You and—Lachlan?—headed for the sand dunes.'

'Of course Lachlan. Who else do you think? Hell, Hamish, someone had to be nice to him. You hardly made the effort.'

But she had coloured. His efficient, cool fiancée was seriously flustered.

'You were nice to him…as in heading for the sand dunes.'

'It was just a bit of fun! This is the modern world, you know.'

'I think I'm old-fashioned.'

'Well, don't be. Hell, Hamish, we lead separate lives. That's the basis of our whole relationship.'

'What relationship?'

'We fit,' she snapped. 'You know we do. Together we can be a serious team. But not if you're going to get jealous every time I let my hair down.'

'I would have thought…maybe you'd want to let your hair down with me?'

'Oh, come on, Hamish. That's not what our relationship's about. We're a *serious team*. Does it matter if we get our fun elsewhere?'

And it was as easy as this. He was being let off a hook he hadn't known he was on until tonight, and suddenly he didn't even recognise what it was that had snagged him.

She didn't love him. He didn't love her. Where on earth had they been headed?

'I'm in love with Susie,' he told her, and she paused in shaking her hair to stare at him in incredulity.

'You have to be kidding.'

'I don't think I am.'

'What on earth do you have in common?'

'I guess…nothing. Are you in love with Lachlan?'

'Of course I'm not. I don't do love.'

'Including with me?'

'We're a sensible partnership,' she snapped. 'You know that. We've talked about it. You let emotion into your life and it's down the toilet. If you were on with the widow—'

'I'm not on with anyone.'

'But you want to be? With her?' Disbelief was warring with incredulity that he could be so stupid.

There was only one answer to that. 'Yes.'

'She'll never be a businessman's wife.'

'Maybe I'll be a landscape gardener's husband,' he retorted, and she gave a crack of scornful laughter.

'This is ridiculous. You're being ridiculous.'

'Yes.'

She paused. Regrouped. 'Let's talk about this. We don't need to break up. I want that title,' she said abruptly, as if it was suddenly the most important factor in the whole deal.

'I think you can buy titles over the Internet if you pay enough,' he said cautiously. 'I'll see what I can do. It can be a breaking-off-engagement present.'

'You're not serious.'

'I'm serious.'

'I've come all this way for *nothing?*' It was practically a yell. She was no longer flustered. She was out and out furious.

'I'm sorry.'

'Not half as sorry as you're going to be,' she snarled.

'You really think I wouldn't mind a marriage where my wife trots off into the sand dunes with other men?'

'This has nothing to do with anything I might have done with Lachlan,' she flashed back. 'Has it?'

'No,' he admitted. 'It hasn't. But I've decided… Marcia, maybe emotion is important in a marriage. Maybe we could both do with some.'

There was a long pause, strained to breaking point.

'Right,' she said at last. 'You want emotion? Let's see how you deal with emotion, you stupid, two-timing wannabe country hick!'

Sitting in the middle of the table was a vast earthenware casserole containing the congealing leftovers. Marcia removed the lid. She lifted the pot—and she threw the entire contents at her fiancé's head.

With pot attached.

Tuna surprise!

Susie heard Marcia come in. She heard their soft murmurs in the kitchen. Then the voices were raised. Then came a crash of splintering crockery.

Should she get up and investigate?

Mind your own business, she told herself, and shoved her pillow over her head so she couldn't try to eavesdrop.

She didn't want to know.

She didn't.

Breaking off his engagement had been as easy as that.

Hamish lay in bed and stared at the ceiling and wondered where to take it from here.

His cell phone rang.

It was three in the morning. Was there an emergency back in the office?

'Douglas,' he said crisply into the phone, trying to sound efficient, and there was a sigh down the line that he recognised.

'You're not supposed to be working.'

'Jodie?'

'You remember me?' His ex-secretary sounded pleased. 'Nick said you mightn't answer the phone if you recognised my number. Are you still in Australia?'

'Yes,' he said cautiously. 'Jodie, it's three in the morning.'

'Since when did you need sleep? I've just seen your photograph.'

'My photograph,' he said blankly.

'Oh, Hamish, it's lovely.'

'Aren't you supposed to call me Mr Douglas?' he demanded, and her sigh this time was totally exasperated.

'I'm not your secretary any more. I'm calling as a friend.'

'Why?'

'To tell you I think she looks gorgeous. To say the baby looks really cute and the dog's amazing and I've never seen you look so happy. I opened the magazine and got such a shock that I almost dropped my coffee.'

'What magazine?'

She told him and he gaped into the stillness. 'How…?'

'You're on the beach,' she told him. 'The baby's asleep at your feet. What's the dog's name?'

'Boris,' he said, before he could stop himself. His mind was racing. A photograph on the beach. Albert and Honey… It had to be Albert and Honey's photograph. This was Susie's doing. She'd told them his real name, they'd have done some research, and now the photograph would be splashed across America.

Did he mind?

'Is she nice?' Jodie was asking.

'Um…yes.'

'One of the girls from the office told me Marcia was following you.'

'Marcia's here. Jodie, what business is it of—?'

'You see, the thing is that I'm pregnant,' Jodie said, ignoring his interruption. 'I thought I was last week and now I'm sure. Nick and I are so happy. But I'm so happy that I want everyone else to be. So I'm worrying about you.'

'You don't need to worry about me.'

'I won't if you end up with the lady on the beach.'

'She won't have me,' Hamish said before he could stop himself, and there was a breathless pause.

'You've fallen in love,' Jodie said at last. 'Oh, Hamish…'

'She won't have me.' It was almost a statement of despair. He was in territory here he didn't recognise.

'You haven't asked her to live in your grey penthouse?' Jodie said anxiously. 'She doesn't look the sort who'd live in a penthouse.'

'Hell, Jodie, it's where I live. It's where I work.'

'I've taken a job as part-time secretary in the church that Nick's restoring,' Jodie said as if she hadn't heard him. 'The pay's lousy. Not a lot of prestige there. I'm happy as a pig in mud.'

'I'm pleased for you. But—'

'Don't stuff it, Hamish.'

'Mr Douglas!' he roared before he could stop himself, and there was a cautious silence—and then a giggle.

'You've got it bad,' she said on a note of discovery. 'Oh, I'm so pleased I phoned. Nick said I was butting in where I wasn't wanted but I so wanted to know, and now I do. I'll ring you back in a few days and find out the next installment. Don't stuff it. And don't shove your penthouse down her throat.'

Where was sleep after that? Nowhere. The castle was almost eerie in its stillness. At five Hamish rose and went out into the bushland behind the garden. He walked the trails in the moonlight, calling over and over again.

'Taffy?'

If he could find her...

He wasn't sure what that might mean. He only knew that Susie was holding herself under rigid control and he needed to break through it. Somehow. If he could find Taffy, he could offer to buy a house on the coast, commuter distance from work. He could see Susie there, but the loneliness thing was an issue. She'd need a dog.

He could buy her a dog but Taffy would be better.

Taffy was dead.

But there was a tiny part of him that was refusing to accept the pup's death. It was the logical conclusion and he'd spent his entire life trying to be logical, but he'd just let this tiny chink of inconsistency prevail. Just for now.

'Taffy...'

He didn't find her. Of course he didn't find her. Logic was the way to approach the world. Logic was always right. Emotion...well, it had no place in his life. Did it?

There was a bruise on the side of his head that said emotion was happening whether he encouraged it or not.

Somehow he had to persuade Susie anyway, but by the time he conceded defeat and returned to the castle, he knew he was too late.

The castle was alive with people. Half Dolphin Bay seemed

to be there. Kirsty was presiding over the kitchen, issuing orders. A mountain of luggage was piled in the hallway. Susie was behind a mug of coffee, with half a dozen women sitting around her.

She looked up as Hamish entered. Their eyes met—and he saw a tiny flicker of hope die behind her eyes.

'You didn't find her.'

She knew what he'd been doing. She wasn't being logical either. She was still hoping.

Someone had to see things as they were. 'No.' He spread his hands, helpless. 'Susie…'

'Hamish, can you help Jake load gear into the car?' Kirsty asked, sounding as if she was annoyed with him, and he met her gaze and knew he was right. She was seriously displeased. 'It's like a huge jigsaw puzzle. How we're going to fit everything in, I don't know.'

'Sure.'

'And what happened to Mrs Jacobsen's casserole?' Kirsty asked.

'I took a dislike to it. Tell Mrs Jacobsen I'll buy her ten more. Susie, can I talk to you?'

But Susie was no longer looking at him. 'I'm leaving in half an hour and I have all my friends to say goodbye to,' she whispered. 'Hamish, we said everything we needed to say last night. There's nowhere else to go.'

'Susie, you're way over the limit for cabin baggage.' It was Jake, appearing at the door and looking exasperated. 'Rose can't need all these toys.'

'One's Hippo, one's Evangeline and one's Ted. They're all too precious to be entrusted to the cargo hold.'

'You'll have to repack,' Jake said, trying to sound stern. 'Evangeline weighs two kilos. Two kilos for a toy giraffe! It's either Evangeline or the nappies.'

Susie closed her eyes, defeated by choice. Blank.

She should be crying, Hamish thought, feeling desperate. She should be sobbing. But her face was closed and shuttered. Dead.

'Please, Susie…' he started, and her eyes flew open again.

'Leave me be,' she snapped, anger breaking through the misery. 'Hamish Douglas, butt out of what doesn't concern you.'

If there'd been another casserole to hand he could have been hit twice over. And maybe he would have welcomed it.

He butted out.

Marcia was packing as well. He went out to the courtyard and found her loading her gear into the back of Lachlan's BMW.

'As fast as that?' he asked, and she gave him a vicious glare. Lachlan, looking nervous, stayed back.

'You don't want me here. I'll be back to you about financial details.'

'Financial details?'

'This has cost me,' she muttered, throwing a holdall into the trunk with vicious intensity. 'I've wasted three years of my life organising our future and you mess it up with one stupid widow. If you think you'll get out of that without a lawsuit, you have another think coming.'

'You did go to the sand dunes,' he said mildly. He looked across at Lachlan, who decided to comb his hair in the car's rear-view mirror.

'I hate you,' Marcia told him.

'You don't do emotion.'

'I so do!' She rallied then, whirling to face him head on, and her eyes were bright with unshed tears. Tears of fury, frustration and bitterness.

'You see?' she snarled, her voice almost breaking. 'I do "do" emotion. It's just that I don't want to. It stuffs up your life. You can't control people. And I don't want it, any more than I want you.' She flung herself into the passenger seat and slammed the door. Unfortunately the window was open and without the engine on she couldn't close it.

'Get in,' she snapped at Lachlan. 'Let's get moving.'

'Sure,' Lachlan said, and grinned at Hamish. 'That's quite a lady you're losing.'

'Rich, too,' Hamish offered.

'You think I don't already know that?'

I'm sure you do, he thought as he watched the BMW disappear from view.

Two unemotional people?

No. There were emotions there all right. Maybe they were in the wrong place but they were still there.

As were his. He just had to figure out where to put them.

He still hadn't figured it out thirty minutes later as he watched Susie climb into Jake's car. Still with no tears. Still with that dreadful wooden face he was starting to know—and to fear.

'Goodbye, Hamish,' she said, but she didn't kiss him goodbye.

Her body language said it all. He had no choice.

He stood back and let her go.

The castle emptied, just like that. One minute there'd been a crowd waving Susie off, a confusion of packing and tears and hugs and waving handkerchiefs as the car disappeared down the road.

Then nothing. The inhabitants of Dolphin Bay simply turned and left, went back to their village, went back to their lives. Which didn't include him.

Hamish went back into the kitchen, expecting a mess, but the Dolphin Bay ladies had been there *en masse* and everything was ordered. Pristine.

There was a note on the table from Kirsty.

> Susie's organised professional cleaners to go through the place tomorrow. Leave a list of what you want kept. They'll dispose of the rest. Mrs Jacobsen says one casserole dish will be fine, thank you, but it had better be a good one.

Great.

He walked back out to the hall where Ernst and Eric were looking morose. Guard duty with nothing to guard.

They'd look dumb back in Manhattan, he thought. Could he write a clause into the hotel sale, saying the new owners had to keep these two?

Ridiculous.

The word hung.

Why had Susie thought his proposal ridiculous? It had been a very good offer, he thought. He'd told her he loved her. He'd look after her, keep her safe, make sure she wanted for nothing.

Ernst and Eric gazed at him morosely.

Ridiculous.

'The whole thing's ridiculous,' he snapped. 'Not me. What does she want me to do?'

Whatever it was, he couldn't do it. He couldn't.

His phone buzzed and he looked at the screen. Jodie. Another lecture.

He flicked it off. Out of communication.

That meant the office couldn't communicate either.

Good. He needed to not communicate.

'You are sure you're doing the right thing?'

'Of course I am.' They were outside the vast metal gates at the airport—gates you could only go through as you passed passport control. The days of waving planes off were long gone. Now the gates slammed on you two or three hours before the plane left and that was that.

Susie and Kirsty were in a huddle. Jake was standing back, holding Rose, giving his wife and her sister space to say goodbye.

'But you're in love with Hamish.'

'He doesn't have a clue what love is. Leave it, Kirsty. It's over.'

'You will come back when our baby's due?'

'I promise.'

'Oh, Susie, I don't see how I can bear it.'

'If I can bear it you can,' Susie said resolutely. She'd expected to be a sobbing mess by now, but the tears were nowhere. She didn't feel like tears. She felt dead.

'I can bear it,' she told her sister. 'You've been the best sister in the world but we're separate. Twins but separate. You have your life and I have mine.'

Yes, thought Kirsty as she stood and watched the gates slide shut, irrevocably cutting Susie off from return. I have my life. My husband, my kids, my dog, my life. Oh, Susie, I wish you had the same.

What the hell was a man to do?

Hamish paced the castle in indecision. He went back into Angus's room and looked at the papers scattered over the floor. Yes, they needed to be gone through. There were all sorts of important deeds that couldn't be left. They represented a couple days' work.

He'd stay for two more days, and then he'd leave.

He rang the airline and booked his return flight for two days hence. Right. That was the start of organisational mode.

Now sort the papers.

It didn't happen. His head wasn't in the right space. The papers blurred.

He went back out into the garden and saw his half-finished path. He's work on that.

Two spadefuls and he decided his hands were just a wee bit sore to be digging.

He'd go to the beach. He'd swim.

Alone?

He had to do something.

He went to the beach.

The water was cool, clear and welcoming. Before, every time he'd dived under the surface of the waves he'd felt an almost out-of-body experience. It had been as if he'd simply turned off. A switch had been flicked. Here he could forget about everything but the feel of the cool water on his skin, the power of his body, the sun glinting on his face as he surfaced to breathe.

Today it didn't work. He couldn't find a rhythm. He felt breathless, almost claustrophobic, as if this place was somehow threatening.

Susie had almost lost her life here, he remembered. And he hadn't been here to help her.

She wouldn't have let him near even if he had been here. Hell.

He looked back to shore. A sea-eagle was cruising lazily over the headland. As he watched it stilled, did a long, slow loop, focussing on something below, and glided across the rocks just by him.

There was something there—a dead fish maybe—but Hamish's presence distracted the bird. For a moment he thought the bird would plunge down, and suddenly he splashed out and yelled at it.

The bird focussed on him and started circling again. Slowly. Still watching whatever it was on the rocks.

It'd be a dead fish, Hamish told himself. Nothing but a dead fish.

He struck out for the rocks, surfacing at every stroke to make sure the bird wasn't coming down. Twelve, fourteen strokes, and he reached the first of the rocks. They were sharp and unwelcoming. He'd cut his feet trying to get across them.

It'd be a dead fish.

But the thought wouldn't go away. He looked skyward and the bird was focussed just in front of him. Two or three yards across the rocks.

He hauled himself out of the water. Ouch. Ouch, ouch, ouch.

A dead fish...

It wasn't a dead fish. It was Taffy, curled into a limp and sodden ball, half in and half out of a rock pool.

He thought she was dead. For a long moment he stared down at the sodden mat of fur, at the tail splayed out in the water, half floating. At the little head, just out of the water.

And then she moved. Just a little, as if she was finding the strength to drag herself out of the water an inch at a time.

The rocks were forgotten. His feet were forgotten. He was kneeling over her, lifting her out of the water, unable to believe she'd still be alive.

'Taffy,' he whispered, and her eyes opened a little. And unbelievably the disreputable tail gave the tiniest hint of a wag.

'Taf.' He held her close, cradling her in his arms, taking in the enormity of what had happened.

What *had* happened?

He looked up and the eagle was still circling. There was another bird now, swooping past, as if the two birds were disputing about who was to get lunch.

Two birds…

He looked down at Taffy and saw lacerations in her side. Deep slices. Something had picked her up…

And carried her out over the sea? And then maybe got into an argument with another bird, and the prey had been dropped.

If she'd been dropped into the white water around the rocks then maybe the birds had lost her. Maybe she'd have been left struggling in the water, to finally drag herself up here.

Only to expose herself again to the birds of prey who'd dumped her here in the first place.

Hamish was crying. Hell, he was crouched on the rock and blubbing like a baby. Taffy.

'We'll get you warm,' he told the pup. 'We'll get you to a vet.'

But to walk over the rocks in bare feet was impossible. He was two hundred yards from the beach.

He'd have to swim.

He backed into the water, dropped down into the depths and felt Taffy's alarm as she was immersed again. He was on his back, cradling the pup against his chest. He'd get back to the beach using a form of backstroke—backstroke with no arms? But if the pup struggled…

'Trust me, Taf,' she said softly, and it seemed she did. The little body went limp.

'Don't you dare die on me,' Hamish told her. 'I have such plans for us. My God, how can I have been so stupid?'

The doors closed behind her.

It was over. Susie walked past the duty-free shops and the huddles of excited travellers and she didn't see them. Her mind was blank.

'I'm not going to let myself get depressed again,' she told

Rosie, hugging her almost fiercely. 'I've been down that road and never again. If I'd let Hamish have his way…no, I've fought too hard for independence to risk it all over again.'

That was the crux of the matter. Maybe she could change him. Maybe she could teach him what it was to really love.

'Oh, but if I failed…' she told Rose. 'I have you to think about now, sweetheart, and I'm just not brave enough to risk everything again.'

The vet was stunned. And beaming.

'Two deep lacerations on the right side but only scratches on the other—the bird couldn't have got a decent grip. But there's nothing vital damaged. We'll run an IV line for twenty-four hours just to be on the safe side but you've got her warmed and dry. I see no reason why she shouldn't live to a ripe old age.'

Hamish stood and stared at the little dog on the table and felt his knees go weak. He'd run up the cliff, wanting help, wanting to shout to the world that he'd found her. The castle had been empty.

He'd opened the oven door, lined the warm interior with towels and laid the pup in there while he'd pulled on some clothes. Then he'd offered her a little warm milk, and had been stunned when Taffy had hauled herself onto shaky legs, shrugged off her towels and scoffed the lot.

Then he'd thought that maybe he'd done the wrong thing in giving her milk—maybe she'd go into shock or something—so he'd bundled her off to the vet. To be given the good news.

'She's as strong as a little horse,' Mandy, the vet, was saying. 'Susie will be so pleased. I can go about sorting out the quarantine requirements again.'

Taffy would leave, Hamish thought blankly. Of course. Taffy was Susie's dog.

She didn't feel like Susie's dog. She felt like family.

'Can I take her home?' he asked.

'Back to the castle? Can you keep her still so the IV line stays in place?'

'Sure.'

He carried her out into the morning sunshine and shook his head, trying to figure where he was.

Things had shifted. Important things.

What plane was Susie on?

He started doing arithmetic in his head. The new rules for international flights meant you had to be there three hours ahead of departure. Kirsty and Jake's car had been overloaded, and they'd left leeway, expecting delays. If he left now…

Taffy was in a box in his hands, the IV line hooked to a bag slung over his shoulder. He'd have to rig it up carefully in the car to get her back to the castle.

He didn't want to go back to the castle.

He'd have to find someone to care for Taffy.

He didn't want someone else to care for Taffy. At least…not completely.

'You haven't found the puppy?' It was Harriet, Dolphin Bay's postmistress, emerging from the post office and carefully adjusting a sign on the door to read 'Back in Five Minutes'. 'Oh, my lord…'

'I'm not *my* lord,' he said absently. 'I'm Hamish.'

'You're my lord to me,' she said, resolute. 'Ever since I saw you in that kilt.' She peered into the box and her mouth dropped open in shock. 'You've found her,' she whispered. 'Oh, my lord. Where was she?'

'An eagle had her,' he said, but he was moving forward. 'Harriet, see that sign?'

'The sign?' She turned back to where she'd written Back in Five Minutes. 'Yes?'

'Can you make it five hours?'

She looked at him as if he was crazy. 'Of course I can't.'

'Yes, you can,' he said encouragingly. 'I'm your liege lord. You just said it. My wish is your command. Harriet, I command you to change the sign, hop into the front of the car and cuddle Taffy.'

'Why?'

'Your liege lord needs his fair lady.'

* * *

'Flight 249 to Los Angeles is delayed by sixty minutes. We wish to apologise for…'

'Fine,' Susie said to Rose, and glowered at the screen. 'Let's go buy some duty-free perfume. You'd like that, wouldn't you, sweetheart?'

'No,' said Rose.

'What do you mean, she can't come in?'

'Sorry, mate, dogs are forbidden in airport premises.' Hamish had parked the car in the multi-storey car park and they were now at the airport doors. Hamish was carrying Taffy's box and Harriet was carrying the IV line.

'You can't go any further,' the man said, and Harriet sniffed, knowing what was coming.

'Harriet…'

'You're going to ask me to sit in the car with Taffy,' she said darkly. 'Just when it gets interesting.'

'Harriet…'

'Don't mind me.' She sighed, her bosom heaving with virtuous indignation. 'I'm just the peasantry.' Then she grinned. 'Go on with you,' she told him. 'But I'm not staying in the car. I'll just sit on the doorstep here and watch the comings and goings. Taffy and me will like that.'

'You can't stay here,' the security officer told her, and she puffed up like an indignant rooster ready to crow.

'There's a sign saying I can't come in with dog,' she said. 'But there's no sign saying I can't look in with dog. That's just what I'm doing.'

And she sat on the rack holding the luggage carts in place. She slung the IV bag over her shoulder, she took Taffy's box into her arms and she smiled.

'What are you waiting for?' she demanded. 'Go fetch who you need to fetch.'

Her flight had been delayed. Oh, thank God, there was sixty minutes' grace. But even then it wasn't easy. There was the little matter of the metal doors at passport control.

'You can't come through,' he was told. 'Not unless you're a traveller.'

'I'm a traveller.' He hauled his passport from his wallet and displayed it. 'I'm from the US.'

'You need to be booked on a plane today. You need seat allocation before you can get through.'

They were adamant.

'We can get a message to whoever you want to see,' he was told. 'But if they come out they'll have to go through security again. No one will be happy.'

Maybe she wouldn't come out, he thought. Maybe a message wouldn't work.

He took his wallet over to American Airlines. 'I have a ticket two days from now,' he told them. 'Any chance of swapping it for today?'

'The flight's fully booked,' he was told. The girl behind the counter eyed him dubiously, and he thought that even if he had been booked there might be trouble. He'd dragged on jeans, a windcheater and trainers but he hadn't shaved that morning and he'd come straight from the beach.

And he knew he looked desperate.

Hell.

The gates stayed shut. She'd be through there, sitting, miserable, maybe crying…

He stared at the screen. There was Susie's flight, leaving in forty-five minutes. Any minute now they'd start boarding.

The flight straight after that was to New Zealand.

Susie's flight was from Gate 10.

The New Zealand flight was from Gate 11.

Act cool, he told himself, trying frantically to be sensible. If you launch yourself at the counter and act desperate, they'll drag you off as a security risk.

So he sped into the washroom, washed his face, bought a comb and a razor from the dispenser and spent precious minutes transforming himself from a beach bum with hair full of sand to someone who might board an international flight with business in mind. Casual but cool.

He stared at himself in the mirror. What was missing?

Ha! Five more precious minutes were spent buying a brief-case and a couple of books to bulk it up.

Then a walk briskly to the Air New Zealand counter, feeling sick with tension and with the effort not to show it. 'Any chance of getting onto the flight this afternoon? I only have hand luggage. I'm booked for a US flight in two days but I've finished what I need to do here and could usefully see some of my people in Auckland.'

His authoritative tone worked. The girl looked him up and down—and smiled. 'Do you have a visa?'

He did. The work he did required travel at a moment's notice and he always had documentation.

'There's only economy available,' she said, and he almost grinned. What value a comb?

'Thank you.'

Which way was New Zealand?

Why would she want to buy perfume?

'Let's have a look at duty-free cigarettes.'

'You don't smoke,' she told herself.

'I might. If I get desperate enough.'

'Are you all right, madam?' an assistant asked, and she blushed.

'Um…yes. Just telling my daughter about the evils of smoking.'

Hell, why was security taking so long? The line stretched forever.

'Passengers for Air New Zealand, please come through the priority line.'

Thank God for that. But when he was through…

'They're boarding already. If you'd like to board the cart we'll get you straight to the boarding gate.'

Fine. But he was jumping off early.

She wasn't in the departure lounge.

Where was she?

'This is the final boarding call for Flight 723 to Auckland…'

Where was she?

'Pardon me, sir, your flight is ready for boarding. You need to come this way.'

'Not until I find who I'm looking for!'

There was a commotion down near her boarding gate. Shouting. Beefy security men, running.

Then a couple of burly giants escorting someone back toward the entrance area.

Susie glanced up from her rows of Havana cigars…

Hamish.

'Excuse me,' she said faintly, stepping out into their path. 'Where are you taking him?'

'Security,' one of the guards said brusquely. 'Step aside, ma'am.'

She was holding a box of Havana cigars in one hand, Rose in the other. She dropped the cigars.

With huge difficulty she managed to hold on to Rose.

'You can't take him away,' she said faintly. 'He's mine.'

CHAPTER TWELVE

'SO YOU see, you need to come home.'

They weren't going anywhere right now. The chief of airport security had raised his eyebrows, shrugged and shown Hamish, Susie and Rose into his office, closing the door on three trouble-makers.

'Take her baggage off the plane,' he growled to his staff as he left them to it. 'American Airlines is already boarding. She's officially missed the plane and if she objects I'll have them booked for nuisance. Or something.'

But there was no way she'd object. The security head was smiling as he closed the office door behind them—and he just happened to nudge a wastepaper bin full of crumpled paper in Rose's direction. He had kids himself and he knew what was needed here was a bit of distraction so the adults of the party could sort themselves out.

Rose obliged. She immediately started emptying the trash, paper by paper, perusing the security memos of the day with all seriousness, then ripping them into tatters, more thoroughly than any shredder.

Hamish wasn't reading anything. He was holding every part of Susie he could reach.

'But I still don't understand,' she whispered when she could finally find room to speak. She'd just been very thoroughly kissed. She was snuggled against him and he smelt of the sea. He tasted of the sea. Her Hamish. 'Just because you found Taffy...'

'I cried when I found Taffy,' he told her. 'It felt right. And then the thought of sending Taffy to you in America felt wrong.'

'So you're saying…?'

'I want to marry you. I want to marry you more than anything else in the world.' Then he hesitated. 'No. That needs improvement. I already asked you to marry me and you very rightly threw it back in my face. But it's different this time. It's more than just the love thing. Susie, I want us to be a family more than anything else in the world.

'Which means?'

'Reorganising,' he said bluntly. 'Not taking you back to my life. Not being part of your life. Making a new life for all of us where all the pieces fit in a new whole. Where all of us are a part of it.'

'Just because of Taffy,' she whispered, awed.

'Just because of you,' he told her. 'When I found Taffy, I thought how fantastic it was that I'd found her, and then I thought that I'd found our dog but I'd lost the most important person in the world. Here I was, crying about a pup when my life was gone. And I suddenly realised why you cried—and why you stopped crying. You must love me. You must. Please, Susie…'

'Of course I love you,' she said, and tried to smile. 'How could I not love those knees?'

'A woman with taste.'

She silenced him with a kiss, and the kiss lasted deeply and satisfactorily through the shredding of at least ten more security memos.

It was a kiss where all questions were answered. Where there was no need for words.

It was a kiss where two people found their home.

'The first time I asked you to marry me I was dumb,' Hamish whispered at last, when he could finally find the space to get the words out. She was cradled on his knees and he was holding her as if he'd never let her go. 'But, Susie, I swear this is different.'

'I know it's different,' she said scornfully. 'You think *I'm* dumb?'

'I'd never think you're dumb.'

'You don't mind that I've been married before?'

He answered that with another kiss. 'You don't mind that I almost married Marcia?'

'No, but this is different, too,' she said, trying to be serious. 'Marcia and you…you weren't really engaged. But I did love Rory. I never thought I could love again, but his love, this love…it's just…'

'This is a love for who you are now,' he said, hugging her tight while the world steadied on its axis. 'Are you worried that I'll be jealous of Rory? That I'll make you put away his photographs? Hell, Susie, Rory's part of my family and I need all the family I can get.'

'No, but—'

'Rory is part of who you are,' he told her, refusing to be interrupted. 'He loved you and he cared for you and how can I ever be anything but grateful that he found you out in the wide world and brought you into the Douglas clan?'

'As Angus brought Deirdre,' she whispered. 'And all of us…somehow we're all together. She wriggled on his knee, feeling suddenly like bouncing. The shock was wearing off and what was left was a searing blast of joy so great it almost overwhelmed her. 'Oh, Hamish. Do you think we'll live happily ever after with Ernst and Eric?'

'They expect nothing less.'

'In our castle?'

'Sure, in our castle. With our pumpkins.'

'As in all good fairy-tales.' Her thinking was extending, past the confines of the man she loved to the world outside. 'Where's Taffy now?'

'Out in the trolley racks.'

'*Where?*'

'With Harriet. Come and see.'

And when they finally found Taffy she wasn't alone. The trolley racks were loaded.

Kirsty and Jake had shown the girls round the airport and had finally emerged to find the postmistress—and dog—in residence. So they'd settled down to wait, too—hoping that Hamish hadn't talked himself onto Susie's flight—and when Susie and Hamish and Rose emerged from the airport, it seemed half Dolphin Bay was waiting for them.

'So you've come back to us,' Jake said, but he wasn't talking to the woman he'd said farewell to a couple of hours ago. He was talking to Hamish, gripping him on the shoulder as a man gripped a friend he hadn't seen for years.

'I guess I have,' Hamish said, thinking of the impossibility of futures broking from Dolphin Bay, and then shrugging and thinking that impossibilities were made to be overcome.

'I guess I have.'

E-mail From: Hamish Douglas
To: Jodie Carmody
Subject: Suggestion

Dear Jodie

Susie and I are delighted to hear you and Nick will be at our wedding next month, here in Dolphin Bay. With your pregnancy and your job as church secretary, we thought you'd be deeply embedded in your choir stalls.

But your letter, saying the stalls are finished and you and Nick are after adventure before the arrival of your little one, set us thinking. Maybe you'd like to share our adventure?

As you egged me on to discover, my life has changed. We have a castle, we have a little girl, we have a dog and we have a pumpkin patch. I have my financial training, Susie has her landscape gardening and we've been looking for ways of putting them together.

I can do some sharebroking from here, easily, with only the occasional trip to New York. But I need a secretary.

Susie can garden here to her heart's content, but she needs people to enjoy her garden and eat her vegetables.

The castle is aging and maintenance is screaming to be done. The conservatory alone needs someone to care for it—someone who loves wood.

The castle needs people.

So we've decided to open our Castle By The Sea. It will be styled as a Cottage By The Sea, which is a famous holiday camp for children in need. Disadvantaged kids will come to us for the holiday of a lifetime. They'll come in times of family crisis, they'll spend two weeks here, on the beach, learning to garden, learning to farm in the experimental farm Susie's planning. They'll take time out from whatever crisis is in their lives. We've talked to the authorities. We have enthusiasm!

But we need someone with experience with disadvantaged kids. They'll come with their carers, but we'd plan their experience. And—you see, Jodie, I do pay attention—I remember you telling me that Nick is a social worker. That he worked with disadvantaged kids and he loved it. We wondered whether he'd like to dip his toe in the water again.

Jodie, we're not offering Nick a full-time job as a social worker or a woodworker, or you a full-time job as a secretary. Susie and I don't intend to be full-time gardeners or sharebrokers either. But we are offering full-time commitment.

What we'd like is for you guys to have a house in the castle grounds—maybe helping build it could be Nick's first job—and for you both to be Share-Castlers. Like share farmers, only different. This castle needs two families. We're inviting you to be our partners.

You don't need to answer at once. Terms need to be negotiated. There's no way I'll let you do this as a temp. What about it, Jodie? Will you share our happy ever after?

Think about it and let us know. With love from:

Hamish and Susie and Rose and Taffy and Ernst and Eric

Text Message from Jodie Carmody to Hamish Douglas

We're on our way. P.S. Who are Ernst and Eric?

THE THROW-AWAY
BRIDE
ANN MAJOR

Ann Major lives in Texas with her husband of many years and is the mother of three grown children. She has a master's degree from Texas A&M at Kingsville, Texas, and is a former English teacher. She is a founding board member of the Romance Writers of America and a frequent speaker at writers' groups.

Ann loves to write—she considers her ability to do so a gift. Her hobbies include hiking in the mountains, sailing, ocean kayaking, traveling and playing the piano. But most of all, she enjoys her family. Visit her website at www.annmajor.com.

I dedicate this book to my late, much-beloved mother, Ann C. Major, even though I know she was really a true-blue horror fan.

One

Central Texas, near Austin
Abigail Colins's ranch outside Bastrop, Texas
Early morning, first of June

Predictable Leo Storm had seemed like a safe choice.

When you go to a bar on the rebound intending to dance with a wild cowboy or two, and you end up sleeping with the dullest, safest, most-buttoned-down guy there—your next-door neighbor of all people—you don't expect earth-shattering consequences…in his bed or afterward.

Abigail Collins's eyes burned, and not from mucking out her horse Coco's stall. She was suffering from a bad case of Poor-Me Syndrome.

Greedy, ambitious CEOs like Leo Storm were supposed to play it safe when it came to sex. They were supposed to carry wallets full of condoms and fall asleep after doing it once.

Apparently Leo hadn't read his CEO rule book on said subject. His skill and enthusiastic ardor as a lover had made Abigail's toes tingle and her bones melt. She'd opened herself to him in ways that had caused her to despise herself and blame him the next morning. They'd done it so many times, she'd been tender for days. Needless to say, she'd avoided the heck out of him ever since.

So, the discovery that she was pregnant—by Leo—sucked big-time.

You can have anything you want—as long as you're willing to pay the price, her mother used to say. Trouble was, the price was due, and Abby didn't want to pay.

Ever since she'd found out about her condition last week, she'd been wallowing in self-misery—not that she was proud of such childish behavior.

As soon as she'd gotten up this morning and had finished going to the bathroom, desperation had overwhelmed her again, and she'd flipped the toilet lid down and collapsed on it, sniveling like a baby. A little later she'd had another good cry while knocking her forehead against the wet tiles of her shower.

As if buckets full of tears or regrets—and don't forget whining—did any good. Some things just had to be faced.

Pregnant! By Leo Storm!

She was a control freak and single with no desire for a long-term alliance of any kind after being hurt so badly when her boyfriend, Shanghai Knight, had dumped her.

Since puberty she'd gone for short-term relationships with cowboys like Shanghai; not for boring, bossy, calculating, corporate, money guys without souls like Leo. She'd been the brains, and the cowboys been the brawn.

She licked her lips and wiped the sweat off her brow. Well, she wasn't going to cry again. No use indulging in any more pity parties. She was a big girl—whether she was acting like one or not. She could handle this. She *had* to handle this.

Which was why she was telling Leo today. Surely she'd feel better once that was behind her. She closed her eyes and tried not to think about Leo's white, drawn face and blazing black eyes the last time she'd seen him. He'd been furious at her. Not only furious—he'd said he was through with her.

Usually being in the barn with Coco, her gentle palomino, soothed her. Not today. Not when she dreaded driving into San Antonio and telling a certain stubborn, macho CEO, who was now refusing to take her calls, that *they* had a little problem.

Every time she bent over to scoop another pitchfork load of manure and dirty straw into the wheelbarrow, the zipper of her jeans slid a little lower, reminding her of *their* mutual problem and *that* night, that one night with him that she'd tried so hard to forget.

Not that he'd wanted to forget. He'd made it very clear he'd wanted her—again and again. He was nothing if not determined. He'd called her both at home and at her office. He'd dropped by, but finally when she'd rejected him for about the tenth time, he'd become so angry he'd issued his ultimatum—which she'd ignored.

Having rid himself of her, he wouldn't be happy to

learn that *that* night was now every bit as impossible for her to forget as it had been for him.

Heaving in a breath, she rested her pitchfork against the wheelbarrow and tugged her zipper back up. She was panting by the time she'd managed it, so she didn't even try to snap the waistband. The jeans had been tight when she'd bought them, but since she'd planned to take off a couple of pounds, she hadn't worried about it.

No chance of losing those pounds anytime soon.

As she stooped to pick up the pitchfork, the cell phone in her back pocket vibrated against her hip. She threw the pitchfork back down hard, and it stabbed a mound of hay so violently that Coco, who was just outside the stall, danced backward, her hooves clattering on the concrete floor.

Oh, God, what if her big darling slipped because of her thoughtlessness?

"Easy girl," she whispered, her tone gentle even as the stench of straw and urine and horse in such close quarters caused nausea to roil in her stomach.

She hoped against hope that Leo had relented and was returning her call like a reasonable individual. Maybe he'd even agree to stop by her ranch house tonight to talk. Much as she would dread seeing him, it would be so nice if she could avoid the drive to San Antonio and the humiliation of fighting her way into his office after he'd made it clear he never wanted to see her again.

Not that she could blame him for that. Her heart knocked as she remembered accusing him of not being able to take no for an answer and of stalking her. He'd hissed in a breath. But she'd seen the acute pain in his black eyes right before he'd whirled, pitched the roses he'd brought her into the trash and quietly walked back to his truck. Later he'd called her and had delivered his ultimatum, which, for some weird reason, she'd replayed at least a dozen times in her mind. Did she enjoy suffering or what?

Instead of Leo's name, the number of In the Pink!, Abigail's own company located on a side street just off Congress Avenue in downtown Austin lit up the blue LED of her mobile phone.

Kel, her executive secretary, best friend, unpaid therapist…and of late, her number-one shoulder to cry on, was calling.

Damn.

Abigail sagged against the wall of the barn. A tear rolled down her cheek as she caught her breath. Then she swallowed and squeaked out a hello that she'd meant to sound chirpy.

"Hey, Abby, do you have a cold or something?"

"Or something." Abigail felt frozen. "This thing has me all messed up."

"I know. Hormones."

Or the terror of Leo Storm, of what he would say and do to her this morning at her news, especially after the way she'd treated him.

"Other than feeling like I'm about to have a nervous breakdown, I'm fine. Never better." Somehow she managed a hollow laugh. "As fine as someone with morning sickness can be, mucking out a stall…before they face a firing squad."

"You need to hire somebody for that yucky-mucky stuff now."

A city girl through and through, Kel didn't get horses.

"I know. You're right. I will."

"So, anything I need to know before I start scheduling your day?"

"Yes. I-I'm going to tell him…today."

"Oh? When exactly?"

"This morning! First thing!"

"Wow. Well, finally!"

"Putting it off is driving me crazy. The only problem is it looks like I'm going to have to track him down. He won't return my calls."

"You should have listened to your smart secretary. Didn't I tell you, you should call him and apologize—"

"Smart-assed secretary!"

"Big-assed, too." Kel laughed. "And getting bigger. Jan brought in two dozen donuts this morning coated with yummy strawberry goo. I'm inhaling my second."

"Okay. Well, I didn't call him back or apologize. And ever since, he's avoided the ranch and me. Now he won't even take my calls or call me back."

"Why are we surprised?"

"I said it was urgent. I've left several messages with his secretary, too. Yesterday, she actually got snappy and said he had no intention of returning my calls. I can't tell you how humiliating that was. I'm not about to tell a witch like her to tell him I'm pregnant with his child, so I guess I have to drive over there."

"Right. You think you'll get back here this afternoon?"

"After lunch. I'll probably be a basket case after seeing him."

"Do you want me to cancel your afternoon?"

"No!"

"Is there anything I can do?" Kel's voice was soft with concern.

"Just be your smart-assed self and put out any and all home fires."

"Don't worry about us," Kel said. "Just take care of you."

They hung up.

Abigail's hands began to shake again as she slid her phone in her back pocket. Compulsively, she began marching back and forth in the barn, straightening tack that didn't need to be straightened, lining up bottles and brushes on shelves, trying to feel she controlled something. She got a broom and began to sweep the feed that Coco had shaken out of the feed sack when she'd grabbed it by her teeth earlier.

Coco walked up and lowered her head almost apologetically. It was her way of begging for her favorite treat, a mixture of oats and molasses.

"Not today, big girl. Not after this big mess you made!"

Setting the broom against the wall, Abby pushed the wheelbarrow full of dirty straw outside the barn and up a small hill where she dumped it before heading toward the house. Coco, who adored her, trailed behind her in the hope of being stroked or fed, but Abby was too distracted to notice her as she usually did.

Pregnant! By Leo....

Even though Abigail had taken the pregnancy tests a week ago—three of them—she still couldn't believe she was in this mess. She was a businesswoman, an entrepreneur with a staff of forty, the owner of her own ranch. Make that a ranchette. But still...she was *la capitana* of her ship! Even if she'd sailed headlong into the rocks.

She reached into her pocket and pulled out her phone. Quickly she scrolled down to Leo's cell number and punched it. Once again she listened to it ring until his voice mail picked up. So, he still refused to answer. She flipped her phone shut and began to pace.

So what else was new? She'd watched him screen his calls, so it was easy to imagine his black eyes grimly eyeing her name before his jaw tightened and he thrust his buzzing phone back in his pocket.

How eager he'd been for her to call him just two weeks ago…until she'd accused him of stalking her. He'd stormed home, but had called her back. She hadn't answered, but he'd left a message.

"Stalking? Is that what you think? I thought you were just embarrassed and wary because we sort of took our relationship too far and too fast that first night," he'd said. "I was hoping I could convince you that I think you're great, as a person I mean. That I was willing to slow things down. But if you really want me to leave you the hell alone, I will. Call me back today, or I'm through, and I mean through."

She didn't know him very well, but she imagined he was probably a man who meant what he said.

She clenched her fist. It was ridiculous how crushed she felt that he wouldn't return her calls now. She'd told herself all he'd wanted was more wild, uninhibited sex. Had she taken the intensity of his interest for granted? Had he meant more to her than she'd known?

In any case, when she hadn't done exactly what he'd wanted, he'd quickly thrown her away. Like her mother and her father had…after Becky, her twin, had vanished. Abigail killed that thought. She didn't like to think about her long-missing twin or that she herself had never mattered very much to anybody.

She drew in a sharp breath. Yesterday after calling his secretary, she'd tucked Leo's business card in her dresser under her lingerie. Fisting her hands at her sides, she marched toward her house. She had to find that card again and call his office. Then she'd punch his exact address into her GPS and drive there.

Letting her screen door bang behind her, she rushed inside her kitchen and washed her hands before heading toward her bedroom.

She took her time at the faucet. Why had she let him pick her up that night in that bar? Why had she gone to that bar when she'd felt so lonely and rejected and vulnerable after Shanghai had dumped her for Mia Kemble?

Why had she thrown herself at Shanghai, a wild-bull rider who'd never been particularly fascinated with her in the first place?

It was no use asking questions like that. She had to go from here. She'd been hurting, so she'd had a night of wild sex with Leo Storm. As a result, the next pair of jeans she bought would have an elastic waistband.

Had he even used a condom? She wasn't sure. Except for a few shamefully sizzling memories, the night was a horrible blur.

Once inside her bedroom, she yanked the top drawer of her dresser open and began ransacking her underwear. When his card wasn't there, she looked up and caught a glimpse of a pale, thin woman with guilt-shadowed eyes and clumps of butterscotch tangles falling about her shoulders. She stood up straighter and sucked in her stomach.

Even though her jeans wouldn't snap, her tummy didn't look the least bit fat…*yet*. Still, thoughts of her future big belly panicked her.

Oh, God. Pretty soon she'd have to tell her staff. Shaking even harder, she squeezed her lashes shut and then yanked the second drawer open so hard it fell to the oak floor. She knelt and began clawing through her nightgowns and T-shirts.

Never again did she want a repeat of a week like the last one. After a visit to her doctor, Abigail had realized that she couldn't go through this alone…or end it as Kel had suggested. So, if Leo thought he could play Mr. CEO jerk and just give her that ultimatum and then walk away…the way everybody in her life had always walked away…well…at least, she'd tell him off first.

A final image of her mother packing her suitcase and telling her she was leaving her father—and leaving her—made her heart ache as she opened a third drawer.

Abby didn't know much about babies, but she knew enough to know her baby would want her to at least tell its father about the pregnancy.

She suspected that Leo had been staying in San Antonio and avoiding his ranch. Or rather the Little Spur, the ranch he owned with his brother, Connor, which was next door to hers and to Shanghai's Buckaroo Ranch. She hadn't seen him or his black truck—not once at the Little Spur—since his ultimatum, and lately she'd been watching. *Well, too bad, Mr. Rich Know-It-All, Macho CEO! You should have kept your pants zipped.*

The last thing she wanted to think about was that night in the bar after they'd danced dirty and she'd become as intensely aroused as he'd been. He'd kissed her, a second time, his tongue in her mouth, his hands sliding all over her, caressing, cupping, possessing. She'd melted, utterly melted like a slab of rich chocolate too near a flame.

Later in his loft in downtown San Antonio, she'd climbed onto his dining-room table and stripped. The next morning when she'd awakened next to his tanned, naked body, all she'd wanted was to run from him and forget.

She dreaded facing him again. He'd probably suggest the modern options just as Kel had.

"So, why even tell him?" Kel had said. "Just take care of it. In a week you'll forget it ever happened."

"You don't have my memories, Kel."

Some things, one never forgets.

Abigail hadn't ever told her about that fatal afternoon two identical eight-year-old little girls had run up a twisting trail after a wild turkey in the Franklin Mountains. The sun had been setting. The thin, impish face of her twin, Becky, had been rosily alight, her hair backlit with fire.

"Wait!" Becky had screamed. "Wait for me!"

Abigail had yelled back. "No! Come on!" Then she'd turned, expecting her twin to follow as she always did. But that had been the last time she'd ever seen her sister.

Abby opened the last drawer. She still dreamed about Becky, and now she dreamed about her baby, too. She'd never wanted to be part of a family again and open herself up for more hurt, so being pregnant was very risky for her. Still, she wasn't about to throw away her precious unborn baby. Not when she knew how sacred family was if you were lucky enough to have it and how easy it was to make irrevocable mistakes.

Don't think about Becky.

Abigail's hand closed around a card. Not Leo's card, but a Christmas card...from her father.

The money, fifty dollars in cash that he'd carelessly tossed in the envelope as a last-minute gift, was still inside it. Not that he'd spent Christmas with her. His only gift had been the card with that single bill, and it had arrived two weeks late, long after she'd given up hope he'd even thought of her at Christmas.

For a fleeting second she remembered that last Christmas before Becky had disappeared. She and her twin had conspired to make sure their parents didn't know they no longer believed in Santa Claus. They'd made cookies for Santa and set out small pink teacups filled with milk near the fireplace.

A dark feeling of loneliness washing over her, she hugged her tummy. When she'd been a little girl, she'd never felt alone. She'd had a twin, someone to share everything with. They'd both taken ballet and had had identical pink tutus and tights.

Don't think about Becky.

Abby was shaking as she tucked the Christmas card back under her sweaters. She smoothed the dark blond tangles out of her eyes. One thing she knew—no matter what Leo did, she intended to love her baby with all her heart. Bad as things seemed right now, maybe this was her second chance.

Finally, her hand closed numbly on Leo's expensive, engraved card. Lifting it, she stared at his name in bold black type. Dreading his condescending baritone, she swallowed hard, grabbed her cell and punched in his office number before her fear could escalate.

"Golden Spurs. Leo Storm's office. Miriam Jones. How can I help you?" The crisp, no-nonsense voice that had so annoyed her yesterday was as impersonal as ever.

"I need to see Mr. Storm. This morning. It's urgent."

"Mr. Storm makes his own appointments, and I assure you, he makes as few as possible. He's quite busy today. Perhaps you could send him an e-mail and outline the reasons why you need a meeting."

"N-no...no e-mail!"

"Your name please?"

She gave it—as she had yesterday. There was a long pause. Then his snoop of a secretary asked more questions before excusing herself to confer with Leo. The woman's voice, chillier than ever, came back on the phone almost immediately. The nosy witch was nothing if not efficient.

"He says he can't see you, and that you'll know the reason why."

"What? Did you say it was urgent?"

"Yes. Just like I did yesterday." Another long pause so this could sink in. "Is there anything else I can help you with, Miss Collins?" the impossible woman asked, her chilly tone holding polite finality.

"Did you really tell him it was urgent?"

The next thing Abigail knew, the woman had said a dismissive goodbye and Abby was listening to a dial tone.

Her heart pounding, Abby punched redial. "When is the best time this morning for me to see him?" she blurted before his secretary could say anything.

"I told you what Mr. Storm said—"

"You don't understand. He doesn't understand. I *have* to see him. Work me in."

"That could take hours. And even then, I can't promise—"

"Just do it!"

"He's been down in South Texas at the Golden Spurs for the last four days. I'm afraid he has a lot to catch up on. And...I'm afraid he was most emphatic about not wanting—"

Abigail snapped her phone shut. Scooping up a handful of clothes off the floor, grabbing a pair of heels, she stomped into her bathroom. Five minutes later, she looked more or less presentable with her hair in a tight coil at her nape and her body clad in a pair of black slacks and a blue knit top. Slinging her black jacket over one arm and her purse over the other, she barged out her front door and raced toward her white Lincoln.

Coco looked up and whinnied expectantly, but Abby marched past her.

She had to tell Leo her news—whether or not he wanted to hear it.

She hoped she ruined his day, his week, the rest of his life—just like he'd ruined hers.

Two

Immense paintings and photographs of the world-famous Golden Spurs Ranch, which was two hundred miles south of San Antonio, decorated two walls of Leo Storm's impressive outer offices. Sheets of glass along another wall looked out over the winding San Antonio River fringed darkly by cypress trees and buildings. Not that Abby was impressed by his showy office or the dramatic view as she scribbled a note to Leo and folded it again and again until it was a tiny wad.

If she'd been agitated when she'd walked in, she was totally charged after sitting here an hour, watching his secretary pointedly ignore her and escort others who'd come in after her, in to see him, the last of whom had been an elderly, unhappy-looking rancher.

She tried and failed to distract herself by studying his office. The massive photographs were of cowboys, oil wells, cattle drives and the legendary big house where the Kemble family he worked for had entertained presidents and kings, and lately, Arab sheiks. She'd been there— once. The museum-quality, nineteenth century oil paintings were mostly scenes of cowboys and Native Americans, although there was the inevitable clichéd landscape of Texas hill country, live oaks and bluebonnets.

The opulence and grandeur of the Golden Spurs headquarters were meant to impress, but Abigail merely felt incensed as she continued to languish in a huge red leather chair that dwarfed her.

Impatiently, Abigail looked at his secretary again. Naturally, the tight-lipped, string bean of a redhead with that awful knot screwed at the top of her head rustled papers and pretended to ignore her in that arrogant way waitresses in posh restaurants do when you need silverware and wave madly while trying to signal them.

Abigail glanced at her watch and then up at the photograph of the big house again. She'd been there once and did not have fond memories of it.

Damn his hide! Leo owed her. He'd ruined her life, hadn't he? She was through playing his games! She looked at her watch. If she didn't do something, Leo would never see her.

Getting up from the chair, she rushed up to his secretary's desk to plead her case for what had to be the fourth or fifth time.

Her forehead puckering, the redhead, who was clearly losing patience, pursed her mouth. "Yes, Miss Collins?"

"Would you give him this note—*please?*"

Arching her brows, the woman narrowed her eyes as she studied the tightly folded wad. Finally she took it, rolled her chair back and got up without a word. Abigail watched her walk briskly down a long, wide hall and open his door. A few minutes later she repeated that stiff-legged march, her heels clicking all the way back to her desk. Then she spun her chair and sat down.

"Well?" Abby said.

The woman shook her head. "Mr. Storm says he's very sorry, but he's busy—*all day*. I tried to tell you that you'd be wasting your time, that you'd be better off sending him an e-mail. He told me to remind you that you made the decision to break off your relationship with him."

What? He was blaming her and humiliating her at the same moment?

Rage and embarrassment sent fire blazing through Abby. How dare he deliberately humiliate her?

Relationship? Since when did they have a relationship?

Somehow she resisted the impulse to scream. "I have to see him," she repeated softly. "It's important."

"I'm sorry."

Clearly, she wasn't. She'd probably read some manual that told her never to meet anger with anger. Embarrassed for Abby, the woman stared down at her desk.

"I've told you repeatedly this is urgent."

"And I've told you he said he can't see you."

Abigail could feel herself hurtling toward some edge. She knew she had to get a grip. "Oh, really? Can't or won't?"

Behind her, she heard heavy footsteps. When she turned, two large, beefy men in dark suits were heading toward her. They looked like cops. Their purposeful gazes and tread both energized and terrified her.

His secretary followed her gaze. "I'm truly sorry, but he said he wants you out of the building. I'm afraid he called security. They'll escort—"

"Damn him!" Abigail barged past the impossible woman and raced down the hall toward Leo's office.

The men shouted her name and then thundered after her. His secretary cried, "Wait! You can't go in there!"

Just you watch me!

Abigail banged his door open, walked inside and slammed it so hard pins flew out of her hair and sprinkled onto Leo's polished oak floor.

"Maybe a lot of people admire you because you're the CEO of Golden Spurs, but I know you too well. You're a ruthless, cold-hearted bastard." Mike Ransom had to yell to make himself heard over the raised voices behind the door.

Leo's focus was on Abby's voice, too, and he grew angry that just knowing she was out there could rattle him. Security must have arrived to handle Abby, but it didn't sound like his men were succeeding. She'd made it crystal clear she dated cowboys—only cowboys and only short-term. That she disliked him, that she thought his type serious, dull and greedy. So what the hell did she want with him now?

"I work with dull city guys like you all day long, men who don't ever think about anything but making money," she'd told him at one point. "I don't want to play with them at night when I'm looking for a little excitement."

Why the hell had she broken her sacred rule then and slept with him?

More importantly, why the hell had he broken his

own sacred rule—which was never to combine business with sex? Dammit, the Golden Spurs board had hired him to find the late Caesar Kemble's missing twin daughter. He in turn had hired his brother, Connor, a security specialist, to look for her. Connor had stunned him when he'd informed him that their own neighbor, Abigail Collins, and her missing twin were probably the Golden Spurs heiresses.

Leo had tracked Abigail to that bar that night to obtain a DNA sample from her, not to bed her. The beer bottle he'd bagged proved she was a Kemble.

With immense effort he forced himself to concentrate on Mike Ransom. The old man looked frail and weathered. Despite his blustering, his thin shoulders were slumped in defeat, the fabric of his jacket hanging against his body like a broken bat's wings.

The snap and toughness damn sure hadn't gone out of the old man, and Leo suppressed twinges of admiration and sympathy. "If I'm a bastard, the world has you to thank."

"I wouldn't sell the Running R. Not for twice your offer. And never to you."

"You don't have a choice. Just like I didn't have a choice when you kicked me the hell off the Running R for getting Nancy pregnant when I was eighteen and didn't have a dime to my name. How does it feel to know you're helpless and at *my* mercy now?"

Strangely, Leo didn't feel nearly as happy as he'd thought he would now that he'd turned the tables on the old man.

The ruckus Abby was stirring up outside was growing louder. Not good.

Leo longed to storm past Mike and deal with Abigail himself but forced himself to remain at his desk.

"This is revenge, pure and simple," Ransom said, still glowering at him.

"You would know," Leo replied.

"You don't even want the ranch. You're just after it because you know I love it and want Cal and Nancy to inherit it someday…and because you've never gotten over…."

No, he hadn't gotten over his pregnant girlfriend, Nancy, refusing to marry him because he was broke and homeless. No, he hadn't gotten over Nancy marrying Ransom's son, Cal, instead. No, he hadn't gotten over losing his daughter. Not when he knew Ransom had caused all these things.

"Think what you like…."

Leo would have said more. He'd waited years for this day. He'd been psyched to finish Ransom off this morning in a cool, bloodless business battle of wills.

Suddenly he heard racing footsteps. His door opened and slammed. He shot to his feet just as Abigail locked herself inside his inner sanctum and whirled on him, her dark, gold hair tumbling over her shoulders like a silk curtain.

"Get out!" Leo yelled even as the memory of his hands in her hair as he held her close so he could kiss her came back to him. The memory made heat pulse through him.

Frozen, she stared at him with the wide, frightened eyes of a doe caught in his sights as she tried to smooth her wild hair. Her face was worrisomely thin and much too pale.

He remembered how her eyes had blazed after their

first kiss, her pupils dilating with passion that night. Now dark blue circles shadowed her lovely hazel eyes. Except for the bold blue of her knit top and all that butterscotch hair falling over her shoulders in such wild disarray, she was dressed as primly as a schoolteacher in a black jacket and slacks.

She stooped and retrieved several pins from the floor. Pulling her hair back, she secured it again, so that she looked much more severe. He remembered how sexily she'd been dressed in the bar that night. Still, despite Ransom's raised eyebrows and her attempt to look all prim and proper, her haunted, condemning gaze both burned him and drew him. He felt his body harden and heat even as Ransom's cold eyes drilled him.

Hell. He had to get rid of her. She'd made it abundantly clear that she considered sex with him a huge mistake and that she despised him and his type intensely and not just for seducing her, as she'd put it—which was a laugh if ever there was one.

Ever since she'd slipped from his arms and run away without a goodbye, she'd been telling him to go to hell in various ways. But she'd been as eager for it as he'd been. Then she'd had the gall to tell him she'd been pretending he was Shanghai that night. The final straw had been when she'd accused him of stalking her. Damn her, he was through.

He wasn't about to admit that that night had opened doors into his heart that had been closed since Nancy, Cal and Mike Ransom had ruined his life when he'd been little more than a kid.

"I'm busy," he said. "You're interrupting an important meeting."

"Believe me, I don't want to see you, either! But like I told your secretary, this is urgent! And, Leo, I swear— it won't take long," she whispered in a voice that cracked. "I've got to talk to you. After you hear me out, you don't have to see me again."

I don't want to see you, either. Both those words and her raw, hateful tone cut, but her shadowed eyes were scaring the hell out of him. What was wrong?

With an effort, he fought his concern and curiosity and kept his gaze and voice hard. "As you can see, I'm busy."

"Not anymore you're not. I'm just leaving," Ransom growled. "The bastard's all yours, sweetheart. Enjoy." His last word seething with sarcasm, Ransom shot him a murderous look before pivoting. Unlocking and opening the door, he slammed it behind him.

Seeing their chance, the two security officers rushed the door, but Abigail was faster. Swiftly, she shot the bolt. When the officers banged on the door, she leaned against it, her mouth trembling.

Her face was ashen, and the lack of brilliance in her wide eyes was beginning to frighten him. She was scared to death of him. She swallowed, or, at least, she tried to.

Gagging, she gave a little cry. Then, cupping one hand over her mouth, she lurched toward his desk. Was she seriously ill?

Fear gripped him even as her eyes grew even wider in panic. With her hand still covering her mouth and the other crossed over her stomach, she sank to her knees and retched violently. For another long minute she made horrible, dry-heaving sounds as she held on to his wastebasket.

"What the hell is wrong with you?"

Finally, when she lifted her desperate gaze to his, her hair wild again as it fell over her shoulders, he saw Nancy's white, terrified face from the past.

"Can't you guess?" Abby whispered.

And he knew.

Still, he had to ask her. "Morning sickness?" he muttered, hoping to hell and back he was wrong.

When she nodded, the stark pain in her mute eyes tore off a corner of his soul. Shuddering, he shut his eyes and took a deep breath, attempting to clear his head. Not that the trick worked. The air suddenly felt too thick to breathe. Or maybe his heart was thudding too violently.

"You'd better not be trying to nail me for somebody else's kid...for Shanghai's..."

She blushed, and when a single tear slid down her cheek, he bit his tongue so hard he tasted blood.

"I hate you," she whispered. "I think you're... you're horrible."

God, she was right. How could he have said that? He was the worst creep on the planet.

When she spoke again, her eyes flashed with real hatred and her voice had sharpened. "But it's yours. I wish it wasn't, believe me. I never wanted to see you again, either!"

Her barbs stung. "You would have preferred Shanghai! Even if he is married. You made that abundantly clear."

She ignored his comment. "There are tests that will prove it's yours...if you don't believe me. There's DNA."

He felt his neck heat guiltily. He knew way too much about DNA.

"That won't be necessary," Leo said through clenched teeth. "Look, I'm sorry...."

"Relax. You don't have to apologize. I hate you just as much as you dislike me."

"Right." No surprise that she didn't want his child any more than she'd wanted him.

He ran his hand through his hair, staring at her for a long moment while her eyes damned him to hell and back. When she knew the whole truth—why he'd been in the bar that night—she'd have even more justification for hating him. If the Golden Spurs board learned the truth, this could spell the end of his career.

Abruptly, Leo strode across his office and opened the door that led to his private washroom. He turned on the faucet and dampened a towel with cold water. He poured water into a glass. When he returned, he handed the towel and the glass of water to her.

"Sit down before you fall. Bathe your face, and we'll figure out what the hell you need to do next."

"I need to do? It's yours, too," she repeated dully.

"Right. I get that."

"But you didn't believe—"

"I said I get it—okay? It's mine. Unpleasant realities have a way of sinking in fast. Now this is what we're going to do—"

"You can't just boss me around. I don't work for you."

"You're carrying my child."

"You're supposed to be smart! Did you even use a condom?" she accused.

"Yes, dammit. Several."

She flushed as if it embarrassed her to remember once hadn't been enough for either of them.

"I wasn't some kid, in such a rush and so madly in love, that I didn't think…."

He'd done that once, years ago with Nancy when he'd been eighteen. Still, that aside, he'd been wild for her. He hadn't just happened to go to that bar. He'd known she'd be there. He'd had something very important to tell her.

Something very important to get from her.

Too bad for them both that she'd dressed so sexily and had looked so sad that he'd let himself get derailed before he'd obtained what he'd needed.

He remembered how many times they'd done it, and how every time it had just gotten better and better. How she'd moaned and sobbed and opened herself utterly, clinging to him with her legs and arms until he'd hardened again while still inside of her. He'd felt sexy and big and powerful.

He remembered her taking him between her lips, kissing him until he'd felt himself in a hot swirl of soft, wet satin and had climaxed in her mouth. She'd been sweet, hot and good. He'd been on a high for several weeks after that night. He'd been unable to believe that she would want to throw him and what they'd had that night—which had been that mind-altering, at least for him—away.

As if she read his mind, color flooded her face. "I—I don't remember much about that night."

"Right. Lucky you. I wish I could forget you and all that happened between us as easily."

"Well, I'll have the baby now as a constant reminder."

"So you want to keep it?" His rush of relief stunned him.

She sprang out of her chair, sputtering at him angrily. "D-don't you even dare suggest anything else the way Kel did, or I'll…or…."

"Hey…hey… Calm down." He rushed to her and placed his hands on her shoulders.

At his touch, something raw and true sparked in her eyes. Then hatred followed in its wake.

Heat flashed through every nerve ending in his body. As if burned, she jumped back, and as always he felt stung by her rejection.

Impossible relationships with women. Were they his specialty or what? But this was worse—because it involved his career. He was screwed on every level by this turn of events. Dammit, he liked being CEO of the Golden Spurs, and if he didn't think fast, his career was charred toast.

"Settle down," he muttered, but his voice was deliberately gentle now. "I-I'm glad you want my baby."

"Your baby?" she repeated, backing even farther away from his blunt, broad hands.

When he nodded, relief flooded her face. He fought the softening he felt as she sank slowly back into her chair. He had to remember she was dangerous, exceedingly dangerous on many levels.

He went to his own chair, and she sat in hers staring across his desk at him as if she were in a daze.

"What are we going to do?" she finally whispered. "This is such a shock."

It sure as hell was, and it was far more complex than she knew. He would have to act before she figured out that she held all the trump cards.

"You've had more time to get used to the idea than I have. I'm sure my secretary told you I've got a really jammed schedule today. Why don't I come over tonight? Say around seven? And we'll talk about options."

"I—I would really prefer to meet you in some public place."

"At night? Then you'd have to drive back to your ranch alone. Are you more afraid of me than of some stranger who might follow you home?"

"You don't have to worry about me. I'm used to living alone, to driving home alone."

"If you're having my baby, you and the baby are my responsibility now."

She bristled. As he stared at her narrowed brows, he could almost see a dozen arguments buzzing in that micromanaging brain of hers.

"Okay, forget I said that. I don't want to argue. But are you afraid of me?"

She shook her head furiously.

"Okay, why didn't you want to see me again?"

"I didn't want to see you again because you're pushy and arrogant, and because you're not the kind of man I like."

"Right. You prefer bull riders. Shanghai Knight in particular."

Why was he repeating himself? Because knowing that hurt, dammit. "You pretended I was him, and you wish this was his kid."

She wouldn't meet his gaze. "At least I didn't lie to you about him."

"Didn't you?"

Shanghai. Leo was sick to death of hearing about the guy. Goaded, hardly knowing what he was doing, he leapt out of his chair.

She jumped up, too, but he clamped his hands around her arms and pulled her to him before she could run. The heat of her body nestling against his torso and legs reminded him of her wet, enticing silkiness that night and why he'd been unable to stick to his original agenda in the bar. Hell, she'd filled him with a hunger it might take a lifetime to satisfy.

"Why are you so afraid of me? Did I hurt you? Have I ever hurt you? Forced you?"

He'd done worse than that by getting that DNA sample without telling her, by not informing her who she was. There was no telling what she'd do when she found out. But it was better to kill one snake at a time. He had to know what she thought of him.

"No, but—"

"Yet you called me a stalker…."

She was shaking as he tightened his grip.

She felt good. So damn good. She smelled of wind and trees, of wildflowers.

"I only said that so you'd leave me alone."

"All that Shanghai crap… Are you really in love with him? Or were you just throwing him at me because you couldn't face me after what we'd done?"

She didn't answer, but something in him relaxed a little.

He'd sensed her inner demons right from the beginning. He knew all about inner demons, and like a fool, he'd sympathized.

He should let her go now, but he couldn't. "If you didn't want me, then why did you make love to me again and again that night?"

"I don't know. I can't remember."

"Can't? Or don't want to remember? Do you really hate me the way you said?"

"Y-yes."

"Go on."

Fixing him with her huge, hazel eyes, she tried to form the words but couldn't.

Suddenly he noticed her heart beating in her throat as she swallowed convulsively. Did she want him... just a little? He remembered burying his face in her breasts. How soft she'd been. How sweet she'd tasted when he'd licked each nipple. How eagerly she'd kissed him back.

"Okay, so maybe you don't totally hate me. But we're still in a helluva mess, aren't we?" he said.

Cursing, he ripped off his glasses and crushed her mouth beneath his. Again, she tasted exquisite...like honey. He expected more fight, but like a terrified animal that had exhausted itself after being caught in a trap, she went absolutely still. Finally, when he didn't release her, when the heat of his body seeped into hers, she grasped his muscular shoulders and pressed her soft lips closer to his, opening them to him.

He loosened his grip. Not even then did she run. Slowly her tongue slid against his, mating with his, and she pushed herself tightly against his body. She didn't draw back, not even when she discovered that he was fully aroused. When he pushed himself against her, she caught her breath.

Moaning, arching her pelvis against his erection in bold invitation, she circled his neck and then caressed his cheeks with her hands, framing his face in her palms as she kissed his mouth again and again.

Instantly the sweetness and the passion and the primal perfection of that night she'd spent in his bed flooded him, and everything made sense again. No wonder he'd been unable to believe she didn't want him. No wonder he'd gone back again and again only to endure more painful rejections.

Her response to his kiss and his male arousal was instantaneous and instinctive and true—unlike the negative garbage she'd been dishing out ever since. He wanted this woman.

When he realized how acute and complex his need for her was, and what a terrible, complicated mess he was in, he jerked his mouth from hers and backed a safe distance away. As if there were a safe distance.

His breathing was hard and labored, but so was hers. Maybe she was pregnant, but he was equally trapped.

"Seven o'clock," he muttered, his tone low and fierce. "Your house. If you prefer to be in a public place, I'll drive you into town in my truck."

"You have no right to just take charge."

"Like I already said, you're having my baby. I think that gives me certain rights."

"This—and what just happened—is exactly why I didn't want to tell you. You'll take advantage...."

Hell. She'd liked it—every bit as much as he had.

"But you did tell me. So, I'll see you at seven. Unless you want me to finish what that kiss started...here on my couch."

Her eyes widened as she stared past him to his long, leather couch. Involuntarily, she touched her lower lip with a fingertip in a way that caused desire to pulse in his blood. "No...."

She must have seen the heat in his eyes that signaled how close he was to the edge because she turned and stumbled toward the doors. Twisting the knob, she seemed to panic when the door wouldn't open and began to beat against the wood with her fists.

He walked across the room. Without touching her, he turned the appropriate lock.

"Seven o'clock sharp," he murmured dryly against her ear before she jumped and ran through the open doors, past his secretary and the still-waiting security guards. Leo motioned for them to let her pass.

Watching her slim hips encased in black silk swing back and forth as she disappeared down the hall, he broke out in a sweat. He had to quit lusting after her and think. All hell would damn sure break loose when she and the board discovered who she really was—which meant it was time to consider damage control.

He shut the doors, went to his desk, punched a button and told Miriam to reschedule his late-afternoon appointments.

Sinking into the chair, Leo's mind flashed back to the afternoon his brother, Connor, had barged into his office and tossed his Stetson and several 8 x 10 pictures onto his desk of their cute neighbor from the ranch next to theirs, riding her palomino bareback.

"I'm pretty sure Abby's one of your missing twins, but we need a DNA sample to confirm it," Connor had said.

"Abby?"

"Like I said, we won't know for sure until you obtain the DNA sample."

"Me? You're the hotshot security specialist."

It hadn't taken Connor long to convince him that all he had to do was buy her a cup of coffee and bag her cup.

Leo called her office late one evening to make an appointment and had told her secretary he was Abby's neighbor. In passing, Kel had mentioned where Abby and she were going that night. He'd shown up at the bar and had taken it from there.

A week after Leo had slept with Abby, Connor had called and said they had a DNA match. Abigail was one of the missing Golden Spurs heiresses. Which made her long-vanished twin, Becky, the other one.

Abigail was the last woman he should have slept with. If he didn't figure out a way to turn this new disaster to his advantage, her pregnancy could cost him everything.

Three

Leo sat down in front of his computer, adjusted his webcam and moved his mouse. He was a firm believer in the theory that when the shit hits the fan, the best defense is almost always a good offense.

So, whose ass better to kick than his baby brother's?

Several mouse clicks later, Connor's square-jawed face and broad shoulders filled Leo's screen. They both nodded and said hello. Then Connor, who was obviously having a better day than he was, leaned back in his chair and flashed his trademark lady-killer smile.

"How can I help you, big brother?"

Connor swept a lock of blond hair out of his blue eyes. He'd put in quite a bit of hard time playing the baby brother from hell and wasn't always as easygoing as his present-day smile might indicate. Baby brother had definitely shown his dark side on more than one occasion.

Leo, who'd raised him after Mike Ransom had kicked them both off the Running R Ranch—not that Connor had been to blame for that—had bailed his baby brother out of plenty of messy jams before a nasty altercation with the police had finally convinced Connor to stay on the right side of the law. Connor had joined the Marines, served in Afghanistan, married and had been widowed.

Leo cut to the chase. "So why the hell don't you have any promising leads on Becky Collins? You been sitting on your thumbs or what?"

Connor loosened the knot of his tie and shifted in his leather chair. Not that his cocky, lady-killer smile wavered. "I have my top agent on the case, but so far…nothing. It's as if she vanished into thin air out there in that El Paso park. Hey, ever since I sent you the DNA report that confirms who our sexy neighbor really is, I've been waiting to hear from you. How'd she take it when you told her who she is?"

Counter-kick-in-the-ass. Baby brothers were good at that, especially baby brothers who'd grown up to be talented P.I.'s and in addition owned a large, multifaceted security business with branches in several major Texas cities. Hell, it could be argued that Connor was even more successful than he was. Not something Leo, who was as competitive as hell, liked to think about much.

"I haven't," Leo hedged testily. "Not yet."

"It's been weeks since I found her. A week since I sent the DNA results. What the hell are you waiting for?"

Maybe Connor was sitting in his office in Houston, but the gaze of his big blue eyes shaded by dense black lashes felt as hot as a laser beam.

"It's complicated." *And getting more complicated.*

"You were as excited as hell when I gave you the file on her."

"Yeah, I was."

"You said if the DNA proved I was right, you were going to tell her first thing."

"I intended to." Leo frowned, not liking the interrogation. "When I met her that night, she was still on the rebound because Shanghai, our neighbor, had dumped her to marry Mia Kemble."

"Right, Mia Kemble of the Golden Spurs Ranch; her famous half-sister, or is it cousin?

"Cousin. Only Abby doesn't know who she really is."

"My point. So why don't you tell her?"

He'd been trying to when she'd accused him of stalking her.

"She was pretty vulnerable that night…and in a sort of self-destructive mood. She was acting crazy, and I got crazy. Things got personal pretty quick."

"Usually you put business before pleasure."

"Too bad I didn't that night."

"Tell me you didn't sleep with her."

"I didn't sleep with her," Leo repeated as if by rote. He probably could have fooled anybody but Connor. Connor had an uncanny knack for smelling out a lie.

Connor's smile changed into something more dangerous, and he leaned forward. "Don't just repeat what I said like a damn idiot. Say it like you mean it."

"I wish I could. Hell. Look, she didn't agree to that DNA sample I sent you. Worse, she's pregnant. I'm meeting her tonight to figure out where we go from here."

Connor whistled. "You knocked up the long-missing

secret Golden Spurs heiress you hired my agency to find? How will the Golden Spurs board react to that?"

"Favorably—if I figure out how to make this work for me...."

"Leo! Don't work it! Not this time! Just keep it simple."

Leo didn't say anything.

"Leo! You'd better listen to me. For once, keep your damned ambition in check and just tell her and the board the truth. This is your kid. You don't want to mess things up the way you did last time."

"The way I did? Have you forgotten how Mike Ransom and Cal threw both of us off the Running R when Nancy turned up pregnant, probably because they'd always wanted Nancy's family's ranch? How they convinced her to marry Cal instead of me because they could do so much more for the baby? For little Julie," he amended softly. He swallowed as he remembered Julie, his dark-eyed daughter, a defiant teenager now, a slim woman-child he barely knew, who hated him.

"No, I haven't forgotten, but you don't want that to happen this time, do you? Look, I know what you've been through. But I know these kinds of situations, too. People make incredible messes when they keep secrets or cover shit like this up. Things spin out of control."

"I'm not going to promise you anything. You know as well as I do that honesty got me into a helluva lot of trouble. So much trouble I lost everything. Nancy... Julie... And you—nearly. I used to think I'd never see myself clear."

"It wasn't your fault I went a little wild after Mother died, when it was just the two of us and you were working all the time."

"Maybe it was. I should have paid more attention to you. I shouldn't have let Cal adopt Julie. I should have fought harder be a part of my daughter's life."

"You've gotta forget...like I have."

"You're not me, little brother. If Ransom hadn't thrown me off the Running R...and cut off my college money, then maybe Nancy wouldn't have left me for Cal. I can't forget that."

"Right. Praise the Lord. You're swimming in success, and you still want that old man's head on a spike."

"You know something funny—Mike Ransom was in my office today. I had the bastard in the palm of my hand, but instead of squeezing, I let him walk out the door."

"Good for you! After all, he is Julie's only living grandpa."

"No! The only reason he got away was because Abigail showed up, looking haunted and ill. I started feeling sorry for her, and then she let me have it with both barrels."

"God speaks to us in strange ways. He has a plan. Why do you think she showed up at that exact moment—pregnant? Maybe to give you a chance to count your blessings and reconsider getting your revenge. Ransom made a mistake. A long time ago. Yeah, he was too rough on you, but haven't you ever made a mistake? He's an old man now. His wife's sick. The ranch has been in his family for generations. If you hurt him, you hurt Julie."

"I'm through with this conversation."

"Just think about it. Ransom's got plenty of problems without you going after him. Life has a way of making us pay for our sins. If you use Abigail to suit some ambition of yours, you'll regret it."

Connor said goodbye. Leo clicked his mouse, and the computer screen went blank. He sat staring at himself in the gray glare. Then he ran his hands through his hair. After a long time he got up, went to his bar and poured a shot and a half of scotch into a highball glass. Leaning his head back, he bolted it.

Normally, he never drank during the day, and never at his office. The stuff burned his mouth and throat as he sat back down in his leather chair for a long moment and waited for the liquor to ease his pain. When it didn't, he eyed the bottle across the room, yearning for another shot.

No. He'd been down that hellish road. It was always better to face pain, better to stay in control.

Instead, he opened up his top desk drawer and pulled out the file folder with Abigail's name on it that his brother had triumphantly pitched on his desk six weeks ago. Opening it, Leo thumbed through the various documents and photographs.

Several glossy 8 x 10 photos taken with a high-power lens of Abigail riding her golden horse, Coco, fell onto his desk. The DNA report was there, too. He'd told Connor that it was a helluva coincidence her ranch was next to theirs and Shanghai Knight's.

"More than a coincidence," his newly converted, ex-bad-boy brother had retorted with sickening, self-righteous assurance and an easy smile. "It's nothing short of a miracle. God definitely has a plan."

"I don't believe in miracles or plans."

"Someday you will. Maybe sooner than you think."

Leo went to his bookshelf and picked up Julie's picture. She had black hair and black eyes. He'd called her on her last birthday and she'd refused to talk to him. Nancy said that every day she looked more and more like him.

Julie was a teenager now…nearly as old as he'd been when he'd gotten Nancy pregnant. She had a bad attitude about school, said she didn't want to go to college, said she didn't want to do anything but hang out with her friends, who were creeps for the most part. She wanted a tattoo and some piercings. She wore tight clothes and too much makeup. Nancy said it was because she craved attention. Cal said it was because she felt abandoned by her biological father. But what could he do about that when Julie refused to take his calls or see him?

He'd never played a big part in her life, so for all intents and purposes Cal was her father. Now she was nearly grown, and Leo regretted having let his daughter slip away.

Bottom line: how far was he willing to go to prevent that from happening again?

All the damn way, he thought. All the damn way. He'd do whatever the hell it took.

Just one more minute….

The sun was low in the sky, and the shadows of the oaks and pines swept across the gravel road and the lush grasses where Coco grazed nearby.

It had to be close to seven. Abby knew she should get up from the stone bench and go back to the house to wait for Leo. But her heart was thudding because she felt so anxious at the thought of facing him again. She was exhausted, and the balmy warmth soothed her.

Why was it that she could go and go and go—until she stopped? Still, Leo Storm didn't strike her as a patient man, and it would only make things worse if she kept him waiting.

Not that she got up. The soft breeze caressing her cheek was too seductively delicious, and her body felt heavy as she continued to lie flat on her back on the cool stone bench. So instead of doing the intelligent thing, she stayed where she was, procrastinating, enjoying this fleeting moment of peace.

From her first dread-filled, wakeful moment, her day had been long and tense. This was the first second she'd had to herself, if she didn't count the hectic commutes from the ranch to San Antonio, from there to Austin, and then the commute home. The high-speed traffic had been dense and fierce, so there was no comparison to this alone-time lying underneath this wonderful tree.

Trees looked completely different when viewed from such an angle. Lying here took her back to her childhood, and she remembered how much she and Becky had loved climbing trees.

For a moment longer she forgot Leo and lay quietly, staring up at the spreading branches of the immense live oak tree and then beyond at the sparkling sunlight and brilliant blue sky that peeked between the dark leaves. The world was big and the universe even bigger. The problem of her pregnancy and dealing with Leo seemed tiny in comparison until she heard him thrashing clumsily through the trees, calling her name.

"Abby! Abby!"

She shot to her feet at the sound of his deep baritone and brushed a leaf out of her hair. "Over here!"

The intensity of his dark gaze had her trembling long before it slid knowingly to her belly and caused heat to scorch her cheeks. Could he tell that her waist was a little fuller?

She remembered standing on his table. He'd been beneath her as she'd undulated to "Wild Thing" and peeled her red jersey top over her head. When she'd wiggled out of her spandex denim skirt, his avid fascination with her body that night had made her feel feminine and reckless and strangely empowered. Like Pandora's box, once opened, needs had been let out that she was having a hard time containing again. But she had to.

Flecked with gold and rimmed with thick black lashes, his gorgeous eyes had followed her every move. When she was naked, he'd strode to the table, clasped her waist and had pulled her into his arms in such a way that she'd slid down the length of his body.

For a long time he'd simply held her. Then he'd kissed her hair, leaned her back down onto the table very slowly and tongued her body until she'd thought she'd surely turn to flame. She'd wanted wild sex and oblivion from the hurt of years of loneliness. He'd wanted more, and that had scared her.

Don't think about that night. Don't let him that close ever again.

He was tall, six-two at least, and rugged, as well. She knew he did hard, physical work on his ranch, and often when one of her fences had needed mending and she'd driven past while he'd been working on the Little Spur, she'd felt a twinge of envy. It would be nice to have a man around who could do things like that.

His skin was dark, the angular planes of his face thoroughly masculine even when he wore his glasses. He must have gotten home earlier than usual because he'd taken the time to discard his suit and glasses and put on a pair of freshly pressed jeans and a long-sleeved, blue chambray shirt. The soft collar was open at his tanned throat and his sleeves were rolled halfway up his muscular forearms.

Suddenly she wished she'd changed into something more flattering, but she'd been too tired to do anything other than shed her jacket.

She sucked in a breath because just looking at the V of dark hair, and his strong, tanned arms made her feel curiously weak. She had to remind herself that he was serious and dull, not her type at all, that she preferred cowboys and, of course, that he'd taken advantage of her.

Calm down. All you're going to do is talk to him.

"I saw your car, so I knocked," he said. "When you didn't answer, I went around back and found the door open. I yelled, and you didn't answer, so I'm afraid I went on in. When you weren't anywhere…" He stared at her again in that intent way that communicated his fear for her. "Well, never mind now. I've found you. I'm glad you're okay."

His evident concern and even his anger pleased her, which was ridiculous. She didn't want him to care. Most of all, she didn't want to need for him to care. There was nothing to like about him—not now—not after he'd gotten them into this horrible mess.

"Have you eaten?" he asked.

Men and their appetites; they either wanted sex or food.

She shook her head.

"We could drive into town."

"I've driven a lot today. I'm pretty tired. Maybe we could just talk…and then you could go."

"You want to get rid of me as soon as possible?"

"I thought I made it clear that I didn't think we had anything going for us."

"Except good sex…and now the baby."

She didn't deny it, so he pressed his point. "That's a lot to have in common, wouldn't you say?"

"Not nearly enough."

"Okay. Truce. Do you have a beer? It's been a long day."

"You're telling me."

His cell phone went off, and he flipped it open, frowning when he saw who it was. "Sorry. I can't talk now, Connor. Yeah, I'm at her place. No, we haven't gotten to that yet. Hell, no!"

Clearly irritated by whatever his brother had said, he hung up abruptly.

"You told your brother…about us?"

"Yeah. He likes you, so I did. Then he got religious on me. Thinks it's a miracle." He glanced toward her, his eyes both cool and yet disturbingly dark and sensual. "Haven't told anybody else, though. Not yet."

"You're close to your brother?"

"Close enough. We've been through a lot together."

"And you own the Little Spur together, too, right?"

"We both thought it was a good investment. Neither one of us can be here all the time. But we both know a thing or two about ranching, and the physical work after a long day or week at our offices releases a lot of tension."

"I love it out here, too."

"That makes three things we have in common."

Coco walked up and nuzzled him.

"Four. See, your horse likes me."

Abby got up and began to walk toward the house. He

and Coco fell into step beside her. His strides were long and easy, yet his pace matched hers. When she reached her front steps, Abby paused.

"I've got to put Coco in the barn."

"I'll do it," he said.

"But she won't let anybody but me—"

"I've been seducing her with little treats of oats and molasses when I see her along our fence line for quite a while."

"What?"

"Just go inside, and I'll join you in a minute." He headed to the barn with Coco following right behind him.

A few minutes later, when he opened her kitchen door, she nodded for him to come inside. He flashed her a smile and then made a beeline for her refrigerator.

"Give a guy an inch," she began, fighting a smile of her own. "Any problems with Coco?"

"She's a breeze compared to you. Too bad you don't crave oats and molasses…."

He grinned. She grinned back. Then, stooping, he opened the refrigerator and got out two bottles of beer. "Want one?"

"No. Not for the next nine months."

His long glance gently touched on her brow, her nose and last of all her mouth. Heat climbed her neck and scorched her cheeks.

He looked a little embarrassed himself before he turned away to rustle through a drawer. He found an opener and popped the top.

Pulling out a chair, he straddled it. Then, leaning back with a pretense of casualness, he took a long pull from the bottle.

"You certainly know how to make yourself at home," she said.

"Would you prefer to wait on me?"

Turning her back on him, she poured herself a tall glass of water.

"This is probably a bad idea, but I'm prepared to marry you," he said.

She whirled. "Don't do me any damn favors, Storm."

"I was thinking more about giving my child my name."

"Your child? My child, too."

"My point exactly. Our child. People with children do occasionally marry each other."

"For the child's sake?"

"Right. There could be other compensations."

Being a man, he was probably thinking about sex. "We're practically strangers!"

"I disagree. On several counts." His burning black eyes were locked on hers, causing her to blush as dozens of shared intimacies she'd fought to forget flooded her mind. She remembered lying on his bed, her legs parted as he lowered his head to kiss her. Cowboy or not, she hadn't been able to get enough of dull, corporate Leo Storm until long after she'd shuddered against his lips. And not even then. She'd clasped the back of his head and had held him against her for long moments, wanting more, several times. Never had she felt so open, so vulnerable, so completely trusting…or so connected.

Why him? She'd told herself that she couldn't ever let herself feel so vulnerable and trusting again.

She swallowed. "I won't marry you."

"You got a better game plan?"

"Not yet."

"Then that leaves me an open field. But, hey, I'm too hungry to come up with plan B." He set his beer on her kitchen table and went to her refrigerator again. "Why don't I cook us both something for supper?"

Before she could say no, he said, "Or I'm happy to take you out."

He was being entirely too agreeable. "But that would just make everything take longer."

"You mean if I cook, you'll get rid of me sooner?" He was chuckling as he knelt and removed a bag of carrots, two potatoes, mushrooms and two thick, frozen steaks.

Fuming because he didn't appear nearly as upset about all this as she was, she watched in silence as he poked holes in the steak's cellophane wrapper and stuck it in the microwave to defrost.

"You want to watch TV or listen to music while we cook?" he asked as he began clanging pots and pans as if their being together didn't bother him in the least.

"How can you act like everything is perfectly normal, when I'm pregnant and feeling so crazy?"

He put the frying pan down on the unlit stovetop. "I thought maybe we should take our mind off the crisis. And that maybe dinner would help us both to relax a little and get used to each other. That maybe then we could think better."

Relaxing with him was the last thing she wanted to do, but maybe he had a tiny point. "Okay. You're right."

She found her remote and turned on her TV because music sounded romantic and being romantic alone in her house with him scared her. Instantly, she regretted her choice when the news stories were all about crimes of passion. When there was one story after another about men killing their girlfriends, he cursed beneath his breath, picked up the remote and changed the channel to one about the hunting habits of large African cats.

Not that she could focus on pouncing cats tearing throats out of zebras. At least, not with Leo's huge, muscular presence filling her kitchen. His black hair was iridescent as he bent over the stove, and she found herself staring at it and remembering how soft and silky it had felt when she'd slid her fingertips through it. He was so broad-shouldered, she wondered if he'd played football in high school.

Gulping in a quick breath, she got up, grabbed a cutting board, a bag of carrots and a knife, and turned her back on him. Trying to ignore him, she began to cut and chop. But she was very aware of him when he edged closer to her as he washed the lettuce. Only when he went outside and lit her grill could she breathe normally again. But he was back in less than a minute, and so was her tension.

He knew his way around the kitchen; she'd give him that. Dinner preparations certainly went faster when there were two in the kitchen. Twenty minutes later the table was set and the side dishes were simmering. Saying the coals outside were perfect, he salted and peppered their raw steaks and then forked them onto a platter.

"Sun's going down. You want to sit outside and relax with me while I cook our steaks?"

Relax? "What is all this to you? A game?"

"No. But do we have to hate each other forever just because this has happened?"

"Yes. I've taken a vow."

"Have you now?" He headed out the door without

further discussion, letting the screen door bang noisily behind him.

Did he know he was totally stressing her out? Like a little kid with a hankering to bicker, she grabbed a bottle of water and stormed after him.

Not that she said anything when she plopped down in the chair across from his. The instant she sat down, she realized her mistake. The sun was going down in a blaze of scarlet. Stars were popping out in the purple afterglow. The fire and the night air and his closeness made her think romance even though all he was doing was sipping his beer while he watched their steaks. She unscrewed her bottle top and gulped, but an ever-thickening tension caused by the night and his nearness and the intimacies they'd shared was building inside her.

Finally, she blurted, "You know, I was doing just fine before you came along and ruined everything."

"Were you now?" he said easily. "That's why you were in that bar that night dressed in a pickup outfit."

She jumped up off her bench. "I'm single. I'll have you know I have every right to go out with a girlfriend."

"No argument here."

"Nobody tells me what to wear."

"Some outfits do strike a chord in the primitive male psyche, as you probably know."

"I don't have to take this."

For some reason instead of stalking back to the relative safety of her kitchen, she stayed put, her breasts heaving. His dark gaze skimmed the labored breathing of her chest much too appreciatively before he grabbed her wrist and pulled her back down.

"I liked what I saw. Too much. I still do." He paused, his eyes roaming lower than she liked.

"Look at my face, dammit."

He met her glare with an amused look. "Tight denim skirt. Short, too. Tight red jersey top."

"You've got a good memory."

"For things I like. You're a beautiful woman. You wouldn't have worn a getup like that if you hadn't wanted to go home with somebody."

"You took advantage."

"I took what was offered."

"Kel talked me into the bar that night. She said a wild cowboy was the only cure for a broken heart."

"But instead of a wild cowboy, you ended up with me…and a baby."

"Because you pushed."

"Sure I did. I wanted you. I go after what I want."

She'd gone with him because she'd felt lost and vulnerable, and he'd given her the illusory feeling of being protected.

He leaned closer. "And you wanna know something? Despite the way you've treated me lately, I still do. That's why I asked you to marry me. The way I see it, your horse likes me, we wouldn't be so good in bed together if you didn't like me a little, you're pregnant and we've both got places out here. That's a start. Maybe we're not madly in love, but if you tried to get along with me half as hard as you put yourself out to be cantankerous, who knows what might happen?"

"If I tried—"

"Yeah, you! If you did, who knows, maybe things could work out between us."

"You're a calculating guy. I can't believe you're serious about marrying me."

"Believe it."

"What you are suggesting is medieval."

"The Western idea of romantic love is far from universal. Lots of countries believe marriages should be based on more practical reasons. Take the Indians...."

"I am not Indian."

"Their divorce rate is probably lower than ours."

"Something is wrong here. I can feel it. Why are you being so nice when you wouldn't even talk to me this morning?"

"Did anyone ever tell you, you have a suspicious nature?" He shrugged. "Think what you like." He pretended to turn his attention to the fire.

When the steaks were nearly done, he tore off a piece. The gesture was savage, and she wondered if he was as calm and practical about all this as he pretended. "Want to test it?" he asked.

She'd barely nodded before his broad, tanned finger placed a bit of beef on the tip of her tongue.

"Delicious," she murmured, savoring the juicy tidbit.

He let his finger linger against her wet mouth until she turned her head away.

He caught her frightened glance. "What do you say we go inside and eat, woman?"

Four

Leo set his plate on the table, went to the counter and turned off her TV. "I've had my fill of lions. How about some music?"

"No! No music!"

"I seem to remember you got pretty excited over 'Wild Thing.'"

Which had led to a long night of lovemaking.

She remembered tossing him her red jersey top, remembered how he'd inhaled her scent while he'd watched her. The next memory that hit her was how she'd felt when she'd awakened the next morning with his long, lean body sprawled on top of her. She'd been naked, and her body had felt well-used. Her mouth had been bruised from too many kisses and sour with the taste of beer. She'd pushed him away, dressed and run. And she'd never wanted to look back.

But she had, first in her dreams, and then all the time this past week.

"Don't get started on that night!"

"My lips are sealed." He smiled as he sat down across from her at her tiny table. His thigh slid against hers. Funny, how mere denim against black silk could send a frisson of heat up her leg. She jumped back, bumping her knee into the table leg.

"Ouch!"

"Are you okay?" he asked.

Before she could stop him, he knelt to inspect her leg, running his hand beneath the silk and up her calf with unbearable tenderness.

"Good. You didn't even break the skin."

"I'm fine," she muttered through gritted teeth, tugging her pants leg back down.

Smiling broadly, he returned to his seat. "You're mighty jumpy."

Who wouldn't be with him so close? Even seated, he seemed huge. Dangerous. Was he bigger inside her kitchen? Or did the room just seem smaller and more intimate now that darkness pressed its velvet fingertips against the windowpanes and she knew they had the whole night ahead of them.

Slicing off a piece of steak, she tried to concentrate on chewing the tender meat. Impossible with his big muscular body so near…not to mention her memories.

He attempted polite conversation, but when she didn't encourage him, he soon stopped talking. After that, there was only the clatter of forks against china and the beating of her heart. Once or twice they reached for bread at the same time, and their fingers accidentally brushed. Both times she felt a jolt and jumped again while he smiled as if he enjoyed her uneasiness immensely.

The night grew ever darker, and she became ever more intensely aware she was all alone with him in the privacy of her house. A house with bedrooms…and beds. She was as bad as he was. She couldn't get near him without thinking about sex.

Oh, would this interminable meal never end? Would he never finish and get to what they had to discuss and leave?

Marry him? Eat with him every night like this? She would go mad!

He devoured his meal with more relish than she and was finished when she still had half her steak untouched. She wished he'd get up and go out on the porch or something so she could eat in peace, but no, he sat politely watching her toy with a bit of potato until finally she dropped her fork in frustration.

"All done," she whispered raggedly.

"You're sure? You're supposed to be eating for two now, remember?"

As if she needed reminding.

She seized her plate and stood up. "We talk now, and then you go. I've got an early morning just like you do."

"No. First we clear the table and wash and dry your dishes."

"You did say you realized that I'm anxious to get rid of you."

"I suggested dinner. I'm not sticking you with a sink full of dishes. Not when you have an early morning."

"As if you care about that."

"I do. I'm told pregnant ladies tire easily."

He turned from her and put his plate down and

splashed detergent into her sink. She heaved in a breath as he began scraping food into her garbage disposal. There seemed to be no stopping him once he was determined on a path.

"All right…we wash the damn dishes," she muttered, surrendering. "Then we talk and you go."

He was silent at first. Finally he said, "We can talk now. You said no to marriage. Does that mean you prefer money? A large check maybe? Or monthly installments?"

She frowned. "No large check. That sounds so…so cold."

"I agree. I want to assume responsibility for you and the baby. I'd like to know my child…be close to him or her…."

"Under the circumstances, the less you're around, the better."

"Does our baby get a vote?"

She thought better before answering that. Besides, she was too tired to argue.

"In any case," he said, "we'll have to make some legal arrangements—to protect ourselves and the child."

"I can't believe we're having this conversation."

"If we were a normal couple, we'd have fallen in love first."

"But we didn't." The thought made her strangely sad. She didn't believe love made you happy. What it did was make you ache for the impossible.

Studying her face, he lapsed into a thoughtful silence.

He couldn't know that he was making her feel guilty, making her long for things she did not want to long for. Damn the man.

When he dried the last glass, she yanked the dish towel

out of his big tanned hand and threw it on the counter. "Now, you can quit acting so concerned and nice and—"

"Careful." He took a step toward her. "Maybe you shouldn't have reminded me that you go for the bad boys. I might take it as permission to be bad. I've had more experience in that role than you might imagine, and we are very much alone."

"No...." She tried to back away from him, but her hips hit the counter edge.

He followed. Placing a hand on either side of her, he gripped the counter, imprisoning her. "You did go to that bar because you wanted a wild cowboy."

"Stop it."

"Who says only cowboys are wild?"

"Leo, this isn't funny. You were being so nice and so reasonable."

"Nice and reasonable doesn't seem to be working. Maybe you're not the only one here who's been made kinda crazy by what happened that night. I crossed lines, too, lines I've never—" He broke off. "Never mind! I haven't had a date or...woman since that night with you. You want to know why I've been sleeping in town? Well, I'll tell you. Out here I kept wondering about you, wondering if you were over here sleeping alone. Wondering if you'd been out with anyone. Some damn bull rider, maybe, who reminded you of Shanghai. Well, have you? Have you seen other men since me?"

Suddenly he was watching her so intently, she couldn't catch her breath.

"Y-yes... Yes! Many times! That's why I didn't want to see you again."

"I wonder." He was staring down at her mouth, which had suddenly gone dry.

She licked her lips. She wished he'd look away, but he didn't. His gaze burned her mouth. She hoped he couldn't tell she was trembling. She traced her upper lip with her tongue to cool it off. "I think you should go."

"Again we disagree," he said too smoothly, his eyes on her lips.

"You're the enemy."

"Depends on your viewpoint. I'm the father of your child. I want you. Even more now that I know you're pregnant and scared and vulnerable."

"I'm not any of those things!"

"You are, and I think that's a big part of the reason you're so mad at me."

She wasn't about to admit he had a point. She didn't want to feel dependent and needy.

"I hate being pregnant! Why do you get to be so strong and sure of yourself?"

"If you'd let me take care of you, maybe you wouldn't be so scared. Maybe you wouldn't hate being pregnant so much."

"What are you saying?"

"Marry me…at least until after the baby's born."

"But—"

"Look, when the sun came up this morning I didn't want to get married any more than you, but there's our baby to consider now. He'll be legitimate. I think that's important."

"He could be a she."

"Could be, but that's not really the point, is it? People don't think as much of babies who don't have fathers. Don't you want to give our baby the best possible start?"

She hated to agree with him about anything, but she was more old-fashioned than she'd realized. If she didn't marry him, she'd dread telling the baby why she'd never married its father. She'd told Kel, but she felt embarrassed about explaining this mess to the rest of her staff.

"We'll sort it all out as we go along," he said.

He was so close, so tall and dark and strong, and she felt so weary and sad and scared. Would marriage make things better or worse?

Despite her determination to dislike him and blame him, his nearness had an intoxicating effect on her. His clean male scent mingled with something tangy and lemony that she remembered from that night. Her skin had smelled of him afterward. Why couldn't she forget how their bodies had strained together in perfect harmony?

And her dreams... Fragments of half-remembered dreams about him had haunted her when she'd awakened hot and perspiring and clutching her sheets against her breasts in the middle of the night. Did she subconsciously hunger for him even though she fought thinking about him every waking hour?

"This conversation about marriage is ridiculous."

"For a minute there you had the look of a woman seriously considering my offer."

She actually had been. "You've got to go." Desperately, she began pushing at his thick chest.

"Not a good idea," he muttered thickly, crushing her closer.

She knew that if she fought him or screamed, dull,

gentlemanly Leo would let her go. For some reason she stood still in his arms and waited. Maybe to see what he would do next.

When she didn't fight him, something hot and exciting flashed in his dark eyes, but he didn't rush her. His arms stayed around her for another long moment. Then he leaned down, tipped her chin back with a fingertip and kissed her ever so lightly. The instant his mouth grazed hers, a ripple of hot, carnal need trilled from her lips all the way down to her toes.

Not that she was quite past the ability to think and admire his technique. Dull Leo was a superb kisser, her mind noted with cold approval.

His kisses at the bar that night had been the spark that had lit the conflagration that had landed them in this mess.

From that first kiss—a teaser, he'd called it—she'd been his. She remembered his second kiss after he'd told her he was going for broke. Talk about a meltdown.

Her breath came unevenly as she opened her lips. She hadn't realized until his tongue slid against hers how much she'd wanted his mouth and hands on her body again. Was that why she'd dreamed of him and feared him?

Quivering, she threaded her fingertips through the soft black hair that curled over his collar. Then with a little cry, she bunched fistfuls of his shirt, pulled him closer. Breathing hard, he was fully aroused. Holding on tight, she reveled in his passion.

"Where's your bedroom?" he demanded huskily after they'd kissed for a while.

"Right behind us," she answered.

"How convenient."

As his mouth left her lips to explore her neck and

trailed kisses upon her heaving breasts, the enormity of what she was doing washed over her. Weakly, she shoved at his chest. Then she began to push at him and struggle in earnest. But her efforts were puny and half-hearted at best because what she really wanted was Leo naked and wild on top of her. She wanted his knees to spread her legs. She wanted to open herself. She wanted him deep, deep inside her.

"Don't run out on me again," he begged between kisses. One of his big hands slipped down her waist to her knees, and he lifted her into his arms.

When she shook her head and murmured no, he kissed her again and again until she shivered. Then quickly, carrying her, he moved down the dark hall to her bedroom. He set her down on the bed and continued kissing and stroking her. His gaze lit her entire being as he tugged her blue top over her breasts and then over her head. She closed her eyes and lay still as he unhooked her bra and removed it. Very gently he lowered his head, causing her to gasp when he began to lick each rosy brown nipple.

Cupping her breasts, he murmured, "They seem larger." He ran his hand down and rested it on her belly, holding his palm there for a long moment with an attitude of such awe and possession that she began to feel on fire.

His reverence caused a tightness in her throat. Not since Becky had she felt this close to another human being.

Finally, she splayed her fingers against his warm chest. Beneath whorls of dark hair, she felt the violence of his pulsing heart.

He wanted her, but he was a man. He'd said he hadn't

had a woman since he'd been with her. What she couldn't account for was the fierceness of her own urgency.

"Leo…"

Wrapping her arms around him, she leaned her head against his chest with a sigh, reveling in his scent and heat and strength. "I'll regret this. I know it."

She sighed, unable to help herself. Being in his arms felt so right and safe.

What was wrong with spending one more night with him? She was already pregnant, wasn't she? The worst was done…horse out of the barn and all that. She felt strangely light-headed, almost happy knowing she had nothing more to lose and that she could gain such immense pleasure and comfort from letting him make love to her.

"I want you naked," she whispered, knowing she must be mad.

"What?"

"Your turn to strip for me. I stood on that table, re-member."

His gaze burned her.

When he didn't move, she said, "Well, go on."

He gasped as her slim, white hands ripped at his shirt, encouraging him as she yanked it out of his waist-band. When he still did nothing, she undid his belt and unbuttoned his jeans. Last of all, she tugged his zipper down. Never had any sound been more erotic than that rasp of metal as denim parted. When she touched him down there, he groaned loudly.

"Go on," she urged, "take your jeans off."

She removed her hand and stared at his dark body, her heart in her throat as he tore his jeans and shirt and briefs off and tossed them on the floor. There wasn't much moonlight, but there was enough for her to marvel at the heart-stopping perfection of his sculpted, male body. Maybe he was a CEO, but he did more than push pencils. Every inch of his lean body was hard and tough, as lean and tough as any cowboy's.

Dull Leo didn't seem so dull all of a sudden. He danced. He rode. He was great at kissing and great at sex. At least, he was with her. What other hidden talents did he have that could thrill a girl?

She closed her eyes, wanting to know more of him, and yet afraid. So afraid. He was what she'd been running from her whole life.

"Damn you! You'd better not be pretending I'm Shanghai! Not tonight!" he growled fiercely.

Her eyes snapped open, and she saw his cold fury mingle with hurt. "No," she whispered, feeling a strange sympathy. "Only you."

"Good. Tonight I don't want any ghosts in this bed. Just the two of us, understand?"

Swallowing, she nodded. Then she scooted across the bed into a pool of moonlight and kissed him, long and lingeringly on the mouth until they were both breathing so hard, she knew it was way past time for her to take off the rest of her clothes.

He helped her undress. When she was naked, he pulled her beneath the sheets and against his body, which was so blazing hot, she kicked off the covers.

"Why the hell have you been so damn set against me?" he growled.

She arched her body up to meet his. Just to tease him, she began to writhe. "Did anybody ever tell you that you talk too much, Leo Storm?"

And that was the last thing either of them said for a very long time, not until she was sobbing and he was crying her name hoarsely and crushing her so close she felt they were one.

Five

Abby awoke to burning heat. Why was she so hot?

When she began to squirm out from under the covers, she realized that she was buried beneath a tumble of sheets and quilts, and her legs and arms were tangled in Leo's. Her first thought was she'd better get out of bed and call Kel to warn her she'd be late getting into the office again. But Leo's warmth lulled her.

Who cared about the office anyway? Kel could handle anything, and from what Abby had seen of Miriam, she imagined Miriam could, too. Unlike the first morning after they'd made love, Abby did not disentangle herself and run. Instead she lay there, savoring the memories of his touches and intimacies of the night before.

Last night, dull Leo had definitely been anything but. Again and again she'd driven him over the edge until he'd clasped her, rasping for every breath, groaning her name as he'd shuddered in her arms.

He'd been so reasonable and nice all evening, cooking supper, washing dishes, putting up with her mood. Had he been intent on this happening all along?

He'd made love to her with such passionate, primal determination—as if he'd been staking his claim and making her his. It had all been very primitive and wild, and just thinking about it made her shiver and feel reluctant to leave the bed.

She stretched, reliving each and every one of the torrid memories. No man had ever wanted her with such intense urgency, and she had certainly responded in kind.

A black lock fell over his dark brow. She marveled that the sharp angles of his virile features could seem so much softer this morning. He'd been so driven and relentless last night.

Despite his dark, unshaven chin, he looked as innocent as a small child. At the same time he looked like a man who'd gotten exactly what he'd wanted.

She was still marveling at his look of contentment when his black eyes lazily opened and met hers, claiming her.

His arm came around her possessively, and he grinned, showing off his perfect white teeth. "Good. You're still here."

"It's my bed. My house," she said. "Where would I go?"

"So—are you going to marry me?"

"There are a million logical reasons why that's a very bad idea."

"You're pregnant. If we're unhappy, we'll get a divorce. Big deal."

"Divorce *is* a big deal."

Her parents had divorced. She still wasn't over it. She'd always dreamed of a romantic start at marriage, of making it work. "I can't just marry—casually."

When she started to ease away from him, he bolted upright, and the tension became palpable between them. He looked fiercely masculine.

"Stay here a minute," he whispered.

She sucked in a breath and swallowed.

"Please. I need to tell you some things."

"Okay."

"I got a girl pregnant when I was a kid. I won't go into the whole story now, but I couldn't marry her. For one thing, she wouldn't marry me. Hell, maybe it was for the best. That's what I try to tell myself. But, I hardly know my daughter, Julie, and I regret that more every day. So, your pregnancy isn't just about me and you, you know."

The pain in his voice touched her deeply.

"I'm older, settled in a career. I have plenty of money. I can afford a wife and child. I would try very hard to make our relationship work."

But he didn't love her, and she didn't love him. Maybe that was a good thing. Maybe when they divorced, she wouldn't suffer so much. If they married, at least their child would never have to be ashamed of the circumstances surrounding its birth.

She mulled over his proposal for a long time. Finally, she met his gaze again. "I know this is crazy. I know it won't work. I'll regret it. But for the baby…yes."

"Hey," he said gently. "How can you still be so damn negative after last night?"

Before she could tell him that sex, even great sex,

wasn't really all that important in marriage, he rolled onto his back and pulled her down on top of him.

"So, we're getting married," he said as if that was going to take some getting used to. "How about that?" His gaze was tender as he kissed her lightly on the brow.

When she didn't budge—fool that she was, was she actually hoping for more?—he said, "I'd better brush my teeth and shower so we can get to our offices."

He went into her bathroom, and her shower ran for quite a while. Later, when he appeared in her kitchen, his wet black hair gleamed, and his breath smelled like peppermint.

Dull Leo Storm was nothing if not fastidious.

"How about a cup of coffee, *dear?*" she quipped.

"*Dear?* I like the sound of that. Coffee sounds good, too, but I can get that anywhere. I'd rather have a kiss…from my bride to be."

"Hmm." Slowly she went into his arms and nestled close as if she belonged there.

He grinned. "I've just got time for one kiss, so I'd better go for broke. Don't want you changing your mind as soon as I drive off."

"Going for broke… That's what you said the night you got me pregnant."

He smiled as she lifted her lips to his. One taste, and they were both starving again. She really did think maybe she ought to promote Kel and give her more executive responsibilities.

"I've got an early meeting," he muttered several kisses later when things had really begun to heat up. "Buy a white dress and veil and decide who you want to be at our wedding. I'll handle the rest of the arrangements and call you back about the date. Let's get married as fast as possible—say in a week or ten days."

"A week? Weddings take a lot of time."

"Trust me. A week!" His quick male smile was both superior and all-knowing.

Men. Women could spend a year orchestrating a wedding. Being a CEO, he'd probably dictate his guest list, turn the arrangements over to the hard-hearted Miriam and think nothing more about it.

Ten minutes later when he loped out to his truck, Abby followed him, still feeling bemused. He kissed her again on the bottom step. Then she stayed there, licking her mouth, tasting him as she watched until his truck disappeared in clouds of red dust.

Her bruised lips were still warm from his kisses. She was wondering if he'd come back tonight and make love to her again. How could she want that? How she could feel almost happy about this, when so much could go wrong?

Was it because he was so good in bed? Yes, that had to be it. After last night, she was still in a brain fog. When she came to her senses, would she even like him?

Doomed. Abby felt trapped and alone as she stood beside Leo one week later before the carved altar of Mission San José in front of a hundred wedding guests, pledging herself in marriage.

If only her father had showed up, just this once. She thought about Becky and her long-dead mother and the perfect marriage and family she'd dreamed about having someday.

She missed the family she'd lost so much, missed

her father. Here she was, alone, marrying a man she barely knew.

"You may kiss the bride," the preacher said, his deep, sonorous voice ringing inside the thick stone walls of the ancient mission chapel.

As Leo's warm lips touched hers, Abby began to shake with the realization she was now married to this darkly handsome stranger. Was it only a week ago that he'd proposed and she'd marveled that he'd thought he could arrange everything so quickly?

Except for the night he'd dropped by to slide a three-carat engagement ring onto her finger, she'd hardly seen him. Miriam, however, had called her constantly to confirm various details. If Miriam was surprised by this sudden turn of events, she'd given no indication. She'd been deferential, respectful and, above all, exceedingly capable and efficient.

All Abby had had to do was buy a dress, invite her father, her friends and her staff…and show up. Not that her father had made the effort to do even that. He'd promised he'd be here to give her away, but an hour before the wedding, he'd called her on her cell with an excuse, wishing her the best wedding day ever but saying that his flight out of Colombia—where he was interviewing terrorists in the jungle—had been cancelled. As always, the adrenaline high he got from hanging out with a dangerous terrorist was a bigger lure than anything having to do with her, so Leo's brother, Connor, had given her away.

Even as Leo's warm lips lingered over hers, her father's absence tugged at her heart.

"It's okay," Leo whispered, releasing her. "He'll make it next time."

How had he known what she was thinking? That seemed sweet until a thought occurred to her and new fears filled her eyes. Was he already thinking of their imminent divorce and her future marriage to another man?

"Next time?" she asked in a tremulous tone.

Sensing her doubt, he squeezed her hand. "When the baby's born."

Still gripping her hand, Leo turned to face the congregation with his new bride. For an instant she was aware of Leo staring at his brother. In a sea of happy faces, Connor was the only man who looked grim. Leo smiled, so she forced a smile, too. When everyone stood, Connor was the last to rise, and he didn't join in the joyous applause for the couple. Was Connor, who knew the situation, as dubious about their union's ultimate success as she?

Leo's guest list had turned out en masse. Not counting his glum-looking brother, most of the guests worked for the Golden Spurs. She'd met many of them when she'd gone down to the Golden Spurs to wait for Shanghai to bring Mia back from Mexico after he'd rescued her.

Joanne Kemble, the late Caesar Kemble's widow and the mother of Mia and Lizzy Kemble, was the first to rush up to them and congratulate Leo.

"My, you're certainly a dark horse," she said a little too brightly. "You didn't even bring a date to the ranch for our Memorial Day family reunion. And a week later you call me and tell me you're getting married? Who is this woman who could make you change course with the speed of light?"

Leo's face darkened. "It happened suddenly."

"You're an ambitious man. You never make a move without thinking about it from every angle. You hardly seem the type to rush into marriage."

"It's called falling in love," Leo said, shooting Abby a tender glance. "Cupid's arrow is but one of the many reasons why it is impossible to predict the behavior of any human being."

"Well, someday I hope to learn the whole story." Joanne's all-knowing, speculative gaze zeroed in on Abby and stayed there, making her feel the woman saw too much. "Your bridegroom called every guest and invited each of us personally. He bragged and bragged about you. He said you were beautiful and smart. He sounded so in love. It was really…quite sweet. I had to change some vacation plans, but I wouldn't have missed this. Not for the world! Leo married. Who would have thought?" She paused. "I can't tell you what an asset he is to the Golden Spurs. And you will be, too, I'm sure."

Only she didn't sound sure.

"Still, this will certainly take some getting used to. I'm afraid we keep him hopping with all our crises. But he's so cool and collected. So logical. So ambitious—globally—for the ranch. He has a way of solving problems with the least emotional energy and the greatest efficiency, which is great, since we Kembles seem to have a flair for drama." She paused, her eyes growing even more intense. "How's your father?"

At the sudden unfortunate change of topic, Abby started guiltily. "He couldn't come."

"And I was so looking forward to seeing him." Joanne looked away.

"You know him?"

Joanne blushed. "Y-yes. Not all that well—I mean, personally—but he is a famous man…at least in some circles."

Abby felt she was missing something. She had never considered her father famous even though he was a multipublished, award-winning, nonfiction writer. "He's in Colombia, working. His plane was cancelled at the last minute. He really wanted to be here."

"I'm sure. Your father is so dedicated." Joanne's forceful, veined hands were cool and yet perspiring as they clung to Abby's. "I admire his work so much."

"Many people do."

"I wish…." The older woman blushed again and then frowned. "Never mind. Just tell him that I—I…that Joanne Kemble said hello."

"I will."

Joanne's gaze held hers a moment longer. There was depth and hope and an inexplicable tension in her gaze, but before Abby had time to dwell on this, a woman named Mona called to her, and Joanne turned and ran eagerly, as if welcoming the chance to escape a conversation that had felt increasingly awkward to them both.

What had that been about?

For a long moment, Abby felt confused and a little lost even though she was surrounded by people and Leo stood at her side with his hand on her elbow.

Joanne seemed to know her father very well indeed, and she'd taken much too great an interest in Abby for comfort. She would have to ask her father about Joanne Kemble someday.

Mia and Shanghai Knight and their dark-haired little girl, Vanilla, were the next to come up. Shanghai held her hand too tightly and kissed her a little more passionately than was proper for a former boyfriend. Was he relieved to have her safely married?

"You're a lucky man, Storm," he said gruffly, shaking his hand after releasing Abby. "You'd better take good care of her. You know you can't work as hard with a new bride."

Leo nodded, rather fiercely she thought.

"Hey, maybe you two could buy me out of the Buckaroo Ranch since your ranches both touch mine on different corners. I don't get up there much since I married Mia."

Leo nodded again. He didn't look like he was enjoying Shanghai kissing Abby or talking to them much. Then Vanilla raced away. Shanghai laughed and, catching Leo's eye, said, "Well, that's my cue. I'd better go," and chased after her. Mia laughed and followed after them at a more leisurely pace.

Funny, Abby didn't feel the least bit jealous of Mia anymore.

"Maybe we *should* buy him out of the Buckaroo," Leo said.

Shanghai's brother, Cole Knight, strode up with his wife, Lizzy, Mia's sister.

Kel, who was next in line, hugged Abby and quietly told her that if she was going to keep the baby, marriage to a guy as cool as Leo was definitely the best way to go.

"He's not the least bit dull. And he holds his own pretty well with all these hunky Golden Spurs cowboys. He's handsome and suave. And he's got to be smart. Still, I can't believe a straight guy could pull this off," Kel said.

"This?"

"You. This wedding. I mean, an historical mission—

the queen of missions, no less—what a great venue for a wedding! So memorable and romantic. And he did it in a week! Cool! Everything's simply gorgeous. Even the weather cooperated." She began to rave about the band and caterer.

Kel knew a thing or two about event planning since everybody who worked at In the Pink! had to constantly arrange photo shoots and coordinate media events, too often with very little notice.

"It's a little too perfect, and it was a little too easy for him, if you ask me," Abby said moodily.

"You'd prefer to be marrying a doltish, wild cowboy with no social aptitude?"

"Let's not go there. Just don't give him too much credit. His secretary probably did everything."

Kel, who thought secretaries ran the world, nodded. "Well, who hired her? Who keeps her happily working? You'd better watch out. Now that he's got a smart wife to go along with his super-brilliant secretary, he'll be invincible."

When the next person in line nudged Kel, she said, "I think I'll go introduce myself to his hunky brother. What was his name?"

"Connor. Over there…."

She nodded toward Connor, who was standing beneath a live oak tree with a glass of champagne in his hand. Why did he keep studying his brother so deliberately?

Connor was an investigator, she told herself. He was probably suspicious by nature. Maybe he thought she'd trapped Leo and felt protective of his older brother.

There were champagne toasts and dancing. Not that Abby drank anything other than sparkling water. Leo held her close when they danced, too close, and she was reminded that dancing close was what had led to that first going-for-broke kiss in the bar that had made her decide to go home with him.

She and Leo cut the cake and fed each other, licking cake and icing off each other's lips. When she passed on the white wedding cake and ate only the groom's chocolate cake, he made her confess that she was something of a chocoholic.

On the surface the reception was gay and happy, but Abby couldn't ignore Connor's unsmiling face every time his glance fell upon his brother or her. Nor could she forget her own doubts or Joanne's awkward comments. This was a marriage of convenience—not a real marriage. And, therefore, not a happy occasion.

Still, why dwell on those things? Maybe she would have stopped worrying if she hadn't overheard a snippet of the brothers' hushed conversation when they thought she was distracted by Miriam.

"So, have you told her?" Connor demanded.

"Butt out!" Leo replied.

"If you don't, and someone else… If she learns what you did that night from someone else, there will be hell to pay."

"You heard me," Leo said.

Abby must have made some sound, because they turned, and, when Connor met her gaze, he broke off in mid-sentence. Flushing darkly, both men rushed up to her.

You married a stranger.

She'd been a fool to go through with this, she thought miserably even as Leo took her hand reassuringly and tucked her possessively against his tall body.

"Told me what?" she asked.

"Sorry?" Leo said, frowning as if in confusion.

"I couldn't help overhearing...."

"We were talking about business. Dull stuff. I hire Connor from time to time."

"What do you need a private investigator for?"

Joanne, who'd been standing nearby chatting to Mona, was suddenly beside them again. "Oh, that's Lizzy's fault," she said, staring at Abby in that way that made her so uncomfortable. "I don't know how much you know about our family, but my late husband had two daughters by another woman, who was rather famous. Electra Scott. Have you heard of her?" A shrill edge had crept into her voice.

Leo's mouth thinned. The color drained from his face. Everyone around them fell silent and looked uneasy, too. Not that Joanne backed off. She seemed hellbent on making some point.

"Oh, yes," Abby finally said. "I believe I have. Electra Scott. Didn't she die recently? In some jungle?"

"Yes." Joanne's eyes were as coldly blue as ice shards.

"And she took wonderful pictures of children and animals and wildlife?"

"Among other things," Joanne said.

"I think maybe my father may have collaborated on a book with her," Abby said.

"Did he? Well, that wouldn't surprise me. They were both well-known."

Leo was frowning and shifting his weight from one foot to the other, but again Joanne ignored him.

"Electra was my best friend in college. She was incredibly adventurous and very...independent. Lots of fun back then. She wasn't made for marriage. She always said, she'd never settle down. That life had too many possibilities. 'Why should I only live one little life, in one country, with one man?' she used to say.

"I brought her to the ranch, and Caesar fell madly in love with her the second he set eyes on her. I was in love with his older brother, Jack, who died, back then."

"I'm sorry."

"Thank you." An ugly shadow passed across Joanne's face. "But it was a very long time ago. I'd grown up knowing the Kembles, so after Jack died and Electra went away, Caesar and I eventually married. Not long after his death, I came into possession of Electra's journal and discovered that Electra had secret twin daughters by Caesar. Eventually Lizzy insisted we ask Leo to find them, and he hired Connor." She looked from Abby to Connor, her eyes seeming to ask much more than her question. "So, how's that coming?"

Leo's hand tightened ever so slightly on Abby's. When she glanced at him, he smiled and deliberately relaxed his fingers.

"I've made some real progress, but lately I've hit a few snags," Connor said, his eyes glued to his brother like an actor waiting for a cue. "Hopefully we'll have some good news for you before long."

Leo heaved in a breath and managed a thin smile. Not that his eyes warmed.

"How old would his daughters be now?" Abby asked, curious about these secret sisters.

"Twenty-six…nearly twenty-seven."

"Like me." Abby looked at Connor. "And these missing twins…they have no idea that they're Kembles?"

Joanne froze. "No. I am quite sure they don't. And it may come as quite a shock when they find out." Then, without another word, she turned and walked away.

Lifting his glass of champagne, Connor gulped it dry. "It's late. I'd better go." He turned to leave without so much as a glance toward his brother.

His abrupt departure, as well as Joanne's, struck Abby as odd.

"Is your brother happy about our marriage?" Abby asked when she was alone with Leo.

"Of course. What makes you ask?"

"I don't know him, but he seems...worried. And Joanne... I don't think she likes me."

"You're wrong about Joanne. As for Connor, he's always been moody. I should know. I raised him. I'm sure it has to do with work. He takes his work very seriously."

Leo's mouth was tight, and he seemed edgily defensive. Abby sensed he probably knew more than he was willing to admit. "Like you say, you know him. I don't. Whatever his misgivings, at least Connor showed up. Unlike my—"

"Your father would have been here if he could have been."

"It's easy for you to believe that. But then you don't know him like I do, do you?"

"Right." As if stung, he shut up.

She was remembering all the school performances her father had missed. He hadn't come to even one, not even those in which she'd starred. She thought about the Christmas card in her drawer that had arrived two weeks late.

This wasn't a real marriage. What did it matter if Joanne acted strange or Connor disapproved or her father wasn't here? Leo, who looked as tight and strained as she felt, took her hand and brought it to his lips. "I'm sorry," he said, squeezing her fingers.

She looked away just as an older man, who introduced himself to her as B. B. Kemble, came up and began to rant about the high winds and drought in South Texas. Leo fell into this discussion with relish, probably because he was anxious to forget her and about their tense conversation. Soon he was smiling again, and she was sure he'd forgotten her entirely. So, feeling lost and forgotten, she let go of his hand and wandered away.

All too soon the reception was over and Leo and she were holding hands again. Bending low, they ran through their guests, who blew environmentally correct bubbles over their heads as they made a dash for Leo's waiting stretch limousine, which whisked them toward the center of the city.

Leo hadn't attempted conversation since they'd discussed Connor and her father. When the driver didn't take the downtown exit that would have taken them to Leo's loft apartment, Abby tugged at Leo's sleeve.

"Airport. Weekend honeymoon," Leo said brusquely. "Sorry I can't get away for longer. Didn't Miriam tell you to pack a bag?"

"She said, 'Be prepared for warm weather. Two nights. And be sure to bring a bathing suit.' I thought she meant you had a pool in your building."

"I do. But Miriam was wrong about the bathing suit. Where we're going, it's so private, we can swim naked. I hope you'll want to."

The sudden heat in his eyes made her breath catch. "Where are we going?"

"It's a surprise."

She couldn't stop looking at her lean-muscled husband. With his black hair and tanned skin, he was devastatingly, moody-broody handsome. Fierce looking, too.

Her heart sped up. Boy or girl, their baby would be beautiful if it looked anything like him.

Leo held out his hand. When she took it, he pulled her closer. Her head fell against his shoulder, and the rasp of his warm breath in her hair made her scalp tingle.

That first night they'd made love, he'd held her curled against him like this for hours. She'd fallen asleep as if drugged from his lovemaking, never wanting to leave his arms—only to wake the next morning to profound guilt at her wanton behavior.

They'd both been forced into this marriage. They barely knew each other. What chance did their marriage have?

Six

When Abby and Leo got off the Golden Spurs jet, warm, humid, salt-laden air blew her hair back from her face. The inky sky swam with stars, and she could hear the surf pounding noisily.

The airport was a strip of asphalt laid on top of sand. Palm fronds clattered noisily beside a lone hangar at the end of the strip.

"Where are we?" she cried as he hurried her through blowing grit toward a strange-looking beach buggy.

"A private barrier island off the Texas coast. It's owned by a Texas rancher and oilman who owes me a favor or two. He offered to let me use his beach house for our honeymoon. His house is about a mile down the beach."

Even if the beach house hadn't been vast, yet cozy, she would have been glad to get inside and out of the wind. Nestled behind towering sand dunes and surrounded by dense vegetation, which included lots more noisy palms, the mansion had the ambience of a Caribbean plantation house. Big open rooms made for stunning interiors with soaring beamed ceilings and furnishing in beiges and browns with the occasional bright plump cushion and potted plant.

Leo ended his tour of the immaculate house in the master bedroom. Beside a massive, textile-draped, four-poster bed, a magnum of champagne and a bottle of sparkling water stood side by side chilling in a silver ice bucket.

As Leo deftly opened the champagne and poured himself a glass, she wondered who kept the mansion in such pristine shape and where Leo's pilot would sleep tonight. Not that she asked.

Leo opened the water and poured a glass for her. When he handed her hers, he tipped his glass toward hers, and she did the same. Crystal clinked.

He didn't make a toast out loud, however, she eyed the bed and made one silently. *To luck. To miracles. To happiness…together…forever.* She knew she was naive to even entertain such hopes.

"You look scared," he said. "At times like this, try to remember that Coco likes me."

"That's definitely a big point in your favor." Another point was the fact that he'd hired an excellent groom to take care of Coco while she was pregnant.

"I'll take all the points I can get," Leo said.

He smiled at her as she lifted her glass. When she gulped deeply, his smile broadened. He was about to lift his to his lips, when his cell rang.

He frowned when he saw who it was and excused

himself. "I've got to take this. Why don't you get ready for bed?"

The word *bed* was still hanging heavily in the air as he let himself out onto the balcony so he could speak privately.

Why was he being so secretive? Was this a business call or personal? She remembered Connor's grim attitude. What was going on?

Have you told her?

What if Connor had been referring to her? Leo had definitely seemed more strained since she'd asked him about their conversation.

Well, the empty bedroom wouldn't give her any answers. It was late. She decided to take Leo's advice and get ready for bed.

A wedding dress wasn't the only purchase she'd made when she'd gone shopping. She'd bought several sheer nightgowns, as well.

Hesitating for a moment, she went to her suitcase and removed her toiletries and the filmiest of all her new nightgowns, which was a transparent beige.

In the marble bathroom, she undressed and showered. She opened her legs and lathered herself. For long moments she let the warm water run down her neck and her breasts to her belly and thighs. Even after all the bubbles were gone, she stood under the water thinking about the two nights she'd spent with Leo.

He was so sexy. He could do anything, everything to a woman. She'd thought a corporate type like him would be unimaginative in bed, but he had no inhibitions. And he'd made her forget hers. Now that they were married, she wondered if he'd be willing to fulfill her wildest fantasies.

The tensions of the wedding and the reception drained away, and an all-consuming fiery hunger ate at her. He hadn't slept with her since she'd agreed to marry him. She wanted him—again. Just thinking about it made her heart beat faster and faster.

She turned off the water, stepped out of the shower and ripped a towel off a bar. Drying herself and her hair, she pulled the nightgown over her head. Last of all, she brushed her teeth so that she'd taste of peppermint, since peppermint seemed to be Leo's favorite flavor.

Racing into the bedroom, she turned out the lights, got into bed and waited for him to return. When thirty minutes passed and he still hadn't come, she got up and opened the doors to the balcony.

There was nothing out there but the screaming palms, the roar of the surf and the blowing sand. She slammed the doors and leaned against them. Where was Leo? Why hadn't he come to bed? Didn't he want her?

Had he had his fill of her already? Did he feel trapped and therefore uninterested? Some part of her wasn't quite ready to believe that. And yet…how well did she really know him?

Without bothering to search for her robe, Abby left the bedroom in search of Leo. When she heard his deep baritone issuing commands as decisively as a general, she ran down the hall. Pushing open the last door, she found him seated at a huge desk in the study, holding two phones, one against each ear.

She paused in the middle of the door so that the hall light came from behind her.

His gaze met hers and then ran the length of her backlit body before returning to her face. Something dark and powerful made his eyes flame. She read male appreciation and maybe more. Whatever his emotion, he turned it off with an abruptness that chilled her. Closing his eyes and then opening them, he regarded her levelly.

"Just a second," he said in a hard voice to whoever was on the phones.

Frowning, he shook his head at her. "Sorry. There's a grass fire at the Golden Spurs. It's huge, and it's my fault because I authorized a controlled burn yesterday. The fire jumped a road and got away from our men. The grass is dry and the wind is horrible. I should have gone down there myself to see to it. But I didn't."

Because he'd married her.

Not that he seemed to blame her.

"I have to deal with it now. Go to bed. I'll sleep in here near the phones. No need for us both to be up all night."

"I don't mind the phone ringing, if only you'll come to bed."

"We'll see," he said. "Maybe later."

"It's our honeymoon."

"I know." A muscle in his cheek jumped, but he lowered his head, his complete attention on his callers again.

Feeling rejected and desolate, Abby lay awake most of the night. She tossed this way and that, her emotions tearing at her. When she did sleep, she had weird dreams. Connor kept appearing in them like a dark spirit with his constant refrain.

Have you told her?

Every time she woke up, she felt like a fool for wanting Leo so much and even more of a fool for feeling so hurt because he preferred the study to being with her. Three weeks ago she hadn't ever wanted to see him again, and now she was pining after him like a lovesick idiot—just because she was a romantic when it came to marriage.

Around five o'clock, she got up and tiptoed down the hall to check on him. She found Leo, still dressed in his tux, asleep in the big leather chair in the brilliantly lit study. He looked so tired, she didn't want to wake him and urge him to come to bed. All she did was turn off the lights and cover him with a soft throw. Then she returned to the master bedroom and lay down alone. Finally, she fell into a dreamless sleep.

An hour or so later he walked into the bedroom and checked on her. She heard him, but false pride made her pretend to be asleep.

He neither spoke nor touched her. He simply stood there watching her "sleep" as she'd watched him. He walked back to his study, and her heart ached as she listened to his retreating footsteps falling ever softer as he moved back down the length of the hall.

Once more she drifted to sleep, awakening a few hours later to the smell of coffee. She combed her hair, put on her makeup and dressed in white shorts, a T-shirt and sandals. Hoping the fires were out and his mood improved, she scampered down the hall and found him in the kitchen talking on his cell again. Only this time, when he saw her, he ended the conversation abruptly.

"Sleep well?" he asked, his face grave.

She nodded, not wanting to admit how much she'd longed for him.

"And you?" She tried to sound casual.

"Not the best night, but I've had worse." His weary

smile failed to reach his eyes. "I'll make you some breakfast."

"What about the fire?"

"Not good. I'm afraid I have to go down there as soon as possible. I'll fly you to San Antonio. Then I have to go to the Golden Spurs. Ten thousand acres have burned. We've lost several structures. The fire seems to be getting worse. We need to cut or hose down the grass on either side of more ranch roads to make firebreaks and move cattle."

"Wouldn't you get there faster…if I went with you?"

"Yes, but I don't expect…" His black eyes narrowed. "I mean the Golden Spurs is my concern. Not yours."

His expression changed, and she wondered what he was thinking

"What?" she said.

"Nothing," he muttered grouchily.

"I'm going with you then. It's my concern now, too. I'm your wife."

"Suit yourself." His face remained guarded and impossible to read, but he nodded.

After a long moment, he said, "Look, I'm sorry I'm such bad company. I just got word that Black Hawk and Chinook helicopters capable of pouring hundreds of gallons of water in one sweep can't join our firefighters until the winds decrease. By the way, my pilot's standing by."

"I can be ready in five minutes."

"No, first we eat. I'm pretty tired after last night, but it wasn't anything compared to what's in store for us."

Like before at her house, he was at ease in a kitchen. Within minutes they were seated at the table in front of freshly squeezed orange juice, eggs, toast and bacon. Even though a maid would probably be flown in to tidy the place, he cleaned the kitchen perfectly. Then they packed, and he carried her bags to the dune buggy.

"Sorry that we didn't have much of a honeymoon," he said once they were airborne and she was glancing wistfully down at the house on the island and the strip of long white beach in front of it.

Not that he seemed sorry. His face was tense and drawn. He was completely preoccupied by his worries about the fire. Still, every few minutes she caught him watching her, almost in the same way that Connor had watched him during their reception, as if he really were worried about something concerning her, too.

Connor's question kept repeating itself in her mind. *Have you told her?*

Was she being self-centered to think he'd been talking about her?

Fifty miles out from the ranch headquarters of the Golden Spurs giant plumes of smoke billowed higher than a mountain against a hellish, purple-orange sky. When they got closer she could see cowboys on horseback were moving cattle. Leo went to the cockpit and ordered the pilot to fly low all over the ranch. He took pictures and made notes while talking constantly to Kinky Moore, the ranch's foreman, on his cell phone.

When they finally landed behind the tall, red-roofed Big House and its outbuildings, the air was heavy with the acrid smell of smoke. A white sun burned a hole through the slate-gray sky. Winds whipped the mesquite and palm trees on every side of her. Kinky ran up to them and told Leo that because of the wind direction, the house wasn't threatened.

"We've got a hunting lodge to hose down and cattle to move just south of Black Oaks. Mia, Cole and Shanghai are down there now trying to save the old Knight homestead at Black Oaks."

Leo studied the black sky and then turned to her. "I shouldn't have brought you down here. The fire's bigger and closer to the house than I realized."

"There was no time to do anything else. I'll be fine."

"Stay inside until I come back. Keep your cell phone charged and handy." He turned to go.

"I want to go with you."

"No!"

She would have argued, but Leo's expression was harsh and unyielding. And the situation was too chaotic. Fire trucks and bulldozers were everywhere. Adrenaline charged the air. Exhausted-looking firemen streaked across the lawn in dirty orange overalls, shouting orders over cell phones and bickering with sweat-streaked, soot-faced cowboys about how best to fight the fire.

When the cowboys saw Leo, they shouted and waved to him, and before she knew it, he'd left her to join the quarrel between the cowboys and the firemen.

The firemen wanted to start some controlled burns, but the cowboys yelled that if the wind changed, they'd lose valuable livestock and maybe the Big House. Leo battled long and hard, speaking in a firm, rational voice, but the firemen refused to listen and soon sped away in their fire trucks to start more burns.

A second later Leo was on his phone again. "Shanghai! The firemen are going to set pasture seven on fire! We've got hunting lodges down there, and if the wind changes—"

Then Leo was running, shouting to Kinky. As the two men got in Kinky's big black SUV, Abby ran up to them and grabbed Leo's door handle.

"Leo… Take care."

His hair was unkempt, his countenance hard and carved with exhaustion and worry. She wanted him to get out of the SUV and pull her into his arms and crush her close, to press his mouth to hers, to say something, anything, before he left, but his dark face remained frozen even as his black eyes seared her.

Kinky twisted the key in the ignition, and the big vehicle roared to life.

"Leo… Don't leave me."

He clenched his jaw and nodded to Kinky to go.

Her last glimpse of him etched itself into her mind. Broad shoulders, steel-like jaw, anxiety emanating from him, virile sexiness.

What if he never came back?

Her heart felt hollow. A fist squeezed her throat closed.

Except for two nights of sex, she barely knew this man. How could she feel this intensely about him when, obviously, he didn't return her feelings?

Her shoulders sagged hopelessly as she backed away from the SUV. She didn't matter. She never mattered. He was leaving her, just like Becky had…just like her parents had. Everybody always left her.

Speechless, motionless, she watched Kinky back the big vehicle out of its space and then edge out onto the road. A minute later the SUV vanished in the thickening smoke.

She notched her chin up. Nothing had changed. She'd been alone for years and years. She had to get a grip. She couldn't let illusions about marriage and what it should mean and her growing attraction for this man make her hope for something impossible.

When she went into the house and descended the stairs to the basement, she found Sy'rai Moore, whom she'd met at her reception, downstairs in the kitchen, cooking and washing dishes along with Lizzy and Joanne. Off in one corner, Vanilla was on the floor building a high wall out of a set of blocks. From time to time, Joanne would fold her dish towel, kneel and add a block to the towering structure, which Vanilla would knock down and then rebuild.

Cowboys and firemen were down at the house between shifts. The men were smiling and laughing, fighting valiantly to pretend they were cheerful and brave as they sat at tables in small dining rooms off the kitchen, eating beans, charred venison, roasted nilgai antelope, gravy and mashed potatoes.

Sy'rai told her they'd hurried home as soon as they found out about the fire and repeated that Mia, Shanghai and Cole were struggling to save the Knight's ancient homestead.

Not wanting to dwell on her fears for Leo, Abby grabbed an apron. "What can I do?"

"Same thing we're doing," Joanne said. "We've got a lot of tired, hungry men."

By six o'clock the smoke was so thick in the basement that Abby's throat burned and her eyes and nose ran constantly. News reached them that things were bad near Black Oaks. Panicking, she tried to call Leo to find out what was going on over there, but he never answered.

The television anchormen gloomily reported that more than thirty thousand acres were on fire and that a wind shift was expected. "There have been two fatalities on the Golden Spurs Ranch over near Black Oaks, but the names of the individuals are being withheld until their families can be notified."

Panic cut through Abby. With her heart pounding in her throat, Abby dialed Leo again. Still no answer. What if...?

She clutched the phone against her chest as aerial shots showed one hunting lodge exploding in flames. Just as the camera panned to the homestead at Black Oaks, reduced to a pile of burning, red-hot rubble, Kinky stalked into the kitchen.

Sy'rai ran to him and threw her arms around him. His face and clothes were black with soot; his voice hoarse. His dark eyes held no emotion.

"Leo...is Leo with you?" Abby whispered.

He shook his head. Then his weary eyes passed over her. "We're evacuating the headquarters. Everybody get your stuff and be ready to get the hell out of here! We've got thirty minutes max!"

"But have you seen Leo?"

"What about Cole...and Mia and Shanghai?" Lizzy asked.

Without looking at Lizzy, Kinky shook his head. "Last I saw of them, they were in the thick of it over there at Black Oaks. You saw the pictures on TV. You know as much as I do."

"But you drove him over there," Abby cried.

"Drove him into hell. That's what I did."

Kinky stomped back up the stairs and began yelling orders. Soon cowboys were lifting priceless antiques and paintings and carrying them out of the house to load into the beds of their pickups.

Frantic, Abby punched in Leo's number again. When he still didn't answer, she ran outside where Lizzy and Sy'rai had begun hosing down the house and grounds and nearby trees with garden hoses.

Sy'rai was hooking more hoses together to make them long enough for her to haul one up the stairs, so she could climb out on the roof and hose it down, too. The roof was made of red tile, and although Abby wondered if hosing it was really necessary, she offered to help her. Then Sy'rai began hauling hoses into the house and up the stairs while Abby hooked more together.

When the trucks loaded with antiques and paintings were ready to leave, Kinky told her it was time for her to go. Joanne was sitting in the front of one of the pickups holding Vanilla in her arms.

"Leo told me to wait for him here."

"Nobody's heard from Leo in more than an hour. His last order was for me to see about you. Why don't you get in with Joanne."

"I'm staying until he comes."

"Hell, girl. Only really stubborn fools like me and Sy'rai are staying to fight to save the house or die trying. Caesar's ghost would haunt me forever if this old place burned just 'cause I ran off and left it."

"I'm staying, too."

"You've got nothing invested here. We're family."

The way he said the word *family* made her feel jealous.

"Leo's out there! Would he leave if I were out there, and he were here?"

"He wants you safe."

"He told me to stay."

"Funny, you don't seem like the obedient type." Kinky glared at her, trying to stare her down, but she squared her shoulders and folded her arms across her breasts. A full minute passed before he finally shrugged and glanced away.

"There's nothing worse than a stubborn woman," he finally said. A grim smile touched his black-rimmed lips as he glanced toward Sy'rai, who was yanking on a hose. "I should know. Hell, I've been married to one damn near my whole life. Grab a hose then before Sy'rai has a heart attack. Help her spray the Spur Tree and the grass around it."

"The Spur Tree?"

"Over there! On the other side of that far road. It's the puny-assed mesquite with all the spurs dangling off it."

Kinky turned to a couple of cowboys. "Guys, we need a firebreak around the house. Fast!"

Dark, black clouds billowed from the south where Leo was. The smoke was thickening, burning her nostrils and lungs.

"Leo," Abby whispered as she ran toward the tree that was covered with sparkling spurs, dragging a hose behind her.

Seven

Half a mile ahead Leo saw a wall of flame and clouds of black smoke. Behind that was the Big House. The loss of the old Black Oaks homestead was still fresh on his mind. The Big House appeared to be square in the middle of the fire…or gone. He couldn't tell yet.

They'd almost saved Black Oaks.

But almost didn't count. Maybe he didn't really want to know about the Big House.

Houses, even a legendary, historical house like the Big House, were just houses. Kinky would have evacuated everybody hours ago, so at least he didn't have to worry about Abby and the baby.

If he lost them… He refused to let this mind go there. He had to believe they were safe.

Leo's hair and wet clothes were singed. His muscles ached. Every sort of thorn was stuck in his skin. His eyeballs and eyelids felt dry and scratchy from too much smoke. His lungs burned.

He wanted to lie down in the road. He wanted a drink, but he kept walking, one slow, trudging step after another. Behind him, he heard Mia's leaden footsteps and her occasional whimper. She was leaning heavily on Shanghai and Cole. Leo couldn't believe Shanghai had let her fight the fire with him, but then knowing Mia, he could. She'd survived being kidnapped by a drug lord.

They say bad people go to hell when they die. Leo wasn't a damn bit sure about that. Today had taught him you didn't have to die to go to hell.

He remembered screaming "Run!" to Shanghai and Cole and Mia as the flames had swept into the oak mott surrounding the Black Oaks homestead. Blackened tree limbs had crashed around them, splintering into pieces and sending showers of sparks in all directions. One had caught Leo's shirt on fire. He could still hear the crackling wall of flames as he'd dived into the creek; he'd felt the burning limbs crashing into the water on all sides of him as the three of them had huddled under the overhang of a huge rock.

They were damn lucky to be alive. If the creek behind the homestead had been ten feet farther away or the fire faster, they never would have made it. But the flames had raced through the trees without burning all the oxygen, only half burning the branches before sweeping north toward the Big House.

Leo pictured Abby as he'd last seen her. Her eyes had been wide and so fear filled when she'd told him goodbye. He'd wanted to jump down and haul her into his arms and never let her go, but he'd known that if he'd so much as spoken to her, or touched her, he never would have been able to leave her.

Why this woman? Why her? He'd never particularly wanted to be a father again, but ever since she'd told him about the baby, he'd felt strangely protective of her. Was it solely because she was who she was, and he was an ambitious bastard? Or had she always meant more?

Abby clung to Lizzy in the humid dark of the basement that was lit by a single flashlight. A cold, deadly fear gripping her heart, Abby couldn't stop shaking.

The thick walls seemed to close in upon her. All she could think of was Leo somewhere outside in that raging inferno. If Lizzy hadn't been holding her, surely she would have gone mad.

"He has to be all right," Abby whispered. "He just has to be."

"He's a quick thinker," Lizzy said, stroking her arm. "If anybody can take care of himself out there, it's Leo."

"Do you really think so?"

"Yes."

The flashlight flickered and went out, and darkness lapped at Abby in terrifying waves. Even though her arms tightened around Lizzy, she nearly screamed. Then another beam flared, and she swallowed a shallow breath when she saw Lizzy's tremendous smile.

It seemed hours that they sat huddled together, waiting.

Then Kinky threw the lower basement door open. "You can come out! The fire's past us! We lost the garage, but the Big House is safe."

As they climbed the stairs, Lizzy said, "This room

was built to protect the family and cowboys from Native and Mexican bandit raids in the 'olden days.' Who knew we'd ever need it for a grass fire?"

Holding hands, Lizzy and Abby climbed the last of the shadowy stairs. The house was still standing. It smelled of smoke and would have to be thoroughly cleaned, of course. When they got outside and saw the scorched oaks, palms and smoldering lawn and garage, they clung to each other. As far as they could see, blackened grass stretched endlessly to the east and south.

Letting go of Lizzy, Abby's eyes had wandered from the huge mansion to the glittering spurs of the Spur Tree. A deathly quiet wrapped around her when she gazed toward the south again in the direction of Black Oaks.

Where was Leo?

Abby saw the desolation in Lizzy's eyes and sensed her concern for her husband and sister, as well. Not that either of them said anything. They were too afraid of losing control.

Abby folded Lizzy into her arms. "For now it has to be enough that the Big House and everyone who stayed here is safe."

Lizzy bit her lips. "We can still hope and pray, can't we?"

Then Kinky began shouting orders, directing them to grab shovels and throw dirt on top of hot spots. "See if we've got any water pressure. We've got some spare hoses in the basement. Get them and spray the trees again. They could still ignite."

Abby busied herself spraying the trees. A couple of hours later she was sitting on a lawn chair, wiping her brow, when she heard Kinky shouting. She looked up and saw several dirty-looking men in the distance walking up the road, waving wearily. One of the bedraggled figures was a broad-shouldered, blackened scarecrow of a man, his shirt hanging in strips against his tall, lean body. He looked tired and footsore as he shuffled across the burned grasses toward her.

"Abby!" The man's deep voice was hoarse and strange, but it made the hair on the back of her neck stand up. She felt a new alertness, a lessening of her exhaustion. There was something about his walk, something about the set of his wide shoulders.

Her heart began to throb fiercely. Her hand went to her throat. When she tried to stand, her knees buckled, and she had to push herself off the ground with her free hand.

Then Lizzy screamed Cole's name and ran past her and flung her arms around two of the scarecrow's companions.

"Leo?" Abby whispered in a breathless croak that didn't sound a bit like her voice. She felt tears on her cheeks. *"Leo!"*

Abby's pulse leaped, then stopped and then sped up again. She felt sick to her stomach, and she was afraid she'd faint. Leo started running. She sprang to her feet and flew across the yard, hurling herself into his arms.

He winced when she grabbed his back, and she said, "I'm sorry. So sorry." But his grip was still strong as he snuggled her against the long length of his body and bent his dirty face to hers. His kiss was urgent and hot, demanding and devouring. His chin was rough against the softness of hers. He tasted of soot and grime and the brush country.

She didn't care. She framed his filthy face in her palms. He was alive. His mouth was vital, and his kisses filled her with a warm, surging tide of sheer desire and wild joy.

He released her so abruptly, she would have stumbled backward if he hadn't seized her by the arms. "What the hell are you still doing here?" he growled. Then he cursed vividly.

"Shh. The baby might hear. You did tell me to wait for you."

His dark eyes glittered with anger. For long minutes his fingers ground bruisingly into the flesh of her upper arms. "Right, blame me. You little fool, don't you know you could have died?"

"But I didn't, so there's no reason to get so mad."

"No reason? The baby could have—"

"What about you? You scared me, too. Do you think I could leave, knowing you were still out there?"

Something in her expression must have gotten through to him because his harsh face softened ever so slightly.

"Abby… Abby…" He lowered his voice to a soothing purr and cupped her chin with his fingers. "Oh, Abby…"

He crooked his head and kissed her again, gently, tenderly, until her fingers were curled against his chest. He held her as she had dreamed of being held, as if he never wanted to let her go. In that moment she was so happy it was hard to remember that the thought of loving and being loved scared her more than anything.

The early-morning sky was a cerulean blue as Abby, Lizzy and Leo stood in front of the Spur Tree.

"I'm going to miss you," Lizzy said. "Except for that one other visit, I've only known you—what—a day or two, but already you seem almost like a sister."

Abby thought of Becky running away from her down that desert trail in El Paso so long ago. "Maybe because we've been through a lot together."

"Leo, did I tell you she helped me save the Spur Tree?" Lizzy asked.

"Only about ten times."

"I couldn't have done it without her."

As Leo watched them together, his stern face tightened.

"We were lucky," Abby said, taking his hand and trying to draw him closer.

"No, it was a miracle," Lizzy said. "We have many, many miracles to be thankful for this morning."

Abby threaded her fingers through Leo's. He was alive, and so were Mia, Shanghai and Cole. The Big House was still standing, and this morning six brand-new flags hung limply from its wide roof. *The six flags of Texas.* The ranch had survived one hundred forty years of Native raids, war, drought, debt and now fire.

Maybe Lizzy was right. Maybe it was a miracle. The wind had shifted and then had died. The flames were now under control, and a storm in the Gulf that was moving toward shore promised rain.

"There's something we have to do before you and Leo can leave," Lizzy said. "Close your eyes, Abby, and then open your right hand."

With quiet excitement tingling inside her, Abby smiled. "I feel like I'm eight, playing a game with Becky."

Leo's face tightened.

"Becky?" Lizzy asked.

"My twin." Abby explained.

"Now hold your hand out," Lizzy ordered as imperiously as Becky might have.

Something heavy and spiky jingled in Abby's hand.

"You can open your eyes," Lizzy said softly.

Abby gasped. "Why, they're spurs. Thank you. I'll treasure them."

"Oh, you're not going to keep them. You see, since you're leaving us, they're for the tree. We have a tradition here that's nearly one hundred and forty years old."

Lizzy touched a pair of spurs dangling from the tree and made them tinkle. "These are my daddy's spurs." Her hand touched a second pair. "And these are Uncle Jack's. Every time a cowboy who's worked the ranch dies or quits, we hang his spurs here. When people like you, who've been important to the ranch, leave, we hang his—or in your case, her—spurs on the tree, as well. Even Leo keeps a pair on the tree when he's in San Antonio."

Abby's hand closed over the spurs in her hand. "Why…why, thank you, Lizzy."

"My real mother's are hanging on the tree, too."

"But isn't Joanne…"

Lizzy shook her head. "Joanne was pregnant with Mia by Uncle Jack when she married my father. The woman Daddy loved was pregnant with me. A horse threw Uncle Jack, and he died. Electra, my real mother, wouldn't marry Daddy. So Joanne and Daddy pretended that Joanne was pregnant with twins. That way they could raise Mia and me as twins. In fact, we didn't know until a little while ago that we're really cousins, not sisters. I didn't know that my biological mother was really a woman named Electra Scott."

"The famous photojournalist? Joanne told me about her."

"Did she? Well, good, maybe she's at peace with Electra at last. They were best friends once."

"She said Leo is looking for your dad's missing daughters."

"My sisters. Joanne was pretty torn up about them when she first read Electra's journal and found out that Daddy had resumed his affair with Electra after she and Daddy were married."

Leo shifted his weight restlessly from one foot to the other. His mouth was thin, his cheeks darkly flushed. He seemed extremely edgy all of a sudden.

"So how's that investigation coming, Leo?"

A muscle flexed in his hard jawline. "What?"

"So—are there any new clues about the missing twins?"

"Maybe a few." He dropped Abby's hand and took a step backward. "Are you two ever going to hang the spurs on the damn tree or not?"

"Hey, are you okay, Leo?" Abby whispered.

"You said five minutes. The jet is waiting."

"Go on then," Abby said. "I'll just be a minute."

He hesitated, obviously skeptical. Then he pivoted on his heel and strode toward the landing strip.

"Men," Lizzy said. "Cole can be so impatient some-times. But I've never seen Leo like this. He's usually so calm and controlled."

"He's tired. He could have been killed yesterday. We were at the emergency room half the night. I guess it's understandable."

"He's okay?"

"Except for a few cuts and bruises. Smoke inhalation, too. And he seems unusually irritable all of a sudden.

But like you said, we have a lot of miracles to be thankful for."

"You'd better hurry then. If ever a man needed a good night's sleep and a lot of TLC from his bride... You didn't have much of a honeymoon, did you?"

"No. At least, not yet...." Abby felt her cheeks heat.

Last night they'd slept together, but they'd both been so exhausted that they'd fallen asleep the minute they'd lain down in their third-floor guest room despite the fact that it had reeked of smoke. When she'd awakened, Leo's side of the bed had been empty. He'd left without a word or a kiss or any show of affection. She'd found him downstairs in the kitchen talking to Kinky and the cowboys.

Not wanting to dwell on the lack of romance last night or to keep Leo waiting, Abby held her spurs up and approached the tree, where dozens more twinkled.

Finally, after studying every branch and reading the engravings on several spurs, she hung hers on the thick branch right beside Caesar's.

Leo was striding purposefully across blackened ground and had made it halfway to the runway when his cell phone vibrated in his shirt pocket. Impatiently, he jammed it against his ear.

"How's it going down there?" Connor asked. He'd called several times, and they'd talked. He'd been watching the news, so he was up on things for the most part.

"Great. When we evacuated the ranch, Abby stayed. She helped save the Big House and the Spur Tree. Hell, she's the heroine of the hour. The family loves her."

"*Her* family. I'd say that's real, real good."

"Lizzy just gave her an honorary pair of spurs. As I

speak, she's about to hang her spurs on the same tree as her father's."

"You'd better tell who the hell she is then. And fast."

"I'd like to make sure she's on my side first."

"Always looking out for yourself, aren't you, big brother?"

"I'm real short on patience this morning. Real short."

"I can understand that after what you've been through. I don't want to get all sappy on you, but you had me going there for a while yesterday when nobody knew where you were and I saw those body bags on TV. I have to admit I said a prayer or two."

"Illegals crossing the ranch."

"Poor bastards. You know, it might help if you asked Abby about Becky. Maybe you could get her talking about the kid's hobbies and dreams. You never know...it might help me find her."

Leo grimaced. The thought of grilling Abby about her sister made him feel even guiltier than he'd felt the night he'd stolen the DNA sample from her before sleeping with her.

"All right," Leo agreed.

"Good. I gotta go, but before I do, I'll say it one more time. First chance you get, tell her."

"Hey, maybe you're my only brother, but sometimes when you stick your nose in my business, you can be a real pain in the ass."

"What's a brother for?"

Leo flipped his phone shut.

Tell her? The thought scared the hell out of him. What if he lost her?

Eight

Abby's nose was pressed against the jet's window. The sky was bright and cloudless, and the fields beneath her were abnormally brown as the jet approached the outskirts of San Antonio.

Leo, his head bent over a ledger Kinky had given him, had scarcely spoken a word on the flight. Every time Abby had even glanced his way, she'd imagined that his square jaw tensed and that his gaze narrowed.

Why was he deliberately ignoring her?

Was something bothering him? Was it something she'd done? Did he feel trapped by their marriage? He'd been so cool and controlled last night in their bedroom. Did he regret…

Stop with the negative questions. You'll drive yourself crazy. It's not like you wanted to marry him.

They'd been married all of two days. He'd barely

touched her, but somehow she felt bound to him, tuned into him on deep, unconscious levels.

What was wrong? Considering all he'd been through, he'd seemed friendly and normal enough this morning. Until Lizzy had taken them out to the Spur Tree and had handed her those damn spurs. But why would he care if Lizzy had honored her in such a way? He couldn't be jealous because the Kembles seemed to like her. But if it wasn't that, then what?

Thinking of Lizzy and the spurs made her think of Caesar's missing twin daughters. She knew Leo was conscientious to a fault. She knew he felt responsible for the fire. Lizzy had asked him about the twins. Did he feel as guilty about not having found them as she felt because Becky had never been found? Apparently he'd been looking for them for quite a while.

"I hope you don't feel bad because you haven't found Lizzy's sisters," she whispered. She thought about Becky, who'd vanished without a trace. She, of all people, knew the frustration of trying to find a missing person.

He hissed in a deep breath but didn't look up. That telltale muscle tensed in his jaw. She had the distinct impression that he definitely didn't want to talk about Lizzy's missing sisters.

"You'll find them," she said reassuringly.

He swallowed. "I'm tired, okay?"

"Of course. I understand." But she didn't look away.

"Connor's responsible for finding them. I imagine it's on his conscience more than on mine." As if to put an end to their discussion, Leo flipped a page of the ledger loudly and lowered his head over the large book.

"What happened to them? Why is it so difficult to find them?"

He slammed the ledger, and she knew he wished she'd leave him alone. Well, it had been his idea to marry. Maybe it was time he learned that if they were stuck together, she couldn't stand the silent treatment.

"Leo, I asked you why it was so difficult—"

"I heard you, okay?" He drew a long breath. "Look, Electra was famous, and so was Caesar. She didn't want to damage Caesar's marriage, so she was very secretive when she put them up for adoption. She used an agency that agreed to a closed adoption. As a result, getting those records has been extremely difficult and time-consuming."

"But you got them?"

His mouth thinned. He nodded. "But often when two people adopt in a situation like that, they're secretive, too," he said. "Maybe they don't ever intend to tell their children they're adopted. And since the girls would be...er...in their twenties now..."

"You said they were nearly twenty-seven. My age."

He swallowed again.

"Right," he said. "People in their twenties move around a lot. They could be anywhere."

"So, Connor's really, really good at finding missing people?"

"That's what he does."

"You know, I have a missing sister, too. Do you think maybe I could talk to him about her sometime? We lost her when she was eight. Ever since then, it's like a part of my soul is still missing."

He grabbed a decanter of scotch from a low table and

poured himself a glass, which he gulped in a single long swallow. "That's awful," he replied.

"We're twins, too. That's sort of a strange coincidence, don't you think?"

"What? You are? Right! Yes, it is! Damn right it is!"

"Becky, that's my sister who disappeared when she was eight," Abby persisted. "I loved her, and I still miss her. I still wonder if she's alive…if she's happy…if she remembers me."

"I'm sorry," he said. He took her hand is his. "Look, I'm really sorry about her." The jet hit an air pocket just as the blood rushed from his face. He was as pale as a ghost, and his eyes blazed queerly. When she squeezed his hand to reassure him, he jumped. Then the jet hit real turbulence, and his stare became so wild and intense that she sucked in a panicky breath. "What? Is…is something wrong with the jet?"

"No. Just a bit of bumpy air. Sorry if I scared you. See…the jet's leveling out. Nothing's wrong."

"It's such a coincidence, me being the same age as the missing twins…and me having a missing twin."

"Yes, I suppose it is." He took a deep breath as if he were choosing carefully what he intended to say. Then he stopped, shook his head and closed his eyes for a long moment. He took two long breaths, and when he opened his eyes again, she was relieved that he seemed almost his old, assured self. Then he ran his hand through his heavy, black hair, she saw that he had a slight tremor.

She felt profound sympathy for him. It must be the turbulence. She hadn't realized he was such a nervous flyer. Maybe he wasn't usually, but he'd been through a lot. Obviously, he wanted to appear tough and unruffled.

He met her gaze. "You say your twin is missing? How did it happen? When?"

Abby didn't want to upset him. Not when he was this worried about flying. Still, he seemed so concerned and interested, that suddenly she couldn't stop herself.

"We were eight," she began in a breathless rush. "We'd been making too much noise in the tent where we were camping in the Franklin Mountains in El Paso, so our parents had made us go outside. We were playing this silly game, chasing each other and hiding from one another. Then we ran after a wild turkey. When the sun began going down, I suddenly realized how far we were from the tent, so I turned to run back down the hill. Becky yelled for me to wait... But I didn't, even though she sounded terrified."

"And?"

"I thought she would follow me like she always did. She was more afraid of the dark than I was, you see. Oh, why am I telling you all this, when you already have way too much on your mind?"

"Because I asked." His voice was low and soothing.

"I never saw her again," she whispered. "Nobody did."

Leo took her hand in his, and his tense, dark eyes shone with compassion. That's when the worst of the pain that she'd carried inside her for years and years burst forth.

"My father thought it was his fault. He'd been down in Mexico just before that, writing about stuff powerful people didn't want exposed. He thinks she was taken across the border. But I knew it was my fault. If I hadn't run away and left her, maybe she wouldn't have gotten lost. And maybe my parents wouldn't have gotten divorced. Maybe Mother wouldn't have died. And maybe I wouldn't have dated all those cowboys who could never have loved me. I didn't want them to love me, you see. Not even Shanghai. Because then they'd leave me. And maybe if I hadn't run away from her that day, my father would do things with me. Like, for instance, maybe he would have come to our wedding." She felt like a fool when she sobbed out that last.

"Shh. You're being way too hard on yourself." He yanked a tissue out of a little box from the nearby table and handed it to her. "Here. Blow your nose."

"T-this is…is why I never talk about her," she sobbed. "Why I try to never think about her." More hot tears fell. "B-because i-it upsets me too much. She was scared, and I left her out there in the dark all alone. And…and I can't stop wondering what happened to her. All this talk about the missing twins has stirred me up I think."

Abby felt weak and exhausted and absolutely raw after her tearful outburst. Fighting the fire was nothing compared to talking about Becky. She sat back, drained.

"I see." Leo's thoughtful gaze studied her. "A while ago you asked about talking to my brother." He seemed to consider his words. "Maybe you should phone Connor and tell him everything you know about Becky. *Everything*."

"It's been such a long time. I hardly dare to hope that even he can find—"

"Hopefully, he'll surprise us," Leo muttered gloomily. His grip on her hand tightened, and she wondered why he suddenly sounded so morose and hopeless again.

As if sensing she was worried, his arm came

around her, and his touch was so soothing she loosened her seat belt so she could curl up against him. She wished he would keep talking to her, because she'd liked sharing with him about Becky, but he said no more.

Instead, a heavy silence fell between them. His body felt tense and hard. Soon she realized an even thicker wall had gone up, a wall that she had no idea how to tear down. Why was he so quiet and uncommunicative all of a sudden when he'd been so attentive after that first night she'd slept with him? Before they'd married, he'd wanted to see her again constantly. Only minutes ago he'd listened to what she'd shared about Becky, but now he was shutting her out again.

"Leo? Are you okay? Did I say something or do something…"

"I'm fine. Just tired."

His tension seemed to increase. After they landed, he drove them in silence to her ranch house, stopping briefly to buy groceries. Without a word he pulled up to her back porch and unloaded their bags and the food. Then he told her he had a lot to catch up on. He called his office and stayed on the phone with various people for hours. She spoke to Kel briefly. Five minutes was all it took for her to catch up on things at In the Pink! When Leo remained in her second bedroom with his phone, she prepared and ate a cold supper of cottage cheese, carrot sticks and sardines—alone. As she'd done on their wedding night, she bathed and brushed her hair until it gleamed. She put on her sheerest nightgown and left her robe seductively unfastened, but when he finally came to bed, dressed only in his pajama bottoms, he gave her a light peck on the cheek. Then he rolled over to his side of the bed, turned his broad, powerful back to her and was silent.

Blinking back tears, she glared at him.

Why didn't he try to seduce her as he had the night he'd proposed?

"Leo?"

He stirred. "Hmm?"

"Is something wrong?"

"I'm just tired," he whispered. "Go to sleep."

She was a new bride. They'd both come close to death. She'd sat in that basement, terrified he was dead. She wanted him to wrap her in his arms, to make wild, violent love to her. But she would not beg.

Go to sleep?

As if she could.

The bloodred neon of the alarm clock was blinking 2:00 a.m. when Abby's breathing finally slurred to a soft and regular rhythm. At last, Leo thought. Maybe soon, he'd be able to fall asleep, too. God knew, he'd better.

He'd known by her choice of nightgown—the damn thing left nothing to his imagination—that she'd wanted him. Just as he'd known by her crushed tone that he'd hurt her when he'd kissed her coolly and turned his back on her. He'd lain there, his heart pounding with desire while his mind was tormented by guilt.

It had taken her hours to fall asleep. Leo knew because he'd been driven crazy by the blinking clock and by her fidgeting.

Asleep now, she snuggled closer to him, her delicious warmth invading his side of the bed. God. He bit his lower lip and turned to stare at her slim body molded by the quilts beside his.

In the moonlight, her loose, butter-gold hair gleamed like silk on the pillow. His heartbeat sped up.

He wanted to touch her hair, to thread his fingers through it, to kiss it, just as he wanted to brush her pale throat with his mouth. He craved her smell, her satiny softness, her taste. He'd wanted all those things last night, too, but he knew just as he'd known last night, that if he so much as held her hand, he wouldn't be able to stop. His deception and sex had gotten them off to the wrong start, and only honesty would set things right. But was she ready for the brutal truth? He'd known who she was, and he'd set her up.

Leo swallowed. Surely lying beside Abby without touching her, knowing she was awake and as needily restless as he, had been the cruelest of tortures. He'd lain there, remembering the fear blazing in her hazel eyes when she'd walked up to Kinky's SUV before they'd headed out to Black Oaks. Nor could he forget the wild joy in her eyes when she'd realized he'd survived. He'd never forget how she'd flown into his arms after the fire had passed the house.

Nobody could fake such emotions. Her heart and soul had been in that kiss. So had his.

If anything, his feelings were even stronger than hers, maybe because he'd lived most of his life in such a cold place. Ever since that moment in front of the Big House, he'd known he cared for her more than he'd ever imagined possible.

When he'd been in the thick of those flames at Black Oaks, fighting the fire and then fighting for his own life, she and the baby had held an inexplicable, almost mythical power over him. He'd wanted to live, solely to get back to them. He'd wanted a chance to be Abby's lover, her husband and the father of their child.

He'd prayed for a miracle as he'd dived into the creek as the trees on all sides of him had exploded in flames. Then he'd seen Abby again, and she'd kissed him so fiercely in that blackened pasture, he'd almost thought he could have his miracle. But his wild hope had made him more afraid.

How could he trust her not to break his heart when she learned the truth? Somehow he had to figure out a way to win her—permanently. Because if he lost her now, he knew from past experience how unbearable such pain would be. When he'd lost Ransom's respect and support, and Nancy and Julie and his mother, he'd lived in a bleak, lonely place fueled only by the cold brilliance of his ambition.

It had been a long, ruthless climb up from his hellish losses. So he didn't have the guts to face losing Abby. He had to calm down and woo her slowly, deliberately.

Ignoring difficult conversations wasn't going to work very long. He had to talk to her, confide in her, listen to her. But not tonight.

In a few months, after he'd won her trust, maybe then he'd find the courage to tell her everything. He could only hope that by then he would have proved he cared and she'd have enough invested in their relationship to forgive him.

In her dream, Leo was cupping her breasts and kissing her endlessly. Then something screamed outside the window, the owls maybe, rudely awakening her. The next thing she grew aware of was Leo's steady breathing.

Slowly she realized that Leo was on his side of the bed—as far away from her as possible. He lay on his back with his arms crossed. His eyes were open, and he was staring up at the ceiling.

He was awake.

"Leo?" Abby whispered, reaching for him before she thought.

His reaction to her lush voice and caressing fingertips was instantaneous and undeniable. As he grabbed her hand and stilled it against his abdomen, his breath caught in his throat. She could tell by the sheet bunched at his groin that he was hard, erect. His skin was burning hot, and his heart was pounding as fiercely as hers.

He wanted her, every bit as much as she wanted him. Yet he was pretending not to.

"Go back to sleep," he growled, pushing her hand away. Then he rolled to the very edge of his side of the bed and lay facing the far wall.

Why was he rejecting her? She should respect his wishes, shouldn't she? And she would, if only he would tell her why.

"Leo…did I do something…?"

"No, I said—"

"But I'm not sleepy."

"Well, I am," Leo said.

"Are you? I wonder."

Her dream made her bold. Giggling, she scooted beneath the sheets until her soft breasts grazed the warmth of his broad back. Her nipples grew hard the instant she felt his smooth, hot flesh. He hissed in a breath, tensing when she stayed there with her breasts mashed against his back. For a second she thought he might jump from the bed. Just to tempt him, she slid her hand down his side to rest upon his buttocks. Gently, slowly, her fingers kneaded.

"I want you," she whispered finally, splaying her fingertips. "I want you so much."

Her hand traced back up the length of his side with exquisite tenderness. He turned, caught her hand and kissed it. Then he went still, slowly he pushed her away, sprang out of the bed and went to the window, where he stood, fists clenched at his sides.

"Leo?"

He sucked in a harsh breath and stayed where he was.

She punched her pillow in frustration. "All right," she finally said. Getting up, she threw on her robe and walked down the hall into her kitchen. Closing the door, she pulled out a chair. Sitting down at the table, she buried her head in her hands.

Did he hate her? Hate himself for desiring her? He'd been so sweet and understanding on the plane when she'd told him about Becky. If he didn't hate her, what was wrong now?

She thought of their child. Did he feel trapped as she had? She wished her dream hadn't made her so brazen. Her stomach tightened.

Why had she touched him, pushed him? Like her, he was used to being in charge. How could she have been so conceited as to think she could seduce him when he was set against her? Why hadn't she given him the time he needed? He'd been through a lot...the news of her pregnancy, their rushed marriage, the fire, blaming himself for all of it, probably. Then she'd pushed him about the missing twins on the plane.

She began to berate herself as being the most selfish, pushy person ever. She didn't know him that well. He was used to his own space. She needed to slow down, to be careful for a while.

He'd been injured in the fire. Last night he'd been in the emergency room. He was probably still exhausted. Maybe he was in pain.

Scalding tears slipped from her eyelids. He'd probably despise her forever now.

Her sobs blocked the sound of his soft tread, so she didn't realize he was anywhere near until he said her name.

When she looked up, he towered over her. He was still bare-chested, wearing only his pajama bottoms.

He knelt and pulled her into his arms. "I'm sorry."

"I'm sorry, too," she whispered as she threw her arms around his shoulders. "Oh, Leo…I-I'm so sorry."

He pressed her close, stroked her back, her hair. She clung to him and was amazed that she was so starved for any show of kindness or affection from him. Never had she wanted any man's caresses and interest as she wanted his. What were these new feelings?

He stared into her eyes for a long moment with a burning intensity that left her breathless even before he traced the back of his hand against the softness of her cheek and then down her throat.

"My precious wife. My darling…"

Her nipples tightened. She swallowed, hoping for more. Then his hand stopped moving.

"Do you hate me?" she whispered.

"God, no. How could you even think…?"

He crushed her to his chest and held her tightly. She felt the thunder of his heart, the warmth of his powerful body.

Her sobs subsided, and she clung more tightly, laying her head, cheek to cheek, against his. He was alive and so solid and strong, so dear. She liked simply being held in his arms. Her dream had not been nearly so good as this. Closing her eyes, she prayed that he would kiss her. Afraid to encourage him, she remained still and breathless in his arms, waiting.

His hand began to move up and down her back. Then he caressed her neck, her shoulders, her arms, and whispered, "Sweet. You tempt me to…"

But he did not kiss her lips or touch her breasts.

Instead, he said, "Come back to bed, my darling."

My darling. The gentle endearment chimed in her soul. *He'd called her his darling. He didn't hate her.*

Threading her fingers inside his, he led her back down the hall.

As he slid the covers back, she saw that his pajama bottoms were tented at his crotch. So, he did desire her.

When they were both in bed, he said good-night. His voice was husky, and he was shaking slightly. He wanted her as badly as she wanted him. Why was he doing this? Why wasn't he going to take her? Why?

She closed her eyes and took a deep breath, willing him to kiss her. But he didn't.

"Good night, Leo," she finally rasped.

Tears beaded her lashes as she lay in the dark, hungering for more.

"Good night," he muttered in a low, choked tone.

She lay in the dark beside him, too aware of his big, long body just inches from hers. Still, as frustrating as his nearness was, his being there made her feel safe. It wasn't long before she fell asleep, and in her dreams he clasped her to him and made love to her as ardently as she desired.

In the morning when she awoke, he was staring so with such intensity that she blushed.

She realized the sheets had come off, and in her sheer nightgown, she was practically naked.

"What?" she whispered, smiling at him because she felt exposed and liked the way his hot eyes burned through the thin fabric to her skin.

"Sleep well?" His voice was gruff and tight.

She sighed. Then she stretched, just to tempt him. "Never better."

He didn't yield; his eyes remained glued to her face. Was he afraid to look at her body in the revealing nightgown? She could see his pulse knocking in the hollow of his tanned throat. She hoped so.

"Did you know you cried out my name...several times?" he said.

"I must have been having a nightmare."

"Didn't sound like it to me."

"Oh, really?" She got up and threw her pillow at him. Without bothering to throw on her robe or cover herself, she scampered off to her bathroom and locked the door. Not that it was necessary. She'd locked it solely to taunt him.

The heat of his gaze had seared through her nightgown. Maybe he hadn't wanted to stare at her, but he hadn't been able to look away. Once she was safe inside, she leaned against the door for a long time, trembling.

Where did she go from here?

Nine

Later that morning, to Abby's surprise, Leo had supervised the high-school kid he'd hired to see to Coco and had scrambled eggs and cooked bacon by the time she'd showered and dressed. He'd hauled out the garbage, as well.

Now he was dressed in dark slacks, a white shirt and tie. His dark jacket hung over a kitchen chair, and his bulging black briefcase stood by the door.

"You're fast and capable and handy to have around," she said as she sat down at the table on her back porch that he'd set. "I'll give you that."

"Hey, who knows, maybe you'll decide I'm a keeper. Beautiful morning," he murmured as he unfolded his napkin.

Sunlight slanted through the oaks and pines. Birds twittered in their branches.

"Yes."

Why were his knuckles white as he held his fork? Why was his face so hard and set? She'd barely slept. Maybe he was as tired as she was.

They ate in silence. When they were done, he stacked their plates and headed into the kitchen. Obviously in a rush, he began rinsing and putting the dishes into the dishwasher.

"I'll be home at seven," he said when he'd finished. "What's your schedule?"

"It'll probably be pretty hectic, but I'll try to be here by seven, too."

His smiled. "Good. We can cook or go out, whatever you'd prefer."

"You're being so agreeable."

"Why is that such a surprise?"

Remembering his rejection last night, she looked up, but his dark, smiling eyes were unreadable.

He went to the door and picked up his briefcase. Hoping he would kiss her goodbye, she chased after him. Instead, he turned and nodded. Then he said shortly, "See you—"

See you. She was a new bride. They'd missed their honeymoon, and he was treating her like a sister.

He pushed the screen door open. Feeling forlorn, she ran after him and watched from the porch when he drove away.

All through the day, she found herself hurrying to get finished with her phone calls and even her pet projects so that she'd make it home to him at the stroke of seven. And when she did make it, by recklessly speeding, and five whole minutes early, her heart fell when his truck wasn't there.

Thirty minutes later he called and said he'd be home at eight.

"I'll have dinner ready."

"Not sardines and carrots, I hope."

She laughed. "No. Steak and potatoes and green beans and chocolate cookies with ice cream. Store-bought, I'm afraid."

"Maybe you're a keeper, too."

"You think?"

"I think. Let me get back to this so I can get home." The eagerness in his low voice warmed her heart.

That night he brought her a box of chocolates and a single red rose. Not that he kissed her at the door or anything, even though she'd come running as soon as she'd heard his truck.

Sexual tension thrummed in her blood as she found a vase and stuck the rose in it. With shaking fingers, she set the vase on the table. All through dinner she found herself turning from his dark face to the rose and wondering why he'd bought it when he wouldn't even kiss her.

After supper they took a walk with Coco following them as the sky turned violet and stars popped out. Leo told her about his day, which had been every bit as crazy as hers, and she told him amusing stories about her meetings and unreasonable clients. He smiled and laughed a lot, and she was aware of him watching her when he thought she wasn't looking.

How could she have ever thought him dull when just being with him around the house was fun? Not since she'd had Becky around had she had someone to share the little things that made up her life. She'd thought he couldn't possibly be interested in hearing about one client's fit over naming and marketing ideas for a new product, but he was either fascinated and held her talent in awe, or he deserved an Oscar.

When it was dark and the moon had come up, they returned to the house and watched part of an old black-and-white Western on television. He confessed he was a sucker for all John Wayne movies.

"I guess in my heart I always dreamed of being a cowboy," he admitted.

"I'm a sucker for anything with a horse in it, too," she said. "A book, a movie…"

He was attentive from the moment he got home until they went to bed. They did nothing out of the ordinary, but the evening was special in so many ways, at least for her, as only simple pleasures can be special when shared with a friend or lover. Was that what he was doing—trying to become her friend?

But again, when they went to bed, he kept to his own side of the bed. Only tonight he didn't even kiss her on the cheek.

Why didn't he push for sex? She quit asking. She decided to try to be patient. Thus, a week passed in this pleasant if frustrating fashion, and with each new day the sexual tension inside her built. Every night he was a perfect friend, a perfect gentleman, but never her lover except in her dreams.

When Connor flew to Austin Friday afternoon to meet a client, Leo set up a late-afternoon appointment for Abby to meet him in her office to discuss Becky. As always, she promised Leo she'd be home at seven. When Connor didn't make it to her office until six, she didn't think to call Leo and warn him. She was so anxious about the interview, she simply shook hands with Connor, closed her office door and turned her cell phone to silent, so they wouldn't be interrupted.

"Sorry I'm late," he said grinning. "Airport. Airplane. Client."

"Say no more. Would you like something to drink?"

"Just water. Lots of ice."

By the time she returned to her desk with two bottles and two glasses of ice, he had his laptop up and running.

He asked all the same questions about Becky she'd answered too many times before, and as always, as he entered her replies into his laptop, she tensed and hunched over, her head pounding.

"What did Becky want to be when she grew up?"

Abby closed her eyes. If she grew up. "A teacher. But she was only eight. How many of us know at that age?" Funny, how she always thought of Becky as eight…as if her life had stopped…Abby's throat tightened.

"Did she like horses, too?"

"No, she was scared of them. Our horse, Blacky, stepped on her big toe and broke it, and she wouldn't go near the barn after that."

"What else was she scared of?"

"Mostly the dark. Snakes. Bugs, especially scorpions. All the usual suspects little girls are afraid of. Goblins under the bed. Disney villains like the witch in *Snow White*. Oh, and the tooth fairy. We always left our teeth under my pillow."

Connor smiled. "Was there anything unusual about her, anything at all that set her apart?"

"She was very sensitive, unusually compassionate.

She would always notice if anybody's feelings were hurt and try to comfort them."

As they talked, Abby lost track of the time. It was almost seven-thirty when Connor said he thought he had enough to go on.

"But do you really think there's a chance that you might find her?"

"Maybe. But you've got to understand that this case is very cold."

Feeling weary from all the emotions his questions had stirred, she nodded. Without another word, she got up and walked him to the door.

He insisted on following her down to her Lincoln. "Are you staying at the Little Spur or in town?" she asked as she flung her purse and briefcase onto her passenger seat and then sank behind the wheel.

"Neither. I'm flying back to Houston tonight."

"Thanks for looking into this."

"No. Thank you." He shook her hand.

Her mind whirled with memories about Becky as she drove home. Connor seemed cocky, but she was afraid to hope.

She was still thinking about Becky as she drove into the garage. No sooner had she gotten out of the Lincoln than Leo ran out of the house. He looked tall and strong and handsome in snug-fitting, faded jeans and a long-sleeved white shirt as he waited for her in the drive. His black hair fell loosely over his tanned brow. She wanted him to take her in his arms, to hold her. Would he never, ever kiss her again?

She drew in a long, shaky breath. Maybe part of her exhaustion had to do with her pregnancy, but she was utterly drained from her long day, the meeting about Becky and then the drive home.

"I'm sorry I'm late," she said as she wearily picked up her briefcase.

He stood in the dark, silently watching her.

"Is something wrong?" she whispered when his silence began to grow heavy.

"Where have you been? I tried and tried to call...."

"You called? Me?"

"You. I sent a text message, too."

She fumbled in her purse for her cell phone and saw that he had. "Oh, I—I guess I turned it to silent ring when I was in that meeting with Connor. Yes, I did."

"You scared the hell out of me."

"Oh, Leo, I-I'm sorry."

She could tell he was upset. His lips were pale and thinner than usual. When he pushed that lock of hair back, she saw that a vein pulsed in his forehead. Yet, the next time he spoke, his voice sounded remarkably controlled, even calm. "It's okay now that you're here, safe."

He grabbed her briefcase. "So, how'd the meeting with my brother go?" he asked as they began to walk to the house.

"He asked me so many questions. Talking about Becky made me so tense I have a headache and a backache."

"I was afraid. I imagined all sorts of wild scenarios. A flat...your Lincoln spinning out of control...a wreck...you hurt..."

He certainly didn't sound like an indifferent husband.

"Oh, dear. Leo, the last thing I wanted to do was upset you."

"I wasn't upset," he said, but his teeth were tightly clenched.

"Why were you so worried?"

"Break in routine, I guess. Let's forget it."

His strides became so long and quick, she had to run to keep up with him. He wasn't dull or cold. His emotions were fierce and all-consuming. Tonight she needed passion.

She needed to be kissed and held. After talking to Connor, she was afraid she'd never see Becky again. After the interview had ended, all she'd wanted was to get home to Leo. She'd imagined his arms around her, longed for them. Tonight she wanted Leo the lover, not Leo the friend.

When she stepped into the kitchen, he had a pasta dish ready to serve. She knew she was being thoughtless and selfish, but she wasn't in the mood for one of their friendly evenings.

"You know what I really need tonight, Leo?"

He turned and glanced past her. Sparks lit her blood. Not that he met her gaze.

She felt awful chasing him, but she couldn't stop herself. "I—I feel as if tension has settled in every nerve and muscle and ligament. If I weren't pregnant, I'd have a beer or a glass of wine. I'll never be able to relax unless I take a warm bath and maybe…maybe, if you wouldn't mind, you could massage me a little."

He closed his eyes and clenched his fists. "Not a good idea."

She shouldn't—she wouldn't—beg him.

Swallowing her pride, she did. "Please…"

The silent kitchen surrounded them. When he

frowned, she felt a horrible certainty that he was about to refuse her.

"Leo. I got so upset thinking about Becky…"

"All right," he said. "You win."

"I'm ready," Abby called to him huskily.

Leo's heart was rushing way too fast as he pushed open the door. He went still, staring at her.

He couldn't do this. But he had to.

Vanilla candles flickered, their soft glow bathing the exposed curve of her slim back in warm, golden light. Sheets were bunched at her rounded hips. Her hair gleamed like dark gold. Hungrily his eyes devoured her. All week he'd held himself in check even though he'd lusted for her constantly. Every night her nightgowns had seemed to grow thinner. Now, tonight, she was naked.

Soft, serene music played. A bottle of her favorite, lavender-scented lotion stood on the bedside table.

Leo was convinced they needed more time, several weeks maybe, to get to know each other. He had taken a long walk, telling himself that he could massage her without letting it go any further…that he had to.

He knew what talking about Becky did to her. Abby was pregnant, shattered and exhausted tonight. He kept reminding himself that they'd gone to bed before they'd trusted each other, and how ashamed she'd been of the dark, wild things she'd done with a near-stranger. He wanted to become her friend, someone she trusted before he touched her again. Tonight was too soon.

He must have made some sound because her fingers tensed, clawing the sheets. Desire raced through his veins and made every muscle in his being tense even as he fought it.

He went to the bed and fumbled to loosen the bottle's cap. Squirting a big blob of cold lotion into his hands much too violently, he waited awhile for it to warm.

"Leo?"

"Just heating the lotion up a bit."

"Or stalling?"

She had him there. "Sorry." He hastily knelt beside the bed and placed trembling hands on her bare shoulders.

For a long moment his hands remained still as her heat seeped into his fingers, causing his muscles to wind tighter. He sank his teeth into his bottom lip until it bled.

He couldn't do this.

"Your hands feel so good. Big and warm. I feel safe tonight with you," she murmured.

Damn. His heart was pounding like a drumbeat gone wild. He was as hard as a brick. He felt like a beast. She was naked under that sheet. Was she trying to drive him crazy or what?

Desperately, he swallowed. Then he forced his hands to move in ever-widening circular motions.

"That feels so good," she whispered huskily.

He shut his eyes, but he still saw her golden hair, the slope of her shoulders, the curve of her hips, and imagined the rest.

His breathing grew ragged. His pulse raced out of control. He wanted her so much he couldn't trust himself a second longer.

His hands stopped. For a long moment he stayed beside her, frozen.

Then she turned, the sheets falling away so that he

saw the triangular wedge of gold curls that concealed the secret of her womanhood. Her pale breasts with their shadowy nipples were uncovered to his gaze.

"Leo, I want to touch you, too. Please...please let me."

He stood up and stared down at her lush golden body, at her soft, wet, red lips. Then he ran.

"Leo?" she whispered in a tiny, bleak voice.

Every organ in Leo's body pulsed with blood and felt on fire as he stood in the guest bathroom splashing cold water onto his face and hair.

"Don't you want me at all?" she murmured from the doorway.

She was probably naked. And so close.

Hell. He stiffened. Why couldn't she just leave him alone?

When he glanced up into the mirror, he saw that her golden hair tumbled about her shoulders in wild disarray and that she wasn't naked anymore. She was wearing a thick red robe that was tied loosely at her waist...and probably nothing else. Her mouth was trembling. Her big sad eyes were asking questions he wasn't sure how to answer. The last thing he wanted to do was to hurt her.

"I think you know I want you," he said.

"Then why have you...or maybe I should ask why haven't you..."

A dark flush crawled up her neck and stained her cheeks.

"Dammit. Because I selfishly seduced you the first night and made you hate me. Then you told me you were pregnant and miserable because of me, and I seduced you to get you to agree to marry me. I've been a bastard. Because of our sexual history, I thought that maybe we should try to become friends before we did it again."

Her face softened. "Really? You were trying to be considerate?"

He nodded.

"That's so sweet."

"Believe me, I'm the last thing from sweet."

"What if I don't choose to believe you?"

"I assure you, my motives are extremely selfish."

A huge smile lit her face. "I'm so glad." Then she laughed and came into his arms, gasping when she felt his male hardness pressing against her pelvis.

"So you do want me?" she whispered huskily. "You do!"

"I do," he murmured, ruffling her hair.

"I'm glad. Very pleased. But I want more than friendship. We're married now…you know."

He knew. His heart was pounding violently.

The bathroom shade was up. Outside, the night was velvet black with only the faintest shimmer of silver moonlight. In that strange, gray light, her normally fiery hair gleamed like platinum.

His arms tightened around her. He'd never felt so close to any woman. Not even Nancy, the girl he'd loved as a boy. And he'd thought he'd never get over Nancy.

His lips found Abby's in a long, hard kiss, his tongue plunging into her mouth. Fumbling with the tie of her robe, she yanked it loose. When she wiggled, it slid off her body. At the sight of her naked, he gripped her arms so hard she cried out.

"Sorry," he whispered. Then he began to tear off his

belt and jeans. Stepping out of the denim, he tossed his jeans aside.

He pushed her against the wall. She was wet with lotion and as slick as satin, open. He stepped back, panting hard. Beneath her long lashes, her eyes were brilliant. Her lips looked swollen and bruised. He remembered that first night when she'd been so hungry for him. Not that they'd been any hungrier for each other than they were now.

"Wrap your legs around me," he commanded roughly. Grabbing her buttocks and pulling her tight, he drove himself into her.

When he filled her the first time, he went still, and she sighed.

"Yes," she murmured. "I thought you'd never...do this...again...."

She said more, but he didn't hear the rest. Still inside her, holding her bottom tightly against his pelvis, he carried her down the hall to her bedroom. With her legs laced around his waist, he lowered her to the bed and then followed her down.

Her pleadings, or whatever the hell they were, fell against his ears in broken whispers, but his desire drove him. He was past hearing her, past everything but the insane, pulsing need that drove him to make her completely his.

Again and again he plunged, each time more forcefully, each time finding a pleasure and a satisfaction unlike any he had ever known until finally he rushed over that final edge, shuddering as he exploded. She wept, clinging, stroking, trembling.

"Did I hurt you?" he whispered.

She kissed his mouth and shook her head back and forth on her pillow. Then she touched the tip of her nose to his.

Vaguely he hoped it wasn't too soon, but he'd wanted her too much and she'd been too sweet…and too hot to resist. He was still burning up.

He'd intended to go a while longer without sex, to court her slowly, to make her like him. So much for good intentions. There were those who'd said he'd been on the road to hell since birth.

He fell asleep while still inside her, with her arms wrapped tightly around him.

Ten

When Leo awoke the next morning, streamers of pink light drifted across the bed. The window must have been cracked an inch or so because he heard wild turkeys gobbling and morning doves cooing.

Glancing at his watch, he saw it was too early to get up. When Abby whispered his name, he pulled her warm, luscious body close. Then he ran his hand down her arm, which was velvety soft and deliciously warm. He kissed the curve of her elbow where a faint pulse throbbed.

She sighed and then reached over and framed his face with her hands. He stared at her before kissing her on the lips. She opened her mouth, and his tongue dipped inside.

"Wait! I've got to get up and brush my…"

"I can't wait."

He circled her with his arms and slid on top of her,

holding her down and parting her legs. His sex found hers. She was slick wet, and so hot. Satin wildfire.

When he went still instead of entering her, he swallowed convulsively. He kissed her again and again, on her throat, on the tip of her nose, on her lips, until her skin felt feverish all over.

"Now it's me who can't wait," she teased, nipping playfully at his bottom lip.

"All right then." He lunged, and her eyes flashed open as she cried out in pleasure.

"Don't move. I want this to last," he said.

"So do I. Oh, so do I."

He tried to slow down and keep his strokes feather-light, but her body gloved him tightly, causing too many exquisite sensations to course down every male nerve ending. It was as if they were wired for each other.

He'd hungered for her too long, and the taste he'd had last night wasn't nearly enough. She moved, causing hot bursts of thrilling sensations to course through him. It wasn't long before he lost all control and began thrusting faster and faster himself. Then they were both crying out at once and holding each other, swept away in a volcanic riptide that left them shaken and yet happy, too.

When he finally got up that morning, he tiptoed from the room. Several minutes later, when he was dressed for work and sitting down to a couple of fried eggs with his newspaper, dammit if the little minx didn't crawl under the kitchen table, unzip his slacks and make him forget all about breakfast and his office. She was insatiable.

Afterward, he pulled her into his lap and told her that was the most memorable breakfast he'd ever had.

"But your eggs are cold," she teased, nuzzling her lips against his throat.

As if he gave a damn. "I'm calling Miriam to tell her I'll be very late."

"Why?" she asked, but she winked at him.

He ripped off his tie and unbuttoned his dress shirt. "Because I've got a favor or two to return. I like to stay even. Why don't you call your office and tell them you won't be in until ten? I promise you won't regret it."

After he returned the sexual favor that she had bestowed on him, she told him again how sweet she thought he was for trying to make her know he respected her.

"But really, surely you could have done that some other way. Not kissing you, not being kissed, not being held, and all the other things we didn't do, was pure torture…at least for me," she said.

"For me, too. Believe me, I sympathize. But you do remember how mad you got at me after that first night. You called me a stalker."

She blushed. "I'm sorry. I thought I had to say something awful to make you go away."

"Why were you so determined you wanted nothing to do with me?"

"I—I was afraid of you, I think. Of how you made me feel…and lose control."

"Are you still afraid?"

"More than ever."

"Because you lost Becky?"

"And my parents, too. Still, avoiding sex wasn't a very practical idea, since we seem to think about it a lot when we're together."

"You can say that again."

"How long did you intend to stay celibate?"

"I don't know," he said. "A few more weeks. I thought maybe we should get to know each other a little better before—"

"But we're married," she murmured. "Hey, do you think we could stay home today?"

"And do what?"

"Are you going to make me keep chasing you?"

In the end, they stayed home all day. Leo told Miriam since he'd skipped his honeymoon, he deserved to spend one day with his bride. And Miriam, bless her practical, capable heart, didn't put up a single argument. The woman she'd once disliked was becoming one of her favorite people.

Bliss-filled days and nights became the norm for Leo and Abby.

They spent the Fourth of July at the headquarters of the Golden Spurs. It had rained, and except for the scarred trees, much of the damage to the pastures from the fire was brightened by leafy new foliage. Fences had been repaired and buildings were being reconstructed.

The Kembles made a fuss over her and her growing belly. It was funny how she felt so close to Mia and Lizzy. She liked to hang out in the barn with Mia and her horses or just sit and chat with Lizzy. It was strange how easily she got along with the Kemble sisters.

Although the summer was long and hot, and the drought, especially in South Texas was a fierce one, Abby felt happier than she'd ever been.

Not that life was perfect. Despite her frequent conversations with Connor and his determination to find her sister, Becky's disappearance remained a mystery. Nor had her father called or answered her e-mails once since their wedding. It was as if after he'd called to say he wasn't coming to her wedding, he'd disappeared off the face of the earth.

"He doesn't care about me," Abby said to Leo one evening in early September as he lay on the couch, perusing some papers from his briefcase that had to do with a pending oil and gas lease on the Golden Spurs.

"He cares," Leo said. "He just doesn't know how to show it. Sometimes when you're running from the crap in your life you can't face, you bury yourself alive in your work so you don't hate yourself. I should know. I did that for years after Mike Ransom threw me off his ranch. Do you remember that day you came to my office to tell me you were pregnant?"

"As if I could ever forget it."

He smiled. "Do you remember that old man who left when you came in?"

She nodded. "The skinny old gentleman who called you a bastard?"

"My mother worked on the Running R, his ranch, as his housekeeper when I was a kid. My father was dead, so Ransom became like a father to Connor and me. He invited us everywhere he took his own son, Cal. Took us to football games and theater road shows in Dallas. Taught us to ride, shoot and rope. Hell, he was even our Scout leader. I grew up loving him like a father."

"What happened?"

"Cal and I both fell in love with Nancy, a neighboring rancher's daughter. She chose me over Cal even though he was rich, and I was poor."

Leo broke off, remembering.

"Go on," she whispered.

"Money didn't make any difference to Nancy when we were kids. But when I got her pregnant my freshman year in college and I had no way of supporting her, I guess Nancy got scared and thought she had to be practical."

Abby nodded. She could sympathize with an unplanned pregnancy coming as a shock and blasting a frightened girl out of her romantic dreams.

"Well, Mike, the 'gentleman' you met, was an upright, teetotaling, religious sort who never took a false step in his whole damn life. He'd been sending me to college. He'd even promised me he'd let me run his cattle operation after I graduated. When Nancy got pregnant, he kicked me off the ranch and withdrew his financial support, called me trash and worse. I told Nancy I'd marry her, but Mike convinced her I was a worthless so-and-so who'd never amount to anything without his help, so she got scared and married Cal. Now her daddy's ranch is part of theirs." His dark face tightened at the memories.

"Go on," she urged softly.

"Mike had had his eyes on Nancy's folks' ranch for a lot of years, so I guess he could look past the moral issues where she was concerned. Eventually they talked me into giving up my rights to my daughter, Julie, too. Everybody, including me, thought I'd be a bad influence on a girl." He swallowed as if he were ashamed and looked up at her.

"I think you turned out all right."

Still, he'd lost Julie. She couldn't imagine giving up her baby forever, and yet if she believed it was really the best thing for the baby... Even so, it would put her in hell for the rest of her life.

"Back then...I convinced myself it would be better for her not to be divided between two fathers, especially since I was so damned bitter."

"Maybe someday you should pursue a relationship with Julie."

His troubled gaze met hers briefly. "I have. I've always been rebuffed. She thinks I abandoned her, which is understandable, I guess."

"Maybe someday...."

"Yeah. Maybe someday. She's kind of running wild right now. Nancy and Cal got so desperate they even lowered themselves to ask me to help, but she refuses to talk to me. She says she's gotten along without me all these years, so she reckons she doesn't need me now. Hell, maybe she's right."

Abby winced. Imagining how that must hurt, she went over to the couch and sat down beside him. Her thigh touched his. Gently, she took his hand.

He threaded her fingers through his and held on tight. "We have a lot to be thankful for. Maybe we should concentrate on that," he said.

He buried his face against her neck. His breath felt warm against her skin. She took his hand and placed it on her stomach.

Holding hands while resting on her tummy, they sat together like that for a long time. He was right. She knew they should concentrate on the baby and the joy they found in each other, on their successful careers and everything else that they had to be thankful for. She must be a very spoiled person to go on moping about Becky being missing and her father being inattentive.

"You know," Leo said. "I did something crazy earlier this week, something I was ashamed of at first."

"What?"

"For years I wanted revenge on Mike Ransom. A few months ago the chance to buy his ranch cheap for the Golden Spurs fell into my lap. This week I had the papers finalized, and I forced him to come into my office to sign them. I knew taking the Running R away from him was worse than pointing a gun at his head and pulling the trigger. I thought I wanted that until he hobbled in with a cane, still blustering and trying to act tough. But he was as pale as a sheet after he picked up his pen, I got scared he was about to have a heart attack."

"What did you do?"

"I grabbed the papers and tore them in two. I told him to get the hell out of my office. He growled at me and then headed toward the door, yelling he didn't want my charity. I started remembering how patient he'd been when he'd taught me to ride as a kid, so I asked him how Julie was.

"'Wilder than Connor ever was,'" he said.

"Ransom looked so lost and desperate as he stared at me that I couldn't just let him leave, so I said, 'Why don't you sit down while I call my banker? Maybe he could help you.'

"'Don't you think I've been to bankers?' he asked.

"'Not to mine.'

"'Like I said, I don't want your charity,' he told me.'

"'You're stubborn, old man. But so am I. It would just be a loan that you'd pay back…with interest.'

"'But you'd be pulling strings to get it.'

"'Look, whether we like it or not, we're family. You're the only grandfather Julie has. I know what you've done for her. And what I haven't done. Let's just say I'm repaying an old debt.'"

Abby took his hand. "I think that's wonderful."

"I think I was a damn fool."

They say time passes quickly when you're having fun. Autumn rushed by even faster than summer had. The long, hot days with summertime cicadas gave way to cooler, crisper mornings and breezy evenings. Being pregnant, Abby was glad the heat had abated.

She couldn't get into her regular clothes any longer, and when Leo constantly touched and stroked her belly, acting like he found her expanding figure more appealing than ever, she felt beautiful and sexy and loved.

How could a man she hadn't wanted to marry make her so happy? But was he happy?

As the months passed, and her due date neared, she wondered about his feelings. Deep down, did he still feel she'd trapped him? Would those feelings surface again?

She asked him constantly if he loved her. They'd be doing chores and having a conversation about work. Or he'd be getting into his truck to drive to San Antonio and suddenly she would touch his forearm and ask, "Leo, do you love me? Do you?"

One such evening they were walking toward the porch when she interrupted him with that question. He whirled and took her in his arms. Without taking his eyes from her face, he said. "I love you. How many times do I have to say it before you'll believe me?"

"I don't know. Again and again, I guess. Forever."

"Why can't you believe me?"

"Because no one ever has loved me. A least not so that I could count on them...."

"Hell, maybe I should be the one worrying about you loving me," he said.

"Do you...worry?"

"Yeah, I do," he admitted.

"But you know I love you!"

"Do I?"

"Yes!"

"Maybe you think you do now. What if you found out something..." He stopped, his expression tensing.

"Like what?"

"Nothing." But his face was dark and haunted, and his gaze was so piercing.

"Sometimes you watch me, just like you're looking at me now," she said, feeling uneasy. "Is there something you're not telling me?"

That telltale muscle jumped in his jawline, but he said, "I like looking at you because I love you. That's all."

But his voice was too smooth.

Something really was bothering him, eating at him. She was sure of it. Too often, she was aware of him watching her, his face silent and tense. If she asked him what was wrong, he would smile or snap at her that nothing was. He would touch her stomach and kiss her and say she was beautiful and that he'd never been happier. Then it would happen again. She would catch him watching her in that way that was beginning to worry her so much.

She wanted to believe that he loved her and that they

would have a happily-ever-after life, but she'd lost everyone who'd ever loved her, so maybe she'd been damaged in some way that made her be the kind of person people left.

He went out of his way on a daily basis to be thoughtful and kind. Maybe his kindnesses and passionate responses to her at night should have reassured her. Part of her thought that she shouldn't doubt him, that by doing that maybe she would make something bad happen. And yet something lay hidden beneath the outwardly peaceful surface of their marriage. She knew he wasn't being entirely truthful.

Everyone in her life had thrown her away. She prayed with all her heart he wouldn't do it, too.

When she wasn't worrying about her marriage, she wished her father would call or come. She wanted Connor to hurry up and find Becky.

Every time she mentioned her hopes about Becky to Leo, he would tense and then watch her in that worrisome way she hated, like he was afraid. But of what? Why did talking about Becky bother him?

Often Abby wanted to be with Leo so much she carried her computer to San Antonio and worked in his office. They could take breaks together and lunch together beside the lazy, brown river under giant cypress trees. Sometimes when she had meetings she couldn't get out of in Austin, he brought his computer to her office, and Kel would set up a desk for him beside Abby's. All too often Kel would breeze inside without knocking and catch them kissing, which she loved.

In fact, Kel became disgustingly, smugly conceited about Abby's newfound connubial bliss. When she

dropped Abby at the San Antonio airport to meet Leo
for their flight down to the Golden Spurs for Thanksgiving, Kel couldn't resist saying something.

"Look at you," Kel said, patting Abby's tummy. "All
smiles and prettily pregnant. You all are so cute, the way
you kiss all the time. Didn't I tell you he was great?
Can't wait to see him, can you? How long has it been—
all of eight hours?"

"Seven and a half. Hey, but don't you dare act like I
owe all my newfound happiness to you. Besides, who
knows how long it will last?"

"Don't borrow trouble, okay?"

"It's just that… Kel, I'm so afraid that it'll all go away."

"Honey, don't be." Kel's voice was soft with compassion. Then her eyes sparkled. "Hey, who's that tall, dark
guy in the Stetson over there, devouring you with his
black eyes?"

"Leo!" Abby squealed, the sight of him filling her
with joy and fear. Then he swooped her into his arms,
and she forgot to be afraid as his hard mouth claimed
hers. She loved him so very much. Putting her arms
around his neck, she clung, kissing him again and again
while Kel made faces at her from behind his back.

"Abby!"

Abby leapt eagerly away from the foal she and Mia
had been petting. The barn doors rolled open, and the
next thing she heard were Leo's boots clicking on the
concrete as he kept shouting her name. Even though she
enjoyed Mia's company, she'd been missing Leo all
morning while he was in the ranch office, discussing
business with Cole and Shanghai.

Shanghai loped into the barn after Leo just as she pushed the stall door open.

"Mia!" Shanghai shouted.

"No, it's me," Abby said. "She's in the stall brushing Angelita, who's incredibly darling."

"Most young things are," Shanghai said, "which is why the world is overpopulated."

"Kinky broke into our business meeting and said he's ready to cut the turkey," Leo said, taking Abby's hand and bringing it to his lips. "I missed you."

"You've got him besotted," Shanghai said. "His gaze kept drifting toward the barn all morning. He didn't seem the least bit interested in discussing our renovations since the fire."

Abby smiled and squeezed Leo's hand. "It's Thanksgiving. You all shouldn't be talking business."

"Ranchers don't take holidays," Shanghai said.

"Have you made any progress locating the twins?" Mia asked as she closed the stall door.

"Some," Leo said.

"Well?"

"Well—nothing. It's too soon to talk about it."

"Leo?" Abby tugged warningly at his hand. "Why the defensive tone? Mia was just asking."

"I said it's too soon. Hell, can't we forget this? We came out here because it's time for dinner, not to discuss the missing twins."

"Mia didn't mean to upset you, darling."

"I'm not upset. You were the one who said it's a holiday. So let's just forget it."

"Fine," Abby whispered, even as a chill went through her.

Those were almost the last words Leo spoke that day. Whenever anyone asked him a question during dinner, he answered with a yes or a no but didn't elaborate. He remained withdrawn on the flight back to San Antonio, barely speaking to Abby. The next morning, he got up early, even though it was Saturday, and drove to his office.

Hours later, after she'd put up their Christmas tree and decorated the house all by herself, she began to wonder if he'd be home for dinner, so she called him on his cell.

"When are you coming home?"

"When I'm done here."

"Can't you bring your work home?"

"Look—"

"Leo, is there something wrong? Something you're not telling me about?"

"I've got a lot to do, that's all. Of course, I'd rather be with you," he said.

"That's all?"

"That's all."

"Why don't I believe you?"

"I don't know. Why don't you?"

"You always get upset about the Kemble twins...."

"I get upset about a lot of other things at work, too. You just don't see me here."

"You're sure that you're not upset about anything that has to do with us?"

He hesitated a beat too long. "No, dammit. Look, I'm sorry," he whispered, sounding worried. "The last thing I want to do is upset you. I'll be home before supper. Hell, I'll be home as fast as I can get there. It's you I want, though...not supper."

When he'd showed up an hour later, he'd swept her off her feet and carried her into the bedroom, where they'd made love for hours. Later, she'd awakened in the middle of the night and had found him at the window, staring outside, his hands clenched.

Something was wrong. She knew it. But until he told her, there was nothing she could do about it.

When she tiptoed across the room and laid her hand upon his arm, he jumped.

"Problems at work?" she whispered.

"Sometimes my thoughts won't stop."

He pulled her close and kissed her hair, her lips. But even though he held her and kissed her as she lay in his arms, she felt the coiled tension in his every muscle.

"Leo?"

"I love you," he said.

Then why, oh, why, did his bleak tone communicate such despair?

The baby was due around Christmas Day, and as Christmas approached she was so huge that Leo didn't want her on the road alone. So Abby put Kel in charge and quit driving into Austin to work. Abby handled what she could for In the Pink! by phone, fax and e-mail. In her spare time she busied herself decorating the nursery and buying presents for Leo and the baby.

She and Leo had chosen not to be told the baby's sex, so she lived in a constant state of excitement wondering whether they'd have a dark-haired boy like Leo or a beautiful little girl with shining black curls. Never once did she imagine her child looking like her.

Caught up in happy thoughts about the baby, she stopped dwelling so much on her absent father or Becky or even Leo's tension. Surely whatever was bothering Leo at work would soon resolve itself.

Lizzy and Mia e-mailed her constantly, mostly concerning the baby. With every e-mail and photo of her belly that she sent them, Abby's friendship deepened with the Kemble sisters.

Leo loved her. Abby loved him. They were joyously expecting a baby.

What could possibly go wrong?

Eleven

Connor held a photograph of girl with dark golden hair closer to his webcam.

"I've got a lead on Becky. I think maybe I've found her in Albuquerque, New Mexico."

The image on Leo's screen wavered. Connor wasn't holding the picture all that steady, but from what Leo could make out, except for the shorter hair, she looked almost exactly like Abby.

His throat tightened with alarm.

"You want me to fly out there?" Connor demanded eagerly. "Or do you want me to hold off until you gut up enough to have a conversation with your wife?"

"Go!"

"Leo, if this is our girl, you're going to have to tell her."

Leo knew that already. That didn't mean he was in

the mood for brotherly wisdom, spirituality, empathy, sympathy or whatever combination Connor chose to attack him with, so he said a curt goodbye and hung up. Then he picked up the folder on his desk labeled *Caesar's daughters: Abigail, Rebecca*.

For a long time he sat at his desk, thumbing through adoption records and Connor's reports on Abby and Becky. Feeling utterly disgusted with himself, he closed the folder and pitched it back onto his desk. Then he leaned forward on his elbows, steepled his fingers and stared into space for long minutes.

He had to tell her! His hands were shaking badly. His stomach twisted. He hadn't felt this coldly afraid in years. Not since Nancy had told him she was pregnant and Old Man Ransom had thrown him off the ranch and left him penniless and helpless. Not since Cal had called him dirt and had married his girl.

Hell, he was dirt now. He should have told Abby the truth a long time ago.

He was both in love with his wife and in lust with her. He'd never thought he could be this wildly happy with any woman. Or this miserable.

On one corner of his desk sat a tiny red jewelry box with a silver ribbon. Inside was a pricey gold horse pendant encrusted with diamonds along with a gold, choker necklace that he'd bought for Abby. He'd seen the miniature horse in a shop window and had thought of Abby the first time he'd seen her riding Coco. She'd looked slim and vibrant with her dark gold hair streaming behind her. He'd known instantly that he'd had to buy the horse for Abby for Christmas.

Not that the gift gave him any joy. If he didn't tell

her that he'd known who she was, that he'd bedded her knowing it, he stood to lose everything.

But when he told her, she might turn on him again as she had after that first night. As Nancy had.

"Why can't you understand why I had to marry Cal?"

He knew too well what it was like to be out in the cold.

He cursed. How many times had he rehearsed a speech and driven home to Abby, only to decide he didn't know what to say to her. He would see Nancy's shining eyes right before all hell had broken loose. Love was not an emotion he trusted.

Damn.

He had to tell Abby. First thing, as soon as he saw her. Tonight.

When the elevator opened, Miriam glanced up, her eager smile genuine and radiant. "Hello, Mrs. Storm. You're looking…"

"Big."

"But beautiful. How do you feel?"

Abby patted her belly. "Big. Really big. Really ready."

"I'll buzz Mr. Storm and let him know you're here. He'll be so happy to see you."

"No. I want to surprise him. I thought I'd invite him to lunch. If he's busy, I'll just go shopping until he has time."

"Well, you know where his office is."

Abby was smiling as she headed down the hall.

Kel had a meeting with one of In the Pink!'s clients this afternoon in San Antonio. Abby was glad that she'd asked Kel to stop by and give her a lift to Leo's office.

"You're sickeningly in love," Kel had teased as

she'd dropped her off in front of Leo's building. "Didn't I tell you?"

"It's rude to say I told you so every single time we talk."

"But didn't I tell you so?"

"Okay. Okay. You were right about happily ever after."

Abby was still smiling as she opened the doors to Leo's private office and found herself staring across the office at his empty black leather chair. "Leo?"

He didn't answer, so she shut the doors and then went over to his gleaming desk. She couldn't help but admire how neat his desk was compared to hers. A red Christmas present with a silver ribbon and a single file folder were the only items on top of the immense expanse of polished cherry that was his desk.

After reading the tag on the gift and realizing it was for her, she picked it up and shook it. Pleased that he'd taken the time to shop for her, she set it back down. She wished it was Christmas now so that she could open it and watch him open all his presents from her. But she had to wait. The elements of surprise and loving expectancy were part of the fun of Christmas that she'd always missed. Only this year, she would have what she'd always longed for: Leo and their baby and presents, lots and lots of carefully chosen presents. As soon as the baby was born and they could travel, they'd go down to the Golden Spurs to see Lizzy and Mia.

Vaguely Abby was aware of water running in Leo's bathroom as she leaned across his desk and lifted the folder. When she saw her name on the label, she started. Curious, she was about to open the file and read it when a door opened behind her.

"Darling, I'm so glad—"

She turned and smiled at him, but instead of running into his arms, she turned back because of what she'd just read on that label.

Caesar's daughters: Abigail, Rebecca.

When her eyes met his again, he froze. He was darkly flushed, guilt staining his cheeks.

As if in a daze, Abby flipped the folder open so violently adoption papers flew out onto his desk and floor. So did several all-too-familiar photographs of herself and Becky. She picked up a picture of Becky in braids and jeans and had to fight tears because her own memories flew at her like birds of prey.

Scattered among the photographs and adoption papers were several stapled reports from Connor's security agency about the missing twins. There was a DNA report that had to do with several beer bottles Abby had drunk out of that night Leo had picked her up in the bar.

With a little cry, Abby flipped pages in one of the reports about Rebecca Collins.

She began to shake. As she read, the awful feeling dislodged from the pit of her stomach and began to slowly crawl upward until it constricted her throat and cut off her breath.

Connor had been all over Texas and Mexico looking for Becky, but Abby knew that already.

Because she'd hired him.

What she hadn't known was that Becky and she were the missing Kemble twins.

How Connor and Leo must have laughed when she'd hired Connor. Like a fool, she'd played into their hands.

"Abby…"

At the sound of Leo's voice, directly behind her now, the fist around her throat tightened. Then the sadness and horror enveloping her turned into a roaring pain ripping her heart in two. Barely able to breathe, she sagged against the desk.

Leo said, "Darling, I can explain."

Darling. How she hated him calling her that now.

He was always so cocksure and confident, he probably thought he could talk his way out of this. He probably saw her as easy and needy and malleable.

To hell with him!

His tanned face began to spin, and suddenly it wasn't his face, it was Becky's.

Wait! Wait for me!

No! Come on!

Abby was shutting her eyes against the vision of Becky when Leo said, "If you'd just listen…."

Becky vanished, and Leo's tanned face came into sharp focus, his hair as shiny and black as wet ink, his stormy, pain-filled eyes flashing as he yanked his glasses off. He was outrageously handsome.

"You don't need to. I understand everything. Just leave me alone."

Intent on escaping him, she shoved herself away from his desk and stumbled toward the tall doors. But her legs were shaky, her gait uncertain, and since he was standing only a short distance from her, he got there much faster.

When he grabbed her arms and pulled her toward the leather sofa, she was too weak to fight him.

"I was going to tell you," he said.

"Sure you were."

"Connor told me to tell you right from the first."

"Then why didn't you?"

"Because I just didn't know how."

"And when did you first know the truth?" she demanded.

"Abby…"

"When?" she said through gritted teeth. "You've got to tell me."

"A few weeks maybe…before that night in the bar."

The fist strangling her throat, her heart, her soul squeezed tighter.

"Not that I was one hundred percent sure," he said.

"Why didn't you tell me then?"

"I had to make sure."

"By screwing me?"

"I took DNA samples."

"Right. The beer bottles," she mused, more to herself than to him. "You're nothing if not efficient. Why didn't you just do your job and take the damn bottles? Why the hell did you sleep with me?"

"Be fair. Why do you think? That was as much your idea as mine! You're the one who climbed on my table and started taking off your clothes!"

"No! You be fair! You've lied to me all along! About everything! I'll bet our entire life together is a lie! You don't love me. You just wanted to marry a Kemble."

"That's not true! I do love you!"

"You want to know something—I don't believe you! I was right about you in the beginning. CEOs like you are a despicable breed. I should know because I work with them every day. You're as ruthless and ambitious as the worst of them."

"Abby, I love—"

"Shut up! You didn't like being an outsider at the Golden Spurs, did you? Somebody they could hire and fire? You wanted to be an insider, and you saw me as your ticket. You wanted it so badly that you used my pregnancy to further your career by insisting on marriage. That's the real reason you married me!"

"No."

"I can't believe how touched I was when you pretended to be so understanding about Becky."

"I'm sorry."

"I'll never believe anything you say again! Never! Did you see me weak and vulnerable and so in need of your love that you could dupe me into believing what I'd always secretly wanted to believe, that there was somebody out there who could love me?"

"No! Hell, no!"

"You knew I'd thrown myself at Shanghai, didn't you? And that he'd dumped me for Mia? You thought I was vulnerable and easy—"

"No."

"Well, we may be having a baby together, but this marriage is over! I want you and your things out of my house tonight! I'll change the locks first thing tomorrow."

"You're upset. You don't know what you're saying. I'll drive you home."

"I'm upset? Who wouldn't be? But I know exactly what I'm saying. And I mean every word of it. I'm calling Kel. She'll drive me home. Not you! And, Leo, if you're smart, you won't tell the Kembles. They're my family. Not yours. I'll tell them who I am—when I'm good and ready. I don't mean this as a threat, but you'd better be prepared for the worst. You probably won't like my version of events."

Connor's blond head filled Leo's computer screen. "You look like shit."

"Thanks."

Not sleeping, not eating and drinking half the night took their toll in a helluva hurry. Leo didn't need Connor to tell him he had to get a grip.

"So what are you going to do now?" There was no trace of any I-told-you-so superiority edging Connor's voice. He was concerned and worried.

Leo finger-combed his black hair wearily. Last night when he'd gone over to try to deliver Abby's Christmas gifts, she'd forgotten to pull her kitchen shade. He'd caught a glimpse of her through her kitchen window when she'd come to see who was on her porch.

She'd been as big as a house in her white bathrobe, but beautiful—oh, so heart-stoppingly beautiful. And sad. He'd broken her heart.

For a long moment their eyes had met and held. His breath had caught in his throat. So had hers. His pulse had raced. Then she'd snapped the shade shut, and he'd felt lost and lonely—truly horrible. Was she going to hate him forever?

He'd knocked and knocked, pounded, yelled. In the end he'd had to leave her gifts on the porch.

His life was a mess. He was a mess.

He felt sick at heart, exhausted. It had been a long, dismal week since Abby had kicked him out and changed her locks. Even if his nights were hell, he'd been trying to work during the days. Connor and he had just finished discussing Connor's report on his trip to Albuquerque. Connor hadn't found Becky after all, but he thought it wouldn't be long.

"What can I do to get Abby back?" Leo muttered. He felt lonely and pathetic. "The only way she'll communicate with me is through Kel or through her closed door. So I talk to Kel every day and yell through her door." He didn't add that he'd drunk half a fifth of scotch after he'd gone home and was still feeling the effects from the hangover.

"Keep trying. I'll pray. What about the Kembles? How are they taking the news?"

"They haven't said anything, so I don't think she's told them. But frankly, I don't care what she tells them."

"Well, that's a switch."

"All I want is Abby."

"Tell her that."

"I would…if she'd open her door or answer her damn phone."

"You dug yourself a mighty deep hole."

"I just hope to hell it isn't my grave."

"Look, I don't like the fact that you're going through this alone, but I've got too much going on to get down to the ranch anytime soon. So if you end up with nowhere to go on Christmas, you're always welcome in Houston."

Nowhere to go….

"Thanks. But I want to be near Abby, just in case. And Kel's sworn she'll let me know when Abby goes into labor."

"Okay. I've gotta go. I'd wish you a Merry Christmas. But since that doesn't seem appropriate, I'll just pray it gets merrier real fast."

"You do that."

Abby sat sipping milk in her living room. Christmas Day was dark and gray but no darker than her sorrowful mood. She kept seeing Leo's face framed by her kitchen window. He'd looked so sad and apologetic… and handsome, too. She'd wanted to touch him. To feel his body against her own.

He was a rat. An ambitious, lying, scheming rat. Determined not to think about him, she shut her eyes. Her stomach felt tight, but that was probably only because she was so big. The baby was due any day, and she felt increasingly anxious out here on her own. She was huge and unwieldy, and it wasn't easy to get up and down off the low sofa without Leo around to help her.

To hell with Leo. The last thing she needed was a man who only wanted her because she was aligned with the rich family he worked for. At least she wouldn't have to spend Christmas alone. She'd be sharing Christmas dinner with Kel's family, and Kel would be coming over later to drive her there. But that was hours away, so she had the morning all to herself.

When she finished her milk, her stomach tightened again. Gasping, she remained on the couch. She needed to wash some clothes and towels and do a few dishes, but she lacked the energy to attack the mundane chores. With her stomach muscles knotting, she felt increasingly uncomfortable, so she just sat, listening to her own breathing as the walls seemed to close in on her.

She thought about her father and then made herself

push those attachments aside. Trying not to feel sorry for herself, she bit her lower lip and stared at the mountain of gifts Leo had left for her last night and that she'd placed under their tree.

Under *her* tree.

She'd never before had so many beautifully wrapped presents, and they were all from Leo. She shouldn't have brought them in. She shouldn't have put them under her tree, but she'd never had so many presents. She hadn't been able to resist keeping them. She was especially fascinated by the small red box with the silver ribbon that she'd seen on his desk that horrible day when her fantasy world had blown up in her face. She knew it had been the last he'd purchased and couldn't help wondering what it was.

His gifts shouldn't mean anything, not now. Not when she knew the truth. His marriage had been a career move. Period.

She'd hated him that day in his office when she'd read about Becky and he'd confessed about the DNA samples. She'd vowed to hate him forever, but he'd been so sweet and attentive for so many months. And those memories haunted her. Even now he kept up his act—calling her, dropping by, sending her notes. Not that she'd answered her phone or the door. And she'd shredded all his notes without reading them. But only after clutching them to heart and nearly dying of curiosity. And yes, she was such a sap, the bits and pieces were in her lingerie drawer. The guy deserved an Oscar. He really did.

He'd made sure Coco was taken care of, and he'd ordered her to stay away from the barn until after the baby was born.

She knew his interest had to do with his ambition. No doubt he was scared as hell she'd say something to the Kembles to destroy his career. And maybe she would. It would serve him right. But every time she picked up the phone to call Lizzy and tell her what a rat Leo was, she hesitated. She couldn't forget lying in his arms after they'd made love even if she wanted to.

She closed her eyes. If only her father would call. The stillness of the house was driving her crazy. Didn't he know it was Christmas Day and that he should call?

She picked up her phone and dialed her father's cell. He didn't answer, of course, so she left another message.

"Daddy, I...I want to wish you a Merry Christmas. I sent you a gift, and I keep wondering if you got it. Where are you? Did you get any of my messages asking whether Becky and I are adopted? It's really, really important that you get back to me on that. I...I'd like to hear from you. I miss you so much. And, Daddy, I'm going to have the baby any day now. I wish...I wish that you could be here...because, Daddy, I—I left Leo...and I'm all alone. Daddy, I...I need you so much."

A robotic male voice that wasn't even a recording of her father's voice said she had thirty seconds left, so she hung up without telling him she loved him.

Daddy, why can't you be here for me...just this once?

Never had Abby felt so alone, and it was all Leo's fault. For a few brief months when he'd been with her, she'd had the illusion she was loved. He'd made her feel so complete when he'd walked in the door at night and kissed her hello and pretended he was glad to see her. Even when he'd helped her load the dishwasher, or when he'd gone to the barn to help with Coco, she'd felt he'd done those things because he'd loved her.

All of it, every precious kiss and glance and thoughtful act, even the Christmas gifts that mesmerized her, had been part of a big, calculated lie to serve Leo Storm's ruthless ambition.

He was a heartless CEO to the core.

She'd been a vulnerable, stupid, naive fool.

Well, never again!

Twelve

Abby heard Kel's knock on her front door. She was rushing to answer it, when her stomach tightened. This time the pain was so excruciating she doubled over and took several deep breaths. In the next instant, she felt something wet trickling down her leg.

Her water had broken.

Oh my God. The baby is coming.

Her first thought was of Leo. Then she hated herself for wanting him so much.

Slowly she moved toward the door, but when she opened it, Leo was actually there.

"Don't slam it," he whispered, wedging his boot inside.

He looked thinner. Last night she hadn't noticed the lines of suffering etched beneath his eyes and beside his mouth. He hadn't bothered to shave or wash his hair, and there were circles under his eyes. His T-shirt and normally creased jeans were dirt-stained and limp with sweat. He certainly didn't look like the self-confident CEO she'd married, and if he were any other human being, she would have felt compassion.

"Where's Kel?" She tried to stand up straight. She was determined to feel nothing for him even though some part of her—that weak, naive, stupid, fatherless little girl that longed to be loved—was joyously glad he was here.

"Outside," he said. "In her car. She's waiting to pick you up."

"She knows what you did and how I feel. I can't believe that she would—"

"Abby, don't be mad at her. It's Christmas. I had to see you, to make sure you're okay. She felt sorry for me and let me knock on your door."

"Well, you've seen me. I'm okay. I want you to go. Get Kel. I need—"

Her stomach tightened, and the awful pain made her squint to hold back her tears. Even so, she grabbed her belly.

"What is it?" He stepped forward, his voice rough with concern.

"Nothing," she said, but she was gasping. And he wasn't stupid.

Understanding dawned and his tanned face tensed. "It's the baby," he said softly. "How far along are the pains?"

"They're not exactly pains."

"Contractions then?"

"I haven't been timing them, but I've been having them all morning. And I think my water just broke."

"Why the hell didn't you call me?"

"You are the last person—"

"Right." Pain flashed in his eyes and was gone. "Save it," he muttered fiercely. "Do you have a bag packed?"

She nodded, suddenly glad in spite of herself that he was here and taking charge.

She'd missed him. She'd missed him so much. And she needed him.

"Abby, I know you don't believe me, but I love you. Not because you're a Kemble heiress, but because you're you. After losing Nancy and Julie, I never thought I'd get a second chance, and that makes you and the baby doubly precious."

He would have said more, but her stomach tightened painfully again. Then Kel came up behind him.

Torn, Abby bit her lips in pain.

Instantly, Leo was all business. He told Abby to get changed and ordered Kel to find fresh towels for Abby to sit on in the truck. He grabbed Abby's suitcase and something from under the tree. Then he went out and drove his truck right up to the back door.

He was an ambitious, lying rat. She'd been trying to convince herself she loathed him all week. Still, it was hard to throw a man out when he was making himself so useful.

Before she knew what was happening, he lifted her into his arms and carried her down the steps.

"I…I want Kel," she said as he opened his door and helped her climb into the cab. Not that she really wanted Kel. His arms about her felt too good.

"I'll be right behind you," Kel said, taking Abby's hand reassuringly. "Besides, I'm so nervous I might have a wreck. He's a good man," she added. "And he loves you. He's told me that every single day, and I for one believe him." She leaned closer. "Nobody's perfect,

Abby. You should know that. You've never gone out with anybody who comes close to this guy. If it was me, I'd forgive him in a heartbeat and never look back. The fact that you're a Kemble is a plus. Who knows, the guy will probably find your sister for you."

Abby didn't say anything. To his credit, once they were both buckled inside his truck, Leo simply drove. Not once did he try to defend himself again or apologize. He simply kept his eyes glued to the road and concentrated on getting them safely to Austin. Her stomach kept tightening, and every contraction hurt more than the last.

Did he love her? Maybe he wasn't perfect. But if he loved her, wouldn't that be enough? Did he have to be as perfect as some ideal husband like the guys she read about in women's magazines? Did guys who did every single thing right even exist?

The next contraction had her panting.

Vaguely she was aware of Leo's foot on the gas pedal. The pastures and houses on the outskirts of Austin whipped by. He was passing every vehicle on the road now.

She would figure it all out later. Right now they were having a baby.

Their baby.

Tucked into crisp white sheets with her black-haired son making gurgling sounds as he sucked her nipple and Leo standing proudly beside her, Abby felt serene, if a little tired.

Very tired.

Surely the happiest days are when babies are born. As long as she lived, Abby would never forget the explosion of her son's little cry or how warm and loving

Leo's dark eyes had been above his blue surgical mask. She'd felt like a queen giving birth to a prince…and like a beloved wife, as well.

To have a healthy, normal son with a man she loved. A man who loved her. Did life get much better?

"Will you ever forgive me?" Leo asked.

His eyes blazed, but his countenance was suddenly as pale as a man facing a firing squad.

"I already have. Come here, my darling."

When he moved closer, she took his big, tanned hand in hers and turned it over. Then she brought it to her cheek and held it there, needing his warmth, his strength. "I already have. I want our son to know his father."

"What about you?" he demanded huskily.

The dark pain that lingered in his voice made her heart throb.

"I never stopped loving you. I tried, but I can't. You made my life too beautiful, and I missed you too much. When I went into labor, the only thing I wanted was you with me. You make feel safe. I've never felt that way before. Not with anybody. Not even before Becky ran away."

"You damn sure had me fooled."

"I had me fooled, too."

His fingertip traced her mouth lovingly. "Oh, Abby…"

"Do you think you'll ever find my sister?"

"I'll find her…or die trying. As you know, I can be pretty ruthless when I want something. Sometimes that's a good trait. And speaking along those lines…"

When he stopped talking, she met his eyes again, only this time they were sparkling.

"Guess who's outside," he said.

"I can't imagine."

"Your father. I had Connor track him down and haul him here bodily. He was in a South American jungle in a terrorist camp, writing the story of a lifetime. But he can't wait to see you and his grandson."

"First…kiss me and hold me, Leo, my precious darling."

Leo didn't make her beg.

Very gently he leaned over the bed, careful not to mash her IV or their son. Their lips met tentatively, first in love and forgiveness and then with eagerness and desire. A long time later, he kissed the top of their son's dark head.

Then he said, "I'll get your father."

"Merry Christmas," her father said as soon as he walked into her hospital room, carrying an armload of presents.

She imagined Leo had bought the presents for him because her father had never bought a present in his life, or at least not that she knew of. But that was okay. Her father was here.

When he leaned down to kiss her cheek, he reeked of cigarettes and leather and jungle scents. His face was rough against her cheek—he needed a shave, but she didn't care. He was here at last. And all because of Leo.

"Merry Christmas, darling," Leo said as she met his gaze over her father's shoulder.

"Merry Christmas," she replied. "The first of many together…I hope."

"I promise you a lifetime of Merry Christmases," Leo said.

And she believed him.

"I can't wait to get home and open that red box with the silver ribbon," she whispered.

"You don't have to wait. I have it right here." Grinning, he pulled it out of his pocket.

When he handed it to her, she pounced on the silver ribbon with the greediness of a child who'd waited a lifetime for a real Christmas.

Her father laughed, but she cried when she saw the exquisite, diamond-studded horse.

"Coco?"

"I think I fell in love with you the first time I saw you riding her," Leo said.

Circling his neck with one arm as she cradled their son in the other, she pulled him down, and he kissed her for a very long time.

Epilogue

A throng of Kembles pressed close to Leo and his golden wife, who was standing proudly beside him as she held little Caesar Kemble Storm in her arms outside the Golden Spurs Ranch chapel. Everybody wanted a closer glimpse of the baby. Even Joanne, who'd been less than pleased when Abby's true identity had been announced.

The February day was bright and warm. Not that that was the least bit unusual in South Texas.

"Well, I guess this makes you family now," Joanne said to Leo with a slight edge in her tone.

"I guess," he replied lazily.

Mia and Lizzy had been thrilled to learn who Abby really was. While not as pleased, Joanne had not seemed surprised when Abby and Leo had gone down to the Golden Spurs for a weekend right after baby Caesar had been born to tell Lizzy and Mia who Abby really was.

But Joanne had grudgingly accepted Abby as if her presence in their family was inevitable, and she'd even congratulated Leo several times. Then, strangely, as she had at the wedding, Joanne had asked Abby about her father and hung on every word as Abby had told her about his most recent visit.

"Did he ever tell you that you were adopted?"

"Not until I asked him during his last visit. He said he'd always intended to when Becky and I were grown, but that when Becky disappeared, he couldn't face it."

"He always seemed so unafraid to me. I was the one—" She broke off.

Again Abby wondered about Joanne's intense fascination with her father.

"How did you know my father?"

"We were friends, briefly," was all Joanne had said. Abby imagined her father must have neglected her because of his work.

Now Lizzy jingled a pair of tiny spurs in front of baby Caesar's plump hands, causing Abby to forget her earlier conversation with Joanne.

"I thought baby Caesar held up pretty well for the service," Lizzy said with a big smile. "These are his, and when you all leave, I'm definitely hanging them on the Spur Tree. Right beside Daddy's."

Abby felt happier every time she was with her admiring new family and their friends. The chapel and the Big House along with all the other buildings had been freshly painted since the fire. It had rained a lot in January, and there hadn't been a freeze, so lush green grass covered most of the earth that had been black last summer.

"Baby Caesar, you were way, way better than my

Vanilla during the service," Mia said. "She's over there sulking by the barbeque pit because I am here bragging on you." Not that Mia's voice was harsh as she told stories about her lively daughter while tugging at the baby's big toe.

Baby Caesar squirmed and bit his fist as if he were drawing on the last of his reserves to be patient.

"I'm afraid I need to feed him," Abby said right before he let out an anxious little cry.

Bunching his fingers, he jammed them frantically into his mouth. When that didn't soothe him, he began to kick. Then he let out another cry.

Smoke from portable barbeque pits drifted lazily against a cloudless blue sky. Immense white tents had been put up on the back lawn to accommodate the guests, who had been invited to celebrate three new members being brought into the family.

While Mia and Lizzy had been wild to welcome Abby, the baby and Leo into the family, it was Joanne who'd suggested that baby Caesar be christened on the ranch where all family members were always christened. Of course, a christening called for a real celebration, and since they were ranchers in South Texas, a celebration called for barbeque, beer and mariachis. The musicians were setting up near the Big House.

No sooner had Abby agreed than Lizzy had overnighted Caesar Kemble's original yellowed christening gown with a note that said baby Caesar *had* to wear the founder's gown.

So here Abby was, standing by her husband as she held their wriggling baby, and surrounded by her family, too.

Finally, after everybody had gotten to pinch the baby's

toes and arms and talk baby talk to him, Leo took Abby's hand to lead her to a private parlor in the Big House where she could feed the baby before they ate lunch.

When they were alone with their baby suckling at her breast, Leo leaned down and kissed Abby long and deeply. Like all his kisses, this one promised her forever.

Without thinking, she touched the exquisite little horse with the diamond bridle at her throat that Leo had given her for Christmas. Then her hand fell to the dark, downy curls on her baby's head.

Her father was back in Argentina, and she hadn't heard from him since he'd left. Still, on the morning of his departure he'd told her how he and Electra had selected an adoption agency to arrange the adoption.

"Electra was an old friend of mine. We'd collaborated on several books. She came to me when she was pregnant, and I told her how much your mother and I wanted children. And your mother and I were so happy…for a little while—before Becky disappeared and everything went wrong."

"Yes. We were happy."

"If only…." He'd paused. "I drive myself to write, you know, so I won't think about it. I've become something of an adrenaline junkie."

"Maybe you should reach out to someone new."

"I tried that once, not so long ago. And got my heart busted up all over again. No thanks."

"I'm sorry, Daddy."

"It's okay."

Abby wasn't going to think about her father or worry about Becky right now. She had too many blessings to count. In fact, she'd never been happier as she sat in a rocking chair with her blouse unbuttoned and Caesar pressed close, her husband smiling lovingly down at her.

She couldn't have imagined such happiness. Not ever. Not in her wildest dreams.

Maybe, soon, Leo would find Becky for her and her daddy.

If any man could, Leo would.

* * * * *

MILLS & BOON®
The Billionaires Collection!

This fabulous 6 book collection features stories from some of our talented writers. Feel the temperature rise with our ultra-sexy and powerful billionaires. Don't miss this great offer – buy the collection today to get two books free!

2 FREE BOOKS!

Order yours at
**www.millsandboon.co.uk
/billionaires**

MILLS & BOON®

Let us take you back in time with our Medieval Brides...

The Novice Bride – Carol Townend

The Dumont Bride – Terri Brisbin

The Lord's Forced Bride – Anne Herries

The Warrior's Princess Bride – Meriel Fuller

The Overlord's Bride – Margaret Moore

Templar Knight, Forbidden Bride – Lynna Banning